THE LUXURY OF SILENCE

SUSAN ADRIANI

Quills & Quartos
PUBLISHING

Edited by Kristi Rawley and Jo Abbott

Cover design by CloudCat Design

ISBN 978-1-956613-30-8 (ebook) and 978-1-956613-29-2 (paperback)

For Glynis, who has the patience of a saint, a heart of gold, and who loves happy endings more than anyone I know.

"I am worn out with civility," said he. "I have been talking incessantly all night, and with nothing to say. But with *you* there may be peace. You will not want to be talked to. Let us have the luxury of silence."

— MANSFIELD PARK, CHAPTER 28

ONE

*It is not what we say or think that defines us,
but what we do.*

Kent, July 1811

THE HOUSE FITZWILLIAM DARCY HAD TAKEN FOR HIS
sister was smaller than his Brook Street residence in London
but tastefully appointed and situated in a fashionable neighbourhood within a mile of the church. A steady breeze from
the harbour carried the fresh sea air to the doorstep, where its
salty scent mixed with the sweetness of lavender, phlox, and
primrose from the garden. The house was a pleasant walk
from the shore, but Darcy found he preferred the peaceful
solitude of the chalk cliffs to the pomp and circumstance of
the bazaar and the promenade. Although the wind blew more
harshly so high above the coastline, the view was incomparable, and the only incessant chatter to be heard was from the
gulls.

Ramsgate offered everything a stylish seaside resort
usually boasted, but it was the church that had first caught
Darcy's eye: a handsome, medieval structure of fine Caen
limestone that dated back to the eleventh century just before
the Norman Conquest—six hundred years before his own

ancestors had come over from France with an apostrophe in their surname. His great grandfather, the third Duke of Devonshire, had insisted on dropping that connexion, and for the last hundred years the family D'Arcy of Derbyshire had been known as the Darcys. It turned out to be an ironic stroke of prudence. While half of England was currently wild to get their hands on a cask or two of fine cognac—a scarcity since the start of the war—the whole of society was equally ravenous to see the British monarchy oust Bonaparte. An ancient family name linked to a barony in France would have earned him nothing but scrutiny from the aristocracy of Britain.

Upstairs a door was opened and closed with a quiet click. Darcy stiffened, bracing himself for a murmur, a sob, a cry— anything that would indicate some new calamity had transpired in his absence.

He was met with silence.

After releasing a harsh breath that he had not realised he had been holding, he uttered an oath and abandoned his solitary vigil at the parlour window to make his way through the house. As desperate as he was to remain with Georgiana, he could not help feeling an equal desperation to escape.

For most of his life, he had worked tirelessly to live up to his father's expectations of him. Pemberley, its tenants, its servants, and their families depended on him. His sister, Georgiana, of whom he had been awarded guardianship after his father's death six years prior, depended on him as well. His charity and concern for all under his care had earned Darcy the reputation of being an honourable man, a fair and just master, and a generous elder brother; but since arriving in Ramsgate, he had agonised over every admirable quality he was supposedly understood to possess.

Was he still an honourable man when he was determined to preserve his family's respectability by concealing Georgiana's disgrace from the world? Was he still fair and just when he hoped the gentleman that she eventually married would be forever ignorant of her indiscretion? Was he still a generous brother when he had unwittingly consigned his gentle, fifteen-year-old sister to the care of a woman in whose character he had been grossly and unhappily deceived? He was furious, heartbroken, mortified, murderous, and completely alone in his misery and self-recrimination. For that reason, more than any other, Darcy could not bear to be idle.

The front door loomed like a beacon before him and Pemberley's master lengthened his strides. The elderly butler seemed to materialise out of thin air to hand him his hat and his walking stick. Darcy donned the hat without comment but declined the walking stick and threw open the door, stepping from the oppressive interior of the house into a day that blazed so brightly it threatened to blind him.

"Oh! Mr Darcy," a feminine voice called from the street. "Good morning to you!"

The urge to return to the house was immediate and compelling, but he forced himself to shut the door and proceed down the slate path to the street, all the while commanding himself to project an air of indifference. By the time he reached the front gate, he was able to meet the woman with every appearance of equanimity. He bowed to her. "How do you do, Mrs Westinghouse?"

Mrs Westinghouse, a matronly woman from London who looked to be about five-and-forty, seemed to have no less than a dozen daughters. The previous morning, after accosting Darcy in the town, she informed him she had brought them all to the coast for the benefit of their health. Darcy, however, suspected she had most likely come for the purpose of marrying the eldest ones off to unsuspecting rich men.

There were eight young women—*Good God, eight of*

them—arranged on either side of her. The eldest three gazed at him from beneath their lashes. The others, who looked far too young to be out, giggled behind their hands.

"As you can see, we are all very well, sir, I thank you. We are on our way to the shore."

"It is a fine day for it," he replied evenly.

"Will you not join us, Mr Darcy? My girls and I would so enjoy the pleasure of your company."

Of that Darcy had no doubt, but he was not in Ramsgate to entertain ladies, especially ladies who had designs on him. His eyes remained fixed upon their mother as he struggled to form a civil response while he felt no inclination whatsoever to be civil.

He was silent too long.

"Come, sir," said Mrs Westinghouse with a simpering smile, "certainly you are not shy?"

Her gaggle of daughters whispered and tittered and smiled becomingly, and Darcy felt a flush of heat rise along the back of his neck as the last vestiges of his patience threatened to disintegrate. "I have business today but hope you and your daughters have a pleasant outing. Good morning." He executed a perfunctory bow and quickly set off in the opposite direction, towards the high street.

As he hastened along past the bakery, the butcher, the haberdashery, and countless other establishments boasting everything from modistes and tailors to trinkets and books, he received similar looks and greetings from similar women and their charges. If it was not grasping society matrons and their daughters, it was dowager aunts with a niece in tow, or benefactresses indulging poor relations. All were likely pleasure bent from London, Manchester, and everywhere in between. Would that he had brought his walking stick after all! Then, perhaps he could cut a swath through the grating politesse and grasping social climbers and part them like Moses did the Red Sea!

Such thoughts were not only unkind but beneath him, Darcy knew. His mother, had she lived, would be ashamed of him; but his dark mood did nothing to foster feelings of charity within his breast. He felt only biting resentment and indignation. None of these women, whether well-dowered or penniless, saw him simply as a man. When they looked at him, they saw a potential prize with a fat pocketbook. He wondered what they would see if they knew about Georgiana. Would they still seek his society and clamour for his notice if they learnt his sister had consented to an elopement and God only knew what else with a philandering degenerate of the highest order? Darcy bit back a bitter laugh. By the grace of God, he fervently hoped he would never be so unfortunate as to find out.

He walked on, past a quaint little inn and a tavern and a blacksmith's shop and a small, well-maintained green next to a burial ground. Beyond the manicured plots and rows of weathered headstones stood the ancient church. It was as he remembered it—the wide bell tower, the stained-glass windows, and the rudimentary deposits on the limestone from which it was built centuries ago by people who had believed so vehemently in God and His goodness that they had erected this sanctuary in His name.

Swallowing audibly, Darcy ascended the steps and opened the door. It took a moment for his eyes to adjust to the dim interior, which was noticeably cooler than the warm, balmy air out of doors. He stepped farther into the nave and the door swung closed with a resounding bang that echoed off the walls. The aisles, the altar, the nave—all were empty. Darcy exhaled a breath of relief. It was blessedly quiet in this holy place. Solemn. Peaceful. Private. He removed his hat and slipped into a pew at the back of the church.

Since he had arrived in Ramsgate two days prior, the ever-present burden of responsibility that rested upon his shoulders had increased to an intolerable proportion, and Darcy felt himself bowing under the weight of it. He had thought to surprise Georgiana by coming unannounced, but Georgiana had managed to surprise him instead, most wretchedly. What followed had felt like a scene from his worst dream.

Entwined limbs, a flash of exposed skin, and his sister's horrified countenance as she frantically attempted to right her gown had sent him into a white-hot rage. He had not been able to sleep through the night since. Every time he closed his eyes, Darcy saw his innocent, fifteen-year-old sister being tended by George Wickham!

God in Heaven—how was he ever to forget what he had seen that day! How would he ever be able to look her in the eye? How would either of them ever be able to move past it and recover?

Darcy felt a tightness in his throat and the hot pressure of tears in his eyes. He dropped his head into his hands with a quavering exhalation, fighting to remain in control. It was not to be. The devastating events of the last two days had finally caught up with him, and their hold upon his conscience was unforgiving. He covered his face with his hands and wept.

&

The harsh pounding on the front door of the house matched the dull pounding in Darcy's head. He abandoned his chair and hastened into the corridor before the servants were alerted to the noise. It was two o'clock in the morning, and there was only one person in the world he was expecting. He turned the locks and opened the door.

"Fitzwilliam," he said, his voice thick with emotion as he moved aside to allow him entrance.

His cousin, four years his elder and a decorated colonel in the Royal Army's Foot Guards, took one look at him and pulled Darcy into a fierce embrace.

Darcy clung to him for several moments, grateful beyond words that this man he respected and loved—whose loyalty was as deep and unwavering as a brother's—had arrived at last. Colonel Fitzwilliam slapped him on the back as they separated, and Darcy took charge of his bag. "You look awful," he muttered, shutting the door, "but I appreciate you coming into Kent. Thank you."

The colonel tossed his hat, cloak, and gloves onto a bench in the anteroom. "I am sorry I could not arrive sooner. I received your express two nights ago and barely had enough time to pack my bag before catching the mail coach. I was in Newcastle on behalf of the major general, otherwise I would have been here sooner. What has happened?"

Darcy's jaw tightened. "Come into the study. We cannot talk here. How was your journey?"

"Brutal. Other than stopping for a quarter hour to change horses every ten miles, we drove straight through. Once we reached London, I hired a hack chaise to take me the rest of the way."

"Have you eaten?"

"I managed a meal in Bromley at the Bell, but I could use a drink. Brandy if you have it, but I shall settle for port if you do not."

Shaking his head, Darcy paused at the study door. "You should get some rest. What I have to relate can keep until morning."

"I doubt it," said his cousin seriously. "You look as though you are about to run mad. Your face when you opened the door..."

Darcy's throat felt conspicuously tight. "You are exhausted."

"As are you." Fitzwilliam gave him a stern look the men under his command were no doubt well acquainted with. "Darcy, tell me."

Darcy ushered him into the room, then shut the door and walked to the sideboard, where he poured brandy into two cut crystal glasses.

Fitzwilliam accepted his gratefully and raised it to his lips, draining the contents in one swallow.

Darcy poured him another.

"I am much obliged," he said, claiming one of two upholstered chairs set on either side of a painted table. "Now, tell me what has happened. Your express said nothing beyond this address and that I should alert no one to my coming here. Had there been an accident or had Georgiana fallen ill you would have related all without hesitation. Is she well?"

With mounting agitation, Darcy strode to the hearth, then back again, passing his hand over his mouth. "She is well," he said darkly, forcing himself to speak the words aloud for the first time. "As well as can be expected after I arrived on Tuesday and discovered her in the arms of George Wickham."

The colonel gaped at him. "Tell me you are joking."

"I am perfectly serious, Fitzwilliam."

"That contemptible blackguard!" Fitzwilliam abandoned his glass on the table as he rose swiftly to his feet. "Where is he now that I may have the satisfaction of running him through!"

Darcy took a long swallow of brandy. "He is no longer in Ramsgate."

His cousin's expression was murderous. "Of course, he is not, the bloody coward! What of Mrs Younge? Stupid, useless woman! How the blazes did Wickham ever get past her?"

Darcy's ire rose further as he thought of the woman he had hired as his sister's companion. "They knew each other," he said, gritting his teeth as he glared at the glass in his hand. "Georgiana was persuaded to believe herself in love. She confessed all to me, with the hope of garnering my blessing— their meeting 'by chance' over a week ago, Mrs Younge encouraging her attachment to him, her agreeing to elope with him to Scotland! When I confronted Wickham, he confirmed every word. He quit the house with that deuced woman in tow, but only after I told him he would never see one shilling of Georgiana's dowry, whether they married or not. It was only by the grace of God that I arrived in time. I had no prior knowledge of any of it! *None!*" Swearing harshly, he hurled his glass into the empty grate, where it shattered, scattering brandy and shards of broken crystal along the hearth and the carpet. "What was she thinking? Eloping! Behaving like a wanton in the very house I have secured for her comfort!"

"Darcy," Fitzwilliam cautioned. "I know you are upset. I am as well, but you are speaking of your sister, not some West End prostitute! Lower your voice else the servants hear you."

"Damned foolish!" Darcy uttered savagely, raking his fingers through his hair. "Damned foolish! And I, just as much the fool as she!"

A heavy, enraged silence filled the room. Darcy stalked to the fireplace, broken glass crunching beneath his boots. He had not thought the throbbing ache in his head could possibly worsen, yet it had. Shutting his eyes, he propped his elbows upon the mantelpiece and dropped his head into his hands, marvelling at the wretched turn Georgiana's life had taken in the matter of a week. What if Wickham did not keep his offensive mouth shut? What if the insolent reprobate decided to blackmail him? What if he came back, either now or in the future, looking for Georgiana? What then? Was Darcy supposed to hide her away at Pemberley indefinitely? Was he supposed to pay Wickham off like he did his creditors? And to what end?

At long last, Fitzwilliam made a grim enquiry. "I hate to ask this, but is there any chance there will be consequences from this botched elopement?"

The words were no sooner said than the image of his beloved sister, heavy with Wickham's child, threatened to overpower him. It was a devasting possibility Darcy had flatly refused to consider for the last two days for fear that his thinking it would somehow make it a reality. Revulsion and outrage in equal measure pressed against his breast, churned his stomach, and lodged in his throat. His heart had been broken every bit as much as Georgiana's—more so perhaps, because Wickham had once been his friend.

Aside from Georgiana marrying the blackguard, her being with child would be the worst possible outcome. Not only would a pregnancy compound his sister's suffering, but it would cause irreparable harm to the Darcy name in the process and likely delay any chance Georgiana had of making a full recovery by months, possibly even years.

Whatever scant bits of sanity Darcy retained were balanced on a knife edge. Though he made every effort to regulate his roiling emotions and rein in his temper, he could not repress the growing fury he felt towards Wickham for his depravity, towards himself for his neglect, and towards Georgiana for failing to recognise the danger of her situation, despite her youthful age. Seething, he strode to the French windows on the other side of the room, slammed his hand against the casement, and turned the full measure of his anger and indignation on his cousin. "I came upon them in the drawing room when he was unfastening the buttons of her gown! His vile mouth was on her *neck!* What do you think?"

"I think that tells us very little, unfortunately,"

Fitzwilliam remarked with a grave countenance. "Have you asked her?"

"Of course I have not asked her! How can I possibly ask my sister such a thing? I cannot even look her in the eye." Darcy exhaled harshly, then shook his head, thoroughly disgusted with himself for failing to protect that which was dearest to him. "Georgiana is devastated," he said, running his hands over his face as he fought to conquer his emotions. "She is tearful and withdrawn and keeps to her rooms and, God help me, I have not discouraged her from doing so. I do not blame her for what has happened, not entirely, but I do not yet trust myself to remain in control of my temper. I do not wish to make matters worse."

Fitzwilliam exhaled heavily. "I shall speak to her in the morning, then. What are your plans, Darcy?"

"Plans," Darcy muttered resentfully. "What plans can I possibly have now? My sister has yielded to the machinations of a depraved rogue and could well be carrying his child. Should her disgrace become public knowledge, her reputation will be in tatters and both of us will be reviled by society. No respectable gentleman shall ever offer for her, and no woman within London's first circles will ever give me the time of day, never mind consent to become my wife. I *have* no *plans*, Fitzwilliam!"

His cousin rubbed his brow. "I meant how long do you plan on remaining here, in Ramsgate? I am surprised you did not quit the place at once and whisk Georgiana off to Pemberley."

Darcy scoffed. "Pemberley. London. Ramsgate. What difference does it make? Short of removing to Australia, I can think of nowhere I can hide her away where Wickham will not eventually find her if that is his design. Georgiana is distraught. I could not add to her distress by dragging her on a four-day journey across England while she is in such a state. I cannot possibly abide London right now. I need time to think else I say or do something to cause her irreparable harm."

"That is sensible of you, but if we know anything of Wickham, it is that he is remarkably lazy. I doubt he would go to such trouble, especially when you are well within your rights to seek retribution. He must know that I would happily kill him for what he has done, even if you are not so inclined towards violence at present. His blood on my hands would be nothing."

"You would hang for it, Fitzwilliam." Darcy rubbed his forehead with his hand as he sank onto a leather chair. His headache, much like Georgiana's situation, had become intolerable. "I doubt Wickham even considered I would tell you. He believes me too proud to lay my personal dealings open to anyone, even to you."

"Then he is remarkably stupid as well. It is well known that your guardianship of Georgiana is divided with me. I have as much right to demand recourse as you do. I require only time and opportunity." The colonel smiled menacingly. "And perhaps the element of surprise."

"Do not," said Darcy sternly, "make this untenable situation any worse. Let Wickham slink off to the bowels of London for a while or crawl under a rock in some obscure country shire. If I can get Georgiana away from here without any hint of scandal following us, I shall be satisfied."

"And if you cannot?"

Darcy shook his head and looked towards the window, refusing to acknowledge the fresh wave of anger building in his breast. His temper, he knew, was resentful, but he could not allow it to lead him to do something rash and foolish. Georgiana had acted foolishly, but she was a fifteen-year-old girl. Darcy was a grown man, the master of Pemberley, and therefore must exercise caution and decorum, always. There was far too much at stake. He cleared his throat. "If Georgiana's disgrace becomes public knowledge, then I give you leave to act however you like. I will not question your right to exact retribution, nor your method. I ask only that you take care and use discretion."

Fitzwillam's hand found purchase on the hilt of his sabre. "Always," was all he said.

TWO

❧

Friendship is certainly the finest balm for the pangs of
disappointed love.

"You like Mr Bingley," said Darcy to his sister two
months later as they broke their fast in the breakfast parlour
of his London residence. He indicated a letter with a wave of
his hand, hastily but enthusiastically composed by his friend.
"He has been kind enough to invite us to stay with him at his
estate in Hertfordshire. The surrounding countryside is very
different from what we are used to in Derbyshire, but I
understand it has much to recommend it, and many
delightful prospects accessible on foot and on horseback."

Taking care to avoid meeting his eyes, Georgiana laid her
fork gingerly upon the table. "Will Miss Bingley and Mrs
Hurst be there as well?"

Darcy endeavoured to hide his frown behind his teacup.
The last time he had been in company with either of Bingley's sisters was during an evening party last April. It was not
an occasion he recalled with much pleasure. The prospect of
spending a month or more in the same house as either of them
was almost as unappealing to him as spending time with his
cousin Arthur, Viscount Emerson, who was not only an
unconscionable philanderer, but an incessant boor.

That said, however much he was not looking forward to

being an object of Miss Bingley's mindful solicitation and Mrs Hurst's witless conversation, it would be good for Georgiana to mix more with society. Bingley's sisters would treat her with kindness, even if they did not always extend the same courtesy to others.

"Miss Bingley is to keep house for her brother, and the Hursts are expected to visit as well. They adore you, Georgiana, and will be glad to see you. I understand there is an exquisite pianoforte in one of the drawing rooms—a Broadwood grand. Bingley has assured me you are welcome to play it every day from dawn until dusk if you so desire."

"A Broadwood grand," she repeated almost reverently, her eyes alight with a flicker of genuine pleasure that had been absent since the wretched week they had passed in Ramsgate at the end of July.

Darcy held his breath, clinging to that one spot of brightness after so many months of despair. *Finally,* he thought. *Finally, there is something in her countenance besides fear and sadness!*

His relief was short-lived.

Almost as soon as the spark appeared it was gone, and Georgiana averted her eyes to stare fixedly at her plate. "I hear it is a superior instrument. I should like to play one someday."

Darcy repressed a sigh of frustration. Although his sister's continued low spirits certainly concerned him, he was mentally and emotionally exhausted himself, and tired of walking on eggshells in his own home. Something needed to be done to draw her out of her self-imposed exile. Since they had arrived in London, she had made no calls and had shied away from company, even their Fitzwilliam relations. Enough was enough. As cheerfully as possible, Darcy turned his attention to his toast and eggs. "I daresay you will very soon. We shall leave for Hertfordshire in a fortnight."

His decree was met with silence.

"Must I go, Brother?"

"You must," he replied gently but firmly. "It will be good for you to get out of London for a while. You have barely ventured outside and have called upon no one, not even our aunt Carlisle, who has been extremely kind to us. Surely, you desire the companionship of other ladies?"

"I enjoy Mrs Annesley's company. She has been very understanding and patient with me."

"While I am happy to hear that you like Mrs Annesley, my dear, she is your companion, and hardly a young woman. You should have friends your own age. Bingley mentioned that there are four-and-twenty families in the neighbourhood. Although the society is undoubtedly more confined and unvarying than our acquaintance in town, many of those gentlemen are likely to have daughters, some of whom are bound to be your age. Perhaps you will find a friend among them, or at least an amicable acquaintance."

"May I be excused?"

Darcy frowned. "You have barely touched your breakfast."

"I am not hungry this morning, and I have much to do."

"What can you possibly have to do that cannot wait until after you have eaten?"

Georgiana hesitated. "Miss Bingley and Mrs Hurst are so accomplished, and I have not yet mastered the piece by Mozart you were so kind as to procure for me the other day."

"There is no rush. We shall not leave London for two weeks, and you will have plenty of time to practise once we arrive in Hertfordshire if you so desire. Miss Bingley and Mrs Hurst will be pleased to hear how well you get on."

There was a pregnant pause, then a solemn, "Please let me practise now," from Georgiana. "I do not wish to embarrass you in front of your friends."

Darcy stared at her, unable to credit what he had heard. Georgiana was incredibly accomplished herself, far more so than many other young ladies her age, and some who were significantly older as well.

She rose from her chair, but Darcy captured her hand, effectively preventing her escape. "Georgiana," he said seriously. "Your talent at the pianoforte is exceptional. I defy anyone who has the pleasure of hearing you play to find anything wanting. If you do not desire it, you need not perform in company, even for people you know so well as the Bingleys and Mrs Hurst. There is nothing you could ever do that would embarrass or disappoint me before our friends."

"I believe we both know that is not true," Georgiana whispered. "Pray, excuse me." With tears in her eyes, she hastened from the room.

Darcy watched her go with a heavy heart, then pushed aside his plate. He had lost his appetite.

*

"You are doing the right thing," said Colonel Fitzwilliam as he reclined in a leather chair opposite the enormous mahogany desk in Darcy's study. "She has been cooped up in this house far too long. It is not healthy, for either of you."

Darcy laid his head against the back of his own chair and passed a hand over his eyes. "Every day for the last two months I have attempted to lure her out of the house with the promise of some excursion or treat. I have tried persuasion, coercion, reason, everything I can think of to tempt her, but Georgiana begs to remain at home. She attends church, but even gaining that small concession was a battle. Nearly every conversation we have had on the subject of her being seen in public has ended in tears."

"You are well within your right to expect her to accompany you into Hertfordshire. I would not advise leaving her behind while her spirits are still so low. Perhaps Georgiana will be more at ease in a small country society, where she knows no one save for Bingley and his family. It will be a clean slate. In Hertfordshire, she may simply be a shy, fifteen-year-old girl with few expectations placed upon her shoulders."

"Georgiana is a Miss Darcy. There will always be expectations placed upon her," Darcy muttered in annoyance. "It matters little whether she is in town or in the country. People will hear her name, see her quality of dress and her fine carriage, and immediately equate her worth as a young lady with that of her fortune and her ties to Pemberley."

"Unfortunately, the world will do as it likes. Despite your distaste for society, you garner even more scrutiny than your dear sister and her fancy frocks. You have the misfortune of being your own master, you are disgustingly wealthy, and you are overdue in taking a wife. Since your father died, there has been constant talk of your yearly income and your holdings throughout the kingdom, even the number of women you have supposedly known." Fitzwilliam smirked at him. "I do not suppose you would care to hear how many courtesans you are rumoured to have bedded?"

"Absolutely not," said Darcy with repugnance. "Despite my adherence to morality in the face of the *ton's* profligacy, I suppose I have been labelled a shameless libertine as well as a rich catch."

"The highborn of the *bon ton's* gentlemen can be a licentious bunch, but their speculations are nothing you have not heard before. It does not matter in any case. Of late, there are an infinite number of braggarts at White's—Middleton, Dunstan, and their ilk—who do not scruple to advertise every assignation they have ever had in scandalous detail. Trust me, your alleged conquests are inconsequential. Dunstan's gall is staggering. Unless he learns to keep his mouth shut about his exploits, he will find himself facing the wrong end of a pistol one day."

"Conquests," Darcy muttered, scowling as he raked his fingers through his hair. The idea of having any sort of conquest was not only abhorrent, but laughable. He was far too fastidious and upright to engage a mistress never mind dip his pen in a doxy.

"Be thankful those skirt chasers know nothing of your restraint. Thus far you have escaped the crude ribbing other virtuous men have endured at the hands of the first set. While your name has been in the betting books for years, to my knowledge it is for nothing more untoward than which lady of your acquaintance will someday have the honour of becoming Pemberley's new mistress. I cannot say as much for any of the others."

Darcy's mouth twisted with further distaste. "And what, pray, have they to say on that score?"

"Nothing that merits repeating. Your old friend from Eton, Joseph Haversham, wagered ten pounds on Lady Babcock yesterday, while Stotesbury put another two pounds on his bird-witted sister."

"Haversham is reprehensible, and Stotesbury is a ninny-hammer. He will bankrupt himself with his tomfoolery."

"So will they all. There are at least four pages of similar nonsense. Of course, my father maintains you will do your duty and wed Anne, so Mendelson and Sommerchurch each wagered thirty pounds on her. They were so foxed they could barely stand, my father included. Arthur wagered five pounds on Lord Malcolm's daughter."

"Edith Wilcox? She is one of the stupidest girls in England!"

Fitzwilliam scratched his brow. "Her name is Agnes. In

any case, Arthur claims to have seen you speaking with her at Lady Devon's in June. Twice."

"She was standing in my way," Darcy replied irritably as his tolerance for such talk evaporated. "God forbid I glance at a woman, never mind speak two words to one in passing! Dancing with one of them is practically interpreted as a declaration of romantic intent, which in turn *must* equate to marriage! It disgusts me. Nine times out of ten they do not even care whether I am unfailingly polite or abominably rude. They desire my ten thousand a year, my house in town, and the Darcy name—nothing else apparently, not even my civility." He rose from his chair, strode to the window, and propped his forearm upon the casement with a grim countenance. "Mark my words—Hertfordshire will be no different. Miss Bingley will inevitably mention Pemberley, and then every grasping mother within a fifty-mile radius will pursue me for her daughter's sake."

"Perhaps, but I urge you to keep in mind that Hertfordshire is hardly London. Who can tell? Your experience there may be very different from the experiences you have had here in town."

"I doubt it will be anything short of a penance. Georgiana will be no easier among strangers than I. In fact, she will likely be as withdrawn in Hertfordshire as she is in London, and without the benefit of more varied entertainments to divert her and the comfort of home, I fear she will likely suffer further unhappiness and discomfort."

"I believe you mean to say that you will suffer further unhappiness and discomfort. Do not even attempt to deny it, for I know you far too well."

"I have no wish to deny it," Darcy replied. He turned his back to the window, folded his arms across his chest, and fixed his cousin with a look he hoped communicated the full measure of his resentment and dissatisfaction.

Fitzwilliam rolled his eyes. "I honestly do not see a problem here, Darcy. Your disenchantment with the proclivities of London's first circles aside, if the society in Hertfordshire is not to your liking, then restrict your sister's contact with those people, just as you would here in town. Georgiana is not yet out. She should not be often mingling in society in any case. Use that excuse to your advantage as well as hers, but pray do not allow her to sit in her room and sulk for the next month. Engage her. Take her riding. Encourage her to draw." The colonel looked pointedly at him and smirked. "Exert yourself while you are at it and mix with Bingley's neighbours. Invite the ladies to tea."

It was Darcy's turn to roll his eyes. "I shall endeavour to encourage Georgiana in a variety of respectable pursuits, but I draw the line at entertaining a room full of ladies. I shall leave that office to Miss Bingley and Mrs Hurst." He returned to his desk and sank onto his chair with a harsh exhalation. "Georgiana requires a friend her age, not a brother more than ten years her senior clucking over her like a mother hen. She is even more soft-spoken than she was before, and she flinches whenever I happen to raise my voice. She is afraid of me, Fitzwilliam."

"Georgiana is not afraid of you."

"She is afraid of disappointing me, then. She has not yet forgotten the events of this summer, nor my initial reaction when I discovered her with...*him*." Darcy could not bear to think Wickham's name, never mind speak it.

"Nor is she likely to forget. Indeed, she never should forget what occurred! She nearly ruined herself, and your name, your reputation, and your marital prospects would have suffered as well. Thank God there were no consequences to speak of, though I still do not know if she truly understood all I was asking of her at the time."

"Nor do I wish to know. Let us speak of other things."

"As you like. When does Bingley take possession of this new estate of his? What is it called?"

"Netherfield Park. He took possession at Michaelmas. We will join him there in a fortnight."

"Were you not supposed to advise him on letting this estate last month?"

"I was, but we had just brought Georgiana to town from Kent. I could not have travelled to Hertfordshire at that time. In any case, he had Hurst to advise him in my stead."

"It is a wonder that he made do, then. I cannot recollect ever seeing Hurst when he was not in his cups."

Darcy snorted. "He is sober enough when Bingley's sisters are otherwise occupied, believe me. Hurst likes his sport even more than he likes his port, and he cannot hold a gun properly in an inebriated state. He would be more likely to shoot his dogs than a brace of pheasant."

Fitzwilliam laughed. "Enough said."

"In any case, Bingley is a grown man and every bit as intelligent as he is competent. He lacks only confidence, which I daresay he shall acquire after being master of an estate for a while. I cannot always be instructing him on the management of his affairs. Someday he will desire to settle down and take a wife, and I do not relish him asking if I find her suitable enough or capable enough or, God forbid, comely enough to hold his interest in their marriage bed." Darcy shook his head. "I am the last person whose opinion he should seek on any matter. I can barely manage my own affairs of late."

The colonel waved his hand dismissively. "Pemberley is thriving. It is only this business with Georgiana that concerns you at present, and that will eventually work itself out. She will not always be so solemn and withdrawn. Fifteen *is* a most trying age. A girl such as Georgiana, who is inherently shy and uncertain and without the counsel of a mother or elder sister, must feel it even more acutely. Take her into Hertford-shire and see what happens. Who can tell? She may meet a delightful young lady who can coax her out of her shell."

"Perhaps," Darcy muttered. "Or perhaps she will be worse for wear."

"There you go—despairing again! Are you taking Georgiana's companion or are you keeping this sojourn a family affair?"

"Mrs Annesley shall accompany us. She is sensible and has an endless amount of patience, whereas my patience is nearly exhausted. She will be a safe harbour for Georgiana whenever I must attend Bingley, which I surmise shall be often."

"You have obviously thought this through," said Fitzwilliam, linking his hands behind his head, "so enjoy yourself. Spend as much time as you like shooting Bingley's birds and thrashing him at billiards. Bingley's sisters will see to it that Georgiana is entertained, and Mrs Annesley will be there to guide her in your absence. She should do well there, Darcy. You can afford to indulge yourself with your friend, especially if your sister makes one herself." A slow, bawdy grin brightened his countenance. "Who knows, perhaps you might make a new friend as well, although far prettier than the likes of Bingley, I would hope!"

Darcy threw a piece of sealing wax at him. "That is the last thing I need. Attend to your own friends and leave me to manage mine."

Fitzwilliam smirked at him, then tossed the wax onto his desk. "You live like a monk. Should you ever deign to live like the rest of us poor sots, believe me, I shall gladly leave you to manage any pretty friends you might make. Until that day comes, I shall endeavour to tease you until you either beg for mercy or see the merit in my sage instruction."

The large, well-sprung coach-and-four bearing the Darcy crest made its way along the dusty London Road towards Hertfordshire at a slow, but steady pace. The cobbled streets of Mayfair were far behind them, and the unevenness of the ruts made the conveyance rock and sway, despite the efforts put forth by the driver to avoid them.

"At least it is not raining," Darcy muttered to himself, grasping the leather strap attached to the roof as he imagined the added inconvenience of having his coach wheels mired in a foot of thick mud. His spotted Great Dane lay at his feet, and across from him, seated on the forward-facing seat, Georgiana peered out of the window. Despite his intent to bring Mrs Annesley, the elder woman did not accompany them. Several days before they were due to depart, she received word that her daughter had fallen ill. Darcy, lately feeling the absence of his own mother acutely, gave her leave to go to Manchester and nurse her.

With a long-suffering sigh, his eyes alighted on the open book on his sister's lap. Georgiana had barely glanced at it during their journey, and Darcy was of the opinion she had brought it to deter conversation. Of late, she had become as adept at avoidance as she was skilled at the pianoforte.

For the last fortnight, his sister had all but lived at the instrument, striving to master increasingly more complex pieces of music. Beethoven's darker compositions had been her obsession for some time, but she had recently taken up Bach's *Chaconne in D Minor*. Although Darcy would prefer her current repertoire contained some lighter fare as well, he did not begrudge her the challenge and concentration that such difficult compositions afforded her. Constant dedication to her music was the one thing that seemed to bring Georgiana any measure of solace, and Darcy was reluctant to interfere. He hoped her playing would in some way aid her in finding her way, if not to the innocent girl she once was, then perhaps to the enigmatic young woman she would eventually become. The last thing he wished to do was discourage her, so he indulged her complex tastes and supplied her with sheet music and a new London master.

An hour later they arrived in Meryton, the only market town within ten miles of Netherfield Park. It was late in the day, but there appeared to be quite a few people bustling about King Street, many of whom were staring curiously at them as their carriage rolled through the town. The usual shops and accommodations lined the road, including a bookseller, a haberdashery, and a modiste. Darcy pointed out the various establishments, including a small circulating library, to Georgiana. "Perhaps the bookseller has some sheet music," he told her. "Though, it is probably not so wide a variety or current a selection as we are used to seeing in London."

"Perhaps," she replied quietly, offering him a timid smile. "I am always grateful to have new music."

"Then I shall endeavour to ensure that you receive some while we are here."

Georgiana turned her attention to the passing scenery, and Darcy consulted his watch. The journey had taken them a little over five hours, including several stops at coaching inns along the way to refresh themselves and to partake of some light fare while the horses were watered.

"According to Bingley's letter, Netherfield should be within a mile or two of Meryton. I believe we are nearly there."

"The landscape is very different here," Georgiana observed, gazing out of the window as the shops, solicitor's office, and tradesmen's homes faded from view, yielding a softer, more natural environment. The sun hung low over the horizon, giving the landscape a warm, burnished look. "It is beautiful, is it not, Brother?"

Darcy could not disagree. While the deep autumn reds, golden yellows, and burnt oranges of Hertfordshire were not dissimilar to what one might see further north, the terrain itself was unfamiliar. There were no beloved peaks or smooth, majestic boulders, only lush, rolling hills as far as the eye could see and wide, expansive fields. No doubt many of those hills afforded a spectacular view of the surrounding country-side, and Darcy, after spending so much time confined to the coach, felt an almost restless desire to acquaint himself with them. The hour, however, was far too late in the day to sate such a desire. He and Georgiana would likely arrive at Netherfield then rest, bathe, dress, dine, and converse a bit before retiring for the night.

Tomorrow, Darcy told himself, shifting impatiently in his seat. Tomorrow he would rise at the crack of dawn, saddle one of Bingley's horses, and tear through the countryside in quest of the picturesque beauty that awaited him from the top of those rolling hills. He had ridden in Hyde Park every day while in London, laying claim to Rotten Row in the early morning when the members of the fashionable set were still abed; but Darcy had missed the vastness and untamed beauty of the English countryside with a passion he found difficult to ignore.

After passing an emotionally draining week in Ramsgate, he had begun to feel the ever-constant pull of his beloved Pemberley. Instead of heading to Derbyshire, though, Colonel Fitzwilliam had convinced him to bring Georgiana to town, where she could be seen rather than hidden away from the world. To keep her under lock and key at Pemberley, Fitzwilliam had reasoned, would only serve to incite specula-tion about the family's absence from society. As it turned out,

Georgiana had hidden herself away quite stubbornly in London despite their efforts, but since Parliament had adjourned on the thirteenth of August and the air in town was so oppressive, few people of their acquaintance remained to comment on their withdrawal. With the arrival of autumn, everyone of notoriety was either in the country hunting on their estates or attending house parties at the estates of their friends.

Darcy's thoughts turned to Bingley, whose genial nature and easy manners never failed to attract a multitude of acquaintance. Though his friend had assured him their party would be an intimate one, Darcy could not help feeling wary, especially so close to Netherfield Park. Bingley had a frustrating habit of admiring and being admired in turn wherever he went; it was entirely possible the Darcys would arrive to a house full of Bingley's friends instead of the quiet family party they had been promised.

Darcy shut his eyes at the prospect. The entire summer had afforded nothing but disappointment and vexation. He fervently hoped Bingley would not add to it by expecting him to be more sociable than his nature allowed. His temper had barely been under regulation since the end of July, and Darcy knew it was only a matter of time until someone or something would cause him to lose it utterly. For Bingley's sake, he hoped he would be able to prevent a scene and avoid causing offence.

THREE

⌒⊙⌒

It is not time or opportunity that is to determine intimacy;
it is disposition alone.

"How wonderful it is to see you again, Mr Darcy,"
said Miss Bingley as the servants removed an elaborately
painted soup tureen from the dinner table and replaced it
with a steaming haunch of roast venison, boiled potatoes, root
vegetables, and duck ragout. "And you as well, my dear Miss
Darcy. How tall you have grown since the last time I saw you!
I daresay you are nearly my height."

Inclining his head to his smiling hostess, Darcy extended
his thanks for what he estimated was the tenth time since his
arrival and turned his attention to the platter of venison. He
had been in Bingley's house for no more than a handful of
hours and already Miss Bingley and her condescension were
grating on his nerves. How he would survive the next month
under the same roof as her was anyone's guess. For the sake of
his sanity, he resolved to seek employment out of doors as
often as possible.

"I am grateful to you, Miss Bingley," Georgiana replied,
albeit timidly, from Darcy's right. "It is kind of you to invite
me to stay."

"The pleasure is entirely ours, Miss Darcy. When
Charles mentioned that you were to accompany your dear

brother, I was beside myself with delight. Louisa and I have come to look upon you quite as our own sister, have we not, Louisa?"

"Oh, of course! We are both excessively fond of you," cried Mrs Hurst from across the table. She smiled widely at Georgiana before turning towards Mr Hurst, who had demanded someone pass him the potatoes.

Darcy, who thought that was an excellent idea, skewered a piece of venison and placed it on his plate with a slice of apple loaf.

"I think," said Bingley good naturedly from the foot of the table, "there is nothing so pleasant as sharing one's home with one's friends. I am glad to have you both as well. I am only sorry, Darcy, that you were unable to see the place until now. But it is no matter. The house is sound, the summer harvest was bountiful, and the neighbourhood is uniformly charming. In fact, I have received as hearty a welcome as I could have hoped from my neighbours. The gentlemen I have met are most cordial and I have enjoyed receiving them here at Netherfield as much as I have enjoyed making calls at their estates in turn."

"I am glad to hear it, Bingley. I look forward to viewing the estate and seeing more of the neighbourhood. The house appears to be in excellent condition and seems comfortable. Despite the soundness of the place, I am certain you must have some ideas for improvements."

"Oh, indeed, I do, Mr Darcy," Miss Bingley interjected before her brother could reply. "The family quarters, of course, will need to be improved as well as the conservatory, and the main drawing room must be completely redone in the French style."

Hurst snorted as he raised his wine glass to his lips and swallowed a large gulp. "How patriotic of you, Caroline."

Miss Bingley lifted her chin. "War or no war," she said

imperiously, "the French are foremost regarding all that is fashionable." She waved a dismissive hand. "In any case, I long to erect a Grecian temple on the south lawn. Your aunt, Lady Catherine de Bourgh, has one on her estate in Kent, I hear. It must be inspiring!"

"She does," was all Darcy ventured to say in response.

"Perhaps you can advise me. I am determined to send to town for an architect. No doubt, he would welcome your involvement."

"And I am certain he would not, madam. Surely, whomever you retain will do an admirable job. I am no architect."

"You are far too modest, sir! Pemberley is unequalled in beauty, grandeur, and taste, and though Netherfield Park cannot possibly compare to its general majesty, I am convinced that you will have much to contribute as we make improvements to the house and grounds here."

Annoyed and hungry, Darcy glanced from Miss Bingley to the venison on his plate, which he had yet to touch, and sighed inwardly. "Pemberley has been the work of many generations, Miss Bingley. I am hardly responsible for its design, only its maintenance."

"I understand the grand stables are considered quite new."

"They were erected when I was a boy."

Miss Bingley brightened. "Then the man responsible for designing Pemberley's stable is precisely the man who must design our folly! You must write to him and plead our case."

"I am afraid that is impossible," Darcy replied. "Regrettably, Mr Paine—"

"Impossible?" Miss Bingley parroted. "Certainly, erecting a folly is a trifle compared to an entire stable! I am convinced if you only write to him and explain our connexion, this Mr Paine would be only too happy to oblige us."

"Miss Bingley, James Paine has been deceased for twenty years. His obliging you is a non-issue."

"Oh. How inconvenient," she said with a frown. "Well, surely you must know some other person—"

"For the love of Job, Caroline," Hurst cried. "Let the poor man eat! Darcy did not spend his day in a coach only to starve to death at the supper table."

"Oh, Mr Hurst," said his wife with a giddy little laugh as she dumped a ladleful of sauce on her husband's turnips. "You are so droll!"

Although Darcy was used to such brusque commentary from Hurst, his sister was not. "Georgiana," he said gently, "I believe Miss Bingley and Mrs Hurst would enjoy hearing about your progress with Mr Stapleton, your new music master."

"But of course," Miss Bingley replied warmly. "You must tell us every detail, Miss Darcy—though, I cannot imagine you of all people needing a music master, not when you are already so proficient."

"I am hardly a true proficient," Georgiana insisted, addressing her supper. "I have much yet to learn."

"And so modest," Miss Bingley remarked with an indulgent smile. "You have nothing to repine on that score. You are by far one of the most accomplished young ladies of our acquaintance. Why, I cannot think of anyone so talented as you."

"Nor can I," Mrs Hurst agreed as she selected a roll and presented it to her husband for his approval.

After shovelling a fork full of peas into his mouth, Hurst grunted his assent.

"You must play for us this evening!"

Georgiana glanced at Darcy with a look of alarm. "Please do not ask me to play. You are so accomplished yourself, Miss

31

Bingley. I am sure that everyone would much rather hear *you* play."

"Nonsense," Bingley insisted with a bright smile. "It would be an honour, Miss Darcy. I believe I mentioned to your brother that there is a fine pianoforte in the drawing room. Indeed, it looks quite grand. For the life of me I cannot recall the maker, but Caroline and Louisa assure me it is an excellent instrument."

Darcy watched his sister slowly withdraw into herself, no doubt in a panic at the thought of being forced to play in public, and mentally cursed himself for ever mentioning the topic of music masters. He ought to have anticipated Miss Bingley would insist that Georgiana perform, but Darcy had been so eager to change the topic that he had not given the next one any degree of consideration. Feeling almost as wretched as Georgiana looked, he sought her hand beneath the table and gave it a gentle squeeze. "Georgiana," he murmured in her ear, hoping to bring her back to the present conversation so they might soon put it to rest. "Mr Bingley cannot recall the name of the company that manufactured his pianoforte. Do you recall anything of it from his letter?"

Her eyes were fixed on her plate, but she took a fortifying breath and said, "I believe your pianoforte is a Broadwood grand, Mr Bingley."

"And is that a sufficient instrument, Miss Darcy? Would *you* enjoy playing such an instrument?"

"Oh, yes," she assured him. "A Broadwood grand is a truly exemplary instrument. I look forward to playing yours very much, but our journey today has made me tired. Please allow me to postpone performing until another evening. I was so looking forward to the pleasure of hearing Miss Bingley play instead."

"As was I," said Darcy, offering his sister a small, conciliatory smile she did not see.

"Then I will join you in persuading my sister to oblige us," Bingley pronounced in his usual, genial fashion. "I must beg your pardon for making such a presumption. Of course, we cannot possibly expect you to play for us when you have only just arrived. Please, think no more of it."

"Yes," cooed Mrs Hurst, placing a hearty serving of duck ragout onto her husband's plate. "You should think no more of it, my dear."

Draining the last of the wine from his glass, Hurst grunted his approval, though Darcy could not discern whether his approval was for Miss Bingley playing in Georgiana's stead, or for the ragout.

"What say you, Caroline?" Bingley asked. "Will you lead the way this evening?"

Miss Bingley glanced at Darcy with a gratified smile. "It will be my pleasure. I am always happy to play for such dear friends. You must tell me, Mr Darcy, if you prefer a certain composer or if you have a favourite sonata so I may play it for you."

Bingley grinned as he returned his attention to his supper. "Excellent idea, Caroline."

From beneath the table, Darcy felt Georgiana's fingers tighten around his own and breathed an inaudible sigh of relief. She had handled herself well and he was proud of her. With Miss Bingley seated at the instrument, that lady would be unable to engage him in shallow pleasantries and flirtations that would only further try his patience, and Miss Bingley in turn would be at leisure to play and exhibit to her heart's content. It was an arrangement that suited everyone.

To Miss Bingley he said, "I am much obliged to you, madam."

To Georgiana, he murmured his gratitude and pressed her hand.

The following morning dawned clear and crisp. Eager to be out of doors, Darcy was dressed and striding across the lawn towards Netherfield's stables before the last of the stars had faded from the brightening sky. After a quick perusal of Bingley's horses, a sleepy looking stable boy saddled a spirited bay named Agador and, within a quarter hour, Darcy was cantering across the park towards the fields. A cluster of smooth, rolling hills, shrouded in mist and resplendent with the colours of autumn, lay a few miles to the south. The fresh air, as well as the exercise required to reach them, would be a welcome reprieve after the stifling formality of Miss Bingley's drawing room the night before.

Spurring Agador to a gallop, Darcy raced through Hertfordshire's countryside. Acres of fields, reaped of their summer harvests, passed by in a blur as the sun rose above the horizon. Farther afield, tenant farmers tended their winter crops with efficient, determined movements. The fruits of their labour would yield a hearty return of their efforts: a veritable bounty born of toil and vigilant care that would ensure their prosperity and see them through the following year.

As usual, Pemberley was not far from the forefront of Darcy's mind. Even before earning his degree from Cambridge, he had remained on the estate from late summer until well into the autumn to personally oversee the harvest. This year was different. Fortunately, he had an excellent steward, else he would never have dared travel into Hertfordshire. His man Shepherd would have everything well in hand; but that was only a cursory solution to a single problem. Of late, everything, including his dissatisfaction with the world, seemed to come full circle back to George Wickham's attempted elopement with his sister.

Uttering a harsh exhalation, Darcy dug his heels into his horse's sides and rode at a near reckless pace until the landscape changed from that of low-lying fields to higher, greener pastures dotted with sheep and crowned with hedgerows. By the time man and beast had scaled the hillside, Darcy's anger had taken a more sanguine turn.

Breathing heavily, he reined in Agador and dismounted. After tethering the horse securely to a sturdy apple tree that still bore evidence of fruit, Darcy wandered along the perimeter of an outcropping of rock that overlooked endless miles of fertile land. The view was magnificent. The mist had begun to dissipate, and from this vantage point Darcy could easily make out Netherfield and the town of Meryton in the distance. The London Road lay beyond. Directly below, scattered along the mouth of a protective valley, a handful of modest manor houses stood proudly among orchards, farms, and infinite acres of fields that had, until recently, overflowed with golden heads of wheat, barley, and rye.

The manor house belonging to the nearest estate was quite close and appeared to be constructed of smooth, dark hued sandstone. Designed on a grander scale than the rest, save for Netherfield, it boasted a moderate sized park, several gardens, and a pretty little wilderness on one side of the property. A stable and stable yard, a carriage house, a barn, and a series of outbuildings were located some distance from the back of the house. The drive at the front was paved with crushed stone. A road wide enough to accommodate a carriage or wagon wound alongside the pale that marked it, past a fieldstone church, and through the countryside for a mile or so before intersecting King Street in the centre of Meryton. If he had to guess, Darcy would say that most of the surrounding fields, as well as a decent sized orchard and a sizeable pond, likely belonged to this principal estate.

The sharp crow of a cockerel drew his gaze back to the sandstone manor, where plumes of smoke curled in unhurried fashion from the chimney pieces. A woman emerged from the front entrance of the house, far more attentive to securing her bonnet than securing the placement of her feet. The surety of her steps surprised him almost as much as the briskness of her pace. In Darcy's experience, ladies did not rush about—they walked slowly and methodically. They certainly did not venture out alone at the crack of dawn on a chilly autumn morning. Darcy observed her with a curious sort of fascination as she made her way with alacrity through the gardens and across the park towards a dense wood brimming with brightly coloured leaves. With the same decided efficiency and lightness of foot, she entered the forest and disappeared.

Several minutes passed before Darcy realised that he had been scanning the woods below, unwittingly searching for a glimpse of her through the trees. Shaking his head at his uncharacteristic behaviour, he turned his back on the valley, its fields, its orchards, and its insignificant manor houses. Surely, this woman's morning constitutional did not merit his attention any more than the woman herself. He abandoned his station at the rocky edge and returned to his horse.

Across the way, a great murmuration of starlings rolled and dipped in an eerie, undulating dance high above the hillside. Darcy plucked an apple from the tree where Agador was tethered, claimed a makeshift seat upon a large rock, and watched them while he enjoyed his impromptu repast. Their synchronised aerial performance was very different from the perfunctory glide of the gulls who levitated above the coast, patrolling the beaches and tide pools in search of their next meal. A sudden gust of wind blew in from the north, and Darcy closed his eyes. If he concentrated, he could almost imagine he was on the blustery chalk cliffs of the Kent shoreline rather than perched on a grassy hilltop in Hertfordshire.

What transpired in Ramsgate had been incredibly painful, but there were aspects of the town itself that had made the circumstances that necessitated his stay there bearable: the fresh, salty scent of the air; the stark beauty of the bright, white cliffs; the cool, welcoming touch of the sea at sunrise; and the sense of serenity and detachment he felt as he dove beneath the waves, propelling himself through the water as his body embraced the gauntlet thrown by the tide. Bathing in the sea had been his salvation. It was the one place where Darcy found he did not feel strangled by convention or cowed by societal politesse. In the briny embrace of the sea, in his most natural state, he was not burdened by the expectations of responsibility, duty, and honour. He was not the master of a great estate, or a brother, or a nephew, or a son. In those precious moments, however brief their duration, Fitzwilliam Darcy of Pemberley had felt a sense of freedom he had never truly known.

The distinct snap of branches and the rhythmic crunch of leaves recalled his attention to the present. He looked towards a dense cluster of deciduous trees a short distance away and was startled to see a familiar, rust-coloured bonnet emerge from among them. Without so much as a glance in his direction, the bonnet's owner untied the burgundy ribbons beneath her chin and skipped to the edge of the rocks.

No sooner had she removed her bonnet than a cascade of dark curls tumbled halfway down her back. Darcy's breath caught. As if that was not scandalous enough, she was backlit by the sun, and her silhouette was revealed to him in shocking relief. All coherent thought left him, and Darcy found he could not avert his eyes from the sight of her. Her unbound hair, her shapely limbs, her flaring hips, her slender waist—all roused a desire long repressed.

A sudden gale whipped her hair into further disorder and twisted her skirts about her ankles. She made a valiant effort to tame her unruly locks and smooth her billowing gown into submission, but her exertion proved futile. The sound of a rich, musical laugh carried to Darcy on the wind as she abandoned her efforts and tilted her face to the sky.

Darcy was mortified. No doubt this gentlewoman would not wish to be ogled and objectified, especially by an ineloquent stranger who lacked the decency to announce himself. It was the idea of her own mortification and the vulnerability of her situation that restored his presence of mind and with it his gentlemanly inclination. He took a moment to compose himself, then discarded his apple core and made his presence known.

She turned towards him with a start, her gloved hand pressed to her breast. "Oh!" she cried as her countenance coloured with a heated blush. Frantically, she gathered her hair, twisting it into some appearance of respectability as she hastily replaced her bonnet and executed a flawless curtsey. "I beg your pardon, sir. I had not the slightest inkling there was anyone about Oakham Mount this morning. I was under the impression I was alone."

For the briefest moment, Darcy considered enquiring whether she made a habit of running up hills and letting her hair down in public whenever she thought she was alone, but his good breeding forbade his uttering such a thing. It was bad enough he had thought it in the first place. Fixing his eyes upon the ribbon beneath her chin, he offered her a curt inclination of his head and said stiffly, "The fault is mine. I should have made my presence known to you at once. I did not."

She stepped away from the precarious drop at the rocky edge. Linking her fingers together, she glanced towards the woods, the path, and finally back to him. "Pray tell me, why did you not?"

While her figure had captivated him, her eyes, the colour of West Indies molasses, rendered him speechless. Rich, compelling, and utterly beautiful, they were fringed with lashes so long they nearly brushed her cheek. There was a brilliancy and an expressiveness in their depths that hinted at an intelligence and a strength of spirit Darcy had not expected to find in such a young woman. He could not imagine her age to be more than nineteen or twenty, yet her eyes spoke to him of untold mysteries, ancient gardens, and temptation.

"Sir?"

"What?"

One slender brow arched in a most becoming manner. "I enquired as to why you did not make your presence known immediately. You appear to be a gentleman of ample discernment. Surely, you could not have failed to notice my approach."

Darcy felt a flush of heat rise along the back of his neck as he recalled precisely why he had failed to make his presence known. Her disarming frankness felt like an admonishment, something Darcy was not used to receiving in any measure from any lady other than his aunt Catherine, who was impossible to please. That he deserved to be upbraided for his reticence was incontrovertible but being called upon by this inconsequential country miss to answer for his deficiency provoked his ire. Rather than account for himself, Darcy assumed an expression of hauteur and remained stubbornly silent.

While such a blunt, unsociable response had never failed to cow the dogged determination of the ladies of London, it appeared to have little effect on the inconsequential miss. If anything, her brow inched slightly higher.

Darcy's dismay was not easily concealed. *What sort of young woman runs around the countryside without a chap-*

eron, scales hillsides at the crack of dawn, and takes strangers to task at the slightest provocation? Even more astonishing, what sort of people deem such behaviour permissible?

There was no doubt in his mind this singular young lady was the daughter of a gentleman, but the quality and style of her dress, while not exactly lacking, revealed that her father's consequence and yearly income by no means equalled his own. That she was attractive had not escaped Darcy's observation, but her beauty was not that of the classic variety currently so fashionable among the *bon ton*. Had he seen her in London he would likely never have paid her any notice.

As if sensing his conflict—and his slight—she crossed her arms with a look of expectancy and some other emotion he could not quite name.

Good God, she is persistent!

He glanced at his horse, contentedly eating apples beneath the tree, and repressed an oath. While he could simply jump on Agador's back and ride away without uttering another word, the likelihood he would cross paths with this gentlewoman again while in Hertfordshire was considerable. If Bingley ever learnt of it—and Darcy was certain he would—there would be no living with him. He must answer her. There was nothing else to be done. "I assure you, madam," he said crisply, "your appearance here was both unexpected and sudden and took me completely by surprise." There. *Some* measure of honesty and decorum was still within his power.

"Of course," she replied pertly. "I can well imagine *your* surprise."

Darcy blinked at her in astonishment. Arrogant ladies he knew. Grasping ladies he knew. Disingenuous, simpering ladies he knew. An impertinent lady, however, was something of a novelty to a man of Darcy's stature. He decided two could play this game. With a hubristic turn of his brow, he applied for her forgiveness and awaited the inevitable bestowal of it.

Instead of absolving him for his insufficiency, she tilted her head to the side and scrutinised him for what felt like a small eternity. She looked as though she were giving the matter a great deal of consideration, as well as taking his measure. She did not, however, look the least bit moved by his apology. "Very well, sir," she said at length. "I shall forgive you your offence so long as you promise to announce yourself promptly in the future. I shall not have you frightening the other ladies in Hertfordshire out of their wits. They have not my fortitude."

Darcy frowned. Could this simply be another impertinent performance, or could his presence have truly caused her alarm? It was impossible to tell. He repressed a sigh of irritation. His morning had not turned out at all the way he had anticipated. Grudgingly, he said, "I am sorry to have frightened you. It was unconsciously done."

"I thank you for your apology, but your intent matters little. What matters is your sincerity."

He could hardly believe her audacity. "My sincerity is by no means lacking."

To his utter consternation, she smiled at him, but her smile showed her doubt.

"You believe me insincere?" he cried incredulously.

"What I believe is that you are a man used to having your own way and quite unused to explaining yourself, even when the occasion, as well as politesse, requires it."

Darcy pursed his lips. Her discernment was infuriating, but by no means inaccurate.

"Oh, *that* will never do," she said agreeably, "for my courage always rises with every attempt to intimidate me."

"Intimidate you! Madam, I already stated it was not my intent—"

"Oh, I know. It was not your intent to intimidate me *then,* but I doubt you can claim so now. Your countenance may resemble a storm cloud, but I am not afraid of you. You are by no means so fearsome a creature as my dear mother, sir! Your ire when incited, I am certain, is nothing to hers."

Darcy fixed her with a level look. "That, madam, would depend upon how far my patience has been tried by impertinent ladies."

"Oh dear," she murmured. "I see I have poked a lion."

"A habit of yours, I presume."

Her eyes sparkled with something akin to mischief. "Only on very special occasions."

It was at that moment Darcy realised he would not be the victor of whatever battle he was presently engaged in with this impertinent little piece. Every facet of her behaviour baffled him! He had no idea what to make of her, what to say to her, or how to act. He wondered whether all the ladies in Hertfordshire were like this one—daring and impudent one minute and disarming the next. If so, the entire shire would think him inept! As far as this young woman was concerned, his appearing the least bit dignified at this point was likely a lost cause. He shook his head with a self-deprecating twist of his mouth. "It appears I am much out of my element. I have absolutely no idea what to say in reply that would not be misconstrued by yourself as ungentlemanly."

"In that case, I believe you have been teased enough. Do not expect to receive an apology for it, however, for I suspect you could use a great deal of teasing. Instead, I shall apologise for any umbrage my teasing may have incited. Should we happen to meet again, it would be terribly awkward for all if we are unable to do so with at least the appearance of equanimity between us."

When she had finished saying her piece, her fingers fluttered to the hastily tied bow beneath her chin. As she delivered her speech she had smiled, but now that she had finished her smile faded. For the first time since Darcy had come upon her, this confident slip-of-a-woman appeared uncertain.

His gaze darted from her burgundy bow to her compelling brown eyes. Minutes ago, he had witnessed her fingers tug impatiently at those ribbons and cast off her bonnet to reveal her unbound hair. How lovely she had looked with her dark tresses flowing freely about her shoulders and down her back! When the wind had whipped them around her head, she had melted into laughter without a care in the world and soon after summoned the courage not only to face him but to upbraid and tease him. She was a paradox and an enigma and absolutely nothing like the dour, simpering ladies of the *ton*.

For some inexplicable reason, it bothered Darcy to see this spirited young woman looking so serious; for the same inexplicable reason, he found himself desiring something he had never desired from any lady of his acquaintance before—her good opinion. "Pray, do not make yourself uneasy. I was perhaps not as sincere as I ought to have been when I issued my own apology. You owe me nothing. You were entirely justified when you took me to task for my deficiency."

Her complexion flushed with warmth. "While I appreciate your view of the matter, you cannot deny that my frankness offended you. Surely, I owe you an apology for that much at least!"

Darcy studied her for a long moment as a myriad of conflicting emotions churned in his breast. Her blushing countenance, her liveliness, and her dark, soulful eyes inspired a yearning he did not wish to acknowledge never mind contemplate.

Instead of repeating his previous assurance that he bore

her no ill will, he decided to take a leaf out of her own book and try his hand at teasing her. He said, "If my acceptance of your apology will ease your conscience, then so be it. As for your frankness, I can bear *that* with as much fortitude as any other poor, unsuspecting gentleman so unfortunate as to come under your scrutiny. Your impertinence is another matter. While my own ability is woefully deficient at present, I daresay under your tutelage I should soon improve to such a degree as to become a proficient."

"I see you are not so defenceless after all," she replied with a delighted laugh. "Well met, sir. I applaud your mettle, as well as your superior understanding of the matter, especially as pertains to my impertinence. I had hoped to pass myself off with some degree of credibility this morning but now see it is a hopeless case."

"No doubt, because you enjoy professing opinions which are not your own."

Her eyes in that moment were especially fine. Their expression and lustre inspired thoughts of wood nymphs come to entice Darcy to do God only knew what. Although the wind was brisk, he felt a sudden flush of warmth.

"I see you have found me out, and in very little time, too. It appears I have provided you ample opportunity to sketch my character, but I fear the likeness you have drawn has painted me in a most unpropitious light! I ought to repine such a misfortune, but I confess that I cannot. Now, despise me if you dare."

"Indeed," Darcy replied, his lips lifting infinitesimally, "I do not dare."

Far too soon for his liking her smile faded, and her countenance became serious once more. "In addition to accepting my apology, I hope you will be so good as to refrain from mentioning our meeting to anyone. We have not been introduced, after all, and the society here is relatively limited when compared to that of London. News travels quickly and wagging tongues are not always kind."

Darcy was as startled by the earnestness in her voice as he was by her request. He was unused to young ladies and their mothers wishing to keep any sort of interaction with him and his wealth a secret—quite the contrary. He could not, however, disavow the truth of the matter anymore than he could fault her good sense and offered her a formal bow of acknowledgement. "You may be assured of my secrecy. No word of our meeting shall cross my lips. Should we have the pleasure of seeing each other again in the future, it shall be as though for the first time."

One slender brow rose eloquently. "And will it truly be a pleasure?"

Darcy endeavoured to remain decorous, but her sparkling eyes and her teasing mouth made him want to smile. "I shall try to make the best of it, despite the risk I run of falling victim to your unconscionable teasing."

"I thank you for such a generous concession. And now I must return home. My family is used to my morning rambles, but my mother has little patience for them, especially today."

"Then I will not detain you. However dear she is, I would not wish for you to incur the displeasure of so fearsome a creature. I bid you a pleasant day."

"A good day to you as well." With an expedient curtsey and a charming smile, she turned and departed the way she had come. There was no further attempt at conversation. No fluttering of her lashes or pouting of her lips. No backwards glances letting him know she did not wish to part from him. No indication whatsoever that she either wanted or expected anything from Darcy beyond his silence and discretion.

He watched her walk to the edge of the woods, this time at a much more sedate and respectable pace. She stepped onto the path and, for the second time that morning, disappeared from his view. For one incalculable moment, Darcy felt a pang of longing in his breast. As quickly as it had come upon him, the sensation was gone. He shook his head at the absurdity of such a thing, untethered his horse, and prepared to return to Netherfield.

FOUR

To be fond of dancing was a certain step towards falling in love.

"How was your walk, Lizzy? You were gone for some time. Did you happen to meet the highly coveted Mr Bingley on your way to Oakham Mount this morning?" Mr Bennet held up his hand. "No, no. Do not tell me. Upon further reflection, I would prefer to remain in ignorance of such matters."

"As you wish, Papa," Elizabeth replied as she claimed a seat beside her father at the breakfast table. She poured herself a cup of tea and recalled the handsome, staid gentleman with whom she did happen to meet. She had no idea whether he was indeed Mr Bingley or another member of his party. It hardly signified, as they had not been introduced. A sudden flush of heat warmed her countenance as Elizabeth remembered the range of emotions reflected in his dark eyes with startling clarity: seriousness, then arrogance, irritation, disbelief, and finally a spark of amusement. When they parted, he had been quite civil, even teasing. She added cream to her tea and willed her heightened colour to dissipate.

"Have you nothing of any import to relate, child?" her father enquired absently from behind his newspaper.

"I had thought to spare you the tedious details of my morning constitutional, sir, but since you are inclined towards conversation, allow me to relate the temperature is cool and the sky clear. I regret I can offer no comment on the state of the roads at present." She raised her brow archly. "I trust the weather is a perfectly sensible topic of conversation on the day of an assembly?"

"Yes," he remarked. "That will do, my dear."

Elizabeth raised her teacup to her lips and took a slow sip. "Is my mother still abed?"

Her father snorted. "On the morning of an assembly? Perish the thought! She is likely facing the perils of her toilet and working herself into a fit of nerves the likes of which have rarely been seen."

"Fear not," Elizabeth assured him as her lips lifted in a smile. "With five unmarried daughters, there is little chance of her nerves keeping her at home this evening, not when the eligible Mr Bingley must be in want of a wife."

"Quite true," Mr Bennet conceded as he turned the page of his newspaper and shook it out. "I hope your heart is not set on marrying the gentleman, Lizzy. Your mother, no doubt, has ambitions to push Jane on him first and, in the event her beauty, comportment, and serenity of countenance fail to tempt him, Lydia and her animal spirits will surely be next in line. Who can tell? Perhaps he will prefer a silly, ignorant girl for his wife rather than a steady young woman of sense and inclination. He would by no means be the first."

While Elizabeth loved her father dearly, she wished he would not speak disparagingly about her sisters. The two youngest were certainly impulsive and silly enough, but his saying so at every turn did nothing to improve their behaviour. If anything, it made it worse. "I assure you I have no designs on Mr Bingley. If I am so fortunate as to dance more sets than I am obliged to sit out, I shall consider the evening a success."

"That is the spirit, my dear," he said drily. "Be fore-warned that your affectionate mother may be of an entirely different opinion. If you have not captured the interest of a discerning young man by the time the dance is ended, you may well find yourself out of her favour."

"I believe I can bear the deprivation," she responded in a similar tone. "It would hardly be the first time."

"No," her father said with a laugh. "I daresay it would not."

&

"Elizabeth Bennet," said her mother from the forward-facing seat of their family carriage as they entered Meryton. "Stop your fidgeting at once or you will ruin the lace on your gown! We do not need Mr Bingley noticing your poor comportment when he ought to be noticing Jane instead."

Jane, who was seated beside Elizabeth on the rear-facing seat, grasped her sister's hand between her own. "When Mr Bingley notices Lizzy, Mama, it will be for her beauty alone. She looks especially lovely this evening. I defy any gentleman to find her less than handsome and agreeable."

Mrs Bennet scrutinised her second daughter in the dark-ened interior. "Lizzy does look very well, I grant you, but her looks are nothing to yours, Jane. Mark my words. If Mr Bingley is to fall in love with one of you it will not be with Lizzy."

"Thank you, Mama," Elizabeth replied tartly. "Such praise is indeed sobering. I shall endeavour to keep it from going to my head."

Across the carriage, their youngest sister, Lydia, who was but fifteen and already out in society, snorted.

Kitty, who was two years older, huffed. "Lydia, you are squashing me!"

"I am not squashing you," Lydia proclaimed indignantly. "You are taking up too much room!"

"Kitty," Jane admonished. "Lydia, please."

Ignoring their bickering, Mrs Bennet resumed issuing instructions to Elizabeth. "I shall have none of your usual impertinence tonight. No gentleman of means wants a wife who behaves impudently or talks of things no one can understand. If you cannot follow your sister Mary's example and refrain from uttering anything clever, you will bite your tongue and remain silent."

Elizabeth pursed her lips as she watched Mary, their middle sister, endeavour to hide her injured countenance by turning aside her head. Perhaps holding her tongue was a practice best applied sooner rather than later. A murmured, "Yes, Mama," was all she ventured to say on the subject.

As gentle as a lamb, Jane consoled Mary. Unlike Elizabeth's two youngest sisters, Mary was plain, moralistic, and reserved, and did not care for dancing. She preferred books to ballrooms and would much rather remain at home and read than attend an assembly, despite the assurance of a rich, unmarried gentleman being in attendance.

Having said her piece to Elizabeth, Mrs Bennet began fussing over the ribbons on Lydia's gown and chiding Kitty for coughing.

Elizabeth took the opportunity to lean closer to Jane. "Dear Jane," she whispered. "If Mr Bingley *should* happen to fall in love with one of us, surely it will be with you."

"Hush, Lizzy," Jane whispered back.

If the interior of the carriage were not so dark, Elizabeth was certain she would have seen a blush on her sister's fair countenance.

A few moments later they arrived at the assembly hall and all five sisters alighted from the carriage with varying degrees of enthusiasm. The doors of the hall were opened wide, and lively music and the sounds of general gaiety spilled into the streets, creating an atmosphere of merriment and anticipation. With bright eyes and flushed cheeks, they gathered their skirts about their ankles to avoid the leavings of the horses and followed their mother as she made her way through the crowd and into the building.

The first strains of *Grimstock* could be heard floating through the hall. Kitty and Lydia, seeing a surfeit of ladies and gentlemen lining up for the set, pushed their way into the ballroom in search of partners. Instead of admonishing them for their forward behaviour, their mother looked after them with an expression of indulgent fondness while her three eldest daughters remained dutifully by her side.

Mrs Bennet, being the principal matron of their exclusive little society, was soon surrounded by her neighbours and friends. All were eager to discuss those in attendance, their attire, and the suitability and prospects of their daughters and sons. Being a favourite and much admired, Jane was asked to dance immediately and was whisked away to join the set with a rosy blush that complemented the pale blue colour of her gown.

With her mother's attention diverted by the usual news and general gossip, Mary slipped away to occupy a vacant chair in a corner, where she produced a book from her reticule and proceeded to ignore all in the room.

Elizabeth sighed. As usual, there were far fewer gentlemen in attendance than ladies, and all but a small group of much older, married men were engaged with partners at present. There were no disengaged, single young men available to invite her to dance, nor would there be for some time. With her toe tapping to the rhythm of the music, she wondered whether the gentleman she had encountered that morning at Oakham Mount was among the dancers. A quick perusal of those moving about the set informed her he was not.

"Eliza!"

The appellation was accompanied by a happy, affectionate smile, which Elizabeth returned in equal measure. "Charlotte! You are looking very well this evening. Your gown certainly becomes you."

"I thank you for the compliment," her friend replied. "You look as beautiful as ever. I am surprised to find you are not dancing."

"Perhaps,I would be if there were as many gentlemen as there are ladies. So long as my sisters are engaged, I fear I shall be forced to forgo the pleasure. After all, who can possibly compete with Lydia's exuberance and Jane's beauty?"

"Who indeed," Charlotte remarked, looking pointedly at Elizabeth. "You do yourself a disservice, Eliza. You are every bit as lovely as Jane. To a gentleman of the world with more discriminating tastes, you may be considered far more so, as you are clever and engaging in a way your eldest sister is not."

"I am certainly more opinionated," Elizabeth responded with an unaffected laugh. "But, as my mother reminds me daily, such an offence will never be tolerated by any man of means in want of a wife. As I am disinclined to curb my spirited tongue, I shall end up a spinster, destined to teach Jane's future children to embroider cushions and play their instruments very ill. Unless a man of fortune can love an impertinent woman over a beautiful one, mine is a hopeless case."

Charlotte shook her head with an exasperated smile. "Once again, I see there is no arguing with you. Since you mentioned instruments, I shall tell you my father has informed me our distinguished new neighbour has an exceptionally fine pianoforte, although I believe it was an acquisition made by Netherfield's former tenants. Perhaps you will have an opportunity to play it."

"Should our distinguished new neighbour fall madly in love with my most deserving sister, then perhaps I shall."

Casting another exasperated look at her friend, Charlotte appeared on the verge of issuing a rebuttal, but the music stopped, the dancing stopped, and everyone in attendance ceased speaking to turn expectantly towards the door, where three gentlemen and two ladies lingered just beyond the threshold. Their attire was fashionable, far more so than was often seen in Hertfordshire, and their countenances were aloof, save for that of one.

Charlotte's father, Sir William Lucas, crossed the room to greet them. "Mr Bingley," he said graciously. "Welcome."

The most amicable looking of the three gentlemen stepped forward. "Sir William! It is a pleasure to see you again. I thank you for such a ready welcome." He turned to his companions and introduced each one in turn: his sisters, Miss Bingley and Mrs Hurst; his brother-in-law, Mr Hurst; and his good friend, Mr Darcy of Pemberley in Derbyshire.

Elizabeth started as she realised that Mr Darcy and the self-assured, serious gentleman she had encountered on her morning ramble were one and the same. They had parted amicably then, but would that amicability continue now that they were, in fact, thrown into company together? She would simply have to wait and see.

His proclivity for formality notwithstanding, Mr Darcy regarded all in the room with a disinterested coldness that had not been present during Elizabeth's interaction with him at Oakham Mount, even when her teasing and admonishments had tried his patience. He was by far the tallest gentleman in attendance and seemingly the most dissatisfied as well. Soon, all eyes were upon him, taking his measure.

His clothing was elegant. His bearing was regal. He was handsome, and he was rich. Far richer than his friend apparently. The words 'ten thousand a year' and 'Pemberley' travelled through the crowded room faster than a brisk wind through a wheat field and at a volume that likely carried to the gentleman himself.

Elizabeth's lips lifted as she watched him stiffen and stand even taller. While he had certainly shown himself to be well versed in arrogance that morning, she also knew Mr Darcy was capable of being civil and pleasant, and to some extent even teasing. Now, however, he looked only exceedingly miserable and proud.

As though sensing he was the object of her attention, Mr Darcy's disapproving gaze came to rest upon Elizabeth. For a fraction of a moment a flash of recognition appeared on his face, but his haughty mask of composure was back in place faster than the blink of an eye. Before she could so much as arch her brow at him, he turned aside his head. A vivid slap of red coloured his countenance, though whether it indicated embarrassment or vexation Elizabeth could not say. For the moment, Pemberley's master appeared intent upon avoidance.

On any other occasion with any other gentleman, Elizabeth would have been affronted. Instead, surrounded by countless excited repetitions of his yearly income and extensive property, she found herself more inclined towards empathy. Having already met the staid Mr Darcy, she surmised he was not only deeply offended by having his personal business bandied about in such a manner, but also disdained being an object of interest among people he did not know. Elizabeth could hardly blame him, especially when every lady in the room had trained her eyes on him with an expectancy far more likely to inspire irritation than garner favour.

Soon enough the set ended, and Jane's partner returned her to Mrs Bennet's side. Within a matter of minutes, Charlotte's father approached with Mr Bingley in tow.

"Mrs Bennet," said Sir William. "Mr Bingley has expressed a desire to become acquainted with you and your daughters."

Mrs Bennet could not hide her pleasure at the prospect and heartily consented to an introduction.

"Ladies, may I present Mr Bingley of Netherfield Park, formerly of Scarborough in Yorkshire? Sir, this is Mrs Thomas Bennet of Longbourn and her two eldest daughters, Miss Jane Bennet and Miss Elizabeth."

Elizabeth and Jane smiled and curtseyed.

Mr Bingley bowed. "It is a pleasure to make your acquaintance," he said to their mother, wearing a besotted grin as his eyes returned again and again to Jane. He directed a friendly smile at Elizabeth, but his attention soon returned to her blushing sister. "If Miss Bennet is not already engaged, I would consider it an honour to be able to claim her hand for the next two dances."

Mrs Bennet answered for her eldest daughter in a voice that carried to half the room. "Of course, my Jane may stand up with you, sir. I daresay she would like nothing better!"

"I thank you, Mr Bingley," Jane replied pleasantly after her mother had finished. "I am not engaged."

"Capital!" Sir William exclaimed, then indicated Charlotte. "You remember my own daughter, do you not, Mr Bingley?"

The gentleman bowed to her. "Forgive me. Of course. It is lovely to see you again, Miss Lucas."

"And you as well, Mr Bingley," Charlotte replied with a curtsey. Her eyes met Elizabeth's and both friends shared a knowing smile. Mr Bingley was lost to them. He saw no one except Jane.

Rather than return to his own party, Mr Bingley remained by Jane's side until it was time for the dancers to form the set. Elizabeth could not help but feel pleased for her. Every minute in his company showed him to be very gentlemanly with happy, unaffected manners, perfect ease, and good breeding. He was also handsome, something a young man ought to be if he possibly could. He danced every dance and asked Jane to stand up with him a second time, to the great satisfaction of their mother.

Mr Darcy, in contrast, danced once with Miss Bingley, once with Mrs Hurst, declined being introduced to any other lady, and spent the rest of the evening walking about the room, only occasionally bothering to speak to those of his own party. At one point he was reproached for his behaviour by his friend. Elizabeth, who had the misfortune of being seated near them at the time, overheard their conversation.

"Come, Darcy. I must have you dance. I hate to see you standing about by yourself in this stupid manner. You had much better dance."

"I certainly shall not. You know how I detest it unless I am particularly acquainted with my partner. Your sisters are engaged at present, and there is not another woman in the room with whom it would not be a punishment for me to stand up."

"I would not be as fastidious as you are for a kingdom! Upon my honour, I have never met with so many pleasant girls in my life."

Looking to Jane, Mr Darcy replied, "You were dancing with the handsomest girl in the room."

Mr Bingley grinned. "She is the most beautiful creature I have ever beheld! But there is one of her sisters, who is very pretty, and I daresay very agreeable. Do let my partner introduce you."

Mr Darcy raised his eyes for a fraction of a moment to Elizabeth's before turning abruptly back to his friend. "She is tolerable, but not handsome enough to tempt me. I am in no humour to give consequence to ladies who have been slighted by other men. You had better return to your partner and enjoy her smiles. You are wasting your time with me."

Elizabeth blinked in astonishment, then bowed her head, mortified to have overheard such an unflattering account of herself from Mr Darcy's own mouth. Suddenly, all her charitable thoughts of him throughout the evening—every feeling of empathy inspired by the overzealous expectancy of her neighbours—faded. Swallowing her humiliation, she attempted to laugh off what he had said about her being slighted by other men but found it was a task easier said than done. The truth of the matter was that he had slighted her, and worse still, he had done it knowing he would be overheard. Unwilling to remain a moment longer in his presence, she stood and made her way with alacrity towards Jane, who was speaking to Charlotte on the opposite side of the room.

Jane took one look at her and frowned. "Lizzy, whatever is the matter? Are you unwell?"

"I am perfectly well," she replied, feigning a lightness she did not feel. "I am only a bit overheated."

Jane would not let the matter rest. She touched her sister's cheek. "While the room is certainly crowded, there are only coals in the hearth, and you have barely danced all evening. Are you sure you are not ill? You are warm, and your cheeks are flushed with such intense colour."

"I am by no means ill," Elizabeth insisted.

"Then what has happened?"

Elizabeth expelled an exasperated breath and forced a

smile to her face. "Believe me, Jane, it is so ridiculous it is hardly worth mentioning."

"I doubt that is the case," said Charlotte. "You may as well tell us what has occurred. If you do not, you know we shall only imagine the worst."

Biting her lip, Elizabeth allowed her eyes to dart to Mr Darcy, who was deep in conversation with Mr Bingley in the far corner of the room. Neither gentleman looked pleased.

Her ire rose at the sight of him. "Oh, very well," she conceded. "If you insist, I shall tell you. Apparently, a certain gentleman from Derbyshire is in no mood to give consequence to ladies who have been slighted by other men. In his own words, he has declared me merely tolerable and not handsome enough to tempt him to dance."

Jane's brow creased in confusion. "There must be some misunderstanding. Surely, Mr Darcy would never speak so unkindly of anyone, least of all you."

"You assume wrongly, for I heard him quite clearly with my own ears."

Charlotte, who was unfailingly practical, sighed. "It was wrong of Mr Darcy to say such a thing, but I confess it hardly surprises me. Poor humour or not, he has done little to make himself agreeable this evening. Now he has succeeded in making himself even less so."

"True," Elizabeth agreed, training her eyes upon her slippers. "True."

"Come, Eliza. You are made of sterner stuff than this. You cannot desire his good opinion, surely?"

For the moment, Elizabeth hardly knew what she desired. Mr Darcy's cold dismissal of her stung every bit as much as his insult angered her. His behaviour now was very different from his behaviour that morning. Yes, he had been arrogant—even egotistical—but his manners eventually improved. So much so, that he had ventured to tease her. At one point he had nearly laughed. Of course, he had not been packed into a crowded room full of curious, enthusiastic strangers at the time—strangers who appeared far more interested in his fortune and property than they were in his character.

Further discussion of the topic was prevented by the arrival of Mr Bingley and, to Elizabeth's astonishment, Mr Darcy.

"Miss Bennet," said Mr Bingley with a congenial smile. "Pray allow me to present my friend, Mr Darcy. He has expressed a desire to be known to your sister, Miss Elizabeth. May I prevail upon you to perform an introduction?"

Elizabeth gaped at him. *Impossible!* It was impossible what Mr Bingley related was anywhere close to the truth!

Jane, who was incapable of believing any real ill of anyone and likely anxious to redeem his friend in Elizabeth's eyes, returned his smile. "I would be delighted, Mr Bingley." Taking Elizabeth's hand, she turned towards Mr Darcy, greeted him pleasantly, and performed the introduction.

Mr Darcy executed a quick, perfunctory bow. "I am honoured to make your acquaintance, Miss Bennet, and yours as well, Miss Elizabeth."

Refusing to meet his eyes, Elizabeth offered him a brief curtsey. "Mr Darcy."

The musicians began a Scottish air, sending a flurry of happy couples towards the centre of the room to form the next set. Mr Bingley looked pointedly at his friend and cleared his throat, then addressed Charlotte. "Miss Lucas, I do believe I have not yet had the pleasure of dancing with you this evening. Will you do me the honour?"

Despite the belatedness of his invitation, Charlotte's lips turned upwards. "Thank you, Mr Bingley. I am most obliged."

As Mr Bingley led Charlotte towards the other dancers, Mr Darcy said, "Will you dance, Miss Elizabeth?"

Elizabeth, whose indignation at this point was considerable, could do little more than stare. The gloves he wore were very fine, as was his coat and the cascade of knots in his cravat and his posture and every other thing about him. Everything but his opinion of her. She squeezed Jane's hand and released it. "I thank you for the honour," she replied, raising her chin defiantly, "but I am disinclined to dance at present." And with that, she turned her back to him and quit the room.

α

The small balcony was chilly, but also a welcome reprieve after the hot, humid press of bodies inside the ballroom. Elizabeth inhaled a breath of fresh, crisp air as she laid her gloved hand upon the railing and looked out over the meagre garden that abutted the back of the assembly hall.

Never had she been so rude to any gentleman in the entire course of her life! Then again, never had she ever felt such abject humiliation! To be rejected by a man was one thing, but to have his friend force him to accede to an introduction he neither sought nor desired was quite another. Elizabeth did not know whether to laugh at the absurdity of the situation or cry. In any case, the truth would not be long concealed. She had openly spurned a very rich, very eligible man who had insulted her at a public assembly. A man she had initially believed she could *like*. Sooner or later, news of her slight and his would reach her mother—her mother, who, despite all she had to say about her second daughter's clever mind, sharp tongue, and inferior beauty, had expectations of Elizabeth marrying well.

With a long, drawn-out exhalation, Elizabeth covered her face with her hands.

Behind her, the French windows were opened, then

closed with a quiet click. A throat was cleared, and a quiet but firm, "Miss Elizabeth," was uttered.

Stifling a disbelieving laugh, she straightened, smoothed her skirts, and turned. Before her stood the last man in the world she had expected would follow her anywhere, least of all onto an assembly hall balcony; yet there he was, and with a very different demeanour from the one he had shown her neighbours and his friend. Gone was the insufferably disdainful man who had stalked the perimeter of the ballroom throughout the evening and insulted her without a care. In his place stood a man who, although ill-humoured and proud, appeared cautious as well.

"Mr Darcy," she said.

"Pray forgive my intrusion. This morning you told me to announce myself, lest I frighten you."

"I believe I also told you that I am not afraid of you."

One side of his mouth began to lift, but a quelling look from Elizabeth ensured the gesture was short lived. "No," he agreed. "You are certainly not afraid of me, but I believe you are dissatisfied with me."

"On the contrary, what I am, Mr Darcy, is insulted. There is a difference."

"I am sorry. My mood this evening is not conducive to being in company. I did not want to attend this assembly."

Elizabeth nearly rolled her eyes. "Then you ought to have remained at home."

"And so I would have, but my friend would not hear of it."

"And can you not do as you like?" she enquired with an impudence that would not be denied. "Are you not your own lord and master?"

With a bitter laugh, Mr Darcy shook his head. "I no longer know what I am, madam."

There was a wretchedness in his pronouncement, a

caustic note of resentment in his tone that went beyond a general dissatisfaction with the world, and it suddenly struck Elizabeth that this man—this proud, entitled, independently wealthy man—appeared genuinely unhappy.

Despite her anger and indignation, she made a concerted effort to soften her tone. "Well, if you are a gentleman, Mr Darcy, allow me to give you a word of advice—you really ought to refrain from speaking disparagingly about ladies, especially where we can overhear your insults with relative ease. I can assure you that none of us rejoices in hearing we are merely tolerable."

"Again, I must beg your forgiveness. I never should have said that."

"No, indeed. You should have contented yourself with only thinking it."

Mr Darcy rubbed his forehead. "That is not what I meant. It is certainly not what I thought."

Elizabeth waved him off. "Oh, no. You need not go to the trouble of gratifying my vanity *now,* sir. It is far too late for that."

He made no reply.

They stood in silence—Elizabeth, breathing in the night air, and her companion staring fixedly at the ground. Eventually, he indicated the railing with a gesture of his hand. "May I join you?"

Elizabeth shrugged her shoulders. "If it suits you. I have no objection either way."

In three strides he crossed the balcony and settled himself beside her, propping his forearms upon the railing. The space was small, so small that his arm nearly brushed her own. Other than during a dance, Elizabeth had never been so close to a gentleman who was not her father or one of her uncles. To her consternation, Mr Darcy's proximity was as heady as it was disconcerting. Although the night was cool, she could feel the heat of his body. She could smell his scent—a combination of sandalwood, soap, and musk. Such intimate knowledge of him not only felt like an invasion of his privacy but made her blush.

He said, "When I encountered you this morning at Oakham Mount, I was distracted and barely attending to my surroundings. Despite my inattention, 'tolerable' was not a word that came to mind when I first saw you."

"I would imagine not. Wild. Brazen. *Ill-favoured—*"

"Compelling. Engaging. *Lovely.*"

Each word fell from his lips with such succinctness and conviction that Elizabeth found it difficult to doubt his sincerity. These words were far from insulting. They were nothing like the words he had uttered to his friend.

But as gratifying as they were to hear, such contradictory statements were also confusing. "I do not understand what you are about, Mr Darcy. If you are indeed earnest, why did you say what you did to Mr Bingley in the ballroom? Why did you behave so coldly towards me and speak so meanly, so insultingly? I was sitting right there, sir. You saw me with your own eyes. You must have known I would hear you and that others would as well."

"Because I am *tired*," he whispered fiercely. "I am tired of the world having expectations of me! I am tired of avoiding matchmaking mothers and their daughters everywhere I go else I inadvertently greet one too readily, or smile too openly, or pay one too much attention and suddenly find myself alone in a room with her, forced into an imprudent marriage to a woman I barely know, never mind respect or esteem." He exhaled harshly and turned aside his head. "Forgive me. I ought not to have spoken so candidly of such matters."

"No," she agreed. "You should not have. But I shall not reproach you for it. I shall only point out the irony of your making such a statement in the first place."

Mr Darcy turned his head towards her. She nearly laughed at the bewildered look on his face.

"In case it has escaped your notice, you are currently standing in the dark, on an assembly hall balcony during a public ball, quite alone with a woman who is, for all intents and purposes, a stranger to you. A *tolerable* stranger," she said with a flicker of an impudent smile, "but a stranger all the same."

One corner of his mouth lifted infinitesimally. "Well met, Miss Elizabeth," he told her quietly. With only the ethereal glow of a full moon overhead to shed light upon their exchange, his eyes looked almost black.

He had called her compelling. He had called her engaging. He had called her *lovely*. In that moment, Elizabeth found him equally so and it unnerved her. She was not formed for ill humour. Despite the sharp sting of his insult in the ballroom, her anger had diminished. "Since neither of us wishes to find ourselves forced into an imprudent marriage, I should return before my mother or one of my sisters comes in search of me. I have been gone too long and my absence will be noticed. Yours likely will as well."

The trace of a smile Mr Darcy wore disappeared. "Of course. I shall not detain you."

Contrary to his assurance, he did not move aside. He hesitated, then shocked her by briefly touching the back of her gloved hand with his fingertip. Pitching his voice low, more so with emotion it seemed than any fear of being overheard, he said, "I am reluctant to part with you knowing you may yet believe the unkind statements I made to my friend. They were uttered in a dreadful bitterness of spirit and by no means reflect my true impression of you. When I referred to you as lovely, I meant it. I do not make such a profession lightly. Save for my sister, I am not in the habit of paying compliments to ladies, any more than I am apt to follow them onto dark balconies or speak to them alone."

If what Mr Darcy related about other women and their machinations to entrap him into a marriage of convenience was true, then Elizabeth had no cause to doubt him; but this confession puzzled her even more than his previous behaviour. If he rarely paid compliments to ladies other than his sister, why then had he felt compelled to bestow such an honour upon her? Why had he followed her from the ball-room after she had spurned his offer to dance? Why had he apologised to her and spoken so unreservedly of such personal matters?

It made absolutely no sense, and she said as much. "If that is so, why have you honoured me with such a distinction? Surely, in your eyes, I am no different from any other lady of your acquaintance. In fact, you and I are barely acquainted at all."

"Other ladies of my acquaintance, Miss Elizabeth, have a pretension you lack. Other ladies of my acquaintance do not possess your frankness. They flatter. They flirt. They have not your strength of character, nor your perception, nor your sincerity."

The intensity of his words and the intensity of his gaze served as a stark reminder that he was not only eloquent but handsome. He seemed to be full of compliments—compliments Elizabeth had only ever received from Charlotte and Jane and her aunt Gardiner. She realised she was on dangerous ground, and ill prepared to navigate it. The moment required levity, else she end up liking Mr Darcy of Pemberley and his dark, penetrating eyes a great deal more than she ought. "Your manners, I see, have improved a vast deal in the last half hour. That was a pretty speech."

"It is the truth."

"What it is, Mr Darcy, is generous and indulgent and entirely unnecessary, but I thank you for it all the same."

"I would prefer your forgiveness to your gratitude. Can you forgive me for treating you so abhorrently, or will you persist in holding my offence against me indefinitely?"

She smiled. "Holding a grudge indefinitely sounds remarkably uncharitable, not to mention exhausting. You may consider yourself forgiven. We may even part as friends."

"Thank you," he said. His voice was soft, but there was a discernible note of relief in his tone. "I do not plan on remaining in Hertfordshire for more than a month, but I would consider it an honour to be counted among your friends. Will you allow me, or do I ask too much, to prevail upon you to shake hands?"

His request surprised her, but it did not follow that the surprise was unwelcome. She extended her hand to him. "Of course, I shall."

Although the night was cold, Mr Darcy's hand was warm. Elizabeth found both the sensation and the experience soothing and intoxicating in equal measure. She had never held a gentleman's hand before, not like this, and marvelled at the sheer intimacy of what she had always considered to be a seemingly innocuous gesture. How could such an innocent interaction provide such comfort, yet at the same time quicken her heart and threaten to steal her breath?

They remained thus far longer than was deemed appropriate by society's standards for their friendly handshake to retain any appearance of propriety. Both were silent. Both were still. Both showed no inclination to relinquish the other's hand, not even when the opening chords of *Miss Moore's Rant* floated through the windows, signalling the beginning of the last set of the evening. The voices of their Hertfordshire neighbours raised in merriment were a sobering accompaniment.

Suddenly cognisant of the tenuousness of their situation, they separated.

Mr Darcy brought his hands behind his back and glanced towards the door.

Elizabeth smoothed an imaginary crease in her gown with slightly unsteady fingers. By some miraculous stroke of luck her voice did not falter. "Good night, Mr Darcy."

He bowed to her, then cleared his throat. "Good night, Miss Elizabeth. I hope we shall meet again soon."

FIVE

❦

Those who do not complain are never pitied.

"BUT WOE UNTO YOU WHO ARE RICH!" CRIED THE ancient minister to his congregation. His voice was surprisingly powerful for a man of such slight stature. "For ye have received your consolation. Woe unto you that are full! For ye shall hunger. Woe unto you that laugh now! For ye shall mourn and weep."

The fieldstone church smelled of wax and woodsmoke and was damp, despite the considerable press of warm bodies attending the Sunday morning service. The pews were shallow, fashioned from curved oak boards and polished to a gleaming shine. For weary church goers, the smooth finish made remaining upright nearly impossible without expending a copious amount of effort.

For what felt like the tenth time in as many minutes, Darcy straightened his back and endeavoured to ignore the dull pounding in his head. Longbourn's little country church was certainly nothing like the church he attended in London. In London, his family had extensive patronage in the church for nearly a century, a practice Darcy continued as Pemberley's master. Not only did he enjoy the comfort of a cushioned bench during Sunday services, but his family crest was emblazoned on the gate of the pew designated for his use.

"Woe unto you when all men shall speak well of you! For so did their fathers to false prophets. But I say unto you which hear—love your enemies! Do good to those which hate you, bless them that curse you, and pray for them which despitefully use you."

The minister's words made Darcy scowl as he shifted awkwardly in his seat. His back was stiff after sitting for so long in one attitude. Beside him, Georgiana sat perched on the edge of the pew, her head bowed with a solemnity that could not completely conceal her misery.

Love your enemies.

Despite being in God's house, Darcy had to bite his tongue to keep from uttering an oath at the repugnant feelings those charitable words inspired. Love thy enemy indeed! There was a time he had not only loved George Wickham but considered him a brother. Those days were no more. Wickham's unconscionable betrayal had ensured the dissolution of every lingering sentiment of fondness and liberality Darcy had retained towards his former childhood friend. Several successive, vile letters composed by the blackguard had since compounded those sentiments to an almost unscrupulous hatred; but beneath that hatred was fear.

The first letter was dated the second of October, the second letter the ninth, and the third the eleventh, but it was not until that morning—the sixteenth of October—that they had found their way into Darcy's hands.

It stood to reason the letters would have reached him far sooner had all three not been directed at first to Pemberley. His steward had taken the liberty of forwarding them to his London address; his housekeeper there had sent them on to Netherfield. Not two hours ago, when Darcy had come down to break his fast, they were waiting for him on a silver salver with the rest of the post. A frisson of horror, sudden and sharp, had made his blood run cold the moment he recognised the familiar, careless scrawl of Wickham's hand. He had snatched them up, muttered an excuse to the Hursts and Miss Bingley, and returned to his rooms directly, where he tossed the letters on a table and stared at them far longer than it probably took Wickham to compose them.

Finally, unable to bear another moment of wretched suspense, he opened the first one, fully expecting Wickham to demand an exorbitant sum of money in exchange for silence. Instead, he was met with a sickening account of Georgiana's seduction. The other two letters were much the same and appeared to have been written with one purpose: to torment Darcy beyond sanity.

There was no return address, no clue as to where the reprobate might be found and dealt with once and for all. In a way, Darcy was glad. Had he any inkling of Wickham's whereabouts, he would likely have quit Hertfordshire that second, hunted him like an animal, and beat him bloody. The thought of such a painful, mortifying account of his sister's disgrace falling into anyone's hands and becoming public knowledge terrified him. Instead of stowing the letters away in the secret compartment of his writing desk, he threw them into the fire and watched them burn until nothing remained but ash.

From high atop his pulpit, the minister continued to expound upon love and forgiveness. Was it possible to forgive such treachery perpetrated by a man with principles so debase and amoral? As Darcy watched his sister quietly blotting her tears with her handkerchief, he felt a fresh wave of fury descend upon him. Three months had passed, and still she suffered. The sweet, shy, trusting girl he had loved for half his life was now so withdrawn and so full of self-doubt he was at a loss as to how to help her overcome it. He felt her pain and disappointment keenly and worried over her low spirits with an intensity that only ever seemed to increase. While bestowing forgiveness on another was certainly the Christian practice, seeing Georgiana so altered, so markedly unhappy that she would be reduced to tears in church, was no easy feat to ignore. Forgiveness, Darcy knew, was so far beyond his capabilities at that point the idea of it was laughable.

As for *loving* George Wickham, that would never happen. Not in this lifetime, nor in the next. Not even if God willed it.

Exhaling a harsh breath, he offered Georgiana his hand, palm upwards. That she accepted it made the ever-present ache in his heart that much easier to bear.

The minister droned on, and Darcy fought the urge to close his eyes. It was a miracle he had been able to drag himself out of bed that morning, never mind all the way to church. Except for the half hour he had spent on a moonlit balcony apologising to the most unpredictable woman he had ever met, his evening had been nothing but one long, tedious punishment. Even the remembrance of it provoked his ire.

His mood had been abysmal, but Bingley had insisted that he dance. It hardly mattered the impertinent Miss Elizabeth looked even more enchanting in a satin ballgown than she had in sprigged muslin, or that resisting the urge to approach her for half the night had nearly driven him mad. From the moment he had set foot in the assembly hall, exclamations of 'ten thousand a year' rang in his ears, putting him on his guard. After that, he heard little else.

When she raised her eyes to his after Bingley had offered to arrange an introduction, she looked expectant. But the very real possibility that she was not who Darcy thought she was—that Miss Elizabeth Bennet of Longbourn was far more interested in his fortune than his character—not only pained him but incited his anger. The insult was on the tip of his tongue and out of his mouth before he could check himself. The regret he felt was as instantaneous as it was unexpected.

Miss Elizabeth sought the solace of her sister.

Darcy argued with Bingley.

Bingley marched him across the room.

When Darcy attempted to make reparations, Miss Elizabeth not only refused to meet his eyes, but refused to dance with him!

He should have been relieved or even affronted, but instead felt only contrition for having caused her pain. Although a decade of experience avoiding entrapment by fortune hunters rebelled against it, he waited exactly two minutes before following her out of the ballroom and onto a tiny, deserted balcony.

Unsurprisingly, Elizabeth Bennet looked as lovely and unassuming in the moonlight as she did in the sunlight, but she was far more annoyed with him than she had been that morning at Oakham Mount.

When Darcy greeted her, she responded coldly. When he defended himself, she berated him for his gall. When he confessed far more than he had intended, she softened and made him smile. When he apologised, she forgave him. They parted during the last set of the evening as friends; but instead of experiencing a lightness in his breast, Darcy felt a weight descend upon him, much like the pull of a lodestone.

To make matters worse, Bingley, with his open, agreeable manners, had been as well received among his Hertfordshire neighbours as he was everywhere else. Hurst went home with his wife and sister, but Bingley insisted on lingering with a few of the single gentlemen. Hesitant to abandon him to the society of strangers, Darcy decided to remain. When they finally returned to Netherfield, Bingley was in high spirits and in no mood to retire. A good deal of port was drunk, and

Bingley waxed eloquent about Jane Bennet and her sweetness while Darcy pondered her sister in silence.

The pull of the lodestone increased.

Bingley drank more port, but Darcy had imbibed enough.

When Bingley leapt from his chair and proposed riding to Longbourn at once to speak to Miss Bennet's father, then slumped to the floor, Darcy capped the near empty decanter and dragged him off to bed.

By the time Darcy fell into his own bed, it was just before dawn, far too close to the hour when he usually rose to begin his day. As a result, he was feeling the effects of a pounding headache from too much port, too little sleep, and a turbid gut courtesy of Wickham. Fresh air and exercise would certainly help, but that could only be accomplished once the minister finished his sermon.

"And why call me Lord, Lord," said the minister with great zeal, "and do not the things which I say?"

"Damned confusing," muttered Hurst from somewhere beyond Bingley, who sat beside Darcy on his left.

"Shush," said his wife.

Longbourn, a modest estate considered by the neighbourhood to be the highest in consequence after Netherfield, ensured the Bennet family occupied the pew directly behind Bingley's. Darcy could hardly believe his ears when he heard the two youngest girls giggle. At least he surmised it was the two youngest girls. From what he had witnessed of their behaviour at the assembly, they were silly and wild. He doubted the three eldest Misses Bennet would ever behave so indecorously, especially the middle sister, who had spent the entire evening reading scripture in a corner. Bingley's Miss Bennet passed her time dancing and smiling serenely at Bingley, and Miss Elizabeth, with her impertinence and her fire and her heart and her fine eyes, spent the night discomposing Darcy in ways he refused to consider, especially in church.

Annoyed by the immaturity of her youngest sisters, he glanced at Bingley to gauge his reaction, but Bingley looked as green in the gills as Darcy felt. His eyelids were heavy, and he had a slightly glazed look about him as he stared straight ahead, oblivious to everything it seemed, including his own state of unwellness. The minister's voice grew softer, and Bingley's eyelids drooped lower and lower.

Darcy eyed him warily until the frail looking minister suddenly shouted, "But he that heareth and doeth *not* is like a man that without a foundation built a house upon the earth!"

Bingley jerked to attention.

The youngest Miss Bennets resumed their giggling, Hurst snorted, and several amused titters were heard among their neighbours.

The minister cast a disapproving glare at the entire congregation, then cleared his throat and forged onwards with renewed vigour.

From the corner of his eye, Darcy saw Georgiana purse her lips, then quickly hide a smile behind her handkerchief.

Darcy pressed her hand.

❧

"Solomon!" Darcy shouted. "Come!"

But Solomon, usually so obedient and obliging, continued bounding across the field at full speed.

"Damn that dog," Darcy muttered, eyeing the leaden sky with increasing trepidation as he increased his pace. His headache, which had plagued him so severely in church, was essentially gone, mellowed by a cup of willow bark tea and several hours in the fresh autumn air. He had set a brisk pace the moment he left Netherfield. Since then, Darcy estimated he had walked more than four miles through Hertfordshire's fields and winding paths. His boots were caked with mud, and he was beginning to tire, but the picturesque scenery and the exercise were exactly what was needed. Now he was doubling back, eager for a hot bath and a warm fire.

Having crossed the field, Solomon darted into a walnut grove and disappeared between a stand of large trees. Darcy shook his head. Although well trained, the Great Dane was young yet and still prone to bouts of caprice. That would change with time and firmer guidance. He was a beautiful dog, loyal and even-tempered, and Darcy was proud of the progress they had made together since he acquired him in the spring.

The first drops of rain fell before Darcy reached the edge of the grove. They multiplied quickly, and before he could so much as utter an oath, the dark clouds overhead released their deluge upon the land. An ancient walnut tree, resplendent with cheerful yellow leaves, was just ahead. Darcy sought refuge beneath its canopy. Beads of water dripped from the brim of his hat, and he discarded it, raking his fingers through his hair as he scanned the grove for signs of his dog. Where Solomon had run off to was anyone's guess. He could be in the woods by now, chasing after rabbits or digging for voles. There was nothing to do but wait. Resigned to his fate, Darcy took a seat upon a massive root, reclined against the tree's trunk, and crossed his ankles. "Solomon!" he called, linking his fingers behind his head. "Come!"

After little more than a minute, Solomon came.

With him came Elizabeth Bennet.

"Mr Darcy," she said equitably as she performed a perfunctory curtsey. "We meet again."

Darcy gaped at her. The front of her gown was filthy! From the decorative trim at the hem to the covered buttons on the bodice of her spencer, every inch appeared to be spattered or smeared with a muddy pattern that bore an uncanny resemblance to...

"Damnation," he muttered under his breath. He jumped to his feet and summoned his ill-behaved dog to his side. "Solomon! You are a very bad dog today! Forgive me, Miss Elizabeth. I fear he has ruined your gown."

Her eyes bore a flicker of wry amusement. "It is an old gown, so its demise is of little consequence. But I must take offence on behalf of poor Solomon. He is by no means a bad dog! He is merely blessed with the misfortune of being both very large and exceedingly friendly, are you not, Solomon?"

Upon hearing his name spoken with such encouragement, Solomon returned to her side and boldly placed his muddy paws on her chest. Not only did she appear delighted by such unsolicited attention but she began scratching his ears. "Yes," she murmured, "you are a sweet boy, Solomon. You are Mr Darcy's sweet boy."

A low, contented rumble rose in Solomon's throat as he leaned into her touch with apparent pleasure.

Darcy was in awe of her. Despite being only two years of age, Solomon was enormous. The height of his head exceeded that of her waist! The dog had not only accosted her but defiled her gown, yet Miss Elizabeth had not run from him. She had not cowered from him or scolded him. She had defended him, tolerated his energetic attentions, and lavished affection upon him.

"You are gracious, Miss Elizabeth. Most ladies would not reward such discourteous behaviour."

She raised one pert brow and, without taking her eyes from his spoiled dog, replied, "I am surprised at you, Mr Darcy. I had thought the matter quite settled between us."

"I was unaware that anything had been settled between us," said Darcy sceptically. "To what do you refer?"

"Why, to the matter of my being very different from other ladies, of course. You were quite insistent last night, sir.

Therefore, my conduct this morning should come as no surprise to you."

There was a distinct note of archness in her tone Darcy was coming to recognise. Not only was Elizabeth Bennet unique, but she was also refreshing.

Would that he could say the same about Miss Bingley and her platitudes! Recalling the occasion of her first encounter with Solomon, he compared it to Miss Elizabeth's reception of him; truly, there was no comparison. The moment Darcy alighted from his carriage, Bingley's sister had simpered and smiled like anything, but when Solomon leapt from the conveyance a moment later, her jaw dropped open in horror. While Darcy and Georgiana greeted Bingley, Solomon approached their hostess and brazenly sniffed the hem of her gown. It was more than Miss Bingley could bear. She emitted an ear-piercing scream, batted him away, and ran into the house declaring he should not gain admittance to anything beyond the stable else all the furniture be overturned.

Darcy cleared his throat. "Forgive me for my faulty memory. As usual, you are wholly in the right."

"That you have learnt to accept my rightness so readily does you credit. You may consider yourself forgiven, Mr Darcy—once again."

"Thank you, Miss Elizabeth," he responded drily. "I am most obliged to you."

Ignoring him, she whispered some nonsense to his dog, all the while attempting to conceal her smile.

Repressing a smile of his own, Darcy rolled his eyes at her, then directed his attention to the field. The temperature was unseasonably mild for the middle of October, and for that he was thankful. The rain was falling in thick sheets, and large puddles were forming on the ground beyond the sanctuary of the grove. Beneath the thick tapestry of vibrant leaves all was pleasant, if not a bit damp. He wondered how long the rain would continue falling so heavily and whether there was a warmer, more comfortable locale nearby that might provide more thorough protection from the elements in the event the rain did not let up.

Darcy knew he ought to have paid closer attention to the weather when he had set out that morning, but he had been so focused on quitting the house undetected by Miss Bingley he had neglected to consult the barometer. In the drawing room, Bingley's youngest sister was an indolent, accoutred ornament and excessively attentive to Darcy's status as a wealthy, unmarried gentleman. He did not relish the idea of being her dinner partner, never mind being alone with her in the wilds of Hertfordshire, where the necessity of picking her way through a muddy field would likely make her cling helplessly to his arm or worse: faint.

Elizabeth Bennet, on the other hand, appeared more than equal to such a task. Her half-boots were as mud-caked as his riding boots, and her gown...*Good Lord, her gown is a disaster!* Darcy shook his head in bewilderment. If she were any other lady of his acquaintance, she would never have been standing before him calmly patting his dog. She would have been wailing about her ruined gown as she hid behind a tree.

As though she was privy to his inner musings, Miss Elizabeth chose that moment to turn her eyes upon him. "Do you often make a habit of venturing so far from home whenever the sky threatens rain, sir, or were you simply more inattentive than usual to your surroundings this morning?"

"I might ask you the same question, madam, since you are currently keeping me company during this fine weather."

"I assure you it is not by design. While I am fond of walking, I do try to avoid getting caught in the rain if I can help it. Contrary to current appearances, I have not ventured far from home. Longbourn is but half a mile from here. I was hoping to glean a few walnuts before the rain set in, but it is too late in the season and there are none to be found." She gently nudged Solomon's paws from her chest and encouraged him to sit.

He obeyed her without batting an eyelid.

She patted his head and shifted her indulgent gaze to Darcy. "He is a wonderful dog. You are fortunate to have such a faithful friend to accompany you on your adventures. I have long wanted a dog, but my mother will not allow it."

His recent poor comportment aside, Darcy could not disagree with her assessment of Solomon. "He will be your devoted friend for life now. You have indulged him with your kindness and shown him affection. It will not be forgotten."

"Then I shall consider myself fortunate as well. Such loyalty is rare indeed. Solomon is the perfect companion. He is charming and attentive, and I would wager he knows precisely when to say his piece and when to hold his tongue, unlike some other gentlemen of my acquaintance."

Solomon, eager for more attention, nudged Miss Elizabeth's arm with his nose.

"Unlike his master, you mean," Darcy replied with a diverted twist of his mouth. "Solomon is usually exceptionally well behaved, but it appears you have managed to bring out the worst in him this morning, Miss Elizabeth. He was perfectly obliging before he encountered you here in the grove."

"You wound me, sir," she proclaimed as she resumed scratching Solomon's ears. "Had I meant to accuse you of such an offence, my frankness would have demanded I implicate you by name! But that is neither here nor there. We were discussing Solomon."

"Of course. Do forgive me and continue your astute observations about my dog."

Her lips lifted in a smile. "As I was saying, Solomon is restless, sir! Being cooped up in an unfamiliar house with no friends cannot be much fun. He is likely happy to be out of doors after what must have been a long, tedious ride in a cramped carriage all the way from London." She addressed his dog. "You like to be with people, Solomon. Yes, you do. You are fond of being in society. You are very fond of society!"

Darcy snorted. "I shall not even attempt to deny that travelling any great distance in a carriage is unpleasant, nor shall I bother to pretend that Solomon's general disposition is as reserved and unsociable as my own. While I am perfectly content to avoid mixing with society whenever I can manage it, his behaviour is much the opposite, especially when there are indulgent ladies on hand who are willing to feed his vanity and inflate his ego."

"I see the old adage is true," she quipped. "Opposites do attract."

"And now you have wounded *me*, Miss Elizabeth," he declared, feigning offence. "Unlike Solomon, I do not perform to strangers, nor do I have the talent which some people possess of conversing easily with those I have never seen before. I have not Solomon's ease and happy manners. He enjoys being the centre of attention and therefore strives to please wherever he goes."

"Whereas you do not," Miss Elizabeth stated.

"No," Darcy admitted somewhat sheepishly. "I do not."

They talked for two hours. Solomon settled between them, his head on Miss Elizabeth's lap. Eventually, the rain lightened to a misty drizzle and she stood. Dusting off her hands, she invited Darcy to accompany her to Longbourn. Her mother, she assured him, was well known for setting an excellent table. Her father, a self-professed student of human nature, would be pleased to have the company of another gentleman.

She had no brothers and four sisters. All of them were out

and none of them had any fortune to speak of. The youngest two were exuberant and barely out of the schoolroom. The middle one was pious and full of morality. The eldest was angelic and dear and had cast a spell over Bingley.

And then there was Miss Elizabeth, who was like no lady Darcy had ever known. She was impertinent and teasing and intelligent and kind to his dog. She was well read and artless and had the most compelling eyes he had ever seen. Darcy had gazed into those eyes as he sat beside her under a tree in the pouring rain discussing everything from Shakespeare to Plato to the Peninsular war.

Her eyes had captivated him in the sunlight at Oakham Mount. They had enticed him in the moonlight at a country ball. They were expressive and fathomless and bright, and they rendered her heart-shaped face, even complexion, and full, pink lips uncommonly pretty.

Darcy could drown in those eyes.

Unless he exercised caution, he feared he likely would.

"What say you, Mr Darcy? Will you grace us with your presence this evening," Miss Elizabeth asked as her eyes sparkled with mirth. "Or shall we have to make do without your exalted company?"

She was beautiful, desirable even; her situation in life and her family were less so. Last night he had offered his friendship, but to raise her expectations any higher would not only be imprudent on his part, but irresponsible.

No matter how much she intrigued him, Darcy could not afford to become distracted by Elizabeth Bennet. Shifting his attention to his dog, he politely declined.

The taste of his regret was bitter.

SIX

c/&9

**For what do we live, but to make sport for our neighbours
and laugh at them in our turn?**

"Mr Darcy looks at you a great deal, Eliza."

"I cannot imagine why," Elizabeth replied, resisting the
urge to glance in his direction. "I would tell you he looks at
me only to find fault, but I have found him far too sensible to
indulge in such untoward behaviour." She smiled impishly at
her friend. "Perhaps he looks at you, Charlotte."

Charlotte laughed. "The day Mr Darcy looks at me is the
day that pigs fly. No, he most definitely looks at you."

"Who looks at Lizzy?" Kitty asked, pausing beside Charlotte. They were standing in a cosy corner on the far side of
Lady Lucas's drawing room, somewhat apart from the crush
of guests.

"No one," said Elizabeth. "Charlotte is only teasing me,
Kitty."

Lydia appeared behind her, rolling her eyes. "Stop
dawdling, Kitty. Denny is waiting for us, and Chamberlain,
too! You can speak to Lizzy any time." She grabbed her sister
by the arm, and they were gone as quickly as they had come.

Elizabeth watched them cross the room and erupt into
giggles before they joined a group of red coated officers. The
regiment's commanding officer, Colonel Forster, was among

them. He had been married the previous month and his new wife stood at his side, laughing merrily. She was a pretty, lively young woman barely older than Kitty and nearly as silly as Lydia. That Colonel Forster, by all appearances a worldly, sensible man, chose a wife half his age who possessed less than half his good sense baffled Elizabeth exceedingly.

"Pray tell me what has captivated you," said Charlotte, "for I dare not hope it is Mr Darcy."

Elizabeth cast an exasperated look at her meddlesome friend. "I was considering Mrs Forster. Colonel Forster is her superior in age, comportment, education, and intellect. I cannot account for him marrying her. They can have nothing in common."

"Mrs Forster has the brilliance of youth, good humour, and a sizeable dowry. Colonel Forster wanted a wife. Is it truly a wonder that he chose a rich, attractive young woman for his bride?"

"Perhaps not when viewed in such terms. I suppose if I were a gentleman, a large dowry and a pretty face would tempt me as well. But I cannot believe I would ever be happy bound to such a fatuous woman for the rest of my life."

"It is fortunate, then, you are not Colonel Forster." Charlotte inclined her head towards Mr Bingley, who was paying rapt attention to Jane while she conversed with Mrs Hurst in the centre of the room. "And what of our new neighbour? Do you suppose he wants a sensible wife?"

Elizabeth smiled. "I hardly know. He appears to be enamoured of my sister, and I cannot imagine anything more sensible than that. Jane is beautiful, charitable, and good. Mr Bingley is handsome, amicable, and kind. They look well together, do they not?"

"Not only do they look well together, but Mr Bingley looks half in love with her. If Jane wishes to secure him, she ought to leave him in no doubt of her feelings by showing more affection than she feels, not less."

Such advice from her friend surprised Elizabeth. Jane was clearly taken with Mr Bingley and, she suspected, in a fair way of being in love with him. "Surely, he can be in no doubt Jane returns his regard. They have spent much time together over the last fortnight, almost to the exclusion of everyone else. He must see she prefers his society to that of every other gentleman."

"While he may hope for or even suspect her regard, Mr Bingley does not yet know your sister as we do. While his preference is obvious to everyone in the room, Jane's nature is far more reserved. Her composure and her steady, even temperament may well protect her heart and conceal her preference from the rest of the world, but they will do her no favours when securing an admirer."

"Charlotte," she said with an incredulous laugh, "you know Jane is shy. She is demure and proper. No matter how much she likes Mr Bingley, she will never make a spectacle of herself simply to secure him."

"She need not throw herself at him, Eliza. She need only smile a little wider and gaze into his eyes. Mr Bingley looks at her more often than Mr Darcy looks at you. Surely, he will notice and be encouraged by her attentions. With the proper inducement, he shall respond accordingly."

"You know you would never behave in such a way yourself, and neither shall Jane. She is not Lydia."

"I never said she was, but if an eligible, single gentleman of consequence paid me the distinction Mr Bingley pays Jane, I would do all in my power to encourage his interest and ensure its continuation." Charlotte paused to smile slyly at Elizabeth. "Speaking of encouragement, Mr Darcy is staring at you again, to the exclusion of all who speak to him. Whatever could he mean by it?"

"Perhaps he is in a disagreeable humour this evening," said Elizabeth tartly, "or perhaps Miss Bingley has merely bored him with her repetitive platitudes. Not all of us are gifted conversationalists, nor aware of our limitations in such a regard. In any case, you have said quite enough about Mr Darcy tonight. In that quarter, you may lay your romantic notions to rest, for I happen to know he receives an excess of attention in London from ladies of far greater consequence than I."

"Yet Mr Darcy is not in London, but here, staring at you from across the room."

"He wants to discuss books. He does not want a wife."

"Perhaps he only wants encouragement."

"Enough!" Elizabeth cried, laughing at her friend's persistence. "Stop stirring up trouble and save your breath so you may cool your porridge."

"You know I have never cared for porridge," her friend replied.

"Desist, Charlotte, or I shall be forced to take matters into my own hands and tell your mother you played parlour games last winter with Edward Shirley."

"You will do nothing of the sort! Mr Shirley is a third son with no prospects, and I have no money. A union between us would be nonsensical."

"You like him," Elizabeth insisted with a teasing turn of her mouth. "I know you do. As Mr Shirley is not only agreeable, but handsome, I cannot fault your preference. I give you leave to like him. You have liked many a stupider person."

She watched her friend glance towards the far side of the room, where a half dozen neighbourhood gentlemen congregated with her brothers, John and Dick Lucas. Mr Shirley was among them, making merry with his own brothers.

Charlotte sighed. "Liking a gentleman does not make him a prudent option, nor does being agreeable put a roof over one's head or food on one's table. I am not romantic. A woman in my situation cannot afford to be. If given the choice of having a respectable husband with a good income and a comfortable home or having a pittance to live on and a life of uncertainty with a man I like above all others, I must and always shall choose prudence."

"Prudence for prudence's sake is one thing," Elizabeth argued, "but exercising prudence in matters of the heart is quite another. How can you adopt such a rational attitude where love and matrimony are concerned?"

Charlotte answered her with a rueful smile. "Because I am a rational creature, Eliza. At seven-and-twenty, I can ill afford to be anything else. I am not beautiful and sweet like Jane, or handsome and clever like you. I am plain and sensible. I have always believed happiness in marriage is a matter of chance. If I were to suddenly become romantic now, such behaviour would be deemed foolish."

Elizabeth grasped Charlotte's hands. "This will not do! You are by no means plain, nor is being romantic the least bit foolish."

"I am plain enough. As for being foolish, the world would certainly consider me so if I chose to ignore the reality of my circumstances. There is little security in life for penniless women determined to marry for love rather than practicality and no guarantee of happiness. I have accepted my lot in life, but perhaps you need not. Perhaps you may choose better."

Before Elizabeth could form a reply, she heard her name spoken in a deep, formal voice she had come to know well during the last fortnight. She pursed her lips at her friend before assuming a more sanguine expression. "Mr Darcy," she said as she faced him and performed a perfunctory curtsey. "How do you do?"

Darcy bowed and was silent. As expected, there was no hint of the amicable, sometimes teasing gentleman Elizabeth

encountered whenever their paths converged in the countryside, which happened to be almost daily. Instead, the staid,
serious version of Pemberley's master stood before her, his
countenance a careful mask of indifference.

Elizabeth resisted the urge to smile. "I trust you are
enjoying your evening, sir?"

His gaze drifted from her slippers to the top of her head
before settling on her eyes. "You look very well tonight, Miss
Elizabeth."

While any other lady would be gratified to receive such
singular attention from him, Elizabeth knew Darcy better
than to think he meant to flatter her by paying her a compliment. His intent had likely been to neatly sidestep her
enquiry and avoid offending Charlotte. Darcy's distaste for
crowds and idle conversation not only ensured his dissatisfaction with this evening, but every evening preceding it. Elizabeth doubted Miss Bingley clinging to his arm or Sir William
regaling him with tales of his honorary knighthood would be
viewed by Darcy as a boon. Such condescension likely
reminded him of being in town. "Thank you," she replied. "I
hope you are in good health?"

"I am, thank you." He glanced at Charlotte. "Good
evening, Miss Lucas."

"Good evening, Mr Darcy. Pray excuse me. I was about to
open the instrument." She looked pointedly at Elizabeth and
said, "You know, Eliza, what is to follow."

Elizabeth shook her head. "You are a strange creature by
way of a friend, always insisting that I play and sing before
anybody and everybody! If my vanity had taken a musical
turn, you would have been invaluable. As it is, I would rather
not perform before those who must be in the habit of hearing
the very best musicians. According to Miss Bingley, Mr
Darcy's sister is remarkably talented. He cannot be interested
in hearing my paltry attempts."

"Georgiana is indeed accomplished," said Darcy, "but it does not follow that her abilities must automatically render yours inferior."

"I beg to differ," she quipped. "You have yet to hear me play, sir."

"Nor shall I be satisfied until I have."

"Nor I," said Charlotte with a flicker of amusement in her eyes. "There is nothing for it, Eliza. Mr Darcy insists upon hearing you."

"I do," he said with a sincerity that surprised her.

"You see," said her friend, "now you have no choice but to oblige us both."

Elizabeth glanced between the two of them and sighed. She was as used to Charlotte's persistence as she was unused to Darcy's. If he truly wished to hear her play, Elizabeth would oblige him, but she doubted he would be impressed by her abilities. "Very well. If it must be so, then it must, but you have been warned, Mr Darcy. If you are disappointed by my performance, you will have no one to blame but yourself."

"I shall consider myself amply forewarned." He gestured to the pianoforte on the opposite side of the room. "Your instrument awaits."

Linking their arms, the two ladies left Darcy and made their way across the room. The instrument was opened, and Elizabeth settled herself on the bench. Her performance, while not exceptional, was pleasing, and her voice as she sang was rich and sweet and clear. When her song ended, an enthusiastic smattering of applause followed, accompanied by entreaties that she play another. On a whim, Elizabeth chose a lively Scottish air she knew was a great favourite. An impromptu set was formed in the centre of the room by her sisters and some of the other young people, who laughed gaily as they danced. Elizabeth smiled and laughed along with them.

When she had finished, she surrendered the pianoforte to her sister Mary, who leapt at the chance to take her place. While Mary's ability and taste did not equal Elizabeth's, what she lacked in polish she made up for in eagerness. No sooner had Elizabeth stepped away from the instrument than a doleful string of chords filled the room. While the complexity of the piece and the talent to effectively execute it were beyond Mary's capabilities, she was determined to play it, despite Lydia demanding she play *La Boulanger* instead.

As Elizabeth made her way across the room, Darcy made his way towards Elizabeth. Professing a desire for refreshment, he accompanied her into the dining room, where rum punch and an assortment of sweets and cakes were arranged in a lovely spread upon the sideboard. "You sing beautifully, Miss Elizabeth. I was impressed with the depth of your expression, and the quality and range of your voice."

Rather than thank him, she teased him. "But not my playing, apparently."

"Not at all," he replied. "You play the pianoforte quite well."

Elizabeth laughed. "I am afraid *quite* well, Mr Darcy, is not the same as *very* well. I did warn you, but you insisted I play despite my protests. I daresay you will be more cautious in the future."

"That I shall not do. Practising fosters mastery."

"In my case, it may well foster a headache."

"Nonsense. I found nothing wanting in your performance, I assure you."

Elizabeth selected a pretty, crystal cup from the sideboard and raised one pert brow. "Nothing, sir?"

Darcy shook his head at her stubbornness, relieved her of her cup, and filled it with punch. "Truly, you play well. If you practise, you shall play better."

"And what of yourself?" she asked, smiling as she accepted her punch.

He looked at her with confusion. "I do not take your meaning."

"You would benefit from some practice as well. It has been two weeks since you first came into Hertfordshire, yet I have noticed you continue to speak primarily to the members of your own party and rarely to anyone else."

"I am speaking to you now."

"True." she allowed. "But with whom else do you speak? Have you spoken to any of the other gentlemen tonight?"

"I do not know them as I know you."

"If you spoke to them," she chided, "you would get to know them better."

Darcy averted his gaze to the punch pot. "You are correct, of course." He cleared his throat, selected a cup of his own and filled it nearly to the rim. "If you insist upon my speaking in general whenever I mix with society—any society—I fear you will be disappointed more often than satisfied. That said, it so happens I spoke to Sir William Lucas not half an hour ago."

"Did you?" she remarked with some surprise, unable to imagine Darcy, so fastidious and proud, conversing with the diffuse Sir William about anything of substance. "And what did you speak of if I may be so bold as to ask? Did Sir William expound upon the splendours of St James's Court? Or the condescension of the king when he was knighted?"

"We spoke of dancing," Darcy replied to his cup. "Sir William also spoke of you."

"Dancing," she said cheerfully. "How fitting, for I know how much you enjoy the exercise. Why Sir William would speak of me, I cannot begin to guess, and so I shall not attempt it."

"He appears to be a great admirer of yours. By all

accounts, he considers you one of the brightest jewels in the country and a capital dancer."

Elizabeth laughed. "Quite the opposite of your opinion, I presume."

One corner of Darcy's mouth lifted. "If you recall, Miss Elizabeth, I have not yet had the pleasure of dancing with you. I shall reserve judgment regarding your abilities until I have."

"As you were already presented with ample opportunity, I fear your wait may be of some duration. Unless Mr Bingley makes good on his promise to hold a ball, I cannot imagine when another occasion will present itself."

The tips of Darcy's ears turned red. "Pray do not remind me of what I said then. My behaviour on that occasion was unpardonable."

Elizabeth's smile slipped from her face. She had meant only to tease him for his reticence, not upbraid him for his rudeness on an evening that was best forgotten. Embarrassment coloured her countenance. "Pray forgive me. On that night, the conduct of neither was irreproachable, but since then I believe we have both improved in civilities."

Darcy shook his head. "You have done nothing to warrant censure of any kind, either now or then. Your reproach was entirely justified, as justified as my manners and conduct were abhorrent." When she attempted to contradict him, he held up his hand. "Pray do not pain me by insisting your comportment equalled mine, for we both know of the two yours was the superior."

Although she disagreed with his assessment, Elizabeth had no wish to argue with him or to punish him by causing him more pain. She yielded to his request and sipped her punch instead, willing the concoction of rum, syrup, spices, and fruit to soothe her conscience as it soothed her parched throat.

While Darcy raised his own cup to his lips, Elizabeth cast her eyes about the room in search of a new topic, only to spy her friend observing them from the drawing room with keen interest. The pointed look Charlotte levelled at her could not possibly be misinterpreted—a man as handsome, wealthy, and consequential as Darcy was too fine a catch to let slip through her fingers.

Charlotte's persistence, however well meant, only served to vex her. She and Darcy were friends. It was unlikely they would ever become more to each other. The night they met, he had made clear his vehement disinclination for marriage and his disgust with the machinations that ladies employed to bring it about. If he adamantly refused to engage in a flirtation in London, where the ladies were not only elegant and titled, but well-dowered and seminary educated, there was little chance he would stand for it here.

His time in Hertfordshire had proven Darcy was nothing if not conscientious. If conversation with the neighbourhood's unmarried ladies and their eager mothers could somehow be avoided, even to the point of appearing rude, it was done. Miss Bingley, Jane, and Elizabeth were the noted exceptions. Miss Bingley was sister to Mr Bingley, Mr Bingley was Darcy's friend, Jane had captured Mr Bingley's eye, and Elizabeth was Jane's dearest sister. She enjoyed Darcy's society, appreciated his company, and valued his friendship. She admired his intellect and his dry sense of humour and, because she liked him so well, tolerated many of his faults. Their conversations were stimulating and never dull. Darcy was interested in her opinions, he respected her views, and he challenged her in ways other gentlemen had never done. Elizabeth had no desire to drive him away.

"Have I offended you, Miss Elizabeth?"

Elizabeth started at the sound of his voice. "Not at all,"

she said, endeavouring to smile. "Pray forgive me, Mr Darcy. I was wool-gathering."

"Are you certain—absolutely certain—there is nothing I have said to cause you distress?" There was an underlying note of trepidation in his tone that not only surprised her but filled her with a pang of remorse. He did not deserve her inattention, nor did he deserve to think she was dissatisfied with him, not when her dissatisfaction originated with none but herself.

"I assure you, sir, you have done nothing to distress me. But perhaps, in the interest of our equanimity, we ought to discuss pleasanter topics. We are friends, after all. We understand one another much better now. That is what matters."

Darcy stared at her for a long moment, his eyes filled with an intensity of feeling that Elizabeth recognised but had yet to learn to interpret. "Friends," he uttered, averting his gaze once more to his cup. "Yes. We are certainly friends. I thank you for reminding me."

The corners of her lips lifted in reply, but Darcy did not return her smile. Instead, he excused himself and walked to the sideboard to refill his empty cup. Elizabeth frowned as she raised her own cup to her lips and took a measured sip, but nearly spilled what remained down the front of her gown when an insistent, "Lizzy! *Liz-zy!*" was heard from the drawing room.

A moment later, Lydia and Kitty came running into the room. "Lizzy," Lydia cried, nearly out of breath. "You must come at once! Mary refuses to play anything besides boring dirges and hymns, and we are desperate to dance!"

"Come and play for us, Lizzy, please!" Kitty implored. "Everyone in the house is at their wit's end."

She gave each sister a stern look she hoped communicated her displeasure with their conduct and said, "Pray lower your voices else everyone in Meryton hears you. I am sorry to be the source of further disappointment, but I have no intention of playing again this evening."

Neither Lydia nor Kitty bore her refusal with grace.

"No one," said Kitty, "wishes to hear Mary's concertos."

"Everyone wants to dance a reel!" Lydia insisted.

Unmoved by their theatrics and mortified by their poor comportment, Elizabeth suggested they take up the instrument themselves. "Once you both learn to play, you may each take a turn on the pianoforte until you have worn holes in your slippers and your hearts are content. Then all your happiness will be dependent upon yourselves rather than others. It is an arrangement that will suit everyone."

"If I had cared to learn," Lydia proclaimed, "I would have, but you know I have no desire to do so. Jane does not play either and Kitty's health does not allow for it. *You* must play, Lizzy. You are our only hope."

Had the sisters been alone, Elizabeth would have pointed out that since Kitty's health allowed her to dance reel after reel with handsome young men, it would certainly allow her to devote herself to learning the pianoforte. They were not alone, however. Darcy stood ten feet away, likely cringing at every word that passed their lips. Elizabeth shook her head at them instead.

Lydia huffed. "I know what that look means, Lizzy, but it does not signify one jot as neither of us know how to play. Even if we did, we would not play very well. Neither does Mary for that matter," she mumbled sourly.

"If your hearts are set on procuring someone who plays the pianoforte *very* well," Elizabeth replied, "I am sorry to inform you I have recently been told that I only play *quite* well. So, you see, applying to me in this instance will hardly serve your purpose."

Lydia gaped at her. "Who would dare to say such an awful thing to you? I shall give them a piece of my mind!"

"Truly, Lizzy. That was terribly rude," Kitty declared, wrinkling her nose. "I cannot imagine saying such a horrid thing to anyone, even to Mary."

It was at that moment Darcy returned to reclaim his place at Elizabeth's side. "It is possible," he said drily, "that your sister misunderstood the sentiment behind the comment." Glancing at Elizabeth, he added, "As she is often wont to do."

Lydia and Kitty stared at him. It was obvious, by their identical, stupefied expressions, they had not noticed Darcy was even in the room. After a moment, Lydia brightened. "Mr Darcy, surely you would like to hear Lizzy play again. Surely, you must long to make merry and dance with the rest of us! You must come at once and ask Mary to dance, then Lizzy may take her place, and everything will be settled to everyone's satisfaction. I shall even dance with you myself, and so will Kitty and Maria Lucas and any other girl you desire to dance a reel with, for no lady in all of Hertfordshire would dare refuse you anything."

While Lydia looked vastly pleased with herself for making such a speech, Kitty appeared far less so. In fact, she looked as though the prospect of standing up with Darcy positively terrified her. Elizabeth could not blame her. In that moment, Darcy's expression portrayed both incredulousness and indignation in equal measure.

Elizabeth did not know whether she ought to laugh or cringe. Not only had her sisters unwittingly called Darcy rude, but Lydia had essentially ordered him to dance with every lady in the country! As usual, she had given no consideration to whether he would enjoy dancing with her friends, or whether her forwardness might offend him. Poor Mr Darcy, to be the recipient of such an affront! Determined to spare him further offence—and herself further embarrassment—Elizabeth cast a furtive look at her sisters. "Very well. I shall oblige you this once provided you do not carry on as you are now. Return to the drawing room and find your partners. I shall be along in a moment."

"Ooh!" Lydia squealed delightedly. "We knew you would never be so unfeeling as to deny us, Lizzy!" She turned to Darcy with an elated smile. "What fun we shall have together!"

Once Elizabeth's sisters returned to the drawing room, a stilted silence settled upon those in the dining room. Although Elizabeth dreaded looking at Darcy, she steeled herself and raised her eyes to his face. "Pray forgive my sisters, sir. They are well meaning, but their means are often poorly executed."

There was no denying Darcy was dissatisfied. It was apparent in the sharpness of his brow and the harsh line of his mouth. She could hear it in his voice. "You are hardly responsible for your sisters' comportment, Miss Elizabeth. That office falls to your parents, not to you."

Elizabeth felt the bitter sting of Darcy's condemnation as deeply as she felt his disgust. Her mother's unchecked indulgence and her father's neglect had always been a source of pain and mortification to her, but never more so than in that moment. However much she wished to refute such a statement, she could not. What Darcy said of her parents was true.

She imagined sinking into the carpet or claiming a headache and returning home; neither option was viable. Resigned to remaining at Lucas Lodge until her mother declared it was time to depart, Elizabeth pointed out a panelled door on the other side of the room. "I fear once the dancing begins you will find yourself at the mercy of my sister. I would not have you made more uncomfortable than you are already. Sir William's library is through that door and down the corridor. His collection is rather meagre compared to Netherfield's, but you will be quite safe there. Lydia will not impose upon you again."

She was astonished when Darcy not only stepped closer to her but reached for her hand. His bow was merely perfunctory, but the brief, steady pressure he applied to her fingers was not.

A sudden sensation of warmth made Elizabeth blush. Flustered, she raised her eyes to his face, expecting his censure, but was surprised to see contrition instead.

"Pray do not overtax yourself this evening," he told her, pitching his voice low. "Tomorrow, should you find yourself too fatigued to embark upon your morning constitutional, you will be missed." He paused to clear his throat. "As you know, poor Solomon will feel your absence acutely."

Elizabeth could not help herself—she laughed.

Tilting her face towards the sky, Elizabeth smiled as the sun burst through the stratified clouds overhead. "It looks as though we shall not see rain this morning after all. The sun is intent upon making its presence known."

"There is a French proverb," Darcy replied, extending his hand to her as she climbed onto an old stile. The wood was rotted and slippery from last night's rain. "*Pluie du matin n'arrête pas le pèlerin.* It means 'Morning rain does not stop the pilgrim'."

Elizabeth accepted his assistance with a grateful smile. "I have always considered the French language to be beautiful. Unfortunately, my father's library contains no books written in French, so I never applied myself to learn more than a few rudimentary phrases. I learnt German instead, and I am able to read Latin and Greek. They serve me well at Longbourn."

Holding firmly to Darcy's hand, she jumped from the stile to the ground and thanked him.

Relinquishing her hand, Darcy gestured for her to precede him on the path. "You are most welcome. But what is this about learning Latin and Greek?" he asked, falling into step beside her. "That is an impressive accomplishment. I became fluent in both while I attended Eton. It was no easy feat."

"My father taught me Latin when I was eight years old and Greek when I was ten. We did not have a governess, but those of us who wished to learn languages, or mathematics, or geography, were given the means to do so. My parents," she informed him with wry amusement, "had hoped for a son, but I was a determined, inquisitive child, impatient for knowledge and content to spend my days obtaining it. Jane attended lessons as well, but once she was older my mother demanded her involvement in more domestic concerns."

"What of your other sisters?"

"As you know, Mary's tastes are mostly ecclesiastical, and my youngest sisters lack the patience required for anything beyond their own interests. I am hopeful, however, that Lydia and Kitty will eventually recognise the value of an education and apply themselves accordingly. As...independent as they are, I cannot believe either would desire their daughters to be as ill-informed and ignorant of the world as they are themselves."

"Your two youngest sisters are very different from you," Darcy observed. "They do not possess your steadiness, your strength of character, or your innate desire to become well-informed through their own application and diligence. They are not unique in that regard. Most of the ladies of my acquaintance prefer idle chatter and gossip to real, meaningful conversation, even the ones whose husbands sit in the House of Lords. Your superiority of mind and your practical nature, Miss Elizabeth, are as remarkable as your frankness and sincerity."

The first time Darcy had complimented her was at the Meryton assembly the night they were introduced. Then, the bestowal of such praise had baffled her. Now, after knowing him better, Elizabeth saw his facility and candour as a testament to their friendship. That he felt such confidence in her perception and such ease in her company pleased her—far more than it likely should.

Assuming an arch look, she said, "I thank you, but there must be some lady somewhere who applies herself to the betterment of her mind with more faithfulness and rapacity than I."

Darcy shook his head. "I have never seen such a woman, but I suspect if ladies were suddenly granted admittance to university that you would be the first to pack your trunks and hie to Cambridge."

Elizabeth laughed; his assumption was by no means inaccurate. "You know me well, sir, but apparently not so well as you believe. My father would insist upon my attending Oxford as he did, and his father and grandfather before him."

"Your father was an Oxford man?"

"He was. For many years, he regaled me with tales of his life there—of the friends he made, and his lessons, and his determination to see whatever he could of the world."

"Then I take it he has travelled as well."

A wayward leaf, mottled with varying shades of red, fluttered in the breeze and became caught on a stand of withered brush. Elizabeth plucked it from its prison as she passed and twirled it between her fingers. "Sadly, Papa has never ventured beyond England, although he saw much of the country in his youth. Now that he is older, he does not care to travel beyond Hertfordshire. To convince him to take us to London to visit our relations there is a chore. He prefers to stay at home with his books and his port, reading into the night."

"And what of yourself?" Darcy enquired, directing her notice to a muddy patch of ground. "Do you wish to see what adventures abound beyond England? Britain's empire is vast, and there is much of value to be gained from travelling to foreign lands and meeting the people who call those lands home."

The mud encompassed but a small area; Elizabeth skipped over it with ease. "I have always wanted to make such a journey," she confessed, feeling a little surge of excitement at the prospect of seeing more of the world than what she knew in Hertfordshire.

Darcy smiled. "I suspected as much. Where would you go first?"

"The world is so vast it is difficult to choose! Greece, Italy, America. I would go all the way to India if I had the means to do so. But venturing anywhere, even somewhere close to home, would be as welcome. I have seen so little of the world. I am certain I would find every new place fresh and interesting. Once there is peace on the Continent, I long to see France. Thus far, I have only ever experienced the sights and sounds and scents of Paris through books."

"I have been to Paris," he confided. A small, wistful smile played upon his mouth. "But it was many years ago. I have family in the French countryside and on the northern coast, just across the English Channel."

With Elizabeth's prompting, Darcy spoke at length of his time there, recounting his impressions of the countryside, and of the cities and towns he visited as a boy. She felt his excitement, his pleasure, and his appreciation for the experiences and adventures he had there, the knowledge he had gleaned, and the people he had met. "My time there," he told her with quiet reverence, "especially the weeks spent with my parents touring the countryside, was among the most memorable of my life. They could have left me at home with my governess. Instead, they took me with them and showed me a world beyond Pemberley. For that, I shall be forever grateful."

"Will you return to France someday?" she asked, envisioning a young Darcy traipsing through fields full of poppies and wildflowers, a warm summer breeze ruffling his hair.

"I will." There was no hesitation in his voice, only a decisiveness that struck her as entirely inherent to his nature. "God willing, the country I remember will not be altered beyond my recognition when I do. There is a brutality in war, complete in its infliction, that not only effects changes in places, but within the very hearts and minds of the people who live in them."

Elizabeth had long believed the same. "It is impossible to imagine anyone, be they man, woman, or child, emerging from such horrors unscathed. The history books have shown us time and again that while war brings change—in some circumstances necessary change—it also brings much suffering. Bonaparte's ambitions for France are supported by the French populace, but there must be some among them who feel differently. I cannot think that France's mothers are glad to see their sons go off to war. I cannot think its wives, forced to bid their husbands farewell under such uncertainty and duress, do so willingly. The pain and terror they must feel within their hearts—for their husbands, for their children, and for their futures—must be unprecedented! I cannot imagine being unaffected by such sacrifices. I cannot imagine emerging from the atrocities of war unchanged."

A stiff autumn wind blew through the field, rustling dried stalks of barley, causing the skirt of Elizabeth's gown to billow and dance. A tendril of hair caught on her lashes. She brushed it aside, feeling peevish, much as she usually did after playing Beethoven too long.

The sleeve of Darcy's greatcoat brushed her arm.

A soft, fluttery warmth bloomed in her belly, further unsettling her and making her blush. Elizabeth turned her attention to the distant hills and inhaled a slow, deliberate breath.

"Your insight," said Darcy, "and your heart, do you credit. We, as a society, would be ignorant indeed to assume that because men desire war that women must therefore desire the same."

His voice was incredibly gentle.

Elizabeth looked at him then, and their eyes met and held. The warmth winding through her belly intensified. How could his gaze, so fervent and steady, make her body feel such sensations? How could the sound of his voice affect her so? Or the touch of his coat sleeve against her arm?

Darcy was not the only gentleman she considered a friend, but he was nothing like the boys Elizabeth had known all her life. He possessed a regal bearing, a staidness she found both comforting and incredibly appealing. He was highly intelligent and discerning as well—a man of deep insight and few words, but rarely was he silent with her. With her, he had much to say concerning a wide variety of subjects.

And sometimes, when he was tired, or when her neighbours had forced him into conversation for too long, he would simply beg a chair beside her, or direct his gaze to the window, and say nothing at all.

He was unlike any gentleman Elizabeth had ever known.

A hare bolted across the path, startling her. It was enough to recall her attention to the present. Collecting herself, she smiled and enquired after Darcy's sister.

SEVEN

I will not say that your mulberry trees are dead; but I am afraid they are not alive.

"Are we going to have some sport or not?" Hurst barked, snatching his fowling piece from his loader while the dogs paced in the grass. His breath was a cloud of vapour in the frosty morning air. "You can speak of Jane Bennet and her myriad charms all you want, Bingley, *after* we bag our supper and have a few glasses of port by the fire."

Assessing his double-barrel flintlock, Darcy silently agreed. Bingley had been full of nothing but talk of Jane Bennet for three weeks—her beauty, her grace, her gentleness, her smile. While Darcy could find no real fault with her per se—other than her appalling family—he felt the eldest Miss Bennet, with her serenity and her classic figure and her blue eyes and her lauded perfection, was overrated.

"She smiles too much."

"I beg your pardon," said Bingley, sounding put out. "Miss Bennet does not smile too much! That is simply absurd."

Darcy blinked in confusion. Surely, he could not have said that aloud.

Apparently, he had.

"I agree," said Hurst. "The lady is pleasant, and she is pretty. But I know nothing else of her, only that she has a ridiculous mother, a gaggle of silly sisters, and a nice set of teeth."

Bingley waved a dismissive hand. "Mrs Bennet is hardly as bad as all that, and her youngest daughters only want a firmer hand from their father. Miss Elizabeth is delightful. As for Miss Bennet, there is far more to her than her teeth. She is nothing but kindness. She is loveliness itself. She is an *angel*. In fact, I would wager I am in a fair way of soon finding myself in love with her." He raised his gun, took aim, and pulled the trigger as a pheasant burst out of the brush and into the sky.

Darcy started at Bingley's pronouncement.

The pheasant plummeted towards the ground and landed in a thicket on the far side of the field. The dogs were off in an instant, splashing through the stream and into the brush to retrieve it. .

He shook his head. Bingley was forever falling in love with one lady or another. Soon enough, Miss Bennet and her vulgar mother would lose their idyllic charm and Bingley would move on to the next girl, whomever she may be. "I do not mean to imply Miss Bennet is lacking, Bingley, only that she seems to regard the entire neighbourhood with the same serene countenance and unaffected air."

"Miss Bennet is charming," he countered.

"Clearly," said Hurst with a contemptuous snort. "She has certainly charmed you. How many occasions have you been in company with the lady? Three?"

"Five," Bingley replied. "There was the assembly where we were introduced three weeks ago. Then we dined at the Great House at Stoke. After that, we were invited to dine at Longbourn, which we did twice, and at Lucas Lodge just last week. Miss Bennet and I were afforded the opportunity to have many agreeable conversations. I look forward to repeating the pleasure in the future."

Darcy rolled his eyes. "Of course you spoke to her. Her mother went to a great deal of trouble to arrange the seating to suit her interests. You were placed beside Miss Bennet on each occasion."

"I was," Bingley allowed, "but it does not follow I was dissatisfied with the arrangement—quite the contrary. It provided me with the perfect opportunity to know her better."

Darcy stared at him. "What more could you possibly need to know? Her mother is an opportunist. Her father is indolent, and his estate is entailed. There are two uncles in trade—one who lives near Cheapside, no doubt within sight of his warehouses. None of the girls have so much as a shilling among them, which means no dowry for your Miss Bennet."

Shrugging, Bingley handed his gun to his loader. "Perhaps not, but there is more to matrimony than making money, my friend."

"On that, we are agreed." Darcy raised his gun and took aim as a pair of pheasants took flight. "The lady, whoever she is, ought to have excellent connexions as well."

He pulled the trigger.

The first bird fell to the ground.

He fired his second shot, but it went wide. "Damn it," he muttered, shoving his discharged rifle at his loader. He motioned impatiently for another, but it was too late. Hurst beat him to it.

"Well done, Hurst," he said with a rueful twist of his mouth while the dogs tore across the field. "I had not counted on missing."

Hurst narrowed his eyes in annoyance. "Whenever there

is talk of women, nothing ever goes according to plan. When we are to shoot, man, we ought to shoot! Women take up enough of our time. They have no business interfering with our sport as well! Had Bingley not mentioned Jane Bennet, you would not have been distracted. You are both distracted, I daresay, and not with the right sort of birds."

Bingley slapped his brother-in-law on the back. "You may say whatever you like, Hurst, but you will not discourage my admiration of Miss Bennet. Nor will you, Darcy. She can have uncles to fill all of Cheapside, and I shall still think her the most wondrous creature I have ever known. My own fortune was made in trade, or have you conveniently forgotten? I may not have ten thousand a year like some people, but five thousand pounds per annum is more than enough to enable me to marry whomever I like. As of this moment, there is no lady I like more than Miss Bennet."

Darcy scoffed. "Because you happen to like a lady better than any other is hardly inducement enough to marry her. Should you bring her to London and introduce her as your wife, I doubt Miss Bennet will be as well received by society as you would hope. She is no heiress."

Bingley shook his head. "For years, you have been pursued by matchmaking mothers and their daughters, none of whom have ever exercised an ounce of discretion, either in their quest for a rich husband or when relating their expectations to their friends. Your vaunted Pemberley, your house in town, your fortune, and your estate in Scotland are all they talk of. Nothing is said of your excellent character or your steadfast nature or your charitable contributions among the poor. Yet, despite this oversight, you dare to discourage my preference for Miss Bennet! You dare to tell me I should disregard her because she is not rich enough or born high enough to satisfy the *ton*. It is ridiculous—nay, it is incogitable."

"Perhaps the *ton* does not always set the best example, but its members have a wealth of connexions, superior breeding, and an excess of money and property. All those commodities give them power, Bingley—power to either recognise your worth and welcome you into their fold or deny you admittance. Marriage is forever. You cannot afford to choose imprudently."

"Miss Bennet is a gentleman's daughter. I am the son of a tradesman. If I were to make her an offer, Miss Bennet would be the one marrying lower, not me."

Darcy shrugged. "In one sense, yes, but any ties you once had to trade are all but severed. Your fortune is considerable, and you have joined the landed gentry by letting Netherfield. Despite Mr Bennet being born a gentleman, he has nothing to give his daughters, and his connexions, for the most part, are beneath you. That is what matters. That is what the *ton* would see in any case."

Bingley laughed. "Then I say hang the *ton!* When was the last time you attended Almack's or accepted an invitation to a rout in town? Admit it, Darcy. You have no desire to mix with those people any more than I care to, not really. With all their fickleness, I wonder how it is those within the exalted first set have not shunned *you* by now."

One corner of Darcy's mouth lifted in a sardonic smile. "Until I am married to one of their daughters, there are few who would dare. I own half of Derbyshire. My uncle is an earl. My great grandfather was a duke. His great grandfather was descended from French aristocracy. You, however, are still relatively new to society." He rubbed his forehead and sighed. "Are you so sure of Miss Bennet that you can honestly say your wealth poses no inducement to her? That Netherfield's status, your eligibility, your income, and your potential to purchase an estate of your own in the future, have no bearing on her choice?"

"Miss Bennet's regard for me equals mine for her," Bingley replied with absolute certainty. "I would stake Caroline's yearly allowance on it."

"And her mother?" Darcy asked pointedly.

Bingley frowned. "What of her?"

Hurst snorted and patted his greatcoat pockets. "Your lady is demure and obedient. Her mother is shrewd and demanding. Surely, you can solve this equation yourself, Bingley."

Bingley shook his head. "You give Miss Bennet too little credit, and Mrs Bennet far too much."

"Fine," Darcy allowed, albeit grudgingly. "Miss Bennet's regard for you may well be genuine and heartfelt, but fondness does not automatically negate the possibility of her playing the part of a dutiful daughter. Her mother is the epitome of mean understanding and ill breeding. In company, the woman has consistently remarked upon your preference for her daughter. She has shown no regard for decorum, your honour, nor for the delicacy of Miss Bennet's sensibilities and the fragility of her reputation. In my experience, such a mother's influence is not to be underestimated."

Bingley pursed his lips. "I am not blind, if that is what you think. I know her mother has designs on me. That was clear from the moment we were introduced. But Miss Bennet is not her mother. I cannot believe her regard for me is anything but sincere."

"You know virtually nothing of her," Darcy insisted. "You would be a fool to trust any woman so readily on such a brief acquaintance."

"Then I am a fool," said Bingley, hefting his gun to his shoulder. "But are we not all fools in love?"

"I would not know," Darcy muttered.

Hurst withdrew a silver flask from his waistcoat pocket

and gave the cap a twist. "Speaking of brief acquaintances, how is Miss Elizabeth, Darcy?"

Darcy nearly dropped his gun. "What?"

Chuckling, Hurst took a healthy swallow from his flask and wiped his mouth with the back of his hand. "As far as I can tell, you seem to have struck up quite a friendship with the lady. You cannot have known her any longer than Bingley has known his own Miss Bennet. Tell me, are you in a fair way of soon being in love yourself?"

"Oh-ho!" Bingley exclaimed with a vindicated grin. "It would serve you right if you were!"

Darcy shifted his focus to his gun and endeavoured to tamp down his irritation. Elizabeth Bennet and the unsettling emotions she inspired whenever they were in company together was nothing he wished to dwell on, never mind discuss with Bingley and Hurst. Pointedly ignoring his grinning friend, Darcy checked the safety on his weapon and said to Hurst, "The operative word in that statement is friendship. We happen to have several common interests and enjoy discussing them."

"And those interests are what, exactly?" Bingley enquired, rubbing his hands together.

"Books, music, philosophy, politics," Darcy replied dismissively. "Miss Elizabeth enjoys walking a great deal. She has a wealth of knowledge about the Hertfordshire countryside."

"You discuss philosophy and politics. With a woman?" Hurst's smirk was insufferable. "How singular."

Darcy rolled his eyes. "I know what you are thinking, and you are both wrong. I respect her. I like her. But I have no designs on her. As delightful as she is, Elizabeth Bennet is too poor for me to consider. You know my sentiments regarding her family. All my life I have been told, 'marry high, marry money, marry a title'. I cannot disappoint my family by marrying a woman whose standing in society will not advance my own."

"Good Lord," Bingley uttered. "Listen to yourself. You are the master of Pemberley and staggeringly wealthy. You could probably marry a chambermaid if you so desired and still be accepted by the first set. Admit it—you are an insufferable snob who will not so much as look at a woman unless she has forty thousand pounds and a title."

Darcy shrugged noncommittedly. "The lady need not have a title so long as she is handsome and clever and does not grate on my nerves. I could not countenance being shackled to a woman with mediocre abilities and virtually no knowledge of the world. As for her fortune, anything above twenty thousand pounds would be adequate."

Even as Darcy said the words, he felt a sharp pang of regret. Elizabeth lacked none of those traits. What she lacked was notoriety. What she lacked was a fortune. What she lacked was a family that would not make him cringe each time he was in company with them.

"So, what you are saying then," said Hurst, "is that you will not be proposing to Caroline."

Darcy levelled a look of utmost disgust at him.

Hurst laughed and offered Darcy his flask. "Pity."

"No, no. The other one," said Darcy to his valet, indicating the green coat rather than the blue. "Yes. That will do, Worth."

Worth assisted him with his coat, then proceeded to make a few adjustments.

Darcy studied his appearance in the mirror with a critical

eye. Although fastidious, he did not usually primp or fuss over his appearance. He knew he was considered desirable by society's standards but thought little of his looks beyond the pressing of his coat and trousers or the intricate cascade of knots adorning his cravat come evening. He had never wondered whether any lady considered him to be handsome. In truth, he had never actually cared.

Why he ought to care now discomfited him. It was not as though there were any single ladies who were worth impressing in Hertfordshire. Surely, Elizabeth would not care whether he was handsome or ill favoured. Nor would she care whether he wore his blue coat or his green one, so long as his conversation was interesting.

As he tugged at his tailcoat, Darcy wondered which gown she would wear that evening. He had developed a fondness for her dark green muslin. It complemented her eyes and warmed her complexion. Despite the style being outdated in London, the cut and fit were flattering—too flattering. He shook his head. Thoughts like these would get him into trouble, especially when he would soon be dining at Longbourn and forced to speak to her father.

Speak to her father.

God in Heaven...

Darcy pursed his lips. Speaking to her father in such a context should never cross his mind. The man was an enigma, but not in the same pleasant, teasing way his second daughter was an enigma. Darcy found Mr Bennet flippant, sarcastic, dismissive, and unforgivably neglectful of his daughters. That the man permitted his youngest two to run as wild in the streets of Meryton as he did in his own drawing room was galling enough, but by failing to check their poor comportment, Mr Bennet's carelessness extended to his eldest daughters as well.

Then there was the matter of his wife.

Darcy frowned as he considered Elizabeth's mother. He had never encountered any woman with such a latent mind and loud, insistent mouth. It confounded him to think that a man who boasted an Oxford education had chosen such a woman to rear, educate, and advise his daughters.

After accepting his pocket watch from his valet, Darcy glanced at the time and hastened to secure it to the fob. The hour had grown late. No doubt Bingley already had one foot in the carriage. If Miss Bennet belonged to any other landed family in England, Darcy would have found his friend's eagerness amusing, but there was nothing amusing in the prospect of passing another tedious evening at Longbourn. The only pleasure he could expect to receive for his sacrifice would come from speaking with Elizabeth.

Assuming he was fortunate enough to speak with her...

That Elizabeth might be engaged with other guests throughout the evening was a distinct possibility, one he found exceedingly frustrating. Longbourn was loud and often crowded with every neighbour and friend Mrs Bennet could think to invite. Tonight, she had thought to invite Georgiana. While Darcy recognised and even appreciated the gesture, he certainly could not consent to his sister attending such a gathering. She was used to small, intimate dinners and quiet, ordered conversations. This, one did not find at Longbourn.

Checking his appearance in the mirror one last time, Darcy tucked his watch into his waistcoat pocket, collected his gloves, and dismissed his valet. With any luck, his evening would not be a total punishment.

To Darcy's consternation, his evening was a total punishment. Not only was he seated as far as possible from Elizabeth at the dinner table, but her mother insisted on seating him beside herself. Conversation was a trial, as was endeavouring to keep his patience while Mrs Bennet talked of Bingley and Miss Bennet and her hopes of a wedding for the duration of the meal.

Elizabeth, in contrast, appeared to bear the benign chatter of her dinner companions with an equanimity Darcy envied. She smiled. She laughed. Each time she spoke to some neighbour or other, he strained to catch the tone of her conversation. As usual, she appeared to enjoy herself in a way he could not. His eyes returned to her again and again, seemingly of their own volition.

When dinner was finally over, the ladies withdrew, but Darcy found little pleasure in their absence. Cigars and port with the gentlemen tried his patience nearly as much as Elizabeth's mother. Sir William's observations were mind numbing, Mr Bennet's remarks were pedantic, and the officers were well on their way to being drunk. By the time the men joined the ladies in the drawing room for coffee, Darcy had not heard two words of sense spoken together since he had set foot in the house.

He sought Elizabeth with his eyes and spied her seated on a sofa surrounded by a veritable fortress of ladies. The room was crowded and noisy. The fire was built up too high. His head ached. He was irritable and impatient and had consumed two glasses of port instead of one. The idea of enduring another hour of nonsensical chatter was intolerable, as was the thought of playing cards. What Darcy wanted was to speak to his charming friend and for her to tease him out of his dark mood, but he was unwilling to forge a path through the multitude of colourful skirts and tittering ladies to reach her. Singling Elizabeth out in such a manner would only garner attention he did not want. For her mother to consider him as anything other than her dinner guest was an inconvenience he could ill afford.

Dismayed and annoyed, Darcy quit the room.

He stalked through the entire ground floor until he discovered a tiny, insignificant parlour tucked away at the back of the house. It was blessedly empty, with a bed of hot coals in the grate and an upholstered couch set before the hearth. It was as good a place as any to nurse his headache for half an hour. He would have preferred to return to Netherfield, but he knew better than to apply to Bingley for the use of his carriage—his sisters would likely insist that Darcy escort them home. In the dark, with only a few lanterns to light the way, travelling three miles in a carriage would be a slow trial; Mrs Hurst's insipid presence and Miss Bingley's barbed tongue would make the experience even worse.

Living at Netherfield had done little for Darcy's equanimity, but it had certainly reminded him never to underestimate a lady's perseverance once she set her cap at something. In Caroline Bingley's case, that something was Pemberley and, unfortunately, him. Despite her aspirations—and her persistence—he had long known Miss Bingley was not a woman he wished to wed. She would use his name and his consequence to raise herself higher, spend his money imprudently, and turn him away from her bed once she had given him an heir.

She would be coy.

She would be polite.

She would be cold and indifferent.

Coldness and indifference were not what Darcy wanted from the woman who would be his wife. He wanted warmth. He wanted sincerity. He wanted a companion and a lover. He wanted a woman who would engage his intellect, ease his burdens, welcome his presence in her bed, and meet his passion with a fair measure of her own.

Suddenly restless, Darcy strode to the window, where he brushed aside the gauzy curtains with an impatient wave of his hand. Nothing but blackness was visible beyond. Allowing the curtains to flutter closed, he abandoned his post to stir the coals in the grate. He added a log for warmth, and soon a small, crackling fire blazed forth, sending bright sparks up the chimney and casting long, dancing shadows on the walls. Darcy sank onto the couch, shut his eyes, and rubbed his forehead with his hands. The mantel clock chimed a quarter past the hour, and he flinched. His headache had grown worse.

A voice he had come to know well addressed him from the door. "Are you so dissatisfied with your company this evening, Mr Darcy, that you sought to remove yourself from the merriment before you found yourself in the unhappy position of being forced to dance a reel with one of my sisters?"

Darcy was on his feet at once, though more out of habit than courtesy. Despite the throbbing in his skull, he was pleased beyond measure to see Elizabeth standing in the doorway, her brow arched and her hands on her hips. "It was not my intent to be unsociable. I have developed a headache. I had thought a few moments of quietude would lessen my discomfort but, in that regard, I have been mistaken."

"Pray forgive my impertinence. I did not know. May I fetch you something to ease your pain? A glass of wine, perhaps?"

Darcy shook his head, then winced as even that slight movement exacerbated his discomfort. "I thank you, but no. Wine will not be effective in this case."

"Some tea, then? I find chamomile or willow bark especially beneficial whenever I suffer from headaches."

He was about to decline—he did not wish to inconvenience her—but something in the expression of her eyes gave him pause. If Elizabeth wanted to care for him, he would by no means suspend any pleasure of hers. "Perhaps some chamomile if it has already been prepared. Pray do not put yourself to any trouble for my sake, Miss Elizabeth."

"It is a cup of tea," she remarked. "It is no trouble."

"Even so, I would not have you neglect your other guests on my account. I would not like for you to come under scrutiny."

"The card tables have been brought out, and my mother and sisters are distracted by whist and lottery tickets. Mrs Long's nieces are seated at the pianoforte playing a duet. As their abilities are superior to mine, I shall not be missed by anyone." She dipped her head, then bit her lip and regarded him from beneath her lashes. "Tell me honestly, sir, is your headache very bad?"

In that instant she looked so lovely it took Darcy a moment to find his voice. That she believed no one would miss her was incomprehensible to him. He had missed her— far more than he reasonably should. "My present discomfort is inconvenient," he admitted, "but it is nothing I have not suffered before on countless other occasions."

Elizabeth studied him for a long time, as though attempting to discern whether he was being truthful, or merely polite. "I shall return in a moment with your tea, unless you would prefer to have a maid attend you."

Darcy knew he ought to tell her a maid would suit his purpose well enough, but parting with her so soon, after having been denied the pleasure of her company all evening, was distasteful to him. "If you believe your absence will not be remarked upon, I should prefer your convivial society to that of a servant. I have seen nothing of you tonight."

The barest hint of a smile crossed her lips. "Then I shall return as soon as may be."

"And I shall look forward to it," he told her softly as she turned to leave.

It was, after all, the truth.

A quarter hour later found them settled companionably on the couch.

Elizabeth raised her teacup to her lips and took a measured sip. "Will you tell me about Pemberley?"

"Pemberley," said Darcy, smiling gently as he stirred his tea, "is my favourite place in the world."

He proceeded to tell her of the house and the park and the wild, untamed beauty of the grounds. He described the stables and the lake and the woods—all held fond memories of boyhood adventures with Colonel Fitzwilliam and his brother.

An engaging smile brightened Elizabeth's countenance as she listened with sincere interest and apparent pleasure. Every so often, she offered an observation, or asked a question —about his house, or his cousins, or his beloved housekeeper, Mrs Reynolds, who had been in service with the family since Darcy was four years old.

That Elizabeth showed such delight and interest in his home delighted Darcy as well, so much so that an image had begun to form in his mind: the two of them at Pemberley, laying claim to its footpaths, exploring its woods, and spending hours on end in the library.

There would be no one under foot to interrupt them, no one to observe them, and no one to judge them. There would be no prying eyes, no wagging tongues, and no matchmaking mother. If they tarried too long on a morning walk, or exchanged an amused look across the supper table, or paid no mind to anyone but each other for the duration of an entire evening, not one soul would dare remark on their conduct never mind comment on their preference.

Instead, there would be pleasant companionship, intelligent conversation, and laughter. There would be arch looks and teasing smiles. There would be joy and real contentment at Pemberley for the first time in years.

Given time, there might be affection, and perhaps, eventually...

It was a seductive prospect—one that could and likely would get Darcy into trouble.

"And what of your sister?"

"Pardon?" said Darcy, disconcerted he had permitted his mind to wander to such dangerous ground. He would do well to remember he was not at Pemberley but at Longbourn, where half the neighbourhood was presently in the drawing room playing cards.

Over the rim of her teacup, Elizabeth regarded him with a curious expression. "I was wondering whether there is a particular room at Pemberley that Miss Darcy prefers."

Clearing his throat, Darcy took a fortifying sip of tea and endeavoured to conquer the unsettling emotions churning in his breast. It would do him no good to dwell upon that which he could never have. "Georgiana," he replied evenly, "favours the music room. Although Miss Bingley is often overflowing with praise for her talent on the pianoforte, such praise is not exaggerated, I assure you. My sister's playing is exceptional."

"I am sure it is," Elizabeth replied warmly as she took another sip of her tea. "And what of yourself, sir? Do you have a favourite room in your comfortable home where you spend most of your time?"

Darcy shook his head. "Regrettably, the better part of my day is usually spent behind the desk in my study writing letters of business, going over accounting ledgers, and meeting with my steward. Where I most *prefer* to spend my time is the library. Pemberley's is one of the finest in the land. Most of the books were brought over from France by my ancestors and are many centuries old—older than the house itself. That countless generations of my father's family are not only responsible for its existence, but its custodianship, is a tremendous source of pride. All things considered it is a remarkable achievement."

"How fortunate," she told him with a teasing lilt to her voice, "that you have such a sensible answer to give. Had you professed to preferring something inane, such as the billiards room or the larder, I would have been forced to reassess my opinion of you."

Shaking his head, Darcy laughed despite himself. "While a rousing game of billiards has provided a welcome distraction on more than one occasion, I find more true enjoyment sitting before a warm fire with a hot cup of tea and a book in hand. But this, of course, is hardly news to you."

"No," she said as her smile softened. "I daresay it is not. I can picture you there quite easily, reclining in a comfortable chair surrounded by shelves as tall as Pemberley's attics, all of them lined with books. The gilded spines and leather bindings and the scent of parchment and leather...I can envision it all very well indeed."

A flush of colour suffused her countenance then, and Elizabeth turned her attention to the tea things. "How is your headache?"

Good God, she is lovely, thought Darcy as a flush of heat rose along the back of his neck. Her skin looked incredibly soft, and he experienced a sudden, alarming urge to caress her blushing cheek with his fingers. Instead, he folded his hands on his lap. "I am much improved, thank you. The tea has worked wonders for my headache."

She said nothing in reply but silently offered to refill his cup.

He surrendered it and watched as she placed the strainer on the rim, catching tea leaves and what looked like lavender and bits of lemon rind. The calming infusion had certainly aided his recovery, but he suspected it was the woman beside him who had affected the most significant change. Her conversation and her smile and her presence had proved instrumental, not only in curing his headache, but in lifting his spirits.

Unnerved, Darcy accepted his tea and sought an innocuous topic, one that would not tempt him to imagine Elizabeth Bennet as anything but his friend.

EIGHT

❧

There is safety in reserve, but no attraction.
One cannot love a reserved person.

"Why should Jane get to dine at Netherfield?"
cried Kitty, slumping onto the sofa beside Mary, who was
pouring tea for her mother and sisters in Longbourn's front
parlour. "Why cannot we all go? It is unfair."

"Kitty," Elizabeth chided, accepting a cup of tea. "Jane
has been invited by Miss Bingley. The rest of us have not. It
would be rude to beg for an invitation when Miss Bingley has
not seen fit to issue one." She smiled her thanks to Mary and
took a sip of tea.

"But Netherfield is supposed to be very grand," Kitty
lamented, picking at a thread on the sleeve of her gown. "You
must long to see it as I do."

"Not I," Mary replied as she passed her a cup and saucer.
"I have no need for such displays of useless finery."

Kitty accepted her tea with a petulant huff. "Of course,
you would not."

"I cannot care two straws about dining at Netherfield,"
Lydia announced to all in the room, licking cake from her
fingers. "There is nothing for any of us there. Mr Bingley is so
enamoured with Jane that he sees no one else, and Mr Darcy
is so dull and unpleasant I would not welcome his attentions

even if he deigned to pay them to me. And his sister! Georgiana Darcy is such a mousy, unsociable thing. If I had such fine gowns and bonnets, I would want to show them off, yet she only ever leaves Netherfield to attend church! Either she is a simpleton, or she believes herself to be above us because she is rich and we are not. Either way, it is vexing. If she cannot be bothered to dine with us, or utter more than a few monosyllables about the weather, then I certainly shall not be bothered with her."

"Lydia, that is unkind," Jane said in admonishment, blushing prettily, likely at the mention of Mr Bingley's admiration. "I believe Miss Darcy is only exceedingly shy. Since she is not yet out, her remaining at Netherfield is to be expected, not criticised. As for Mr Darcy, he is reserved as well. Although his spirits were more subdued than usual when we dined together the other evening, he was perfectly polite. And he always makes a point to speak to Lizzy. It is kind of him to do so."

Lydia snorted. "I cannot see why he would bother. You have clearly forgotten that he refused to dance with her at the assembly because she was not handsome enough for him. His being gallant towards her now cannot mean anything. We all know he does not like her and is only doing it to please his friend. Once he understood there would be dancing at Lucas Lodge last week, no one saw him again for the rest of the night, likely because he found the idea of standing up with Lizzy so off-putting."

Elizabeth held her tongue as she attempted to keep her annoyance in check. It was not the prospect of dancing with *her* that had driven Darcy to seek refuge in the library until the carriages were ordered, but his disgust with Lydia's presumption that he was at her disposal and willing to act in accordance with her wishes.

"Although he is Mr Bingley's good friend," said Mrs

Bennet as she served herself another slice of cake, "I must say I cannot stand the sight of him. Slighting one of my daughters, as though Lizzy is plain like Charlotte Lucas—it is insupportable!"

"While you are entitled to your opinion, ma'am," said Elizabeth, "I do wish you would not speak disparagingly of Charlotte. She is by no means plain."

Mrs Bennet rolled her eyes. "Of course, you would insist upon her being more attractive than she is, being so fond of her as you are, but you cannot expect the rest of us to be blind to her looks. Whatever you think of Charlotte Lucas, Mr Darcy had no right to treat *you* so infamously—and in public, no less!"

"Mama, at the time, Mr Darcy knew no one in Hertfordshire beyond the members of his own party. He had barely even glanced in my direction all evening, and his rudeness was soon rewarded with a fair measure of my own. I am heartily ashamed of my behaviour then, and Mr Darcy is ashamed of his as well. It has been three weeks since his slight. We have made our peace with one another. Now we are friends. All is well."

Mrs Bennet stared at her in astonishment. "Friends? What care you for being friends with such a man? What care you for Mr Darcy at all?"

"He is very rich," said Kitty thoughtfully, contemplating a plate of chocolate biscuits. "If he does not want Lizzy, perhaps he will introduce her to his friends. He must know loads of other rich men."

Lydia looked as though she had smelled something sour. "La, Kitty. I daresay all of them would be just as proud and disagreeable as he is, and likely worse."

"Mr Darcy," Elizabeth insisted, "is by no means disagreeable. His manners and disposition may not recommend him so well as Mr Bingley's, but I have found he improves upon further acquaintance. He is quick witted and intelligent, his opinions are well formed, and his discourse is always interesting. Aside from his being so reserved in company, I cannot find fault with him. He has been nothing but solicitous and kind."

"I am of Lizzy's opinion," said Jane. "I have conversed with Mr Darcy on several occasions and, while he is certainly serious, I have always found him to be conscientious and polite."

"Good Lord," said Lydia. "You cannot mean to say that you actually like him. Especially you, Lizzy! He insulted you where everyone in Meryton could hear!"

"Do not forget," Kitty supplied helpfully, "that he argued with Mr Bingley afterwards, and Mr Bingley *made* him ask Lizzy to dance!"

"And then *she* refused *him!*" Lydia cried gleefully.

"And your sister was quite right to do it," her mother proclaimed with feeling. "Why should any daughter of mine have to oblige such a disagreeable man when he did not want to give her the time of day?"

"It is imperative to remember," said Mary, "that a young woman's speech should be always with grace and seasoned with salt."

Lydia wrinkled her nose. "Oh, be quiet, Mary. Your sermonising has no place here. You are almost as dull as Mr Darcy. By the by, I cannot see what salt has to do with anything."

"Were you to spend ten minutes of your day in pursuit of spirituality and knowledge rather than officers," Mary told her, "perhaps you would."

Lydia rolled her eyes. "Officers are far more exciting than droll clergymen who are always preaching about being virtuous and proper. Moralising is tiresome."

"It will not seem so tiresome should you wind up scandalising all of Meryton someday."

"Thank you, Mary," said Elizabeth as she directed a quelling look at Lydia. "Surely, my interactions with Mr Darcy cannot be of tantamount interest to you. If you recall, you professed him to be unpleasant and dull not two minutes ago. Therefore, I cannot see any point in further pursuing the subject. You had best choose another."

Pushing a few crumbs around her plate with her fork, Lydia shrugged. "Mr Darcy *is* unpleasant and dull, but I suppose it should not signify one jot what any of us think if you truly like him. He would never do for me, of course—"

"Nor for me," Kitty interjected, popping a biscuit into her mouth.

"—for he is old as well as dull, but if you do not mind having such a disagreeable man as your husband, then I say you are welcome to him. What pin money you will have! You can live like a courtier in London and be ever so merry. With all the diversions of town, you will hardly ever have to see each other, for he will likely want to spend all of his time with his friends doing whatever it is rich men do together."

This appeared to cheer Kitty considerably. "And then you can have us to stay with you and find husbands for us all!"

"A happy scheme indeed," Elizabeth replied drily, peering at her youngest sisters over the rim of her teacup, "but impossibly flawed. As I have no plan at present to marry Mr Darcy, nor has he shown any inclination to honour me with a proposal, indulging such fanciful notions is not only impolitic, but pointless."

"Oh, that hardly signifies," Lydia told her. "I am sure if you only flirt with him a bit he will fall madly in love with you in no time. According to Aunt Philips, men—even stuffy, boring men—cannot resist a pretty face and a handsome figure in a low-cut gown."

Mary set her teacup on its saucer with a clatter, her face pinched with disapproval. "A woman's virtue—" she began heatedly.

But Lydia, loath to listen to another word of her middle sister's moralising, said loudly, "If I were you, Lizzy, I would make haste, for you will be one-and-twenty next year and your bloom will likely fade sooner rather than later. If I am not married before I turn seventeen, I shall die of embarrassment. I do not know how you and Jane bear the mortification, for I certainly could not."

Kitty, who had turned seventeen in September, scowled at her.

Wearing an expression of utmost disgust, Mary abandoned the table altogether.

Jane wisely sought to change the subject. "Might I have the carriage, Mama?"

Mrs Bennet cast a shrewd glance at the sky, crowded with rainclouds, and frowned. "No, my dear, you may not. Miss Bingley mentioned the gentlemen are dining out this evening. You cannot possibly go to Netherfield without Mr Bingley having seen you. If it happens to rain, then you will be forced to spend the night."

Jane appeared scandalised by the prospect. "It would not be appropriate for me to spend the night in Mr Bingley's house—he is an unmarried gentleman!"

"And if you wish to secure him," her mother told her matter-of-factly, "you must take every opportunity to put yourself in his way."

"Mama," said Elizabeth on her sister's behalf. "You cannot possibly ask this of Jane. Please allow her to have the carriage. She will be wet through by the time she arrives."

Despite their pleading, their mother would not consent to

any scheme other than her own. Eventually, their father was applied to and, after much begging from Jane and prompting from Elizabeth, Mr Bennet admitted his horses were needed in the field and could not be spared that day.

"You may walk to Netherfield," said her mother with a note of supreme satisfaction, knowing that Jane would not choose to walk three miles while wearing one of her best gowns. "If you do not care to walk, then I suppose you may go on Old Nellie."

Elizabeth imagined Jane—ever concerned with propriety and accommodating to a fault—arriving at Netherfield Park on the back of their father's brood mare and was mortified. The superior Bingley sisters, who had bemoaned the loss of every conceivable convenience of living in town, would likely laugh!

Jane glanced at the darkening sky with a defeated countenance and sighed.

Horseback it would be.

Jane had not been gone a quarter hour when it began to rain hard. Her sisters were distressed for her, but her mother was delighted. The rain continued the whole evening without intermission, beating against the windows with unrelenting force. Thunder rumbled across the fields, lightning streaked across the sky, and puddles formed in the drive and on the roads. Jane certainly could not come back.

The following morning, shortly after breakfast, a note arrived from Netherfield for Elizabeth. It said:

My dearest Lizzy,

I find myself very unwell this morning, which, I suppose, is to be imputed to my getting wet through yesterday. My kind friends will not hear of my returning until I am better. They insist also on my seeing Mr Jones; therefore, do not be alarmed if you should hear of his having been to me. Except for a sore throat and headache there is not much the matter with me.

> *Yours, etc.*
> *Jane*

"Well, my dear," said Mr Bennet to his wife once Elizabeth had finished reading the note aloud, "if Jane should have a dangerous fit of illness and die, it will be a comfort to know that it was all in pursuit of Mr Bingley, and under your orders."

"Oh, I am not afraid of her dying. People do not die of little trifling colds. She will be well cared for if she remains at Netherfield. I would go and see her if I could have the carriage."

The carriage was not to be had, however. Mrs Bennet would stay at home, but Elizabeth, who felt a real and abiding concern for Jane, determined to go to her. She declared her resolution.

Her mother declared her headstrong and foolish. "Walk! In all this dirt? You will not be fit to be seen once you get there."

"I shall be fit to see Jane, which is all I want."

"What will Mr Bingley think of us," bemoaned Mrs Bennet, "allowing you to go all the way to Netherfield on foot after the fields have been soaked with rain?"

"I daresay you ought to have thought of that yesterday, ma'am," Elizabeth replied as she rose from the table, "before you insisted Jane travel to Netherfield on horseback." She swiped a grape from her plate, popped it into her mouth, and quit the room.

The day was cold, but the exertion required to cross field

after field at a quick pace, jump over stiles, and spring over puddles ensured Elizabeth stayed warm. By the time she reached Netherfield, she was as her mother predicted: not fit to be seen. Shortly after setting out, she had removed her bonnet and now her hair was coming down, her hem was covered in mud, and her half-boots were in a dreadful state. With a weary exhalation, Elizabeth set her bonnet upon a bench within a walled garden near the house, peeled off her gloves, removed her hairpins, and attempted to make herself presentable.

It was by no means the work of a moment. Having no looking glass to consult made repairing the damage to her hair more challenging, but eventually Elizabeth knew the satisfaction of success. She twisted the last hairpin into place, attempted to brush some of the mud from her petticoat, smoothed her gown with her hands, and turned towards the house only to come face to face with Mr Darcy.

For a moment neither spoke but stared in startled silence.

"Miss Elizabeth," he stammered, offering her a belated bow.

"Mr Darcy," she replied with a perfunctory curtsey. Judging by the deep flush of colour upon his face and the tips of his ears, his mortification equalled her own. She wondered how long he had been standing there, and how much of her efforts to restore her appearance he had witnessed. She had lifted her skirts well above her ankles to tend to her petticoat. The idea of Darcy—or any man for that matter—seeing her engaged in such impropriety caused her countenance to become heated, as heated as his own.

Despite fervently wishing otherwise, there was nothing she could do to erase what he might have seen, and no way of knowing for certain that he had even seen much of anything in the first place. She would never be so bold as to enquire and ought to take comfort in the fact that Darcy was too much of a gentleman to speak of it, either to her or to anyone else.

To spare them both from further embarrassment, Elizabeth decided to simply pretend nothing untoward had occurred and said, "I have come to see my sister."

His eyes were trained intently upon the wet, muddy hem of her gown. When he spoke, his voice sounded strained. "Your sister."

"Yes," she said as she felt her colour rise even higher. "My sister Jane."

"And you have walked all the way from Longbourn?"

"As you see." Elizabeth could not tell whether he was scandalised or whether he was merely curious, but the sad state of her skirts and her filthy boots indicated she had, in fact, walked all the way from Longbourn.

When Darcy did not offer any further comment but continued to stare at her gown, Elizabeth decided enough was enough. "Will you be so kind as to take me to Jane, Mr Darcy, or should I apply to the housekeeper? You seem to be out of sorts this morning."

Darcy raised his eyes to hers with a start, then quickly averted them as he cleared his throat. "I beg your pardon. This way if you please, Miss Elizabeth." Almost as an afterthought, he offered her his arm.

"Thank you," she murmured as she accepted it and allowed him to lead her in the direction of the house. Both were silent. Both made a point of looking anywhere but at each other. With every step, Elizabeth's discomfort increased. At last, she could stand no more and enquired, "Do you happen to have any news of my sister? I received a note from her this morning in which she mentioned the likelihood of Mr Jones being summoned."

"I understand the apothecary has seen her, but I have no

knowledge of your sister's condition. No doubt, she will be cheered by your coming."

"I certainly hope so," she replied. "Otherwise, I shall have succeeded in raising my mother's ire and ruining a perfectly lovely gown for nothing."

Too late, she realised her mistake as she felt Darcy stiffen. Silently admonishing herself for making such a flippant remark, she removed her hand from his arm at once and made to draw away from him, but he shocked her by capturing her hand and returning it to his arm.

She stared at him in mute astonishment.

His own eyes were fixed firmly upon some indeterminable point ahead of him. His complexion was heightened. His lips were pursed. He said, "Let us hope she is pleased to see you, then...despite the hem of your gown having been dragged through the holy aftermath of a storm."

That he would tease her after all that had come to pass went a long way towards restoring Elizabeth's ease. "I doubt Jane will think anything of it," she informed him, "for she is quite used to seeing me in such a state. Of course, *she* would never dream of arriving unannounced at someone's home looking as though she had been set upon by gypsies!"

"Whereas you have no such compunction."

Elizabeth laughed. "Sadly, I do not. So long as someone I love is in need, there is little that I would not do for them, including traipsing through six inches of mud after a violent storm. But, as you already know, a little dirt is no impediment for me. I would walk all the way to London and back to bring relief to my dearest sister."

"Your devotion to your eldest sister is both touching and commendable."

"I assure you Jane would do no less for me, nor for any of my sisters."

"I gather Miss Bennet is not a great walker like you are,

though. While you share sisterly affection in abundance, it has been my observation your eldest sister does not share your adventuresome spirit."

"Jane is a paragon of virtue. She is steady and reliable and content being close to home. She adheres to propriety in every situation and values unsoiled slippers and pristine hems far more than I, a virtue which my mother never fails to point out to me whenever the opportunity arises."

"If Miss Bennet is as concerned with propriety as she is the preservation of her gowns, I cannot but wonder at her arrival yesterday—alone, on horseback, in the rain."

Such a slight against her sister chafed. "That is hardly Jane's fault. My father keeps but one carriage and the horses were not available to pull it. Jane could have walked, which she would never have done, or she could have gone on horseback. Riding three miles from Longbourn to Netherfield Park on horseback is practically nothing, but the stubborn, unhurried gait of a geriatric horse would make the trip a trial under the best circumstances. The onset of a downpour made it nearly impossible."

Darcy made no reply and Elizabeth offered no further comment.

Their silence continued until they arrived at the house, where a footman opened an exterior door of a sitting room blessedly devoid of occupants. Releasing her hold on Darcy's arm, Elizabeth entered the house.

Darcy followed her inside.

The door had no sooner been shut behind him when the sound of a pianoforte being played by an expert hand floated into the room. The melody was haunting and dark, but beautifully executed. Elizabeth looked to Darcy, prepared to compliment the talent of the performer, but she faltered when she noticed his grim countenance. "Sir?"

He glanced at her and inclined his head in the direction of the music. "My sister, Georgiana."

"Indeed!" Elizabeth exclaimed, impressed by the girl's ability. "I cannot tell you how pleased I am to hear her at last. It is precisely as you said. Miss Darcy's playing is truly exceptional."

"She practises too much."

The distinct note of disapproval in his tone surprised her. "Your sister has a remarkable talent. If it affords her pleasure, surely, there can be no harm in her practising so diligently."

"Her playing brings her solace. I cannot say whether it brings her pleasure or not. Of late, Georgiana expends her energy on little else. She ought to devote at least a few hours of her time to other pursuits—conversation for example. Instead, she is a slave to an instrument."

"Does Miss Darcy have no friends with whom she visits and corresponds?"

"As you have seen for yourself when she attended church, my sister is very shy. She does not make friends easily. Regrettably, the few attachments she formed in the past that appeared promising turned out to be objectionable."

Elizabeth was uncertain of his meaning. "Do you mean to say the stations and reputations of these young women were objectionable? Or was their unsuitability due to some other factor?"

"It was not the position and reputation of the girls themselves of which I disapproved, but their motives. All were from respectable families well established within London society. None of their associations gave me cause for concern. Their parents were born high enough to make their daughters suitable friends for my sister. What I found objectionable was that the mothers and eldest sisters of those girls were far more interested in Georgiana's connexion to Pemberley—namely, to myself—than in being on intimate terms with Georgiana."

Elizabeth's heart constricted as she imagined the disappointment Darcy's sister must have suffered. To be so cruelly used by girls that she had believed to be her friends would have been nothing short of devastating to a shy young woman such as Georgiana Darcy. "Your poor, dear sister," she said with sincere feeling. "I am grieved to hear those girls and their relations would use her so ill! It is no wonder she dedicates so much of herself to her playing. Tell me, does Miss Darcy attend a seminary in town? Has she gone away to school?"

Darcy shook his head. "She is no longer at school, but her education will continue with tutors and masters in London. Attending school...I had believed living away from home would encourage Georgiana to become more independent, but it has only made her more inclined towards reticence and more doubtful of her own judgment. Lately, she has become more withdrawn than ever."

"I trust you have attempted to raise her spirits."

"I have tried everything I could think of to tempt her, to no avail."

Elizabeth had grown up with four sisters, each one possessed of a unique personality, differing interests, and varying abilities and talents. If rearing a child was a trying endeavour for two parents, she could not begin to imagine how challenging it must be for a bachelor to raise an impressionable young woman on his own.

Darcy had lost both his parents. He was master of a vast estate. He was essentially still a young man in his own right—a young man with a staggering amount of responsibility on his shoulders. Miss Darcy was not the only Darcy who had suffered loss. She had her brother to guide and support her, but who did Darcy turn to when he needed guidance and support? Of the two, Elizabeth suspected the brother's loss may have been the greater.

Feeling a sudden surge of empathy for him, Elizabeth

extended her hand and gently touched his arm. "As her dearest relation, I have no doubt you know Miss Darcy intimately, but a gentleman of eight-and-twenty, no matter how attentive and devoted, cannot fulfil the role of mother and sister as well as father and brother. No gentleman, especially one who is nearly twice her age, can possibly comprehend all that is within the heart of a fifteen-year-old girl."

Darcy clenched his jaw but made no comment. Instead, he looked towards the corridor. The melancholy notes of the pianoforte reached a crescendo, and he shut his eyes as though pained.

Elizabeth withdrew her hand at once. He had welcomed her frankness on countless occasions before, but the same did not appear to hold true now. If Darcy felt offended or even angered by her candour, Elizabeth could not fault him for it. Speaking her mind about books and treatises was one thing; offering her unsolicited opinions about his relationship with his sister, and therefore calling into question his ability to care for her, was quite another.

She was horrified to have forgotten her place and felt his silence as acutely as if he had raised his voice and chastised her. "Please forgive my presumption, Mr Darcy. From what I have seen, you are a caring brother and diligent guardian to Miss Darcy, and I am certain you are doing everything in your power to ensure her comfort and happiness. If you will excuse me, sir, I should see to my own sister."

NINE

༄

What strange creatures brothers are!

DARCY SAT UPON THE BENCH IN THE WALLED GARDEN, his forearms braced upon his knees as he held a single kidskin glove in his hands. Its mate and Elizabeth's discarded bonnet had been claimed by a maid commissioned to retrieve them hours ago, shortly after Elizabeth had abandoned him to see to her sister. He had not meant to keep this glove, but for some reason he could not quite explain or even comprehend, Darcy had found his way back to the garden, and the glove had found its way into his greatcoat pocket. His own gloves had long been discarded. It was approaching dusk. The temperature had dropped. His feet were nearly as cold as his hands; yet Darcy was in no hurry to return to the house. While a warm fire, a glass of port, and a friendly game of billiards with Bingley were tempting, the prospect of encountering other members of the household was not. Miss Bingley flirted and deferred to him, Mrs Hurst tittered at him, and Georgiana studiously avoided him.

Then there was Elizabeth, who fascinated him and confounded him and tied him in knots.

Her presence at Netherfield had shocked him, almost as much as the forbidden glimpse of her ankles when she had raised her skirts and attempted to remove the mud from her petticoat. The look on her face after she had righted her gown and discovered him standing there gaping at her spoke volumes—Elizabeth Bennet was horrified, and Darcy, who had always been master of himself in every situation save for what took place at Ramsgate, had found himself completely and inappropriately overwhelmed with desire for her. A recurring theme, apparently, whenever he happened upon her out of doors, bright eyed, dishevelled, and infuriatingly unaware of how alluring she looked each and every time.

Darcy raked his fingers through his hair. Her glove was small, butter soft, and embroidered with an intricate pattern of flowers that perfectly complemented the rich, buff colour of the leather. Although it smelled primarily of the kidskin from which it was made, Darcy detected another scent far more aromatic and feminine. He brought the glove to his nose and gave it a subtle sniff. Lavender, perhaps? He was not practised at identifying flowers by their scent alone. He knew only that Elizabeth had worn a similar fragrance each time he had the pleasure of her company and that he had found it pleasing, almost as pleasing as he found the society of the lady herself.

Good God.

What was he doing sitting in near darkness holding a lady's glove, contemplating the perfume she favoured? When had he ever behaved in such an incomprehensible manner? When had he ever felt such a potent attraction for any woman, never mind one with such appalling connexions and low prospects?

The answer, of course, was never.

And now she was to be a guest in Bingley's house until her sister was recovered and able to return home.

Darcy shut his eyes.

Instantly, Elizabeth's eyes appeared before him, sparkling

with mirth and kindness. He recalled her compassion, her intelligence, her artlessness, and her wit. He recalled her penchant for teasing him and her ability to make him smile. Last, but not least, he recalled her boldness—the uncanny talent she possessed for calling him out, frankly and openly, for his most grievous failings: his overweening arrogance, his unpardonable rudeness, and the complete disaster he had made of his life and Georgiana's by neglecting to be all she required—a father and mother and sister as well as a diligent elder brother.

Elizabeth Bennet was beautiful, she was caring, she was devoted and good, but she was also the daughter of an insignificant, eccentric, country gentleman of little conse-quence. How in the world had she managed to break down Darcy's steadfast defences? How had she come to know him so well in only three weeks? And more importantly, how was he to resist her when every moment spent in her company only increased his attraction to her?

With a harsh exhalation, Darcy slid her glove into his greatcoat pocket and dropped his head into his hands. What he felt for Elizabeth Bennet went beyond physical attraction. He admired her. He esteemed her. He looked forward to conversing with her for God's sake. Her mind captivated him as much as her beauty. Given time, he could find himself in love with her.

It was a thought that terrified him.

Darcy groaned.

Residing in the same house with her was going to be hell.

❧

"Miss Eliza," said Miss Bingley at dinner that evening. "Pray tell us that your dear sister is feeling better."

"I fear Jane has not improved since you last saw her, Miss Bingley."

"How sorry I am to hear it! There is nothing so disagreeable as being ill. I confess I despise it above all else."

"As do I," Mrs Hurst lamented. "It is a most unpleasant thing to be ill. Mr Hurst is never ill."

"Never?" Elizabeth enquired.

"No. Never."

"You must tell us your secret, Mr Hurst," said Elizabeth with an inquisitive smile.

Swallowing a mouthful of mutton, Hurst raised his wine glass in the air, as though about to give a toast. "It is no secret," he told her brusquely, "but more of a philosophy, madam. I drink eight pints a day to keep the apothecary away. And, by God, it works I daresay!" In one fluid motion, he swallowed the remainder of his wine, then returned his attention to his dinner plate.

Mrs Hurst giggled and reached for the decanter to refill her husband's glass. "Oh, how clever you are, Mr Hurst! Is he not a wonder, Miss Elizabeth? Is my husband not the cleverest gentleman you have ever met?"

"Oh, yes. Very clever," Elizabeth agreed, endeavouring to hide her amusement behind her own wine glass.

Bingley wore a congenial smile as he tucked into his boiled potatoes. "Well put, Hurst. I had no idea you were a poet."

"Or a romantic," said Darcy as he contemplated a piece of pigeon pie. "I have often heard poetry touted as the food of love."

Hurst snorted.

A small, engaging smile appeared on Elizabeth's lips. "Of a fine, stout love, perhaps. Anything less would surely crumble under more ardent professions."

Darcy regarded her curiously. They had spent hours

discussing countless classics, prose, and poetry with great spirit and flow. He was no stranger to her literary preferences, which included an almost reverent appreciation of romantic poetry. Her comment gave him pause, enough to say, "I cannot believe that of you, Miss Elizabeth. I once heard you expound upon poetry as being precisely in accordance with what Wordsworth noted in his preface for *Lyrical Ballads*—a spontaneous overflow of powerful feelings. Having professed such decided sentiments, surely you cannot doubt the efficacy of poetry to inspire love."

"Everything nourishes what is strong already, Mr Darcy, but if the love in question is only a slight, thin sort of inclination, I am convinced one poor sonnet will starve it away entirely! Even the most poignant verse by the most celebrated poet cannot possibly inspire affection where none exists."

Darcy frowned. "What would you recommend then, to a man violently in love who wishes to inspire equal feeling in the object of his affection? Suppose this man does not possess the talent for making speeches. Suppose his own meagre words cannot do justice to the powerful sentiments within his heart."

"Surely, a gentleman who has lived in the world, who is possessed of sense and education, is also possessed of taste and decorum. He need not recite poetry to gain his heart's desire. He need only choose his words prudently and speak from his heart. If the woman he loves returns his affection, there can be no need for anything more."

"And if her heart is not in accord with his?"

"Flattery," Hurst interjected, looking pointedly at Darcy as he stabbed a carrot with his fork. "A little well-placed flattery will never lead a man astray."

"Oh, I quite agree," said Mrs Hurst. "There is nothing I like more than pretty compliments and expensive trinkets!"

Miss Bingley cast a sly look at Darcy. "Nor I, Louisa. A

gentleman can never pay a lady he admires too many compliments."

Darcy ignored them all. "And what are your thoughts, Miss Elizabeth? Do you also share Mr Hurst's opinion that flattery will assist a man in winning a lady's heart?"

She raised one impertinent brow. "Oh, undoubtedly, sir. Certainly, a man need not go to more trouble than that to inspire affection."

One corner of Darcy's mouth lifted. "I had forgotten how much you enjoy professing opinions that are not your own."

"You know nothing of the sort," she told him sweetly. "We ladies are vain creatures. As for myself, I am also possessed of an unsociable, taciturn disposition. Rarely am I willing to speak unless I expect to say something that will amaze the whole room and be handed down to posterity with all the éclat of a proverb."

"This is no very striking resemblance to your own character," Darcy observed. "How near it is to mine, I cannot pretend to say. No doubt you believe it to be an accurate description."

"Oh, no," Elizabeth insisted as she turned her attention to her supper. "I shall not be swayed by *your* flattery, Mr Darcy! I am far too intractable for that. Any gentleman who does not share my belief that poetry can reduce an unrequited love to ashes stands little chance of ever garnering my favour."

Resisting the urge to laugh, Darcy reached for his wineglass and gently swirled the contents within. He regarded Elizabeth over the rim. "I would expect nothing less from you."

"Singular," Hurst muttered, eyeing the two of them as he scraped his plate clean. "Louisa, pass the potatoes."

Mrs Hurst passed her husband the potatoes.

For ten minutes, conversation gave way to eating until

Georgiana, who rarely spoke unless a question was posed to her, shocked everyone at the table by addressing Elizabeth.

No one was more surprised than Darcy. He looked from his timid sister, who stared intently at her plate, to Elizabeth, who regarded her with polite expectancy.

"I was wondering," Georgiana stammered, raising her eyes to Elizabeth's, "if you have a favourite poet."

Elizabeth smiled warmly. "I am so pleased you asked, Miss Darcy. Of late, I have enjoyed the works of Walter Scott a vast deal, especially *The Lady of the Lake*. Last month I read Coleridge's *Rime of the Ancient Mariner* and several poems by Wordsworth. Next week I shall pick another volume from my father's library and admire that author's work best of all, so I would not say that I favour one poet or work over another, at least not for long. My opinions are forever changing with each new discovery or fresh reading. Tell me, are you an admirer of poetry as well?"

"I confess I am not," Georgiana replied, glancing at Darcy. "But my brother has added many volumes to Pemberley's collection. He loves poetry and is forever buying books."

"To think," Miss Bingley declared, "that in addition to so many other interests, you and I also share a passion for poetry, Mr Darcy. What a happy coincidence!"

"Yes," Elizabeth agreed, casting an amused look at Darcy. "A very happy coincidence. Tell me, Miss Bingley, which poet is your favourite?"

"Oh, there are far too many to name. I suppose I like all the same ones as Mr Darcy. His taste is superior to everyone's."

"Indeed." Elizabeth's eyes shone with a brightness that usually preceded mischief. Instead of directing some teasing remark or other at Darcy, she raised her wine glass to her lips and took a measured sip, then turned to his sister and asked her a question about music.

For several minutes, Darcy listened to their exchange with something akin to wonderment as Elizabeth coaxed Georgiana out of her shell by speaking of composers and sonatas and fugues and soliciting Georgiana's preferences and opinions regarding all. It was the first time in months he had seen his sister so animated and open to conversation; that she was conversing with Elizabeth, whom she had only ever met thrice at church, astounded him all the more.

When Miss Bingley sought to reclaim his attention by enquiring about his family's plans to reside in London for the winter, Darcy had no choice but to oblige her. Their conversation could not hold his interest so much as his sister's, however, and when he not only glimpsed a smile on Georgiana's face, but heard her laugh, he could not resist sending up a silent prayer of thanksgiving.

When the gentlemen re-joined the ladies in the music room that evening, Darcy had anticipated the pleasure of seeing Georgiana speaking to Elizabeth, much as she had during dinner; instead, his friend was absent, and Georgiana was sitting alone. Concerned, he crossed the room and claimed a seat beside his sister on the chaise she occupied. "Georgiana," he said in lieu of a greeting. "Where is Miss Elizabeth?"

"Miss Elizabeth is checking on Miss Bennet," she replied quietly. Her eyes darted to Miss Bingley and Mrs Hurst, who were seated nearby. The sisters were engaged in a private conversation but speaking loudly enough to be overheard.

"I quite agree," said Mrs Hurst. "Her hair was blowsy, indeed."

"And her petticoats," Miss Bingley cried. "Have you ever seen any lady's petticoats covered in so much mud?"

"Not a one."

"I would have been embarrassed to show my face to the

undergardener, never mind apply to the housekeeper for admittance. What say you, Louisa?"

"I daresay I would as well."

While Miss Bingley continued in the same vein, Mrs Hurst spied her husband standing at the sideboard, pouring himself two fingers of brandy. Without uttering a word, she abandoned her chair—and her sister—and joined him.

Miss Bingley, who had been speaking at the time, appeared startled to see her go, but quickly composed herself when she noticed Darcy. "Mr Darcy," she said as she rose with alacrity and claimed a seat beside Georgiana. "Louisa and I were just discussing Eliza Bennet."

"Were you?" he replied with a terseness that should have given her pause.

It did not, and she said to him, "Of course, you noticed the dreadful state of dishabille in which she arrived this morning."

Darcy offered no comment.

Miss Bingley appeared undeterred. "She arrived on foot, you know, and quite alone!"

Georgiana frowned. "It is my understanding that Miss Elizabeth enjoys walking."

"To be sure, she must, Miss Darcy. But to walk three miles or four miles or five miles or whatever the distance through muddy fields is simply not done. Why, it shows an abominable sort of conceited independence—a most country town indifference to decorum."

Darcy said, "It shows an affection for her sister that is pleasing."

Miss Bingley laughed. "What it shows, my dear Mr Darcy, is that Eliza Bennet is by no means the sort of girl with whom my brother ought to associate, nor any of us for that matter. Why, she looked positively wild!"

"If she did, it quite escaped my notice. I thought she

looked remarkably well this morning. Her eyes were brightened by the exercise."

Miss Bingley blinked at him. "Surely, you would not wish to see your own dear sister make such an exhibition."

"Certainly not, but neither would I expect her to ignore what is right and just. Should she have been fortunate enough to have had a sister, I have faith Georgiana would do all within her power to bring relief to her in times of illness and distress. You, Miss Bingley, would do no less for your own sister, I am sure."

To this pronouncement, Miss Bingley had no alternative before her but agreement.

Darcy looked towards the window and endeavoured to subdue his annoyance. Elizabeth was well-read and clever. At supper, they had discussed poetry, and he had sought her opinion on how to determine the affections of a potential lover—two subjects of which Miss Bingley was woefully ignorant. He suspected it was the attention he paid Elizabeth that incited his hostess's ire, not so much her muddy petticoats.

Like countless women of his acquaintance, Miss Bingley had been educated in one of London's finest seminaries, but her knowledge of the world was lacking. She spoke French and Italian. She painted tables and screens. She played the pianoforte and the harp and the violin with as much proficiency as any other lady in town.

Elizabeth could do none of those things. She sang far better than she played. She spoke German and understood Latin and Greek. She read philosophy and poetry and the London newspaper. The other morning, she had discussed Goethe intelligently and insightfully, with as much animation and depth as any Cambridge scholar. In London, and in society in general, Elizabeth Bennet would be labelled a bluestocking. To Darcy, she was a breath of fresh air in a stagnant room.

"Your pianoforte is very beautiful," said Georgiana with sudden purpose. "I should like to play for you, Miss Bingley—if I may."

Darcy turned towards his sister in astonishment. It was the last thing he expected her to say.

"Nothing," Miss Bingley proclaimed, "would give me greater pleasure! I have longed to hear you play these three weeks if not longer, and I daresay so has Louisa. I absolutely insist upon attending you."

"I was hoping I could prevail upon my brother to turn my pages. We have spent so little time together of late..."

Miss Bingley's smile was indulgent. "Surely, your dear brother would not like to perform such an office! Gentlemen rarely do. They much prefer to enjoy a lady's performance from a more favourable distance. From afar, a lady is always shown to her best advantage."

Such a comment being made to Georgiana, who was not sixteen or out in society, was simply unacceptable. Darcy was about to voice his disapprobation when Georgiana said,

"My brother often indulges me by turning my pages. I assure you he is quite capable."

"Oh, I am certain he is, my dear, but Mr Darcy need not turn your pages while he is at Netherfield."

Darcy's tolerance for Miss Bingley, her prattle, and her contrivances had reached its end. Before another word could be uttered, he turned to his sister and said, "You need do nothing you are unequal to, Georgiana. You certainly need not exhibit this evening if you do not sincerely desire it. We may spend the whole of tomorrow together if you like, or any other day that suits you. As ever, I am at your disposal."

In an uncharacteristic show of affection, Georgiana reached for his hand and grasped it tightly. "I know you are," she said softly, but with an earnestness that surprised him. "You have done so much for me, Fitzwilliam. You have encouraged me and supported me and spoiled me all my life. To play such a superior instrument for half an hour is no sacrifice, especially if my doing so will afford you pleasure."

For the first time in nearly four months, Darcy felt the ever-present tension in his shoulders loosen its grip. Wordlessly, he kissed Georgiana's hand and escorted her to the pianoforte, where he settled himself beside her on the bench.

She played for three quarters of an hour, her fingers flying over the keys with a natural ease and rapidity Darcy had always admired. Her attempts at conversation were less eloquent. Haltingly, she enquired how he had spent his days in Hertfordshire, what attractions the area afforded, and what best pleased him about the neighbourhood.

Her performance was as flawless as ever, but the piece she chose that evening had a distinctly lighter feel than her repertoire of late. Darcy felt lighter as well. To see Georgiana speaking with Elizabeth at supper and exerting herself to play for their friends heartened him and gave him hope that all may yet turn out well.

"Miss Bingley seems intent upon attracting your notice, Brother."

Darcy detected a hint of disapproval in his sister's tone that was uncharacteristic of her. Frowning, he raised his eyes from the sheet music and glanced in Miss Bingley's direction. Whether that lady's eyes were fixed upon him, Darcy could not say. Behind her, standing in the doorway on the far side of the room, was Elizabeth. Her head rested against the casement and a gentle smile played upon her lips as she listened to Georgiana perform Bach's *Toccata and Fugue in D Minor* perfectly.

His demeanour softened.

When the music ended, Bingley applauded Georgiana's performance enthusiastically from the card table. The Hursts, eager to resume their game of commerce, were more reserved. Hurst called Bingley to order, but Bingley's preference for Miss Bennet far outweighed his preference for cards. He abandoned his game, no doubt anxious to hear Miss Bennet was better.

Miss Bennet was not better. She had slept poorly.

After expressing his concern, Bingley offered to summon Mr Jones without delay.

Elizabeth thanked him but declined. Her sister only wanted rest.

At the pianoforte, Miss Bingley bombarded Georgiana with platitudes about her diligent practicing and praised her superior taste and technique while Darcy grew irritated and impatient—for what he could not say.

Eventually, Bingley returned to the card table and Elizabeth made her way to the instrument. Her eyes met Darcy's and she smiled, but rather than speak to him she lingered in the background, patiently waiting for Miss Bingley to finish flattering his sister. When their hostess had finished, she stepped forward and caressed one gleaming, ivory key with her fingertip. "You played that piece so beautifully, Miss Darcy. Will you not indulge us and consent to play another?"

Such a sincerely issued request could not be denied. Georgiana assented with a shy smile, and the ladies chatted politely while she selected another piece: Mozart's *Eleventh Piano Sonata*.

It had once been their mother's favourite and often inspired such deep sentimentality in Darcy that the pleasure of hearing it performed was often overshadowed by the pain of the bittersweet memories it invoked. Unless Darcy requested the piece, Georgiana rarely played it. That she intended to do so now confounded him. Except on one occasion when Colonel Fitzwilliam had visited Pemberley, she had never played it in company, nor had Darcy ever expected she would. "Georgiana," he said lowly. "Perhaps you ought to play something else."

Miss Bingley would not hear of it. "I adore Mozart, Miss Darcy, and this piece in particular! You simply must play it. I am all anticipation!"

"Georgiana..." he repeated.

But Georgiana, at first so determined to please her brother, now appeared intent upon obliging their hostess and would not meet his eyes. "Would you be so good as to turn my pages for me, Miss Bingley?"

With a gratified smile, Miss Bingley assented.

Disconcerted by his sister's singlemindedness and at a loss as to what he ought to do about it, Darcy held his tongue. Anything he said or did at this point would only cause a scene and distress Georgiana. Instead of dissuading her from her course, he steeled himself and offered to escort Elizabeth to the sofa on the opposite side of the room. Once she was comfortably settled, Darcy sat beside her.

"Thank you," she said as Georgiana began to play. "Your sister is a lovely young woman. I have enjoyed speaking to her about a variety of subjects this evening, especially music. Pray, how old was she when she learned to play?"

For once, Elizabeth's presence could not command Darcy's attention as it often did. The anxiety he felt upon hearing the music he intimately associated with his beloved mother was distracting, as was Georgiana's determination to play it. He did not immediately comprehend that Elizabeth had posed a question to him, never mind awaited his answer.

She repeated her question a moment later.

Chagrined, he replied, "Forgive me, Miss Elizabeth. I was distracted. My sister was not six years old."

"So young! Did your father send to London for a music master?"

Georgiana glanced in their direction. Her eyes met

Darcy's, her countenance flushed with colour, and she quickly looked away.

"He did not," Darcy muttered absently. He wondered what on earth his sister could be about. She had never particularly warmed to Miss Bingley. Why she had suddenly developed a desire to please her baffled him. Far more disconcerting was hearing her play his mother's song. With each note Darcy was flooded with memories and emotions he was ill prepared to face, especially in company. He ran his hand over his mouth. His self-possession felt alarmingly inconstant.

"Whoever instructed her must have been truly exceptional as well."

Darcy shifted in his seat, barely attending. He twisted his signet ring around his finger, a nervous habit he acquired as a boy but could never quite break himself of, even as a man. He started to lift his hand, intent upon combing his fingers through his hair, but caught himself and returned his hand to his lap.

Then Elizabeth asked the one question that never failed to bring years of heartache and resentment to the fore. "Was it your mother who taught Miss Darcy to play so beautifully?"

Her words and the implication behind them were jarring. In complete stupefaction he stared at her, galled and hurt beyond measure that she, who understood him so well, would dare mention his mother at such a moment! Elizabeth's name —her Christian name—was on the tip of his tongue.

Their eyes met, and suddenly a powerful feeling of disquiet seized him, flaying what little remained of his equanimity. Instead of realisation, instead of *contrition,* Darcy saw only confusion in Elizabeth's gaze—confusion and heartfelt concern.

Across the room, the music swelled and dipped, as though

carried on the wind from some faraway place, and Darcy's composure eroded further. As intimately as he felt Elizabeth Bennet knew him, in that moment it was abundantly clear she had no idea what this sonata meant to him. She did not know the memories it invoked, or the pain it inflicted upon his soul. Why would she? How would she? As dear as she had become to Darcy, he had known her but three short weeks, and he had never seen fit to tell her.

Suddenly, the room felt unbearably hot, and Darcy's chest felt inexplicably tight. He slipped his index finger beneath his cravat, tugging furtively at the artful arrangement of knots, desperate for relief. His efforts proved fruitless.

"Are you well, sir?"

Darcy hardly knew. The polite thing to do would be to answer yes, regardless of how he felt, but he could not bring himself to say so. In that moment he felt so many things—anxious, disjointed, overwhelmed by a depth of feeling that was somehow both familiar and foreign—but certainly not well.

"Sir," Elizabeth said again, this time with more urgency. "You look quite ill...!"

Her distress was impossible to ignore.

Darcy looked at her then, truly looked at her, and saw her discomposure nearly matched his own. That his failure to master his emotions had disturbed Elizabeth's equanimity to such an extent grieved him exceedingly.

Despite being in the drawing room, despite being within view of Georgiana and Bingley and Bingley's sisters and Hurst, Darcy extended his hand towards her without hesitation or thought. What followed was barely more than a fleeting caress, a gesture of reassurance bestowed upon a dear friend; but the softness of Elizabeth's skin shocked him, the warmth of her hand scorched him, and the tiny, startled gasp that escaped from her lips maddened him beyond anything he had ever known.

Elizabeth just stared at him.

Her eyes were wide and fathomless. They were dark and inexplicably warm. In the candlelight, they shone like the moon reflected upon the sea on a summer night. As ever, they compelled Darcy like nothing else. The urge to kiss her with abandon, to worship her with his words and his mouth and his body, nearly overwhelmed him.

His breath and his heart and his sanity tangled in his throat.

A flush of heat rose along the back of his neck.

In the next instant he paled.

"Pray excuse me," he rasped.

And then he fled.

TEN

⌒◦⌒

None of us want to be in calm waters all our lives.

IF NETHERFIELD LACKED ANYTHING, IT DID NOT LACK comfort. The bedchamber prepared for Elizabeth was elegantly furnished and well-appointed with soft linens and plush counterpanes of the highest quality. The fire was banked by an obliging maid who supplied tea and cake and biscuits on lovely china plates. There were decorated tables and upholstered chairs, a painted screen beside the hearth, porcelain figurines on the mantel, and a bookshelf with a few scant volumes of poetry and a novel that might have delighted her had she been in the mood to read.

Despite being tired and despite her comfortable bed, Elizabeth slept fitfully. She rose shortly after dawn, dressed without summoning a maid, and checked on Jane. Finding her sleeping peacefully, she walked to the window, brushed the curtains aside, and peered out over the park. A thin layer of frost covered the ground, glistening in the pale morning sunlight. With a wistful sigh, she watched starlings soar and swoop in bold aerobatics high above the trees. Fat guineafowl pecked at the lawn, hunting for insects, and one proud peacock strutted along a manicured path paved with pale stones.

Elizabeth longed to be out of doors. The day was too fine to restrict herself to the house while Jane slept. Later, once she awakened, Elizabeth would attend to her sister's every comfort; for the moment, she needed to stretch her legs, clear her head, and breathe fresh, crisp air.

The repetitive ticking of the Chippendale clock in the corridor was all she heard as she made her way towards the grand staircase. She descended the steps, asked a footman to retrieve her bonnet and pelisse, and awaited his return by the door. The main anteroom was cold, something Elizabeth had not expected in so fine a house. It was early however, and Netherfield's manor house was large—much larger than Longbourn's. To sweep out each hearth, lay fresh kindling, and set new fires took a great deal of time. Perhaps when she returned from her walk all the hearths would have been tended and the fires stoked to a roaring blaze.

Wrapping her arms around herself to ward off the chill, Elizabeth made a slow circuit through the room. Ornate chairs upholstered in patterned silks lined the walls. Paintings depicting landscapes and seascapes hung above them. Elizabeth paused before a beautifully rendered painting of the coast. She had never been to the sea and wondered whether it was truly as spectacular as the artist had portrayed it to be. The colours were vibrant, and the work itself was rich with detail. Gulls, with wings extended, soared above the cliffs while smaller birds, likely little terns, decorated the water's edge. Elizabeth smiled to herself. To see the sea and feel its breath upon her face as she stood on the sandy shore would certainly be something!

Her fanciful musings were interrupted by the sharp staccato of footsteps descending the marble staircase at a rapid pace. A moment later, Darcy appeared wearing a wool frock coat, snug-fitting deerskin breeches, and top boots. He looked tired, but no longer unwell. He walked briskly to the door and peered out of the window, likely assessing the weather.

Elizabeth released a breath she had not realised she had been holding. His behaviour the previous evening had both baffled and alarmed her. At supper he had been easy and equitable, but his comportment was very different after she had returned from spending time with Jane. One minute Darcy was master of himself; the next, he appeared deeply agitated and pale, as though he had seen a ghost. When he quit the room, it was abruptly, so abruptly Elizabeth's head had spun.

For the rest of the night, she had thought only of Darcy. Every interaction they had that day was recalled, every conversation dissected, but she could conceive of nothing she had either said or done that might have discomposed him to such a degree. If he had truly resented her for pointing out his ignorance of his sister's heart that morning, Elizabeth doubted he would have engaged her so readily—or so pleasantly— during supper. Any other possibility for his disturbance eluded her. Try as she might, she could think of none.

That Darcy had risen early and was presently dressed for riding must be proof of his good health. Nevertheless, Elizabeth bit her lip in indecision. Until she heard him proclaim that he was recovered, her disquiet would persist, but the question remained: Would Darcy welcome her concern or view it more as an invasion of his privacy? She reminded herself they were friends—friends who would reside in the same house until Jane felt well enough to return home. Surely, enquiring after his health was to be expected. Before Elizabeth could change her mind, she said, "Good morning, Mr Darcy. The weather looks very fine today, does it not?"

The sound of her voice appeared to startle him, but he soon regained his equanimity. "Good morning to you, Miss

Elizabeth. Forgive me for failing to greet you properly just now. I did not see you standing there."

"No," she said as she gathered her courage. "I daresay you did not. Despite your distraction, you appear to be in excellent health this morning. That did not seem to be the case last night."

Clasping his hands behind his back, Darcy made his way towards her. "I am much improved this morning, thank you. I hope my sudden indisposition did not cause you undue distress."

As he came closer, Elizabeth noticed dark circles beneath his eyes, an indication he had probably slept poorly. For some reason she could not explain, she longed to touch his face. Such a bold thought was discomfiting, not to mention improper—as improper as his reaching for and caressing her hand last night in the drawing room. Elizabeth twisted her fingers together instead. "You were quite pale, sir, and you appeared to be in a mild state of shock. Indifference in such a situation would have been impossible."

"I am sorry. I did not mean to cause you to worry."

"I would never accuse you of such," she told him gently. "I am relieved to see you so well recovered."

Darcy cleared his throat. "I was not expecting to see you so early this morning. Yesterday, much of your time was devoted to nursing your sister. You must be tired."

She smiled and shook her head. "I am presently planning my escape."

"You are leaving?" he said with some surprise.

Elizabeth would have laughed if he had not looked so distressed by the prospect of Jane being left to the mercy of Miss Bingley and Mrs Hurst. Neither lady had proved to be of any use in a sickroom. "For shame, Mr Darcy. I would never be so unfeeling as to abandon my sister in her time of need. But spending half an hour out of doors while she is sleeping will provide a momentary respite from near-constant confinement. Once the footman returns with my pelisse, I shall be off to enjoy the fresh air of Mr Bingley's beautiful park."

"The park is lovely in the morning. I hope you find Miss Bennet much improved upon your return."

"As do I. For the moment, she is sleeping soundly and seems comfortable."

"I am glad to hear it." He appeared on the verge of saying more, but his eyes flickered to the painting of the coast, and he stared at it to the exclusion of all else.

The setting sun and the rolling sea and the chalk white cliffs were truly something to behold. Seeing them captured so brilliantly, suspended in time at such a moment of majesty, had certainly enchanted Elizabeth. She longed to hear Darcy's impression. "What think you of the sea, Mr Darcy? As much as I love Hertfordshire's verdant hills and lush fields, I have wanted to see the sea since I first read *Gulliver's Travels* as a girl. It is a beautiful painting and masterfully done. Do you suppose it is a faithful likeness?"

It seemed to take him a small eternity to find his voice. "Yes. Very faithful."

"Do you know it, then?" she asked, heartened by his admission.

"I have been there twice," he said with undue seriousness. "To Ramsgate. I have stood upon those very cliffs."

Elizabeth was barely able to contain her enthusiasm. "So, this is Ramsgate? How wonderful! You must tell me your impression, then."

"I fear there is little I can say that would do it justice. You would do better to see it for yourself."

"I shall not argue that visiting a place is often an entirely different experience from hearing it spoken of, or seeing it depicted in a painting or in a book, but I believe you give yourself too little credit. You attended Cambridge and have a superior command of the English language. Surely, you can string together a few words about the sea to satisfy my curiosity." When he offered no reply but continued to stare at the painting with an increasingly grim countenance, Elizabeth adopted a different approach. "I understand sea bathing is popular among tourists visiting Lyme, Weymouth, and Brighton. I do not suppose you were bold enough to attempt it yourself while at Ramsgate?"

To her consternation, Darcy's eyes remained fixed upon the painting. Clearly, he was disinclined to speak. Elizabeth could not fathom why. The silence between them continued unbroken, taking on an almost tangible quality.

Finally, when she felt she could bear it no longer, Darcy spoke.

His voice was impenetrably grave. "Every morning at sunrise I walked to the shore. Even from the cliffs, the air smelt of salt and brine. The sea itself was never still. It was magnificent, hypnotic—a living, breathing entity impossible to contain. It could break a ship in half or drown a man in a matter of minutes. But there is more to the sea than its malicious beauty and intemperate nature. Beneath its cold surface, beneath its undulating waves, there is tranquillity and peace. Submerged, no idle thoughts disturbed my conscience. Not one soul imposed upon my peace. If not for Georgiana, if not for Pemberley, I could have remained in its embrace forever."

Darcy's recounting of his communion with the sea was as personal as it was poignant. His words and the sincere emotion behind them put Elizabeth in mind of poetry. His sublime descriptions moved her, inspired her, and made her long to experience the sea for herself all the more. But there was also an underlying current of the macabre present, an almost chilling note of despair impossible to ignore.

"You make the sea sound haunting, even terrifying, yet at the same time incredibly romantic and beautiful. It is as though you described a long-lost friend or a lover rather than a great, tempestuous body of water. Your experience at Ramsgate must have been profound, sir."

His reply was a quiet but earnest recitation from *The Seafarer*. "'How his heart would begin to beat, knowing once more the salt waves tossing the towering sea...for no harps ring in his heart. No rewards. No passion. No worldly pleasures. Nothing. Only the ocean's heave'."

"'But longing'," said Elizabeth in answer, her voice soft and steady as she recited the next line of the ancient poem, "'wraps itself around him'. Tell me, Mr Darcy, did you lose yourself in the sea, or happen to find yourself?"

Darcy bowed his head. "The sea was my salvation," he murmured, so softly she almost did not hear.

He looked at her then, and Elizabeth found it difficult to breathe. His eyes, which so often displayed his staunch composure and self-possession, now held a look of such ineffable sadness and yearning that her heart ached. In vain, she searched for something to say to him, some *bon mot* to either cheer or soothe, but all she could think to say was, "I am sorry."

Darcy swallowed audibly. At his side, his hands curled into fists. In his movements, in his expression, and in his dark, penetrating eyes, Elizabeth sensed an almost palpable need for something she could not quite discern or name. She could only assume it had something to do with his time at Ramsgate. She had no idea what could have happened to him there, but clearly something had, and it affected him deeply.

He stepped towards her, closing the distance between them to mere inches. In the chilly anteroom, standing so closely, the heat from his body warmed her like a flame. Elizabeth's countenance flushed with feeling, and Darcy's with some mysterious, unknown emotion she could not identify, but dearly wished she could.

"Miss Elizabeth," he said gruffly, but with considerable feeling. He looked as though he wanted to say more—that he *meant* to say more—but the footman returned with her pelisse and the moment was lost.

"There," Elizabeth said as she finished plaiting Jane's hair. "Now you look much better." She laid the brush on the bedside table then set about straightening the bedlinens and fluffing the pillows.

Jane smiled faintly from an upholstered chair beside the bed. She looked pale and wan, but her fever had broken during the night and had not returned. "I am so glad you have come, Lizzy. Truly, I do not know what I would have done had you stayed at home."

"Nor do I," Elizabeth replied teasingly, "for neither of your new friends seems up to the task of nursing."

"They are not nearly so disagreeable as you believe them to be. Miss Bingley and Mrs Hurst both sat with me yesterday morning before you arrived. It was most kind of them."

"Yes, very kind. I cannot help but notice they have not come to see you since."

"Nor do I expect them to now that you have come. At least not until much later in the day. Miss Bingley is busy running her brother's household and Mrs Hurst, having experience in such matters, must assist her."

Elizabeth pursed her lips. Her sister was too good, especially regarding the superior sisters. She said as much. "I regret to inform you it is far more likely Miss Bingley is busy running after Mr Darcy while Mrs Hurst endeavours to distract her husband else he consumes all of Mr Bingley's port."

This elicited another faint but exasperated smile from Jane. "You are incorrigible. I know you and Miss Bingley are not the best of friends, but she is far too dignified and proper to ever chase after anyone, especially Mr Darcy. He is her brother's friend."

"He is also wealthy, handsome, and single. According to all the mamas," Elizabeth said with a wry twist of her mouth, "he must be in want of a wife. I believe Miss Bingley intends for it to be her."

Jane sighed. "Poor Miss Bingley."

"Poor Miss Bingley, indeed. I fear not even her twenty thousand pounds will tempt Mr Darcy to offer for her."

"I imagine not. Anyone with eyes can see his admiration lies in another quarter." Jane reached for Elizabeth's hand and grasped it with her own. "Whatever shall I do without you?"

"I cannot think what you mean."

"Lizzy, you must see Mr Darcy admires you."

Elizabeth, however, saw no such thing. That he esteemed her was clear enough, but as to harbouring a tendre for her, she heartily disagreed. Unlike Mr Bingley, who promptly sought Jane's society upon every meeting and remained faithfully by her side, Darcy usually lingered in the background, stern-faced, taciturn, and closed mouthed. Whenever he did approach Elizabeth, it was well into the festivities when her neighbours—and specifically her mother—were well occupied and therefore least likely to notice such marked attention. "I shall not deny Mr Darcy appears to enjoy my society, but he has no design on me. He has come to Hertfordshire to visit his friend and to avoid the marriage market in London. He is not searching for a wife but is doing all in his power to avoid being saddled with one. You must have seen how he stiffens whenever Mama mentions Mr Bingley's attentions to you within his hearing."

Jane regarded her with large, glassy eyes as she feigned an innocent expression. "And what pray does Mr Darcy do whenever you speak?"

Elizabeth shook her head with a rueful little smile. "I hardly know. Last night at supper he was animated and inclined towards conversation but incredibly inattentive afterwards. When I left you and returned downstairs, he seemed unwell. This morning..."

Jane's brows furrowed. "This morning...?"

Elizabeth hesitated as she considered what she ought to relate, if anything. The look in Darcy's eyes—the sadness and earnestness and longing—still haunted her every bit as much as his behaviour confounded her. But his longing for what? She could not begin to guess and decided to keep the more intimate particulars of their early morning exchange to herself. "It was nothing. He was amiable and apologetic and then he was distracted and morose. I believe something weighs upon him heavily."

"I understand Mr Darcy has many responsibilities. He is master of his family's estate and guardian to his sister. According to Mr Bingley, Pemberley is one of the most prominent estates in all of Derbyshire. Despite his independence, his wealth, and his consequence, Mr Darcy's cannot be an easy life."

"No, I suppose it is not." Wishing to lend the moment some levity, Elizabeth changed the subject to Darcy's friend. "Speaking of Mr Bingley, he hardly knew what to do with himself yesterday. He asked after you incessantly. It was quite tiresome."

Even in illness, Jane looked lovely when she blushed. "Hush. He did no such thing."

"Yes," Elizabeth insisted with a smile. "He certainly did.

Were it not entirely improper, I do believe he would burst through your bedchamber door and speak to you himself! Come. You ought to be resting comfortably in bed. I have kept you in this chair far too long. Mr Bingley would never approve."

Once Jane was settled in bed and the counterpane arranged, her lips lifted in a tired, but hopeful smile. "Do you truly think Mr Bingley is concerned for me?"

"Without doubt. He has offered to have his cook prepare any dish that might tempt you, be it broth or plum pudding or ices. I have never seen any man so eager to please as Mr Bingley is to please you. You are fortunate to have such an attentive admirer."

"Dear Mr Bingley," she whispered as she closed her eyes and drifted off to sleep.

For the next quarter hour Elizabeth occupied herself with a book, but it proved dull and could not hold her interest. Casting it aside, she walked to the window and gazed upon the park. She nearly laughed when she spied Solomon running circles around an imposing topiary in the garden. Darcy stood a fair distance away, watching him. Eventually, he summoned the dog to his side.

Solomon bounded across the lawn with unbridled enthusiasm. As he approached, Darcy made a gesture with his hand and Solomon not only stopped short but sat obediently at his master's feet. His long, whiplike tail thumped against the ground.

Darcy got down on one knee and rubbed the dog's ears. His mouth formed words Elizabeth wished she could hear as Solomon leaned into his touch with apparent pleasure. After several minutes of indulging his dog, Darcy ceased his ministrations and pressed his lips to the top of his head. Solomon appeared delighted and, in turn, licked his master's face until Darcy pushed him away with a smile and stood.

Elizabeth grinned at their antics. There was no doubt in her mind Solomon was well cared for, but to see such evidence of the affection that existed between this wonderful, unusually reserved man and his sweet dog warmed her heart. The elegant, staid persona Darcy wore in public was nowhere to be seen. He was playful and sweet himself, and completely devoted to his dog.

Touching her fingertip to the glass, Elizabeth traced a silly approximation of Solomon's profile in the frost along the pane's edge. For the second time that day she found herself longing to be out of doors. Earlier, she had sought fresh air and exercise. Now, she longed for employment. She imagined skipping down the staircase and bursting through the front doors into the sunlight. She imagined running through the park until she was gasping and happy and flushed. Solomon would chase her, and Darcy would roll his eyes at their silliness. Then he would offer her his arm. His gaze, as it often did, would linger on her eyes and her mouth when she spoke, and his countenance would be easy, as easy as his smile.

Solomon uttered a series of loud, excited barks as Darcy threw a large stick across the garden with considerable force. The Great Dane bolted after it, his tongue lolling from his mouth. Elizabeth stifled a laugh as he galloped past the stick, then doubled back to claim it. It took him several attempts to secure it between his teeth. Darcy shook his head, but there was no mistaking his broad smile.

Elizabeth smiled as well. How dearly she loved him when he smiled!

A moment later, she felt the colour drain from her face as she realised a startling truth—*she loved him!*

In shock, she sank onto the cushioned window seat and pressed her hand to her breast, directly over her heart. Although their growing closeness had certainly made her aware that she cared for Darcy, it seemed almost incomprehensible to her that in three short weeks he had become much more than simply her friend. He had become *dear* to her— dear to her in ways that Charlotte Lucas and Penelope Harrington and countless other girls were not. It was a sobering epiphany, especially when she recalled Darcy would be leaving Hertfordshire the following week, perhaps never to return.

Elizabeth exhaled a tremulous breath. She could say nothing to him of her feelings, nor did she entertain the slightest hope of their paths crossing in town. Her father had long hated the constant bustle and pomp of London and rarely travelled there if he could help it. Her aunt and uncle Gardiner, who resided near Cheapside with their three young children and with whom she and Jane were particularly intimate, often came to Longbourn instead.

Short of bidding Darcy a pleasant journey, Elizabeth could only hope he would remember her with fondness— enough fondness that, when he availed himself of his friend's hospitality in the future, he would seek to renew their acquaintance as well.

Acquaintance.

What a wholly inadequate word to describe the depth of such a friendship!

Acquaintances did not wind their way through the countryside each morning, meeting by unspoken design to discuss everything from music to philosophy to the state of the kingdom. Acquaintances did not exchange teasing banter across the dinner table or amused glances across a crowded room. Acquaintances did not touch each other, even during moments of distress. Last night, when Darcy had reached for her hand in the drawing room, her entire body had been affected—from the hair on her head to the tips of her toes and everywhere in between. Even now, Elizabeth felt the ghost of his fingertips on her skin—warm and forbidden and divine.

A knock upon the sitting room door startled her, forcing her attention back to the present. With considerable effort, she endeavoured to banish all thoughts of Darcy and her love for him from her mind. The likelihood of the visitor being Miss Bingley or Mrs Hurst, or both, was great. Elizabeth needed her wits about her. Drawing a fortifying breath, she took a moment to gather her composure and to steel herself for the petty remarks and tiresome observations that would assuredly punctuate their visit. A quick glance at her reflection in the looking glass on the dressing table assured her that her appearance was presentable. Nevertheless, she smoothed her skirts, drew another bracing breath, and proceeded to the door.

She opened it, but instead of the superior sisters, Miss Darcy stood before her. Elizabeth nearly sagged with relief. "Miss Darcy," she said with an expression of real pleasure. "What a delightful surprise."

The girl's lips lifted in a self-conscious smile. "Pray forgive my intrusion, Miss Elizabeth. I have come to enquire after your sister. I hope she is better."

"I am happy to report Jane's fever has broken, but she easily tires. She is sleeping for the moment, but you are welcome to come in and keep me company if you like. In fact, I would be indebted to you, for it is very dull otherwise!"

"If I would not disturb Miss Bennet's rest, or inconvenience you, I would enjoy spending time with you very much."

Elizabeth stepped aside so Miss Darcy could enter, then led the way to an upholstered sofa situated before the hearth. A maid had recently built up the fire, so the sitting room felt cosy and warm. "Allow me to ring for some tea."

"Please do not go to any trouble for me," Miss Darcy replied. "I have come to see you, not to be waited upon."

"It is no trouble at all unless you really would rather not

have tea, in which case I would be a wretched hostess indeed to force it upon you."

"Oh, no! I am sure you could never be wretched to anyone, not when you have shown me such kindness."

"It is you who are kind," Elizabeth insisted. "As for absolving me of wretchedness, I urge you to reserve judgment until you have heard me play the pianoforte. Compared to your own exceptional talent, my meagre abilities are nothing short of a punishment!"

"But I understand you play so beautifully. My brother told me he has rarely heard anything that has given him more pleasure."

Hearing her mention Darcy caught Elizabeth completely unaware; hearing he had praised her performance on the pianoforte—a performance she knew he had found wanting—surprised her even more. "I am afraid your brother has grossly exaggerated my talent, no doubt for some mischievous reason of his own."

Miss Darcy's forehead creased with confusion. "That cannot be, Miss Elizabeth. Fitzwilliam never exaggerates. He always tells the absolute truth."

"While I certainly do not doubt your brother's integrity, the only performance of mine he has witnessed was remarkably unimpressive! Owing to my negligence in practising, my fingers fumbled on the keys several times, which I am certain did not go unnoticed by your brother, or anyone else so unfortunate as to hear me. It was very good of him to claim otherwise."

"My brother *is* very good," Miss Darcy agreed, her voice soft. "I could not imagine having a better or a kinder one."

"I confess myself quite envious. I have no brother, only four sisters. Jane, as you know, is the eldest. She and I have always been close, but the other three—Mary, Kitty, and Lydia—although younger, are no less beloved."

A wistful smile tugged at Miss Darcy's lips. "I should have liked to have had a sister." A moment later, her smile faded. "I would by no means have you believe I am unhappy to have Fitzwilliam, though. I assure you nothing could be further from the truth. He is everything I could ever hope for in a brother. There is nothing he would not do for me, or for anyone for whom he cares. When I say he is very good, I speak nothing but the truth."

"Of course you do," said Elizabeth. "I am wholly convinced of your brother's goodness. Although I have taken every opportunity to tease him, the truth of the matter is I have enjoyed the discussions we have had these three weeks. I am very pleased, as well, to be better acquainted with you."

"As am I. Since we arrived in Hertfordshire, my brother has spoken so highly of you, but I suppose that is to be expected, as you both appear to have much in common."

"Do we?" she enquired, knowing perfectly well that they did in fact have much in common.

"Oh, yes," Miss Darcy insisted. "You and Fitzwilliam both enjoy the country and going for long walks. You enjoy music and philosophy and poetry. You are also intelligent and inquisitive, and you adore Solomon." She shook her head in dismay. "No lady who has ever met Solomon has been unafraid of him. You are the only one. My brother loves him dearly, so it goes without saying that he admires you and holds you in esteem. If he did not, he would never have mentioned your name to me, never mind referred to you in such glowing terms."

For weeks Charlotte had insisted Darcy admired her. Not half an hour earlier, Jane had said much the same thing. That he had spoken to his sister, not only of her, but of her interests, gave rise to hope; but that hope was soon quelled by reason. The disparity in their ages rendered Miss Darcy an unlikely confidante of her worldly, much older brother. No matter how much Darcy appeared to enjoy Elizabeth's society, it was by no means indicative of his feeling more for her than friendship. In the grand scheme of things, it likely meant very little at all.

"As it happens," Elizabeth admitted, "I think highly of Mr Darcy as well." To more than that she would not confess. Certainly not to Miss Darcy. She doubted she would even be able to bring herself to reveal all within her heart to Jane.

"Many people think highly of him," Miss Darcy replied with undue seriousness, "but there are so few people in the world of whom my brother thinks well. There are even fewer whom he admires."

Uncomfortable with the direction their conversation had taken, Elizabeth cast about for another topic. She recalled the Darcys were soon to leave Hertfordshire and said, "While I am very glad to have made your acquaintance and that of your brother, I am sorry to hear that you are to leave us next week. Will you return to London, or will you travel to Derbyshire?"

The words had no sooner been spoken than Miss Darcy's countenance dimmed. "I do not know. I regret our time in Hertfordshire has reached an end. Mr Bingley often remarks that your neighbours have been welcoming and kind. They must think I am terribly rude for remaining at Netherfield while the rest of the household attends dinners and pays calls."

"Not at all. I understand you are not yet out. No one in Hertfordshire expects you to move in society as though you are. You attended church. It was enough."

"It is very good of you to say so. I hope you will not think me presumptuous when I confess that I should like to know you better, and your sisters, too, if they would be amenable."

Elizabeth smiled. "That can certainly be arranged. But I feel I must warn you whenever my sisters and I are together at Longbourn, we are an exuberant bunch! If you are used to order and quietude, I fear you will be sorely disappointed. My two youngest sisters especially, can be quite spirited."

"I should like to become better acquainted with them in any case. Do you...do you think that your sisters would find my society pleasing?"

"Of course," Elizabeth assured her. "You would be very welcome at Longbourn."

It was by no means a falsehood. Although Lydia had expressed consternation about Miss Darcy's inherent shyness, Elizabeth suspected the girl's sweetness, elegant manners, and fashionable gowns would soon earn Lydia's approbation. Kitty always followed wherever Lydia led, and Mary would be pleased to have a quiet friend who enjoyed music as much as she did. Miss Darcy's genteel comportment might improve that of all her sisters, and her sisters in turn might instil in Miss Darcy some of the confidence she currently lacked.

What Darcy might think of his sister forming such friendships was another matter.

With that in mind, Elizabeth asked, "Is your brother at liberty to extend your stay at this time? Is he expected in town or at his estate?"

Miss Darcy's face fell. "I do not know, but if he has business with his steward, I am afraid our staying on in Hertfordshire may not be possible. Doing his duty and fulfilling his responsibilities is extremely important to Fitzwilliam. He must consider the needs of Pemberley and its people constantly and with utmost seriousness and care. There are so many who depend upon him."

"I can well imagine, but it cannot hurt to ask. Even if Mr Darcy's business calls you away, perhaps you will be able to return to Netherfield in the future. He and Mr Bingley appear to be great friends, and it is obvious that Miss Bingley and Mrs Hurst are fond of you."

This appeared to lift Miss Darcy's spirits, and she brightened. "Aside from my cousin Richard, Mr Bingley is Fitzwilliam's closest friend, and Miss Bingley and Mrs Hurst have always treated me well. Should they desire our return, I know my brother would be pleased to oblige them."

"Then it is settled. Should your brother absolutely insist on leaving as planned, you will not be without options, or friends, in Hertfordshire."

"And shall I truly be welcome at Longbourn?" Miss Darcy asked hopefully.

Elizabeth reassured her with a smile. "Indeed, you will."

ELEVEN

❧

I may have lost my heart, but not my self-control.

DARCY SHED HIS ROBE AND STEPPED INTO THE STEAMING tub of water. Dismissing his valet, he rested his head against the towel that had been placed on the rim of the copper tub for his comfort and closed his eyes with a weary sigh. As the day wore on, the weather had turned unseasonably cold, and he had spent a good portion of it out of doors inspecting neglected hedgerows and crumbling stone walls with Bingley. Their numbers were considerable and repairing them before spring would be an arduous task, but Bingley was confident it could be done.

Darcy was not as certain. While the house had been well-maintained, there were other aspects of the estate in need of repair. A capable steward would have seen to it all, yet Netherfield's had not. An absent master was no excuse. According to the accounts there had been funds to cover the maintenance costs, including necessary repairs to the tenants' cottages, but as far as Darcy could tell the bulk of the money had been spent on superficial improvements to the main house. Bingley had balked when Darcy suggested dismissing his steward, and Darcy had baulked when Bingley proposed keeping him on. A spirited discussion on the merits of alteration and progression had followed, but at the end of the day Netherfield was Bingley's estate. Although his friend had sought his advice and Darcy had freely given it, ultimately, it was up to Bingley to either heed it or not.

After speaking of estate matters for most of the day, both gentlemen were eager to retire to the billiards room—Darcy, to avoid Bingley's sisters while he enjoyed a glass of port; and Bingley, to wax eloquent about his favourite topic: Jane Bennet.

The lady had been at Netherfield for three days, recuperating from her cold in Bingley's second-best guestroom. Yesterday, her mother descended upon Netherfield to see how she fared, her three remaining daughters in tow. Mrs Bennet had barely spent half an hour upstairs before she returned to the drawing room to take tea and remark upon the poor state of Miss Bennet's health with as much enthusiasm as she did the fineness of the house and the furniture.

It was for Elizabeth's sake that Darcy forced himself to remain at the window with his back to the room, drinking his tea and biting his tongue while the woman rattled away about the benefits of country living, the superiority of their little Hertfordshire society, and that they dined with four-and-twenty families. One look at Elizabeth's burning countenance told Darcy all he needed to know—she was mortified and ashamed of her mother's behaviour.

Bingley's sisters exhibited none of Darcy's restraint. Instead, they fussed with their jewels and smiled condescendingly while their brother listened politely to Mrs Bennet and attempted to interject his own observations, with little success. Eventually, Miss Lydia and Miss Catherine reminded Bingley of his promise to hold a ball at Netherfield, a scheme he agreed to with alacrity, much to his sisters' horror. "Once Miss Bennet is recovered," he proclaimed, "I shall instruct Cook to make white soup enough for the whole neighbourhood and you, Miss Lydia, will name the date."

This pronouncement was received by the two youngest Miss Bennets and their mother as one would expect—their raptures knew no bounds. The pious Miss Mary, however, did not share their unbridled enthusiasm, nor it seemed, did Elizabeth. As soon as her mother and sisters departed for Longbourn, she returned to Miss Bennet's bedside and did not come downstairs again that day—not for supper and not afterwards, once the gentlemen re-joined the ladies in the drawing room for coffee and cards. Bingley, forever desirous of any scrap of news he could glean of Miss Bennet, was disconsolate. Georgiana, too, was saddened by Elizabeth's absence.

Despite his own disappointment, Darcy found himself breathing a sigh of relief. For too long he had felt the danger posed by his pretty friend, her witty remarks, and her fine eyes. For too long he had tamped down any tendrils of tender feeling that threatened to take root in his heart. However much he craved her society, Darcy had hoped an evening's reprieve would aid him in conquering his ardent attraction to her once and for all.

It did not.

As predicted, residing together in the same house was the most exquisite form of torture. Elizabeth was at Netherfield for the express purpose of nursing Miss Bennet, but whenever circumstances provided half an hour's reprieve, she would seek employment elsewhere. Daily Darcy encountered her at the breakfast table, at the supper table, in the library, and out of doors—usually close to the house, walking the manicured paths of the park. That she was installed in the bedchamber across the corridor from his own proved to be as distracting as it was compelling.

Her very first night in the house—when Georgiana's defiant playing had distressed Darcy to such a degree that he had pressed Elizabeth's hand and felt all he had felt—had been sleepless. The following morning proved equally disconcerting. In that moment, with the painting of Ramsgate's cliffs staring him in the eye, Darcy had been so captivated and rattled by Elizabeth's sensitivity and insight, her gentleness and her heart, he had nearly lost his head and his wits and confessed all—Georgiana's near ruin, his guilt for failing to protect her, his furious hatred of Wickham, and the crippling sensation of helplessness and fear he felt every time he received another one of the blackguard's deplorable letters.

By some miracle, his powerful inclination to unburden himself was prevented, not by the return of his own sound judgment, but by the timely interruption of a footman carrying Elizabeth's bonnet and pelisse.

Exhaling harshly, Darcy raked his fingers through his hair and repressed an oath. Water droplets dripped down his arms, his face, and his neck. To expose his own faults and failings would have been foolish enough, but to expose Georgiana to such censure and denigration could have resulted in irreparable disaster. He had been standing within the main anteroom of the house, for God's sake, where the family and servants and any manner of persons could have overheard every word that he uttered! He ought never to have so much as thought of recounting his sister's disgrace to anyone. He was not some gossiping matron or tittering female with a loose tongue—he was Fitzwilliam Darcy of Pemberley. He was private, exacting, and discreet. He did not discuss his most intimate dealings with anybody; certainly not with any person he had known for a mere handful of weeks.

The tightening of his chest and the quickening of his heart were a stark reminder that Elizabeth was not merely 'any person', nor were the last three weeks insignificant. They were among the most enjoyable of Darcy's life. In that short span of time, Elizabeth had not only become his friend, but an unaccountably *dear* friend. It mattered not whether she was ankle deep in a muddy field or wearing an evening gown in her mother's drawing room, Darcy cherished every moment they spent together. He welcomed her society with ever increasing pleasure, sought her opinions on a variety of subjects, and basked in her smiles. In turn, she bore his inherent reticence with equanimity, endeavoured to put him at ease, and took pains to draw him out. She cheered him. She challenged him. She impressed him. She made him think and wish and *want*.

Darcy stared at the ceiling, frowning as the warm, flickering light from the fire cast animated shadows across the wide expanse of plaster and the elaborate cornice that framed the walls. It ought to have been impossible for any lady—especially one whose circumstances were so decidedly beneath his own—to insinuate herself into his well-ordered life with so little effort, never mind secure a place in his heart. And yet Elizabeth had done precisely that and much more. She had made him admire and love her, and she had made him question the essentials he had long held in such high regard: desirable connexions, noble lineage, and considerable wealth.

Darcy possessed them all.

Elizabeth did not.

He expelled a short bark of bitter laughter. His friends—nay, all of London—expected him to marry an heiress. His family expected him to marry his cousin Anne. Darcy wanted nothing of them. He wanted a wife who would care for him. He wanted a wife who would love him. God help him, he wanted Elizabeth Bennet.

Such a monumental revelation ought to inspire feelings of

joy. It ought to inspire shout-at-the-top-of-your-voice elation. Instead, the idea of binding his fastidious relations to Elizabeth's eccentric family inspired only frustration and futility. Two sentiments Darcy did not like.

Nevertheless, he was in love with her—ardently in love with her.

And he was damned if he knew what to do about it.

⅍

"You want to walk into Meryton?"

Appearing to study her slippers with great gravity, Georgiana inclined her head. "I wish to see the town."

"The town." Darcy blinked at her. He could not recall the last time his sister had wanted to walk anywhere beyond the garden. Whenever she desired to visit the shops in Kympton or Lambton while at Pemberley, there was a carriage at her disposal; in London it was much the same. He laid the letter from his steward aside and reclined in his chair.

"Do you disapprove, Brother?" she asked tentatively, lacing her fingers together.

"It is not a question of whether I disapprove of your going or not. Meryton is a delightful country town, but the distance to travel there is over two miles. Once there, you must then walk another two miles back to Netherfield. You will exhaust yourself."

"I understand Miss Elizabeth and her sisters often walk into Meryton."

Darcy endeavoured to ignore the sudden quickening of his heart any mention of Elizabeth's name never failed to incite. He cleared his throat and said, "Having lived here all their lives, I daresay the Miss Bennets are used to the exercise, whereas you are not. Nor are Miss Bingley and Mrs Hurst.

Longbourn is much closer to Meryton than Netherfield—not half the distance."

"Nevertheless," she told him, raising her head and meeting his eyes, "I would like to attempt it. If you accompany me, Brother, there will be no need for Miss Bingley and Mrs Hurst to do so."

Darcy consulted his watch and glanced towards the window. The weather that day was chilly, but there was a bit of sun peeking through the clouds and walking at a brisk pace would likely keep them warm. "Very well. I have business I must see to for the next hour, but we may set out once I have completed it."

Georgiana beamed at him. "Thank you, Fitzwilliam. I am looking forward to seeing Meryton, and to spending the afternoon with you. I regret hiding away at Netherfield instead of putting myself forth to meet Mr Bingley's neighbours, Miss Elizabeth especially. She is lovely. I cannot begin to tell you how very much I like her."

Again, hearing Elizabeth's name—and his sister's preference for her—made Darcy's traitorous heart skip a beat. "Pray be ready within the hour, Georgiana. Walking to Meryton and back is likely to take the better part of the afternoon. I do not relish being late to Miss Bingley's supper table."

The sun was high overhead by the time they entered Meryton, and the clouds that filled the bleak morning sky had since dissipated. Darcy glanced at his sister and enquired as to her well-being.

She answered him with a contented smile. Her eyes were bright, and her cheeks were flushed from exertion as well as from the cold. It had taken them well over an hour to walk two miles along the road that intersected King Street, but Georgiana's pride in such an accomplishment was undeniable. If she was tired, Darcy felt she was unlikely to admit it, and so did not press her further on the subject.

Upon their arrival they wandered through the town at a leisurely pace. Darcy pointed out various establishments, and Georgiana peered into shop windows until they came upon a bookseller he had patronised with some regularity since his arrival in Hertfordshire. While Georgiana browsed stacks of sheet music, Darcy walked the length of the shop. Last week he had discovered a rare first edition of poetry tucked among the newer publications. Today, however, he could find nothing to tempt him. He re-joined his sister, who found a concerto composed by Haydn she did not own. She paid for her purchase, and they exited the shop, whereupon she declared a desire to look for shoe roses at the haberdashery across the street. Eager to indulge any scheme that would afford her pleasure, Darcy consented.

The shop was spacious, inviting, and well kept. Darcy remained close to Georgiana as she examined spool upon spool of ribbon and lace. She had much to say of the high quality and the shopkeeper's refined taste. Darcy was surprised to learn that many of the accoutrements had lately come from London and some of the finest lace all the way from Brussels.

Buttons were admired next, then gloves, and silk stockings, and more ribbons. By the time Georgiana happened upon a collection of shoe roses, the bell above the shop's door tinkled and a gust of cold air blew from one end of the room to the other. Having had his fill of frippery, Darcy asked Georgiana whether she would care to take tea in a private parlour at the inn before returning to Netherfield.

"Oh, yes," she replied. "I would enjoy a hot cup of tea."

After purchasing two sets of satin shoe roses, she accepted her brother's proffered arm. They had barely taken two steps towards the door when Darcy suddenly found himself accosted by Miss Lydia Bennet. Her sister, Miss Catherine, stood just behind her, looking every bit as startled by her daring as Darcy.

"Mr Darcy!" she exclaimed. "What a surprise it is to meet you, of all people, in Mr Worthington's shop. It is very good of you to accompany your sister, for I know men do not like to shop for ribbons and shoe roses and gloves and lace." Before Darcy could greet her properly, she acknowledged Georgiana with a curtsey. "Good day to you, Miss Darcy."

The curtsey Georgiana performed in answer was far more elegant. "Good day to you, Miss Lydia," she said softly, but by no means hesitantly. "Good day, Miss Catherine."

Darcy executed a curt, perfunctory bow. "How do you do?"

"We are both well," Miss Lydia replied, but her attention was on Georgiana. "You look very smart. Are you here to purchase some ribbon? Mr Worthington has a vast selection, but I suppose it is nothing special compared to what you are used to in London."

"Oh, no," Georgiana stammered. "Not at all. I mean...it is true that London shops have a larger selection of goods, but Mr Worthington has some beautiful ribbon as well."

"Which do you mean?" Miss Lydia asked. "I cannot see anything so fine as what you are wearing."

Blushing, Georgiana indicated the other side of the shop with a gesture of her hand. "There is some lovely velvet ribbon to be had on that wall, and some satin ribbon, too, as fine as any I have seen in London."

Miss Lydia looked towards the impressive display of ribbons, artfully arranged according to their various colours, textures, and widths, and frowned. "Come, Miss Darcy. You must show me."

"Yes, please do," said Miss Catherine. "We have come for

some ribbon to retrim our bonnets. I should like to know which is your favourite."

Georgiana glanced at her brother for permission.

Darcy struggled against a powerful impulse to deny it. Lydia Bennet was certainly not the sort of girl with whom he wished his sister to associate, never mind form an attachment. She was brash and outspoken, and her sister, Miss Catherine, although two years older, seemed content to simply follow her lead. He looked at Georgiana for a long moment, but attempting to discern her mind was an exercise in futility. Sighing inwardly, he inclined his head, indicating she may do as she liked, and saw the corners of her lips lift in a small but definitive smile.

"They are over here," said Georgiana, turning towards Elizabeth's sisters.

With a pleasant smile of her own, Miss Lydia linked her arm with Georgiana's and engaged her in an animated discussion on the merits of silk versus satin ribbon as they crossed the room. As he watched his sister point out several ribbons to Miss Catherine, who proceeded to examine each one with interest and then grin and nod her head at something Miss Lydia said to her, Darcy felt something within him shift.

They were drawing her out, much as Elizabeth had done at Netherfield.

Of course, Elizabeth had conducted herself with far more delicacy and elegance, but the result appeared much the same. As far as he could tell, Georgiana seemed as pleased to speak to Elizabeth's sisters of ribbons and frippery as she had been to speak to Elizabeth about composers and music.

Darcy ran his hand across his mouth as he contemplated what that meant.

It was by no means an ideal connexion. Lydia and Catherine Bennet were beneath Georgiana in situation, manners, breeding, and birth; but the comportment and manners of their two eldest sisters were, inarguably and consistently, above reproach.

Not for the first time, Darcy wondered where Elizabeth and Jane Bennet had learnt to conduct themselves with such dignity and grace. Their gentility and refinement were certainly not instilled in them by their parents. Mr Bennet was too often in his book room and not often enough in his drawing room, and Mrs Bennet was often as silly as her youngest daughters. If Darcy had not been able to recognise a slight resemblance to her mother in the fullness of Elizabeth's mouth, he would have suspected her of being a foundling.

Miss Lydia, in contrast, was the spitting image of her mother while Miss Catherine more closely resembled her father. They were fifteen and seventeen, respectively, and idle, indulged, and unchecked. While they were too young to be out, they were certainly old enough to know their behaviour was neither proper nor acceptable. Darcy wondered whether they could yet learn restraint and decorum as their eldest sisters had done, or whether improving their comportment would be an exercise in futility. It went without saying that such an office should fall to their parents, but neither their mother nor their father had bothered to set them a good example before; it was doubtful they would begin now. Nor did the sensible counsel of their elder sisters appear to hold any influence when there were young squires and red coated officers to dance with during assemblies and impromptu reels in their neighbours' drawing rooms.

Miss Lydia and Miss Catherine required a firm hand.

Darcy frowned as Bingley came to mind. His friend's infatuation with Jane Bennet had not waned but continued unabated, despite the fact he had seen nothing of her for days. Should her regard for Bingley be genuine as Bingley claimed, he may well end up marrying her, and all her sisters would then become his own.

But would good-natured Bingley, who had never raised his voice to his own sisters, be up to the task of curbing Miss Bennet's? Darcy could not say. If Miss Bennet and Bingley married, he would give Bingley a year before Mrs Bennet and her officiousness would drive him to purchase an estate elsewhere, leaving Elizabeth's family in Hertfordshire to do as they will. Miss Lydia and Miss Catherine were obsessed with dancing and beaux. Should they end up flirting their way to infamy, it was unlikely Mr Bennet possessed either the resources or the inclination to act as he ought to preserve their respectability. Bingley and his five thousand a year would pay for their forwardness in more ways than one. Without his assistance, the Bennet family would likely face ruination and disgrace.

The idea of his beloved Elizabeth suffering such a fate both sickened and angered Darcy. She deserved better—far better—than an indolent father who neglected his family, an excitable mother who pushed her daughters towards any young man who looked smart in a red coat, and sisters who cared more for amusement than they did their own reputations.

But what could be done?

Nothing can be done, said a stern voice from somewhere in the back of Darcy's mind. *It is neither your concern, nor your responsibility. You must think of your own respectability and Georgiana's. One brush with ruination was enough!*

But they are Elizabeth's sisters, said another voice, less sensible and far more charitable than the first. *Someone must do something before it is too late and Miss Lydia and Miss Catherine are out of reach. Your own dear sister might have been Mrs Wickham by now...*

The prospect of Georgiana as Wickham's wife was

beyond abhorrent, and Darcy could not but thank Heaven, again and again, that he had arrived in Ramsgate in time to prevent such a catastrophe from occurring. God only knew what unspeakable miseries she would be made to endure had he failed to intervene. Even now, the profligate opportunist refused to leave them alone!

Since arriving in Hertfordshire, Darcy had received a total of eight letters written in Wickham's hand, each one more reprehensible and immoral than the last. The two most recent were the most worrisome yet, as Wickham had finally done what Darcy had expected him to do all along: threaten to expose Georgiana publicly unless he was compensated for his silence and compensated well.

In short, he demanded money.

An exorbitant amount of money.

More money than Darcy could reasonably afford to pay.

The first six letters were consigned to the fire the moment Darcy had finished reading them, erasing all evidence of their existence, and ensuring Georgiana's name—and his own—remained untarnished for the time being. The last two, however, were a very different matter. Feeling vulnerable and utterly helpless, he had slammed his fist against the wall with such force a crack appeared in the plaster. Then, after swallowing the bile in his throat, he cursed Wickham to hell and locked both letters away in his writing desk until he could think coherently and decide what, if anything, ought to be done. Thus far, he had not mentioned so much as one word of Wickham's letters to Colonel Fitzwilliam, but it appeared as though he would not be able to avoid doing so much longer.

Being an officer as well as a gentleman, Fitzwilliam would want to call the disgusting reprobate out; but violence, even in the name of honour, had never been Darcy's way. Neither did he want to see his cousin lose his commission or worse: face imprisonment or be hanged. If he had learned anything in the last eight-and-twenty years of his life, it was that sinking to Wickham's level was not worth the trouble or the risk.

But what could be done?

Darcy had no bloody idea.

Just thinking about the entire sordid business made him sick with apprehension and rage.

To subdue his mounting agitation, as well as remind himself that Georgiana was in Hertfordshire, safe and happy and well, he observed her closely as she selected a long length of velvet ribbon the colour of dark chocolate, then pointed out a second ribbon in a similar colour and proceeded to compare their texture, their fineness, and their weight.

Beside her, Miss Lydia nodded her head as though in understanding while Miss Catherine offered her own observations. Georgiana smiled. Despite the quiet, sober tone of her voice, both of Elizabeth's sisters appeared to be paying her rapt attention. The boisterousness and impatience Darcy had come to expect from them was nowhere to be found. To his consternation, the girls were getting on remarkably well.

The audible sigh that escaped him was one of annoyance as much as relief.

It was clear from the direction written on Wickham's letters he believed Darcy was presently in Derbyshire. If he were to go there with the intent of demanding payment for his complicity and find Pemberley without its master, London would be his next stop. For that reason, Darcy had no choice but to extend his stay in Hertfordshire until he could devise some sort of plan to put a permanent end to Wickham's treachery.

Despite his reluctance to have his sister form a more lasting, intimate connexion with Elizabeth's sisters, Darcy was not heartless, nor was he blind to the possible advantages to all three girls should he allow Georgiana to continue the acquaintance while they remained in the area. It appeared they would be there for some duration; having a friend or two her own age would do her a world of good.

Briefly shutting his eyes, he sighed again, this time in resignation.

Then he steeled himself, crossed the room with a determined stride, and invited Miss Lydia and Miss Catherine to join them for tea.

TWELVE

⟨◈⟩

Circumstances change, opinions alter.

THAT MORNING, JANE'S HEALTH HAD UNDERGONE SUCH A marked improvement as to enable her to leave her bedchamber that evening. While Elizabeth was delighted for her, she was equally delighted for herself, as it meant she would be able to return home sooner rather than later. While she could not repine Mr Bingley's kindness and generosity or find fault with the beauty and comfort of Netherfield Park, she missed being at Longbourn. She missed her noisy, affectionate family. She missed walking her favourite paths, reading her favourite books, and sleeping in her own bed. Elizabeth was ready to go home.

Once the supper table was cleared and the ladies removed to the drawing room, she returned upstairs for Jane. Amidst the anticipation of passing a pleasant evening with her friends, Jane had forgotten her shawl on the bed. Fearing she would become chilled, Mr Bingley declared he would send a maid to retrieve it, but Elizabeth requested that he not. To dispatch a servant to do that which she was glad to do herself made little sense. The day had been long and uneventful, she had remained indoors for the entirety of it, and she was desperate for employment. Dinner—an exercise in restraint in and of itself—had only exacerbated her impatience for physical exertion, as had Mrs Hurst's insipid observations and Miss Bingley's disdainful little asides.

Mr Bingley's adoring gaze and happy, attentive manners promised her sister would want for nothing in her absence, even as his own sisters exclaimed over her and spouted inane pleasantries that made Elizabeth want to roll her eyes. As Miss Bingley affected an air of interest and demanded 'dear Jane' regale them with an account of how she had spent her day, Elizabeth took her leave.

Finally free of the superior sisters, she ascended the stairs as rapidly as her legs would carry her. Imagining Miss Bingley's horrified countenance at such a want of proper, ladylike behaviour brought a smile to Elizabeth's face. She reached the first floor in lighter spirits, carefully smoothed her skirts, and crossed the carpeted corridor to her sister's bedchamber at a more respectable pace.

Upon entering the room, Jane's shawl was not to be found on the bed. After searching the closet, the dresser, and even the floor, Elizabeth discovered it at last in the sitting room, discarded on the couch. She gathered it up, shook it out, folded it, and sighed. Returning to the drawing room held little appeal at present.

Hugging the shawl to her breast, she walked to the window and peered at the blackness beyond. No stars graced the night sky, only a sliver of the waning moon. Despite dozens of torches lining both sides of the drive, it was dark; so dark she could barely make out the trees swaying in the periphery. The long line of flames danced and curled with the wind, flickering and flaring and then calming. It was a seemingly endless cycle, mesmerising and soothing in equal measure.

It was then that a coach entered the drive. It was a handsome conveyance—large and elegant, with a dark, gleaming finish. It slowed as it neared the house and rolled to a stop at the front steps. The horses were handsome as well—perfectly matched in size, temperament, and colour. All four made a show of tossing their heads and blowing thick clouds of vapour from their nostrils that indicated the temperature had grown considerably colder than it was that afternoon.

While the driver tugged on the reins from the seat at the front, a liveried footman jumped down from the perch on the back and opened the door. Darcy alighted, raised his eyes to the window where Elizabeth stood watch, and acknowledged her presence with a slight bow.

Elizabeth's eyes widened in surprise. The gesture was entirely unexpected, as unexpected as his having noticed her standing there in the first place. She was, after all, a tiny, lone figure ensconced on the first floor, framed by one of nearly a dozen windows. Before she could acknowledge his gallantry, Darcy's attention shifted to his sister. Accepting Miss Darcy's proffered hand, he assisted her as she alighted from the carriage, tucked her hand into the crook of his arm, and escorted her up the steps and into the house.

The monotonous evening Elizabeth had anticipated suddenly brightened.

With the Darcys' return came the prospect of interesting discourse and a reprieve, however temporary, from Miss Bingley's supercilious looks and veiled criticisms. Elizabeth checked her appearance in the looking glass, tucked a loose curl back into place, then quit the room and made her way towards the staircase with the sensation of butterflies fluttering in her stomach.

Much to Miss Bingley's dismay, Mr and Miss Darcy had not dined at Netherfield that evening. They had accepted an invitation to dine at Longbourn instead. How in the world such an unlikely arrangement had come to pass was a mystery that Elizabeth had yet to solve. Each time Darcy had dined with her family his mien had been dour, especially during his prior visit when he had been awarded the seat of honour at the supper table—the one to the right of her mother's.

On that night, Mrs Bennet had barely ceased speaking long enough to draw breath. God only knew what topic she had chosen to expound upon until the dishes were cleared from the table and the ladies withdrew. It was doubtful Darcy had welcomed any discourse extolling her favourites: gossip, matchmaking, and eligible young men. On the few occasions Elizabeth was able to glance at him without fear of drawing the attention of her own dinner companions, his countenance appeared graver and more implacable than ever. As the meal wore on, Elizabeth did not know what mortified her more: her mother's incessant chatter, or Darcy's increasingly terse replies.

To make matters worse, the house itself had been over-crowded and hot and full of noisy, spirited neighbours, the officers had drunk too much wine, and Lydia and Kitty, being in their father's house, were even more spirited than usual. Before the card tables were brought out, Darcy had made his escape.

Meaning to deliver an impertinent reprimand and encourage him to re-join the other guests, Elizabeth abandoned her friends and went in search of him. At length, she discovered him in the smallest room in the house, nursing a headache. Taking pity on him, she offered him tea, and privacy, and a maid to serve him, but Darcy requested her company instead.

I have seen nothing of you tonight.

He had uttered those words quietly but sincerely, and Elizabeth had been inordinately pleased to hear them. And so, she returned as discreetly as possible with the tea things and remained with him in the little parlour at the back of the house, ignoring a lifetime of propriety in the process.

For nearly an hour they sat before the fire and spoke of Pemberley while sipping chamomile tea. No one, not even her father, noticed their absence. At the time, Elizabeth could not decide whether she ought to feel grateful or affronted. Later, she decided on the former. The stain of compromise was not a stigma she aspired to obtain; nor did she desire a forced marriage, not even to a gentleman so perfectly suited to her in temperament and taste as Darcy. Elizabeth had liked him then, more than any other gentleman of her acquaintance. Now, every feeling of amity she harboured for him, every bit of admiration and esteem, had evolved into love.

The marble staircase loomed, and Elizabeth began her descent, taking each step in rapid succession. At the bottom, she crossed the main anteroom, passed through a second, smaller room, and entered a long, elaborately painted corridor. At the end of it, the drawing room door, with its elegant framework and gilded trim, stood ajar. Elizabeth slowed her pace and then stopped altogether as Miss Bingley's voice floated towards her with a clarity that was shocking.

"...cannot imagine what reason you would possibly have to go to Longbourn, sir! Surely, there can be little inducement to dine elsewhere when such friends await you at Netherfield."

Darcy's voice was pitched lower, and was quieter, but his words were as easily discerned as Miss Bingley's. "I apologise if my accepting the invitation on such short notice inconvenienced you or caused offence. I assure you it was unconsciously done."

"Pray think nothing of it," Miss Bingley replied. Her tone was rich and cloying and implied an intimacy between them that made Elizabeth dislike her even more. "I am not the least bit offended, only concerned for your poor sister. Miss Darcy is used to the very best society. I fear she must be quite undone after suffering such an evening with persons who are so far beneath her in situation and consequence. The youngest girls, especially are—"

"Quite young yet," said Darcy. "Given time and firmer guidance, their manners will likely improve."

"Do you truly think so? I, for one, cannot share your optimism. Why, just look at their mother!"

"Their mother—"

"Set her sights on Charles from the very beginning. She is a fortune hunter, and I am sorry to say, as mercenary as they come."

"No more so than any lady of the *ton,*" Darcy remarked in clipped tones. "Despite Mrs Bennet's aspirations for her daughters, I have found her to be a considerate and gracious hostess. Miss Bennet and Miss Elizabeth are both, inarguably, excellent young women who are a credit to her."

Miss Bingley laughed almost condescendingly. "How droll you have become, Mr Darcy!"

"I am perfectly serious, Miss Bingley."

Anything Miss Bingley had to say in reply went unheard as Elizabeth turned abruptly and marched back the way she had come. She was mortified and indignant and in danger of losing her composure. Hugging Jane's shawl more tightly to her breast, she pressed her back against the panelled wainscoting of the anteroom with a huff. While she was by no means oblivious to her family's faults, to overhear those whom she loved being disparaged by Miss Bingley at such a moment stung. If the hour was not so late and Jane had not that morning just recovered from her cold, Elizabeth would pen a note to her father, begging him to convey them back to Longbourn that instant. Instead, she took a much-needed moment to rein in her temper.

The effort chafed and, unable to remain still as she contemplated Miss Bingley and her dislike of all things Bennet, she began to pace from one end of the room to the other. Miss Bingley had shown herself to be rude, condescending, and above her company on multiple occasions. Why then, did hearing the woman espouse her insufferable opinions on this evening discompose her to such an extent? Was it because Elizabeth had not expected to overhear them? Or was it because Miss Bingley had disclosed them to Darcy?

Beyond a shadow of doubt, it was the latter more so than the former.

She bit her lip. Much to her chagrin, Darcy was no stranger to her family's shortcomings, having witnessed them himself on countless occasions. It was entirely likely he had witnessed them anew not an hour ago. The possibility that her family had once again behaved poorly while in company with him tied her stomach in knots. Yet, instead of agreeing with what Miss Bingley had espoused, he had defended her sisters. He had complimented her mother. And without Miss Bingley having so much as mentioned either Elizabeth or Jane, he had honoured them as well.

However low Miss Bingley's opinion of her family, Darcy had not remained silent or impassive when she had voiced it. He had spoken in their favour, and he had even sounded indignant on their behalf.

Abandoning the anteroom, Elizabeth headed towards the drawing room a second time.

As before, Miss Bingley's voice preceded her as Elizabeth approached. She wondered whether the woman had any idea her voice carried, or whether she would even care if she were suddenly found out.

"...but I suppose there is not much in the way of truly refined beauty to be found in these little country backwaters. By the by, you must tell me what your uncle, the earl, has to say regarding your favourite, for I dare not presume he will approve of your choice. Then again," she said with an intimate little laugh, "perhaps an arch look or two from such fine eyes will soon persuade him otherwise."

Elizabeth pushed the door open and entered the room.

While Darcy appeared to be glaring at the carpet and noticed her not at all, that was not the case with Miss Bingley. The moment she beheld Elizabeth her eyes widened perceptibly, but then she looked much as she ever did—a perfect blend of refinement and hauteur.

"Miss Eliza," she exclaimed. "Whatever are you about this evening, scampering through corridors and bursting into rooms? We did not so much as hear your approach, did we, Mr Darcy? Perhaps you ought to fasten bells to your slippers, so you do not scare unsuspecting persons out of their wits." She laughed at what she likely perceived to be her own cleverness and placed her hand upon her lacy fichu. "You gave me quite a fright, my dear! It really was most ungenerous of you." Assuming a coy smile, she addressed Darcy. "What say you, sir, to such unseemly behaviour? It is, after all, hardly the way of the fashionable ladies we are acquainted with in town."

Darcy's entire demeanour, from the hard set of his jaw to his impossibly stiff posture, betrayed his annoyance with the woman. "Hardly."

In his pronouncement of that one word, Elizabeth discerned the full measure of his impatience and dissatisfaction, but there was also a subtle, underlying note of sarcasm as well. There was nothing subtle about the way he abruptly and rudely turned his back to Miss Bingley, nor in the exaggerated, haughty tone he adopted when he said to Elizabeth, "Pay heed, madam, for not every lady is so fortunate as to possess your fortitude. While I cannot in good conscience suggest wearing a bell, I shall not scruple to recommend that you make your presence known in the future, else the populace of Hertfordshire, and Miss

Bingley especially, suffers unduly from a lack of awareness."

And then Darcy blatantly and deliberately rolled his eyes.

Elizabeth stared at him in amazement. That he had delivered such a speech at such a time—a speech overflowing with words and sentiments so similar to those she had once uttered to him—made it difficult to keep her countenance, especially while Darcy's eyes remained fixed upon her in such a pointed manner, as though challenging her to say something equally provoking in turn.

Before she could manage to string two words together in reply, Miss Bingley, who was apparently none the wiser given the sardonic tone of Darcy's speech, said, "What a way you have with words, Mr Darcy! I daresay our guest will have no recourse but to heed such excellent advice as you have imparted. You must see, Miss Eliza, what a champion I have in Mr Darcy. Such presence of mind he has—and so gallant! He is, of course, never wrong."

"Never wrong, indeed," Elizabeth remarked smoothly, holding Darcy's steady gaze with her own. Rather than delivering a dose of humility, as Miss Bingley had likely intended, her little speech only made Elizabeth want to laugh. She raised one impertinent brow at Darcy instead and, with as much solemnity as she could muster, said, "I find myself, Mr Darcy, in the unenviable position of begging your pardon. Should Miss Bingley be rendered insensible and witless on account of my unfashionable comportment, it would be a great tragedy for our little country society. I certainly would not desire it."

"Nor would I," he replied. One corner of his mouth twitched, as though fighting the urge to smile.

Elizabeth was forced to bite the inside of her cheek to keep from smiling herself. *Poor Miss Bingley!* If Netherfield's mistress only knew that the gentleman whom she so admired was making fun of her right under her nose!

"How good of you, Miss Eliza," said the lady in question, "to be so reasonable. The world will thank you for it, I am sure."

Darcy rolled his eyes once again at this pronouncement, but Elizabeth assumed an unaffected smile. "I have been called many things, Miss Bingley," she replied sweetly, "but I am happy to say that unreasonable has never been one of them." She indicated Jane's shawl. "Pray excuse me. I must deliver this to Jane before she catches a chill."

She sent Darcy a brief, arch look as she curtseyed, but, before she had taken two steps in her sister's direction, Darcy stepped forward and lightly, unobtrusively, touched the back of her arm.

"I am very glad, Miss Elizabeth, to see Miss Bennet looking so well. Your sister is extremely fortunate to have such a devoted and affectionate nurse."

Darcy's gaze was warm, as warm as his voice. As warm as his touch. His proximity, as well as the liberty he had taken—and in front of Miss Bingley no less—startled Elizabeth to such a degree that she could do little more than stare at him.

"Speaking of sisters," said Miss Bingley, ignoring Elizabeth as she slipped her hand into the crook of Darcy's arm, effectively recalling his attention to herself. "You must tell me, sir, how is your own dear sister? I have not seen her since this afternoon, when you walked to Meryton together. I wonder what you could have been thinking, dragging her all that way in the cold! Although we are in the country, taking your carriage would not have been remiss. I fear, should we stay too long in Hertfordshire, that you and Charles will be in some danger of turning into savages!"

Darcy uttered a curt, "Excuse me," and withdrew his arm

from her grasp. Before Miss Bingley could so much as blink at him, he bid both ladies a good night and quit the room.

&

The little porcelain mantel clock in Elizabeth's bedchamber chimed twice, but sleep eluded her. With a frustrated sigh, she threw off the counterpane and reached for her discarded dressing gown. After slipping it on and cinching the waist, she lit a candle in the chamberstick beside the bed with a spill from the mantel, opened the door, and quietly made her way through the darkened hall towards the staircase. The carpet beneath her stockinged feet provided comfort, but there was a chill in the air her nightclothes did little to dispel. Holding her candle aloft, Elizabeth made her way down the stairs with care, determined to retrieve her abandoned book from the drawing room and return to her bedchamber as soon as may be.

She had not counted on hearing the pianoforte being played as she approached.

The music itself was incredibly soft, almost sombre—a quiet, existential movement, as soothing as it was evocative. Although beautifully executed, this concerto bore no resemblance to the vigorous, more complex pieces Miss Bingley and Mrs Hurst favoured. It could only be Miss Darcy on the instrument.

Elizabeth frowned. She had seen nothing of the girl that evening and had wondered—and worried—whether her visit to Longbourn had been pleasant, or distressing, as Miss Bingley had supposed. Knowing how much Darcy's sister had looked forward to being a guest there, Elizabeth hoped all her family had made her feel welcome and easy, despite their unfashionable manners and penchant for disorder and gossip.

The music swelled to a crescendo, then ebbed and flowed

into a more delicate, lighter refrain. The movement, its simplicity, and the emotions it evoked were poignant and lovely. Haunting and heartbreaking, but lovely all the same.

Elizabeth rested her head against the doorframe and closed her eyes. Miss Darcy's talent was as extraordinary as her performance was flawless, but her taste tended towards melancholia. There was something about this piece especially that not only moved one's audience but quietly, almost unobtrusively, overwhelmed. If Elizabeth felt such ineffable longing within her heart simply from listening to Miss Darcy's playing, she could only imagine the powerful feelings Miss Darcy experienced each time she gave herself over to such beautiful, sorrowful music.

The music ended gradually, naturally, and Elizabeth expelled a measured breath. She felt emotional, almost vulnerable in a sense, and hesitated for several minutes, uncertain as to what she ought to do. The last thing she wanted was to intrude upon Miss Darcy's privacy, but neither did she feel as though she should leave the girl to herself. The piece she had chosen had spoken of sadness and longing. It had spoken of loneliness. Surely, this was not an instance where politesse should be observed. Turning her back on her shy, soft-spoken young friend and leaving her to herself would not only be unkind, but unfeeling.

Resolved, Elizabeth placed her hand upon the doorhandle and opened the door.

THIRTEEN

༺✦༻

There are very few who have heart enough
to be really in love without encouragement.

IN THE DIM INTERIOR OF BINGLEY'S DRAWING ROOM,
Darcy closed his eyes. The final notes of the movement hung
in the air, slowly fading until the only sound that remained
was the occasional brittle tinkling of the coals in the hearth.
Slowly, almost reluctantly, he lifted his fingers from the keys
and opened his eyes. Rather than easing his nerves, the music
had only served to further agitate him.

Before he could stop himself, he combed his fingers
through his hair, disrupting his man's meticulous efforts. If his
father could see him now, he would take him to task and
remind him that a gentleman's appearance ought to be impeccable—as impeccable as his comportment and his reputation.

His father's own reputation had been nothing short of
irreproachable. George Darcy was considered by all who
knew him to be an excellent man and a benevolent, liberal
master. He may not have understood Darcy in all the ways
his mother had, but he had loved him. He had trusted his son
to make intelligent, informed decisions and to do what was
right to be done. If he had not, he would never have left
Pemberley, its legacy, its people, and its future in Darcy's
care.

Feeling peevish and infuriatingly sentimental, Darcy wondered what had possessed him to choose Bach's transcription of Alessandro Marcello's *Concerto in D Minor*. He had played it adagio, and its gentle notes and sombre chords had done nothing but further exacerbate his doleful mood. With a frustrated exhalation, he tugged impatiently at his cravat. His coat had been discarded long ago and he was in his shirt-sleeves—another offence of which his fastidious father would have disapproved. Unless a gentleman was in his bedchamber, there was no reason he ought to be without his coat, regardless of the hour. Even now, Darcy could hear his father's deep, steady voice reminding him of his importance in the world, his station in life, and the responsibilities attached to both:

"You must always endeavour to set an example for your lessers, Fitzwilliam. You must set an example for George."

Darcy snorted derisively. *A fat lot of good* that *had done—setting an example for George Wickham!* He would have done better to have cut all ties with the blackguard and exposed him long ago, but he had not. Affection for his father and, later, respect for his father's memory, had prevented him time and again. It was no longer respect that kept Darcy from exposing his father's favourite to the scorn of the world but his fear of exposing Georgiana. Darcy ran his hand over his mouth. He had loved his father, respected his father, and endeavoured to please his father, but, by God, he wished he had revealed the true extent of Wickham's depravity to him when he had the chance!

Scowling, he reached for the untouched glass of port he had abandoned on the lid of Bingley's Broadwood grand, raised it to his mouth, and took a generous sip. Would that George Wickham and his reprehensible demands would go to the devil so he could be free of him once and for all!

Darcy swallowed another mouthful of port and endeav-

THE LUXURY OF SILENCE

oured to suppress his rising temper. As much as he wanted to cut out Wickham's vile tongue, age and experience had taught him the use of violence rarely solved problems; if anything, it created more. With considerable effort, he forced all thoughts of Wickham, his immorality, and his betrayal from his mind and focused his attention on Bingley's pianoforte instead.

The sound it produced was incomparable, and its intentional lines and sensuous curves were a work of art. Darcy ran his hand over the lid. Day after day, the rich warmth of the wood, the highly polished finish, and the salient smoothness of the keys had called to him. It was on this night, however—nearly a month since his arrival in Hertfordshire—that he had finally surrendered to its lure. It was the first time Darcy had played in nearly six months.

As always, his performance was flawless. His mother, who had recognised his potential when he was but four years old, had taught him every aspect of proficiency from rudimentary fingering to the most intricate pieces and complex chords. It went without saying that she would have been as delighted with his performance now as she was when he was a boy. His father, who had placed far more importance on duty and consequence, would have viewed his playing in the same, rigid light he always had—as a thorough waste of a man's time.

No longer of a mind to sit still, Darcy drained his glass, abandoned his seat at the instrument, and strode to the hearth to stir the coals. There was a chill in the room that had begun to seep into his bones, but he was not yet ready to retire. Retiring meant a fitful night's repose. It meant vivid dreams where his dearest wishes were realised, only to be cruelly ripped from his grasp. He shifted his attention to Solomon, curled before the fire on Miss Bingley's prized Persian rug.

The dog raised his head as his master approached. His

large, soulful eyes followed Darcy's every movement, and his whiplike tail thumped happily against the floor.

Despite his incongruent mood, Darcy could not help but smile at his dog. After stirring the coals and arranging several logs in the grate, he got down on one knee to scratch behind Solomon's ears.

With a low, contented growl, Solomon leaned into Darcy's touch; but something across the room caught his attention and he was suddenly on his feet, his long, curious nose straining towards the door.

Darcy rose as well and placed his hand on the side of the dog's neck, restraining him. "Solomon," he commanded, his tone quiet but firm. "Stay." He looked towards the door and saw the soft, incandescent glow of a candle, a slight figure, and a most unexpected but beloved face—*Elizabeth*.

Solomon's tail beat an energetic tempo against his master's leg.

"Stay," Darcy bid him again, but he was distracted—by Elizabeth's presence, by her appearance, and by the quickening of his own traitorous heart.

It was habit, rather than any conscious, gentlemanly notion of gallantry, that induced him to bow, but his execution lacked its usual fluidity and polish. Darcy felt a momentary prick of discomfiture. *Will she never cease to discompose me in some manner or other?*

Given the depth of his feelings for her, he suspected it was entirely likely that Elizabeth Bennet would affect him profoundly until the day he died. Innocent though she was, he had always found her bewitching, but this—*this* was beyond the pale. She wore no gown, no wrap, no jewels, but stood before him clad only in her nightclothes, and her hair, which was usually arranged with such care, was loose and tumbling past her shoulders in a riot of dark curls. She looked like a fey princess—a temptress straight from the pages of some romantic poem. She looked as she had the very first time Darcy had ever seen her, standing at the edge of Oakham Mount.

His eyes travelled the length of her, from her unbound hair to the tips of her toes. They were barely visible, peeking from beneath the ruffled hem of her modest nightshift. Darcy swallowed audibly but, try as he would, he could not bring himself to avert his eyes. The picture she presented was the most alluring combination of innocence and dishabille he had ever seen.

Dear Lord, she is beautiful! Beautiful, guileless, and impertinent...

And, for better or worse, she was in possession of his heart.

In that moment, Darcy knew beyond any shadow of doubt he would never want another woman so long as Elizabeth Bennet existed in the world. He wondered if he were to suddenly abandon propriety and cross the room, take her in his arms, and kiss her, would her heart pound as fiercely as his? Would she hold him close? Would she meet his passion with her own? Or would she recoil from him and ring a peal over him and, in the most severe and painful terms, remind him that they were friends and she had no interest in becoming more?

Before Darcy had met her, the idea that any woman would reject him had never crossed his mind. But Elizabeth was different, as was evident in the way she spoke to him, teased him, and held him accountable for his incivility—however unintentional—every time she perceived he had given offence. She placed an inordinate amount of value on honesty, forthrightness, and affection. It was doubtful she would agree to marry any man who did not value those same qualities. Neither would she tolerate a husband lacking in intelligence or a man whom she could not respect.

The sweet, rich timbre of her voice recalled Darcy to the present with an abruptness for which he was woefully unprepared.

"I believe you have long been desiring my absence. Forgive me, Mr Darcy. It was not my intent to intrude upon your privacy. I came for my book and...I..." Her voice faltered, and she fell silent. "Pray excuse me. I should return to my room."

It took Darcy a moment to comprehend what she had said to him. It was only when she turned towards the door that he recognised her intent to leave. He was loath to part with her. He was always loath to part with her, but most especially now, when providence had been so generous as to grant him time alone with her. The last occasion they had spent more than a few moments together without interruption had been a week ago, at Longbourn. Then, his head had ached. Now, the only ache he felt was within his heart.

"Please, stay," he said to her, taking care to keep his voice low so as not to awaken the house. "The pleasure of your company is most welcome. Allow me to offer you a chair by the fire, Miss Elizabeth. Or perhaps you would like a glass of port. Should you take a chill and become ill, I would be grieved indeed."

When she neither thanked him nor readily agreed to his invitation but hesitated in silence, he felt a pang of disappointment. When she stepped away from the door and moved farther into the room, he felt a glimmer of hope; but it was short lived.

"It is the dead of night, and we are alone, sir. While I appreciate your offer, you know I cannot possibly accept it. My remaining would be inappropriate."

She was correct, of course, but they had been alone before. Darcy recalled each moment with sincere pleasure. Granted, Elizabeth had not been wearing her nightclothes on those occasions, but he had been alone with her nevertheless. Once, when they had found themselves in a secluded glen on an unseasonably sunny morning, she had told Darcy he could be charming when he put forth the effort to do so.

He dearly hoped he was capable of charming her now.

Solomon emitted a pitiful little whine, seemingly torn between obeying his master and longing to greet the woman he adored.

Darcy inclined his head towards his impatient companion. "As you can see, we have a very capable and willing chaperon. If you will not remain for my sake, pray remain for Solomon's, lest he believes you consider him unworthy of performing such an office. Otherwise, I fear his fragile self-esteem will suffer a blow from which it may never recover."

He was inordinately pleased when her lips twitched, lending her serious mien some levity. "For shame, sir," she chided, all the while endeavouring to repress her smile. "I mean no disrespect to Solomon, but I have known him nearly a month and, in that time, it has been my observation that he not only possesses self-assurance in abundance, but he is exceptionally prone to distraction."

"We are fortunate, then, that Miss Bingley's drawing room is conveniently devoid of rabbits and squirrels."

Elizabeth's twitching lips gave way to laughter. "How incorrigible you are tonight, Mr Darcy! Far more so than usual. I cannot imagine what has inspired such a transformation, but I certainly cannot repine seeing you thus. Much as it pains me to admit it, incorrigibility suits you."

Darcy wanted to tell her that *she* suited him; instead, he inclined his head and returned her smile. "My incorrigibility, madam, is owed entirely to you and your impertinence. You are an excellent teacher. As for Solomon, he has grown as fond of you as I have, and therefore will ensure you come to no harm. If you will remember, we have been alone before. Many times."

Her smile dimmed. "I remember. But you know, as well as do I, that our being alone on those occasions does not make our being alone now any less improper. You are in your shirt-sleeves after all, and I am...even less formally attired."

Although it was dark, and Elizabeth was across the room, Darcy was certain her complexion must be painted with the most exquisite blush. He stared at her for what must have been a full minute in silence. The prospect of relinquishing the pleasure of her company was a bitter elixir to swallow. With some effort, he reminded himself he was not a petulant schoolboy being denied a treat, but a grown man—a gentle-man. He ought to behave like one and yield to her. He ought to insist that she return to her bed. And yet, he found his gentlemanly principles were currently at war with his desire to spend time with the woman he loved. The very notion of sending her away when he craved her society so fervently was repellent to him, even if it was what was right to be done.

"Be that as it may, it is my dearest wish that you remain, at least for a little while. To be at Longbourn, surrounded by your parents and sisters, and without you, was not...I am afraid I was ill prepared for the experience."

Elizabeth cast her eyes to the carpet. "I hope they did not tax you or Miss Darcy unduly. As a collective, they are a tour de force. Even the heartiest constitutions are often over-whelmed by my family's liveliness. I can only imagine your poor sister, who rarely attends any sort of—"

"No," he said at once, seeing he had explained himself poorly. "No. You misunderstand me, Miss Elizabeth. All your family were hospitable and welcoming. Your mother, espe-cially, treated Georgiana with a vast deal of kindness, and me as well. My sister was delighted with the visit. It was not the actions of your family for which I was ill prepared. I was ill prepared for what I felt being at Longbourn without you."

He paused to clear his throat. When he resumed speaking, his voice was lower, his tone was softer, and his heart that much fuller. "What I am trying, so inarticulately, to say is that I missed you. While your family was everything gracious and civil, I missed hearing your laughter sprinkled amidst theirs. I missed your witticisms. I missed seeing your smile. I missed having you beside me—teasing me, encouraging me, advising me to be more patient and more affable than I have been on prior occasions. Tonight, when I returned to Netherfield, I had hoped we would have been able to spend some minutes together, but that was not the case. Instead, I have seen nothing of you, and I have not liked it."

"You were missed as well," Elizabeth confessed quietly. "Without your intelligent discourse and sound observations, I am afraid dinner was..."

"Tedious," he remarked, "and interminably long. I am certain you suffered far more so than did I. Your mother, as you know, sets an excellent table, and she aims to please all her guests. Miss Bingley, however, has not always treated you with the kindness or respect you deserve."

He was surprised when the barest intimation of a smile lifted the corners of her mouth. "Not always, no, but she is *tolerable,* I suppose, for the most part."

Her ability to make light of situations which must, to some extent, pain her, never failed to impress him. "I have very much regretted not having a moment alone with you this evening."

"And I with you. Of course, you have uttered a similar profession once before, when you dined at Longbourn last week."

"And, as I recall quite clearly, you were generous enough to oblige me, despite our being much alone."

"I took pity on you. You had a headache and were feeling poorly. It would have been a cruelty to leave you to yourself."

"And so, it would be an unkindness to abandon me now. You may call me selfish, but the idea of relinquishing your society, when duty and affection for our dear sisters have parted us today, leaves much to be desired. I have passed a fitful night, and I am at loose ends. Miss Bingley tried my patience exceedingly. Please," he implored. "Stay."

For what felt like a small eternity, Elizabeth regarded him in silence. The flame of her candle flickered and danced with each expelled breath, casting her pretty features in ghostly relief.

Darcy's fingers toyed with his ring, his mind racing as he watched her in turn. She would tell him no this time, and her answer would ring with finality. She would deny him, turn from him, and leave.

At long last Elizabeth did turn from him, but it was not with the intent of abandoning him as he feared. Instead, she walked to the door and quietly shut it, in effect, ensuring their privacy while reducing their risk of discovery. The click of the latch was unusually loud in the dim interior of the room. There was an ultimacy in accordance with the sound it made. A permanence that resonated within Darcy's very soul.

As though Elizabeth sensed it too, she did not come to him but chose to remain where she was—across the room with her back pressed to the door, clutching her candle with one hand as her other fidgeted with the belt of her dressing gown.

She had never looked more lovely.

Nor more uncertain.

That she had decided to remain with him despite the impropriety of the situation made Darcy feel wanted and cared for in a way he had not since his mother's death. It was as though his happiness meant something to Elizabeth, just as hers meant something to him. Were they to be discovered now, he would marry her without hesitation or reserve—for her sake, for Georgiana's sake, and for his own most of all. But Elizabeth knew nothing of his heart. She had no idea how much he had come to admire and love her. For that reason alone, he could not help but love her even more.

"Thank you," said Darcy softly.

Her eyes were fixed, not on him, but on Bingley's Broadwood grand. In lieu of a reply, she teased him. "It is no wonder you were so underwhelmed by my playing, Mr Darcy. Perhaps, the next time the opportunity presents itself you ought to consider taking my place at the instrument. I am certain the neighbourhood, and Miss Bingley especially, shall thank you for it."

So, she had heard him, then.

A wry smile tugged at Darcy's mouth. "I have no wish to usurp your place, now or ever. I have neither the need, nor the desire to exhibit, especially before Miss Bingley."

"While I perfectly comprehend your wish to avoid Miss Bingley's raptures, you play so beautifully. It would be cruel to deny your friends the pleasure of hearing you, especially at the expense of having to listen to *my* unequal attempts."

Darcy rolled his eyes. While he was pleased beyond measure that she had enjoyed his performance, he was in no mood to discuss his talent, nor his mother's, nor to explain his father's disapprobation of his playing. Not tonight, when he already felt so much. "Presently, you are the only friend of mine who possesses any knowledge of my ability, therefore, yours is the only pleasure that is of concern to me. By now, you must know that I would deny you nothing, so long as it is within my power to give it, but I beg you not to speak of my playing to another soul. It is far too personal to me. I have no desire to share it with the world, only with those whom I hold most dear."

He extended his hand to her then, a silent entreaty for her to come to him, but Solomon, who had waited so patiently throughout their exchange, misinterpreted the gesture. Without warning, he abandoned his master and raced across the room with his tongue lolling out of his mouth.

"Solomon, heel," Darcy called in alarm and frustration.

Although his command was not enough to curb Solomon's determination, it was enough to make him check his exuberance before he reached Elizabeth. He came to a stop just short of where she stood and sat expectantly at her feet, panting happily as he gazed at her.

With an indulgent smile, she greeted Darcy's ill-behaved dog in her usual way—by lavishing affection upon him, whispering nonsense to him, then gently but firmly calling him to order. It was fortunate the Great Dane had not jumped upon her or else the entire house might have been set ablaze.

Still grinning at his dog, Elizabeth straightened, but when her eyes returned to Darcy her smile faded. Then she simply stared, much in the same manner as Darcy was presently staring at her.

Realisation dawned as he recalled he was still in his shirt-sleeves. Muttering an apology, he retrieved his coat from the wingback chair by the fire, where he had tossed it hours earlier. It was snug fitting and fashionable, which had made removing it difficult. Thankfully, donning it required less effort. "Forgive me," he said as he tugged it into place and fastened the covered buttons. "I am not usually prone to such informality when I am not in my own home. I hope I have not offended you. It is the last thing I would wish."

"You were hardly expecting company at such an hour, sir, never mind the company of a lady. Pray think no more of it." It was then, after he was more properly attired, that Elizabeth ceased her vigil by the door and moved to join him.

Solomon, ever her devoted servant, padded after her.

When she reached the pianoforte, she stopped to admire it with a wistful smile. "It is a wonderful instrument. The same can also be said of your playing. I believe your talent may even exceed that of your sister." Setting her chamberstick on the lid, she positioned her fingers on the keys and began to play the first few chords of a short, sweet melody she had sung the other evening at Darcy's request.

"Will you play now?" he asked, coming to stand beside her. "I should dearly like to hear you."

To his consternation, Elizabeth laughed. "No. I would much rather hear you play. Your abilities put my own to shame. Do not dare attempt to deny it, for I happen to know you abhor deceit. Despite your honourable nature, I would not believe you—not in this case."

She raised her eyes to him then, and Darcy, unable to help himself, reached for her hand.

"As you wish," he said, bowing ever so slightly.

After seeing her settled comfortably on the bench, he claimed the spot beside her. The bench was small. While it was by no means the first time that he found himself in such proximity to Elizabeth, it was the first time he had been close enough that her shoulder, her arm, and the length of her thigh brushed his own. The contact sent a shiver through Darcy, one he could not bring himself to regret. In desperate need of a distraction, he moved to the very edge of the bench, cleared his throat, and enquired, "What would you like to hear?"

Elizabeth shook her head. "I have no preference. You may play whatever you wish, and I promise I shall love it."

Her hair was loose, her dressing gown was loose, and she smelled faintly of lavender and some other scent Darcy could not name but which he found incredibly pleasing. He itched to touch her in any manner of inappropriate ways—to sweep her hair aside and comb his fingers through her curls; to press a kiss to her cheek and, perhaps, if he felt particularly bold, to the enticing curve where her neck met her shoulder. Instead, he pressed his fingers to the keys of the Broadwood and began to play Beethoven's *Tenth Piano Sonata in G Major*.

No sooner had he played the first few notes than Elizabeth expressed her delight with his choice. The music was light and pleasing, sometimes energetic, and often delicate. As was his wont, Darcy immersed himself in his playing, but there was no ignoring the woman seated at his side. Her very presence warmed him from within and made him feel as though he could do anything in the world so long as she listened to him, and smiled at him, and comprehended him as she had these weeks—with more clarity and more sensitivity than anyone else.

All too soon, the piece came to an end. Lifting his hands from the keys, Darcy turned towards Elizabeth and felt his heart stutter in his chest. She was so beautiful, so vibrant, so full of heart and joy and life. Her eyes, with their long, inky lashes, were as dark as he had ever seen them. Her lips were full and pink. She was so utterly lovely that he found himself lifting his hand without thought or care and gently brushing a curl from her cheek. He tucked it behind her ear and watched as Elizabeth's complexion flushed with the most beatific colour.

Darcy was charmed. He was enamoured. He was deeply, irrevocably in love. Her blushing countenance, her sweetness, and the expressiveness of her incomparably fine eyes tested his hard-won self-control beyond its limits. It was as though Elizabeth was the moon and he the tide. Try as he would, Darcy was helpless to resist her lure. He felt the warmth radiating from her body. He felt each exhalation of her breath on his face. That he had closed the distance between them to mere inches did not even register in his besotted brain.

"How I adore you," he whispered, giving in to the urge to

caress her hair and her cheek with a featherlight touch of his hand. And then, before he could stop himself, he leaned in and captured her lips in a tender, heartfelt kiss.

It lasted but a moment—the briefest touch of lips—before Elizabeth gasped, and Darcy found himself jerked unceremoniously back to the present.

He released her at once as realisation and alarm sent his heart plummeting towards his stomach.

"Pray forgive me. I had no right to take such liberties." His voice had never sounded so foreign to him—so full of self-castigation and loathing as it did then. How could he have forgotten himself to such an extent? How could he have allowed his baser instincts to override his gentlemanly conduct?

Touching her fingertips to her lips, Elizabeth regarded him with wide-eyed astonishment. That she had not slapped him for his audacity, or berated him, or attempted to quit the room was incredible; but neither had she offered Darcy any sort of encouragement, either before or after the fact.

Eventually, she found her voice. "Why did you do that?"

Darcy averted his eyes. To explain himself would be the equivalent of opening Pandora's Box. He had been inexcusably careless with her, and he had been inordinately selfish. Now, he must answer for it. But what answer was he to give?

Because the moment you entered the room every semblance of rational thought left my brain?

Because you are so very lovely, inside and out, that having you so near makes my heart ache?

Because I have fallen in love with you and have dreamt of kissing you for weeks?

In the end, they were not grand words that Darcy uttered, or romantic words, but honest words. "Because I think of you. I think of you all the time."

He had not believed it was possible for Elizabeth's blush to deepen, but deepen it did before his eyes.

"I daresay it is only natural, as we have become such friends."

Her response to his declaration, so deliberate, almost dismissive, made Darcy's heart ache. Did she honestly consider him her friend and nothing more? He could not bear to think that this woman whom he loved so ardently perceived him in such an innocuous light. He could not bear to think that friendship was all they were destined to share. "We are friends, that is true," he said as he struggled to keep his emotions at bay. "You have become my dearest friend in the world."

He extended his hand to her then, all the while willing her to accept it. More than anything else, he had to know whether Elizabeth intended to hold the liberties he had taken against him. Should she be unable or unwilling to overlook his unconscionable behaviour, he would be devastated. Regardless of whether she loved him or whether her feelings were, in fact, unequal to his for her, Darcy could not imagine his life without her now. In the weeks he had known her, Elizabeth had become necessary to him. Of late, he had imagined her as his wife. He could not imagine having to give her up.

By some miracle, she did not shy away from him as he feared, but slipped her hand into his, clasped it with her own, and applied a firm and steady pressure. In that moment, Darcy was torn between exquisite relief and heart wrenching despair. Although she had given him her hand, and thus some measure of reassurance, she had done so without meeting his eyes.

Darcy grasped her hand tightly. The urge to confess his love was overpowering in its intensity. Though he willed himself to keep his admiration to himself and his composure under regulation, it proved a task easier said than done.

At length, he surrendered to the dictates of his heart. "When I think of you, it is not merely my esteem for you that compels me. It is my admiration of you, my affection for you. It is the love I feel for you—a love that transcends the boundaries of friendship."

In that moment, Darcy dearly wanted to call Elizabeth by her name, but the profound intimacy and privilege attached to it restrained him from doing so. He had taken too many liberties that night, none of which were his by right. He would not claim another; not unless she accepted him. Instead, with his heart in his throat, he said, "I think of sharing my life with you. I think of sharing my love and my secrets and my bed. I think of the children I want to give you, and of growing old with you. And I think of how very happy all of those things would make me."

"I think of you, as well," she admitted in a tremulous voice the moment he had finished. "All the time, in all of those ways."

For the briefest moment Darcy shut his eyes. He was overjoyed and overwhelmed at once. He sent up a silent prayer of thanksgiving, then pressed an enduring kiss to Elizabeth's hand. "There is nothing I want so much as to go to your father this instant. But I understand that my preference for an expedient marriage may not be in accord with your own wishes. Nor am I insensible of all a lady must give over upon entering the marriage state. While a man gains a companion and a lover, a lady must leave her family, her friends, and her home—all that is familiar and dear." He shook his head. "As a lover, I have been unforgivably remiss. We have not courted."

"Have we not?" Her tone was as gentle as her expression was affectionate. "You, sir, are my friend, and are as dear to me as my family. Despite our short acquaintance, we have walked out nearly every day. We have spent countless hours in one another's company and discussed all manner of subjects, from our interests and our hopes to our most deeply held convictions. While there are still aspects of your life with which I am yet unacquainted, in essentials, I believe I know you intimately." The corners of her lips lifted with the hint of a smile, revealing that mixture of archness and sweetness Darcy had always adored in her. "If I have not taken your measure by now, Mr Darcy—if I have not already come to love you—I am afraid it is a hopeless business."

"In that case," he said softly, but with considerable emotion, "know that I love you beyond measure—beyond my wildest dreams." Surrendering to his compulsion to slide his hands deep into her hair, he traced the contour of her cheek with his thumb, then her lips. He touched his forehead to hers and inhaled deeply. Her proximity and her scent and the softness of her skin enchanted him beyond anything he had ever known. "Marry me," he murmured. "Marry me, my wonderful, darling friend, and do me the honour of becoming my wife as soon as may be."

"Yes," Elizabeth replied with an incandescent little laugh, wiping tears from her eyes with an impatience that made Darcy smile. And then, to his immense astonishment and pleasure, she touched his cheek with unexampled gentleness, cradled his face with her hands, and kissed him with as much tenderness as she did in his dreams.

FOURTEEN

ᘓᘒ

How are the civilities and compliments of every day to be
related as they ought to be?

THE FOLLOWING MORNING DAWNED CRISP AND COLD,
and the sky, heaving with clouds, thwarted the appearance of
the sun. Netherfield's grounds were coated with a layer of
frost, but inside the manor house, thick, limestone walls and
cheerful fires ensured its inhabitants were cosy and warm.

Despite having only a few hours of repose, Elizabeth
made her way to the breakfast parlour at her usual hour anticipating the delight of a new day. The time she had spent with
Darcy in the drawing room had exceeded her dreams. As she
recalled his beautiful playing, his tenderness, and his heartfelt
declarations of love, her lips turned upwards in a sentimental
smile. He had kissed her last night, over, and over again, and
the sensation of it—of his mouth on hers, and his hands in her
hair—had awakened an exquisite yearning that made her ache
in the most wonderful, transcendent way.

Even now, the memory of his ardent kisses coupled with
the surprising gentleness of his touch aroused the most beautiful longing for more of the same. Elizabeth brought her
hands to her cheeks, willing her heightened colour to dissipate. Everything he had done had been perfect—perfectly
spoken and perfectly expressed.

Darcy *loved* her.

He would be her husband, and she, his wife.

He would be her companion and her confidant and her lover.

And through it all he would remain her friend—her dearest friend in all the world until death saw fit to part them. They would make a life together, and see the world together, and fill Pemberley's nursery with children conceived of their love. Dear, sweet Georgiana would become her sister, and, in turn, Elizabeth's own sisters would become Darcy's. Her father, she was certain, would come to appreciate his keen intelligence and his dry sense of humour, and her mother...

Elizabeth sighed as she thought of her mother, whose sole mission in life was to see all her daughters married to eligible men. She had sent Jane to Netherfield ahead of a rainstorm with the hope of securing Mr Bingley; instead, a dreadful cold had kept her in bed for the better part of a week and Elizabeth had become engaged to Darcy. Although Mr Bennet would certainly see the irony of her mother's scheming taking such an unexpected turn, her mother would likely be vexed. She was in ecstasy over Mr Bingley's attentions to Jane from the beginning. Darcy, however, had made a poor first impression by insulting Elizabeth and avoiding conversation with most everyone in Hertfordshire. Although Elizabeth was hardly her mother's favourite, she was still her daughter. Mrs Bennet would tolerate no slight against her, despite Darcy's ten thousand a year.

Pausing at the top of the stairs, Elizabeth ran her hand over the smooth, polished marble of the newel post and wondered whether her mother had sincerely behaved graciously yesterday, or whether she continued to hold Darcy's initial offence against him. According to Darcy, her mother had been welcoming; but perhaps he had sought to spare Elizabeth the mortifying truth—that Longbourn's mistress had paid him little notice and even less civility. Elizabeth pursed her lips. Of one thing she was certain: whether Mrs Bennet had forgiven him or not, once she learned Elizabeth was to be the mistress of Pemberley, it was entirely likely her approbation of its income would exceed any lingering disapproval of its master. Hopefully, Darcy would not be present to witness her raptures first-hand.

Cringing as she imagined her mother regaling their neighbours with suppositions of new carriages, pin money, and jewels, Elizabeth descended the stairs and continued towards the breakfast parlour, where she discovered her future husband seated at the table reading the London newspaper. A steaming cup of tea was beside him, and a plate containing a slice of toast and the remnants of what looked to be bacon. Smartly dressed in a light blue coat, Darcy looked even handsomer than usual.

Or perhaps, she mused, *it is simply the knowledge that he is mine.*

She greeted him softly, affectionately. "Good morning, sir."

Darcy was on his feet at once, discarding his newspaper on the table and executing a low bow. His eyes, so warm and intense, inspired feelings that were completely inappropriate for the breakfast table. "Good morning to you, Miss Elizabeth. I hope today finds you well."

A veritable flood of images from their late night together filled her head. She endeavoured to put them aside, but it was easier said than done. "While I am not nearly so well rested as I ought to be, I have nothing to repine. I was so fortunate as to have had the very sweetest of dreams."

Darcy's eyes darkened with a look that was entirely familiar. As there were servants present, there was not much he could say in reply without betraying what had passed between them. For a long moment, he simply stared at her, his gaze determined, steady, and soft. "I, too, experienced the sweetest of dreams. In fact, my contentment was such that I was reluctant to awaken."

"Surely, you must know you have nothing to fear. Not now, or ever. The sweetest dreams, after all, are those whose roots are cultivated by reality."

"Thank you," he told her quietly. "I shall endeavour to remind myself of that with great frequency."

Feeling all the danger of continuing their current conversation, Elizabeth introduced the safest, most innocuous topic she could think of: the weather. "Do you believe we shall see rain before the day is over, or will the sun burst through the clouds before long and brighten this dull weather?"

Glancing towards the window, Darcy cleared his throat. "As of yet, I am uncertain. Hopefully, the weather will continue to hold for a few hours at least. I had thought to take a turn in the park after breaking my fast. I would be honoured if you would consent to join me."

Elizabeth smiled with real pleasure at the prospect. "I can think of nothing I would like better. It has been two days since I have taken any fresh air and exercise. I am afraid being confined to the house for another would try my patience exceedingly."

A slow smile tugged at the corners of Darcy's mouth. "I can well imagine your dissatisfaction. Taking a turn in a drawing room is by no means as liberating as walking in a garden or the woods. Now that your sister is better, I cannot suppose she will have need of you so very often throughout the day. Solomon, of course, will be delighted to hear of Miss Bennet's improved health. It has been too long since he has had the pleasure of your company on a sojourn through the countryside. Regrettably, my own society has tried his patience exceedingly. I fear I am not nearly so indulgent, nor so obliging, in his relentless pursuit of voles."

The picture he painted delighted her, and she laughed. "You may tell Solomon that I look forward to joining him as soon as may be. If he is amenable, and if the weather holds, I shall gladly embark on a long walk this very afternoon. Despite my lack of sleep, I am restless today."

In several long strides, Darcy rounded the table to stand before her. "I, too, am restless, Miss Elizabeth." His eyes travelled the length of her, from the tips of her slippers to the top of her head before settling where they always did—on her eyes. He extended his hand to her. "You are exceedingly lovely no matter the day," he told her, pitching his voice low so the servants would not hear. "But you are most beautiful when you smile."

"And you, sir, are very bold," she replied as she placed her hand in his. "You know very well why I smile so prettily."

"I do, indeed, just as you know I am the happiest man in the world knowing your pretty smiles are for me alone. Since my boldness is the result of such felicity, I trust your generous nature will make the appropriate allowances." Without further ado, he led her to the seat beside his own. "I imagine you must be hungry as well as restless. Permit me to fix you a plate before the weather takes a turn for the worse and we are forced to remain inside for the entirety of the day." Pulling out her chair, he saw her settled upon it, then set off in the direction of the sideboard, where the usual offerings were arranged in chafing dishes and on elegant silver platters.

Elizabeth spread her napkin on her lap and watched Darcy select fresh, seasonal fruit, bread and butter, and bacon as though he had served her breakfast a thousand times before. Not only was he familiar with her preferences, but he was familiar with *her*. How fortunate she was to have gained the love of such a man—a man as eager to hear her opinions as he was to promote her comfort and pleasure!

"I know you prefer mint in the morning," Darcy

remarked as he looked over the tea things with a critical eye, "but there is none to be had today." He lifted the lids of several silver pots until he found one that pleased him and poured the contents into a cup. Then he collected her plate and returned to the table, setting both before her. "I thought you might enjoy some chocolate instead. I hope it meets with your approval."

"I assure you, sir, that everything you have set before me meets with my approval. You are very good. Thank you."

"You are most welcome," Darcy replied warmly as he reclaimed his chair. He began to reach for her hand but caught himself and retracted it, then reached for his newspaper instead. "Forgive me," he murmured contritely, shaking out his paper.

Elizabeth repressed a smile as she speared a slice of apple with her fork.

Last night, they had agreed to reveal nothing of their happy news until Darcy had applied to Mr Bennet and received his consent. Knowing they would be courting speculation and gossip the longer she remained at Netherfield, Elizabeth had taken the liberty of writing to her father that morning to request the carriage from Longbourn. Now that Jane was recovered, there was no reason for the sisters to stay another night under Mr Bingley's roof. Although Elizabeth would miss living in the same household with Darcy, Miss Bingley and Mrs Hurst were another matter. Their insipid tittering, superior looks, and snide comments would by no means be missed.

A reply to her letter came as she finished her breakfast, while Darcy recounted a boyhood adventure with Colonel Fitzwilliam, a horse chestnut tree, and a broken arm. Returning her cup to its saucer, Elizabeth thanked the footman and glanced at her letter. Her intent had been only to observe the direction, but the large, swooping script in which her name was written indicated the missive was not from her father, but from her mother. Elizabeth's heart sank.

Darcy touched the back of her hand with his fingertip. "I hope that nothing is amiss."

Elizabeth scrutinised her letter, turning it over and over in her hands. "Would you mind very much if I were to read it now?"

"Of course you may read your letter. Surely, you and I need not stand upon ceremony."

Thanking him, Elizabeth broke the seal and began to read, but what her mother had to communicate only caused vexation. She quickly set her letter aside and raised her eyes to the ceiling, willing herself to remain composed and not give voice to her ire.

"Elizabeth, what has happened?"

Despite being irritated with her mother, Elizabeth experienced a lovely little lurch in her belly upon hearing Darcy refer to her by her Christian name. He had done so without batting an eyelid, as though it was perfectly natural for him to refer to her so intimately in the middle of Mr Bingley's breakfast parlour. "I must beg your pardon, sir. It was not my intent to disturb your breakfast."

"You have disturbed nothing, but you are distressed."

"I am perfectly well. Rest assured all my family are in good health, as am I."

Darcy looked to the window, where a few fingers of weak, winter sunlight were attempting to break through the clouds. "Would you care to walk out now? Although it is likely to be cold, I am confident we will not see rain this morning. We will be quite safe."

Elizabeth recalled a Sunday morning spent in a rainy walnut grove with Darcy, his dog, and a significant amount of mud on her gown, and nearly smiled. "You, of all people, know I am undeterred by a little bit of rain. But to answer your question, yes. A walk would be wonderful. Thank you."

Ten minutes later, they set out along the path that led to the walled garden where they had encountered each other days ago, when Elizabeth had first arrived to see Jane. Then, she had been mortified by the possibility of Darcy having seen her ankles; now, her hand was tucked securely into the crook of his arm. Once they married, he would likely see far more of her than her ankles. That he might *want* to see more of her—to touch more of her—warmed her from within as a delicious little ache bloomed along the base of her spine and wound its way through her body. Elizabeth turned her face into the wind, welcoming the cooling effect of its gusts on her heated cheeks.

At last, they reached the garden. Constructed of field-stone and mortar, its walls stood eight feet high and provided ample protection from the wind. Darcy led Elizabeth to a wide stone bench situated in a well-protected corner, but she was too agitated to be still. She craved employment and exercise and proceeded to walk a circuit around the perimeter of the garden. The various plants—peonies, hydrangeas, and roses—that had sported colourful blossoms throughout the summer months were nothing more than dried stalks in November, made brown and brittle by the onset of winter. Leaves crunched beneath her boots on the slate path. A sudden gust of wind buffeted the outer walls and Elizabeth shivered, rubbing her hands together to generate warmth.

She was startled when Darcy stepped forward, claimed both her hands, and kissed them. "Pray forgive me," he said with some distress. Without ceremony, he produced a familiar butter-coloured glove from his greatcoat pocket and pressed it into her hands. "It is unpardonable of me to have kept this when you have clearly been in need of it."

"Mr Darcy," she exclaimed in wonderment. "You have

found my glove!" She pulled its mate from the pocket of her pelisse without delay and slipped them on. "I am indebted to you. I had believed this glove was lost forever. The pair was a gift from my aunt Gardiner, who resides in London. I see her but rarely, only a few times each year, but she is extremely dear to me. I did not know how I was going to tell her I had lost one."

A vivid flush of colour appeared on his countenance and the tips of his ears. "I have been remiss. I should have returned your glove to you the moment I found it."

"I assure you, sir, I feel nothing but gratitude."

Darcy shook his head. "You ought to upbraid me. I did not do as I ought to have done. I did not return it to you, and for that I am sorry. I gave no thought to your not having another pair. In this weather, it is unpardonable."

"I do have another pair," she told him gently, laying her hand on his arm. "At Longbourn. And you have returned this one now, so there is nothing to repine. All is well."

"You are generous," Darcy replied. "Too generous." He reached for her hand, and she surrendered it willingly. "I shall buy you a pair of gloves for each day of the week and anything else you desire. When we are married, you will want for nothing."

"You will do no such thing. I am not so vain a creature as to make such demands of you. I do not require ten pairs of gloves and twenty shoe roses to make me happy."

"No. I daresay you do not, but you must allow me some leeway to spoil you."

"You may spoil me with the delights of your library. You may spoil me with your superior society, and with long, rainy afternoons curled together before a warm fire as you read all my favourite stories and poems aloud to me. And when you grow tired, or your voice becomes hoarse, I shall return the favour and read your favourites to you."

"And shall I also kiss you?" he asked, tenderly stroking her cheek. "Shall I spoil you with affection as well as books?"

"Whenever and wherever you wish. I shall not object...Fitzwilliam."

In that moment the manner in which Darcy regarded her, as though she was the dearest, most beloved woman in the world, made Elizabeth's pulse quicken; but from somewhere beyond the haven of the walled garden, the sound of voices intruded upon their privacy and the moment was lost.

Reluctantly, Darcy removed his hand from her cheek and stepped away, quietly clearing his throat. "You received a letter from Longbourn, but I have yet to comprehend why it distressed you. Will you not confide in me? I should dearly like to be of use to you."

The mention of her letter had all the effect of being doused by a bucket of cold water, even more so than hearing the voices in the park. Frustrated but resigned, Elizabeth sighed. Although she would rather he remained in ignorance, the idea of keeping secrets from Darcy did not appeal to her. She said, "This morning, before breakfast, I wrote to my father and requested the use of his carriage so that Jane and I may return home today. Instead of receiving a reply from him, my mother wrote to deny my request."

"Perhaps the horses are needed in the fields."

"The horses are not needed in the fields, sir."

"Are you certain?"

"Quite certain," she said, blushing with mortification and annoyance. "My mother has written that she intended for us to stay until Tuesday. She does not desire to see us returned to her before then."

"I see," Darcy muttered, bowing his head as he passed his hand over his mouth.

Elizabeth could well imagine what he was thinking. Her mother, although affectionate and well-meaning, was absolutely determined to see Jane wed to Mr Bingley. Darcy abhorred such machinations. That her mother had sunk so low as to orchestrate this one likely turned his stomach. She glanced at him and saw that his expression not only appeared disapproving, but grave. Was he regretting his soon-to-be connexion to her mother, or was he regretting his proposal to her? Too agitated to remain still while Darcy looked so solemn and dissatisfied, Elizabeth turned from him and began to pace the length of the garden.

On her second pass, Darcy reached for her hand and bade her stop. "You are upset. I wish you would not be, Elizabeth."

"It cannot be helped," she replied, refusing to meet his eyes. "What you must think!"

Darcy shook his head. "Clearly, your mother desires a marriage between my friend and your sister. Am I correct in assuming Miss Bennet is also in favour of such an outcome?"

"Please do not ask me to betray Jane's confidence. Or her heart. I cannot do it. The most I can tell you is that my sister would be mortified to know what my mother has done. She does not approve of her contrivances to 'help matters along', nor would she ever consent to be a party to them. It has been many years now that Jane and I have promised each other that only the deepest love would ever tempt us into matrimony."

Darcy's expression softened, and he raised her hand to his lips to bestow a kiss.

"I am beyond embarrassed by my mother's actions. I would send another note to my father, but I have no confidence he will ever receive it."

"There is no need to send another note. Your mother will not be easy until she sees you and your sisters well settled. While I cannot approve of her methods, I can comprehend a mother's desire to see her children safe and cared for, Elizabeth. Let us hope, once you and I are wed, that she will cease acting with such a single-minded purpose and allow the rest of her daughters to resolve matters on their own."

Although she was certain Darcy had meant to reassure her, Elizabeth felt only an increased sense of chagrin. "I fear you ask too much. I cannot imagine my mother simply leaving anything to providence. She will always want to arrange things as she sees fit."

"A quality she shares with my aunt," Darcy replied ruefully as he ran his thumb across her knuckles. "I have never met another person so determined to have her way in all things, regardless of the sentiments of the rest of the world —not even your mother. In fact, Lady Catherine's machinations put Mrs Bennet's to shame. But most people who know her tend to overlook her interference because she is wealthy and titled and takes every opportunity to make sure they know it."

Elizabeth stared at him. "Are you intimating that you have an imperfect relation, Mr Darcy?"

"Among other things," he said with the hint of a smile. "As for myself, I have striven for perfection my entire life but have repeatedly fallen short of obtaining it. Now, I only wish to be happy. Despite our imperfect families, I have found perfection in you."

"That is hardly fair," Elizabeth cried. "I am by no means perfect—"

But Darcy silenced her protests with a kiss. "Enough," he told her softly, firmly. He caressed her cheek and traced her bottom lip with his thumb. "You are perfect for *me*. I must own that, when I first arrived in Hertfordshire, I was quite jaded and bitter. But every day spent in your company has made me a better man. A happier man. With you, the world is not nearly so dissatisfying a place as it once seemed. With you, I feel as though I can face anything. Even scheming mothers who are intent upon seeing their daughters wed to rich men."

Elizabeth laughed and boldly kissed his thumb.

"Now, tell me what you would like to do."

"What I would like is to stay in this garden with you and hide from the world for the remainder of the day. But I fear that is neither a reasonable nor a feasible request." She averted her eyes to their joined hands. "You must know it is no longer appropriate for me to remain at Netherfield now that we are engaged. Jane is greatly improved. As much as I shall regret parting from you, it is time for us to return to Longbourn. You and I cannot continue as we are in Mr Bingley's house, nor should we endeavour to keep our engagement a secret from those who would wish us joy."

"No," he agreed, giving her hand a reassuring squeeze. "I should say not. We shall soon be found out in some manner or other, and I would not dishonour you or your family by putting off speaking to your father. To disguise what I feel for you would go sorely against the grain in any case. I do not wish to hide our happiness from the world. It would be poorly done."

"We are in accord, then."

"We are, and since your heart is set on returning to Longbourn today, I shall convey you and your sister there whenever you are ready to depart."

Elizabeth shook her head. "I cannot ask that of you."

"You need ask nothing of me. I have offered to do it."

"I do not wish to inconvenience you."

"The only inconvenience to me will be the loss of your society. We are to be married," he told her. "And I am both anxious and eager to obtain your father's permission. Above all things, seeing you comfortable and happy is of utmost importance to me. On this, I shall not be moved."

Elizabeth bit her lip, her heart full of gratitude and affection for the man before her. Inclining her head, she uttered no further objection but raised herself upon the tips of her toes, slid her hands along his shoulders, and pressed a gentle and deliberate kiss to the corner of his mouth. "Thank you," she whispered.

Darcy's hands found purchase on her waist, and Elizabeth kissed him again.

§

That evening, Elizabeth sat before the well-worn oak desk in her father's book room. Darcy had gone before her nearly an hour ago, intent upon obtaining her father's consent the moment her mother and sisters had withdrawn from the dining room after dinner. She fingered a piece of lace on the sleeve of her gown as her father stood before the window, rubbing his forehead with his hand.

"Are you certain, Elizabeth?" he enquired with more solemnity than she had ever heard him utter. "I have given him my consent. He is a man whom I would not dare refuse anything. But are you certain he is the man with whom you wish to pass the rest of your life? He is rich to be sure. You will have many fine carriages and jewels, but will Mr Darcy make you happy, my dear?"

"Mr Darcy does make me happy, Papa," she insisted as she abandoned her chair and joined him at the window. "For weeks he has made me happy. I know you think him proud, but I assure you he has no improper pride. He is perfectly amiable. Despite our initial misunderstanding at the assembly, he has shown me nothing but kindness, deference, and respect. In that time, we have become good friends, and I have grown to love him dearly."

Her father exhaled a weary sigh. "I feared as much."

"Papa," she chided. "Mr Darcy is the very best of men."

"And his estate is clear across the country," he muttered. "Why you would wish to marry such a disagreeable man and travel to such a place is beyond me."

Elizabeth shook her head, knowing that his complaining had nothing to do with any real objection he harboured against Darcy or his estate, but with the distance he would have to travel in order to visit his favourite daughter. "As I have stated before, sir, he is by no means disagreeable. He is honourable and good and owns half of Derbyshire." With a slight tilt of her head, she raised one brow in an arch manner. "According to Miss Bingley, there is no grander prospect than Pemberley in all the land. Would you rather I had refused him in favour of a red coated officer with limited prospects, a penchant for drink, and a silver tongue?"

"I should say not," her father replied. "The officers in Colonel Forster's regiment, although entertaining enough for your sisters, would never do for you. You are much too clever for any of those young men to hold your interest for long, never mind gain your respect. You must forgive me, my dear. I am getting old, and you and Jane alone possess all the grace and discernment to be found in this house. Once you are gone, I fear there will not be two words of sense spoken together for many years to come."

As ever, his flippant dismissal of her younger sisters pained her. "Forgive my frankness, sir, but Mary, Kitty, and Lydia are not dim-witted. They are bright, although easily influenced young women in possession of their own unique talents. They simply require direction, encouragement, and maturity. Perhaps they ought to go to school."

"How very much you sound like your future husband," her father remarked drily. "After receiving permission to marry my favourite daughter, he had much to say on the subject of the others."

Elizabeth stared at him in shock. "Mr Darcy suggested sending my sisters to school?"

With a derisive snort, Mr Bennet crossed the room, where he settled onto the leather chair behind his desk. "Not only did he suggest it, but he also offered to pay for it. As well as a music master for all three, whether they are desirous of one or not." Despite his annoyance, one corner of her father's mouth lifted infinitesimally, likely at the idea of Kitty and Lydia diligently applying themselves to learn anything, never mind an instrument.

It was then Elizabeth recalled how both had begged her to play the pianoforte at Lucas Lodge so they could dance. Instead, Elizabeth had recommended they learn to play for themselves rather than rely on others to provide their entertainment. In truth, she had hoped to encourage an interest in something other than idleness and the pursuit of officers. Darcy had overheard the conversation, but she would never have thought he would have proposed hiring a music master to make her suggestion a reality. Elizabeth was as touched that he had taken her words to heart as she was impressed by his ingenuity. "It is generous of him. Do not you think?"

"Generous indeed," her father admitted, albeit grudgingly. "But having another man tell me that my own daughters lack employment and guidance chafes." Drumming his fingers upon his desk, Mr Bennet sighed. "He is correct, of course."

"Papa, you know that Jane and I have long believed our sisters would benefit from receiving an education that extends beyond the limited opportunities they have at home. Kitty and Lydia are not great readers, and although Mary's nose is forever buried in a book, the subject matter she chooses is hardly diverse, never mind conducive to independent thinking." She paused. "You have not declined Mr Darcy's offer, surely?"

Reaching for the crystal decanter on his desk, her father poured himself a glass of sherry. "As yet, I have given your young man no reply. Considering there would be little inconvenience to myself with the business, I am tempted to take him up on it, if only to have some peace and quiet once you are gone to live in Derbyshire." He raised his glass and took a measured sip, whetting his lips as his expression turned thoughtful. "If only your Mr Darcy would be so obliging as to take your mother off my hands as well, I shall be quite satisfied with the arrangement." He took another sip of sherry and smiled.

Averting her eyes to the fire crackling in the grate, Elizabeth sighed.

FIFTEEN

ↄﾉ☉ↄ

How clever you are, to know something of which you are ignorant.

"WHAT A SENSIBLE YOUNG MAN YOU ARE, MR COLLINS," said Mrs Bennet as the parson tucked into his dinner with a self-satisfied countenance and an appetite reminiscent of the Prince Regent's.

Although it required some effort, Darcy refrained from rolling his eyes. Sensible was not a word he would ever use to describe the man who would inherit Longbourn once Mr Bennet was dead.

Insensible.

Nonsensical.

Imbecilic.

Daft.

Those words, he decided as he served himself a moderate helping of boiled potatoes, *are far more fitting for the second son of Mr Bennet's cousin.*

"I flatter myself by saying it has always been so," Mr Collins replied from his place at Mrs Bennet's right. "Sensibility is an honourable, gentlemanly characteristic no man should ever eschew. Especially a clergyman such as I, so fortunate as to enjoy the condescension and affability of so estimable and noble a patroness as God has granted me. I assure you, madam, that nothing is below her ladyship's notice, even the arrangement of my own comfortable establishment, which is separated from her great house by naught but a lane."

He speared a parsnip with his fork and popped it in his mouth, chewing with considerable energy. "The other morning, as I attended her ladyship in her second-best breakfast parlour—for her ladyship has several—she told me, 'Mr Collins, you must marry'." He glanced at Miss Bennet and all her sisters in turn with an indulgent, almost patronising smile. "Such loveliness I have rarely seen in my five-and-twenty years on this earth. Your daughters are certainly a credit to you, Mrs Bennet."

Longbourn's mistress smiled becomingly while her husband, seated at the opposite end of the table, reclined in his chair and steepled his fingers beneath his chin. Diversion danced in his eyes, especially when he glanced at Elizabeth.

Darcy, on the other hand, was far from diverted.

"Lord," Miss Lydia uttered incredulously from his left as Mr Collins prattled on about the delicacy of elegant females between bites of his dinner. "Does he imagine one of *us* shall agree to have him? What a joke!"

Across the table, Miss Catherine stared at the parson in alarm. Clearly, such a possibility had not occurred to her. Even Miss Mary, whose practice it was to read scripture and play hymns and dirges instead of Mozart and Beethoven, looked as though the prospect of being Mr Collins's wife held little inducement for her. He glanced at Georgiana, who was seated between Miss Catherine and Miss Bennet, and was relieved to see her attention was on her dinner rather than her future sisters' distress.

Although Mrs Bennet's enthusiasm to see her daughters wed gave Darcy pause, he could not imagine Mr Bennet approving of such a man for his future son-in-law. Shrugging his shoulders, Darcy raised his wine glass to his lips and took a measured sip, but nearly choked on it as the parson said, "Cousin Jane, I believe, is the eldest, so of course it is only right that she should be given preference." He bestowed a wide smile upon the lady. "After all, the younger sisters cannot marry until the eldest is wed."

With some effort, Darcy managed to swallow his mouthful of wine before setting himself to rights by gulping down another. A previous dinner engagement with the officers had kept Bingley from dining at Longbourn that evening. Had he been in attendance, Darcy suspected his friend would likely declare himself to Miss Bennet on the spot.

Good God. If Miss Bennet ends up married to this ridiculous man, Bingley will never forgive me.

Darcy need not have worried, as Mrs Bennet promptly informed the parson of Bingley's existence. "As it happens, Jane already has a suitor, Mr Collins. It will not be long now, I am sure, until the gentleman makes her an offer. He is much attached to her. It has been so from the moment he first saw her nearly a month ago. We are all excessively fond of him, but none more so than my dear Jane."

Miss Bennet, who had the honour of being seated to Mr Collins's right, coloured deeply, though whether it was from mortification or from narrowly escaping an alliance with such an obsequious ninnyhammer, Darcy could not say. Although he did not approve of Mrs Bennet's method of deterring the parson from her eldest daughter, at least she had not mentioned Bingley by name. Hopefully, she would deter him from Miss Mary and Miss Catherine as well. Even a blind man could see Miss Lydia was far too young to be out never mind wed.

Mr Collins's smile dimmed, but he soon recovered his spirits and, with renewed vigour, said, "Of course. I would not dream of interfering where the seeds of love have taken root in fertile soil. Though my profession as a clergyman and my situation in life must certainly recommend me to my dear cousin as an equally desirable suitor—"

Miss Lydia snorted.

"—I would not dream of coming between two young people so sincerely attached to one another. I have no doubt," he continued in the same unaffected tone, "that another of my fair cousins will welcome the compliment of my most particular notice. Pray permit me to read to you several passages from Fordyce's sermons this evening, Cousin Elizabeth."

This time, Darcy did choke.

Georgiana's fork clattered to her plate.

Miss Bennet attended her with concern, Miss Catherine began coughing, and Miss Lydia said, "La, Mr Collins! Lizzy is to marry Mr Darcy. Although he often looks as though he is dissatisfied with the world, you need not fear him, for he is kind as well as clever. I did not think much of him at first—he seemed an impossible snob—but I have found he improves upon further acquaintance. Now I like him just as much as I do Jane's Mr Bingley."

"Lydia," Elizabeth whispered harshly behind Darcy's back as Georgiana and Miss Catherine hid their amusement behind their hands. "You forget yourself."

Rather than repentant, Miss Lydia only appeared indignant. "I cannot see why you are cross with me, Lizzy. It is, after all, the truth. And Mr Darcy deplores disguise. He told me so himself."

Before another word could be uttered on the subject, Darcy cleared his throat. "Yes," he said with as much dignity as he could muster. "Thank you, Miss Lydia. Rarely has any young lady paid me the compliment of such a glowing commendation."

Although all her sisters, including Darcy's own, shared a

look of suspended disbelief, she smiled brightly and served herself a second helping of kidney pie. "You are welcome, Mr Darcy. If you only smiled more often, you could easily be the handsomest gentleman of my acquaintance. Despite your severity, your countenance is pleasanter than that of most officers in the regiment, except for Captain Carter's. But it is rumoured that he is to be married soon, so I suppose it hardly signifies how handsome he is in the end. Do you not agree?"

At first, Darcy could do little more than stare at her. But her expression as she turned her eyes upon him was so expectant that he soon found himself muttering, "Of course. Wholly and completely. Thank you, Miss Lydia," before returning his attention to his dinner as a flush of heat rose along the back of his neck.

Beside him, Elizabeth endeavoured to conceal what he supposed to be a mixture of mortification and amusement, taking care to avoid meeting his eyes.

"You are engaged to this gentleman, Cousin Elizabeth?" the parson enquired, albeit with less enthusiasm than he had previously exhibited.

"I am, sir," she replied.

Darcy admired her composure.

"In that case," Mr Collins declared, "pray allow me to extend my heartfelt congratulations to you and your betrothed. I shall be very glad to counsel you both during my stay here, and, if her ladyship grants me leave to do so, I will not hesitate to perform the ceremony as well, for my duty as a clergyman compels me to be of use to those in need of my services and to act in that manner which shall ever promote the holy state of matrimony as a most highly advantageous institution under God."

"Do you hear that, Lizzy?" said Mrs Bennet. "Mr Collins desires to be of use to you by paying you and Mr Darcy such a compliment as to remain until your wedding. That shall likely be six months at least."

Darcy did not know who looked more shocked by Mrs Bennet's pronouncement of the wedding date: Mr Collins, Elizabeth, or himself. He certainly did not wish to wait six months to marry Elizabeth. He wanted to begin his life with her as soon as possible, he wanted to spend Christmas in his Brook Street residence in London, and he wanted to take her home to Pemberley before spring.

"That is generous of you, Mr Collins," said Elizabeth, "but our pastor, Mr Reager, has known me all my life. Much as Mr Darcy and I appreciate your offer, we intend to apply to Mr Reager to officiate. We would not wish to slight him. It would be most unseemly considering my family's long-standing association with him. As for our engagement," she added, glancing at her mother, "I believe Mr Darcy would prefer to marry much sooner. In a month's time, perhaps two."

"A month," her mother cried. "You cannot possibly be married so soon! Why the breakfast alone—" and on she lamented as Mr Bennet took a leisurely sip from his glass.

As he appeared to be as hearty in spirit as he was in appetite, when Longbourn's mistress paused to draw breath, Mr Collins said, "To slight such a well-respected man as your Mr Reager, Cousin Elizabeth, especially when he has devoted his life to attending his flock with such diligence, would indeed be most unseemly. Your loyalty to your parish rector certainly does you credit."

He then turned to Darcy, and, with a gracious smile, inclined his head. "How fortunate you are, sir, to secure the affections of my fair cousin. And if I may say so," he said with mounting enthusiasm, "I find myself in a unique position. It so happens that you share the distinction of having in common the very surname belonging to the nephew of my esteemed patroness—Mr Darcy of Pemberley in Derbyshire. He is a very wealthy gentleman of superior breeding and rank, or so I was told by her ladyship."

All in the room looked from the parson, who appeared inordinately pleased with himself, to Darcy, whose stomach felt as though he had eaten lead rather than Mrs Bennet's excellent duck ragout. *Good God, this imbecile is Lady Catherine's parson?* Of all the clergymen in England, what unforgiveable sin had he committed to have been awarded the misfortune of sitting down to dinner with the one beholden to his overreaching aunt?

"Superior breeding and rank you say?" Mr Bennet quipped as he eyed his future son-in-law with interest. "That is quite a coincidence."

Before Darcy could so much as order his thoughts, Mrs Bennet spoke.

"Mr Bennet, you must not tease Mr Darcy as you do the rest of us. He has not been brought up to suffer such unseemly behaviour as you are wont to subject your own family to, and I daresay neither has dear Miss Darcy. You know very well that Lizzy's Mr Darcy must be the very gentleman of whom Mr Collins speaks. I know you think me daft, husband, but even *I* know there cannot be two Mr Darcys of Pemberley."

It was then that the oddest look came over the parson—an expression that was half excitement, half horror. "But that is impossible," he stammered. "Lady Catherine's nephew is to wed her daughter, Miss de Bourgh..."

Darcy barely repressed an oath. *Bloody hell. Does Lady Catherine exercise no restraint? Why must she blather her nonsense to every person she knows!*

Elizabeth stared at him in stunned disbelief, as did her sisters and mother. "What is he saying, sir?" she enquired as the colour drained from her face. "Are you engaged to your cousin?"

"Absolutely not," he replied, fixing Mr Collins with a look of severity that would have silenced a more sensible man. "I am engaged to you."

Instead of being intimidated, Mr Collins appeared indignant. "Sir, you cannot know what you say! Miss de Bourgh is a treasure—a diamond of the first water. To renounce such a lady is incomprehensible." He wiped his brow with his napkin. "And so," he continued confidently, "I must therefore assume that you are perpetrating a jest. Although my delightful young cousin has charms aplenty, her situation in life pales in comparison to that of dear Miss de Bourgh. I can have no doubt that you fully intend to oblige her ladyship by honouring your engagement to her daughter." He half stood and offered Darcy a sort of deferential bow, smiling insipidly as he resumed his seat.

"I do not understand what is happening," said Miss Catherine, glancing warily between Mr Collins and Darcy. "Why would Mr Collins think Mr Darcy is engaged to this Miss de Bourgh person when he asked Lizzy to marry him on Saturday?"

"I assure you, Miss Catherine," said Darcy, trying and failing to rein in his annoyance with his aunt's parson, "that I am very much engaged to your sister and only your sister."

"My brother never lies," Georgiana said quietly, but with more confidence than Darcy could ever remember her exhibiting in company, even before her encounter with Wickham and his debauchery. "Whatever he says is the absolute truth." She lifted her chin, as though daring Mr Collins to contradict her.

Mr Collins choked, then coughed, then quickly reached for his wine glass. "Blasphemy," he wheezed after draining his glass of wine. "This is as good as blasphemy! It would be the highest honour for any man, regardless of situation and rank, to receive Miss de Bourgh's hand in matrimony. Not only would such a man know the supreme joy of having the most charming companion for his future life, but he would thereafter claim a connexion to the noble House of de Bourgh! Therefore, you cannot mean to denounce your own flesh and blood in favour of mine, though I do thank you for the honour of your compliment." He dipped his head with a practised smile that had likely placated Lady Catherine countless times but which proved ineffective upon her nephew.

"Since you seem to admire my cousin so much, Mr Collins, I give you leave to solicit the honour of her hand yourself. Much as I respect my family, Anne will never receive an offer from me." Tossing his napkin on the table, he addressed Mr Bennet. "If I may have the privilege of speaking to Miss Elizabeth privately, sir, I would be most obliged to you."

"And put an end to such an entertaining spectacle?" the elder man replied with a flippant turn of his mouth. There was a familiar gleam in his eye as well—a mixture of amusement and mischief that reminded Darcy much of his second daughter.

On Elizabeth's countenance, such an expression delighted him. On her father's, and in such a circumstance as this, it was poorly done. Darcy pursed his lips. His patience was nearly gone.

Likely recognising the look of an angry man, Mr Bennet dismissed him with a wave of his hand. "Be off with you then, Mr Darcy. My book room should serve your purpose well enough. I would join you myself, but confess I am curious to see whether the rest of the meal provides equal diversion."

"Papa," Elizabeth murmured disapprovingly as she accepted Darcy's outstretched hand and rose from her chair.

"Please do not make light of the situation. Can you not see Mr Darcy is upset enough?"

Mr Collins rose as well. "Cousin Elizabeth, I must caution you—nay, I must *insist* that you remain with your family. Mr Darcy cannot be ignorant of the consequences—"

"It seems to me, Mr Collins," said Mr Bennet before he had ceased speaking, "that Mr Darcy marrying his cousin is a hopeless business. Although you have had the pleasure of his acquaintance for the whole of two hours, we have known him many weeks—long enough to comprehend that contrary to your wishes, Mr Darcy will do precisely as he likes. I have granted him permission to speak to Elizabeth. Therefore, I have no doubt he will do it, despite your disapprobation."

"Sir," said Mr Collins indignantly, "I must protest. Lady Catherine de Bourgh—"

"Is not the master of this house," Mr Bennet informed him. "Nor are you. Until I am dead, Mr Collins, do be so good as to allow me the luxury of presiding over my own daughters, as well as my own supper table."

"But—"

"Sit. Down. Mr Collins," Mr Bennet demanded.

Mr Collins obliged him.

❧

"Darcy," said Hurst in greeting. "Come and have a glass of port."

"I do not mind if I do," he replied from the doorway of Netherfield's billiards room. After Mr Collins's insufferable presumption, he could use a drink. "How was your evening, Hurst?"

"Not nearly as entertaining as yours I imagine."

"I would not call it entertaining so much as trying. The Bennets have a house guest—a Mr Collins, who is to inherit

Longbourn after Mr Bennet's demise." He strode to the side-board, poured himself a glass of port, and raised it to his lips.

"Is he a decent sort?"

"He is a bombastic imbecile who wants a pretty wife. He is also parson to my aunt, Lady Catherine de Bourgh, of all people."

Hurst propped his feet upon a hassock and crossed his ankles. "Is she the one who fancies you engaged to her dull daughter?"

"One and the same," Darcy muttered, making his way to the hearth to stir the fire.

"I would have paid good money to have seen the look on your face during that performance," said Hurst. "I shudder to think what Caroline might say. You had best prepare your-self. Once she hears Longbourn's heir is under the thumb of your titled aunt she will not be nearly so sympathetic as I."

"Nor would I expect her to be," Darcy replied as he prodded the logs in the grate with a shining brass poker. He glanced at the mantel clock and frowned. "When is Bingley due to return do you think?"

Hurst took a long swallow from his glass and shrugged. "Colonel Forster likes a late night, and Bingley, as you know, is obliging. I doubt he will return before we retire."

"And Mrs Hurst?"

One corner of Hurst's mouth lifted. "Upstairs consoling Caroline. My sister has barely left her rooms since she heard you are to marry Elizabeth Bennet. It has been the most relaxing day and a half I have spent indoors in the last month."

"I am glad to be of service," said Darcy drily.

Hurst chuckled. "She laughed when Bingley told her, you know. When it finally sunk in that it was no joke, I thought she would have a fit of some sort. Do you know she could not talk for a full ten minutes?"

"I did not, but I am glad not to have been present."

"You were wise to stay away. If you remain wise, you will spend all your time at Longbourn until you are wed and take poor Miss Darcy with you. God knows what Caroline will take it upon herself to say to the girl of the matter. She is far too sweet to stand up to the likes of my sister."

"For the moment, yes. But my future wife is not known to mince her words. I have no doubt she will instruct Georgiana in the fine art of speaking her mind at some point or other."

Hurst laughed. "Is Miss Darcy pleased, then, to be gaining such a sister?"

"She is. Georgiana has always wanted a sister, and I am certain Miss Elizabeth will fulfil her every expectation."

"And the others? There are five Bennet girls, not just the two you and Bingley happen to like."

With a rueful twist of his mouth, Darcy discarded the poker. "Despite what I have said of them in the past, they are not without promise. If Mr Bennet is agreeable, I plan to send them to school as soon as may be, especially the two youngest. Preferably to separate schools."

He took a long swallow from his glass as he thought of Lydia Bennet, who had boldly informed Mr Collins that she liked Darcy just as well as she liked Bingley. In his experience, that was a first. Since he and Bingley had become friends at Eton, no one who knew them both had ever liked Darcy as well as they liked Bingley. Bingley was eager, open, and accepting. Darcy was reluctant, recalcitrant, and difficult to please. Since Miss Lydia possessed a tendency to say precisely what she thought whenever she thought it—and usually without consideration as to whether it was appropriate or not—Darcy did not doubt she was, in fact, sincere.

Swirling the amber liquid in his glass in an absent fashion, Darcy claimed the chair opposite Hurst's and made himself comfortable in it. The fire, burning brighter now, crackled in the grate as he further contemplated the anomaly that was Elizabeth's youngest sister.

As the youngest of all Mr Bennet's daughters, Miss Lydia was spoiled and self-centred and on the cusp of becoming a ridiculous flirt. But when he and Georgiana had encountered her and Miss Catherine the other day in Meryton, Darcy had glimpsed a side of her he had not previously known existed. In Mr Worthington's shop, she had been welcoming and kind to Georgiana. She had taken pains to draw her out. Yes, she had talked excessively of frippery and fashion, but she also solicited his sister's opinions regarding both, and was attentive and interested in her answers.

When they took tea in the private parlour at the inn, she had been equally loquacious, but in between bites of cake, Miss Lydia had spoken of her sisters and their interests and similarities, and she had done so with fondness and affection while Miss Catherine filled in the gaps.

Every endeavour at conversation Darcy put forth was answered, and Miss Lydia had posed questions to him in turn. She had even listened with interest to his replies. As a result, Darcy's opinion of her, and of Miss Catherine as well, had begun to shift. By the time they saw the girls back to Longbourn, Darcy had begun to feel an ease with them he would never have previously believed possible. Georgiana, too, appeared comfortable, enough so that when Mrs Bennet invited them to stay for supper, Darcy took one look at his sister's hopeful countenance and readily agreed.

He was almost shocked to find that he had enjoyed his evening, not only because Georgiana appeared happier and more relaxed with the Bennets than Darcy had ever remembered seeing her in the company of their own relations, but because Elizabeth's family had made him feel welcome as well. Save for the hour he had spent entirely alone with Elizabeth in the little parlour the week prior, it was beyond doubt the most pleasant evening he had ever passed at Longbourn. The only way Darcy could have enjoyed himself more was if Elizabeth had been there beside him. Smiling at him. Teasing him. Tempting him.

Hurst chuckled into his port, and Darcy was brought back to the present. "You are quiet."

Darcy cleared his throat. "I apologise. I was lost in thought."

"Thoughts of your Miss Elizabeth I surmise. That is hardly a surprise. The way you two carried on at the supper table, in the drawing room afterwards, and presumably on all those walks you took through the countryside, I was certain you were in love with her. Admit it, man. You were a goner long before she ever set foot in this house."

"I shall admit no such thing. I shall say only that I admire Miss Elizabeth exceedingly. She is a remarkable woman."

"Remarkable," Hurst repeated with an insufferable smirk. "That will do I suppose. Now," he said, shifting his weight in his chair. "What think you of Bingley and his Miss Bennet? Will he ride to Longbourn and ask for her hand tomorrow, do you think? Or will he wait until after he gives his ball?"

Darcy snorted. "It depends on how much he has drunk tonight with the officers. On the night of the Meryton assembly, he consumed an appalling amount of port, declared himself in love, and announced his intent to call upon Mr Bennet directly. It was four o'clock in the morning. Bingley could barely stand on his own feet, never mind ride a horse three miles in the dark."

Hurst barked a laugh. "I shall say this much for my brother—when he fancies himself in love with a lady, he wastes no time overthinking the situation. Despite his flippancy, I have never seen him so taken with any woman as he is with Miss Bennet."

"No," Darcy murmured in assent, thinking of Bingley's

past infatuations, of which there were many. "He has never been so constant in his attentions to any lady, nor so sincere in his admiration."

Hurst cleared his throat. "Despite what you think of her serenity and her smiles and her reserve, Jane Bennet *does* return Bingley's regard. I have seen evidence of it, and Louisa has as well. They are not unlike you and your own Miss Bennet. One is loquacious, the other is less so. In the end, the heart wants what the heart wants. There is nothing for it."

Darcy averted his eyes to his glass.

In his relationship with Elizabeth, the reserve belonged to him.

So was Jane Bennet reserved with Bingley?

Or perhaps she was not. Perhaps Bingley, with his amiable nature, drew her out when they are alone, much as Elizabeth drew Darcy out with her frankness and her penchant for laughter.

Staring fixedly at his glass, he wondered what would have happened if Elizabeth had not seen past his hauteur and restraint to the man beneath. Would they have become such friends if she had not ventured to tease him as she had done on Oakham Mount? Or upbraided him for his rudeness to her at the assembly? If she had not spoken frankly and demanded that same frankness from him in return, would she have formed a mistaken impression of him and written him off as an arrogant churl? The idea that Elizabeth could have ended up disliking him rather than falling in love with him sent a sharp pang of urgency through his chest. In that moment, he felt a powerful inclination to return to Longbourn, where he could look upon her beloved face, touch her, and kiss her, and reaffirm she was in fact his.

Is this how Miss Bennet felt with Bingley? She, like Darcy, kept her emotions hidden and her heart guarded, but that did not mean she was incapable of love. When she spoke, it was not for the sake of hearing her own voice like Caroline Bingley or countless other ladies he knew, but to add something of substance to the conversation at hand. Darcy had seen evidence of her compassion, her goodness, and the adoration and affection she inspired in Elizabeth and Bingley both. God help him, Jane Bennet was probably every bit the angel Bingley insisted she was.

And she would be Darcy's sister. He shook his head.

"Bingley," he said to Hurst, "could do far worse than Jane Bennet. If he has been so fortunate as to secure her regard, then I wish him every happiness. I would be a poor brother indeed were I to offer any further objections to the match."

"Well said," Hurst told him. "Of course, I have told Caroline as much, but she is stubborn, far more so than you."

"Let us hope, then," said Darcy, "that she will soon be in love herself."

Hurst laughed. "I would not hold my breath. Any man interested in securing her favour would have to be either clever enough to outwit her, or pliable enough to please her. And then there is the matter of fortune. Either way, I fear we shall be awaiting an introduction to such a man for a long time to come."

SIXTEEN

⁂

Little dependence can be placed on the appearance of merit or sense.

SLIVERS OF FLICKERING FIRELIGHT SLIPPED THROUGH the gaps in the bed curtains, lending the intimate, cloistered space a soft, burnished glow. As a girl, Elizabeth had loved the feeling of being sequestered within the private, cosy space she shared with her eldest sister. In truth, she loved it still. Although she was grown and about to become a married woman, it remained her favourite sanctuary within Longbourn House—a quiet, quilted haven, where she could wrap herself in soft counterpanes and reflect upon the events and tribulations of her day.

Beside her Jane slept like the dead, her breaths deep and even. For Elizabeth, repose remained elusive. It was no wonder, for Mr Collins's arrival had been heralded by all the pomp and circumstance to which Longbourn's heir was entitled. This meant anticipatory curiosity on her father's part, vexation on her mother's, and indifference on behalf of her youngest sisters once they saw his preaching bands and lack of a red coat.

As consistency was a fickle creature at Longbourn, her father's curiosity had since been replaced by disinterest and annoyance. Her mother, upon learning the parson possessed an excellent living and an attentive benefactress, decided the man who might one day cast her out deserved every courtesy. Only Kitty and Lydia held fast to their initial impressions. Sharing a meal and passing an evening in Mr Collins's company had done nothing to recommend him to any of the Miss Bennets. Although there was certainly no meanness in him, he possessed pomposity in abundance, a figure of considerable girth, and an unhealthy admiration for Lady Catherine de Bourgh and her daughter. Their verdict was unanimous: despite his happy situation in Kent, Mr Collins would make none of them happy in general.

That had been Darcy's opinion as well. For a man such as he—the master of a vast estate used to the respect afforded him by his station—a lecture on duty and obligation from his aunt's supercilious parson had gone sorely against the grain. Said aunt, Darcy claimed, was overreaching, overbearing, and used to having her own way. His cousin, Miss de Bourgh, to whom Mr Collins insisted Darcy was promised, was her mother's opposite in every respect. Words such as meek, disinterested, and intolerably stupid tumbled from his mouth in agitation. In the next breath, he apologised for speaking ill of her, citing it was hardly Anne's fault that her mother had discouraged the improvement of her mind.

Elizabeth had watched him pace the length of her father's book room as he told her of his aunt, his uncle the earl, and their expectations of him. His distress could not but add to her own. Darcy's family, although imperfect in his eyes, was wealthy and titled. They moved in society's first circles. Appearance and consequence were important to them, and they had long expected their nephew to marry as they had done—to strengthen his family's bloodlines, to increase his coffers, and to expand the scope of his ancestral estate. That Darcy was not following their edicts but throwing off convention and marrying where he liked would undoubtedly displease them. Being that Elizabeth was unknown to them and practically penniless would make the situation worse. While Darcy had not mentioned the objections that his relations were likely to raise against her, she was by no means insensible that they would eventually be raised. Once his ire had run its course, she said as much.

His response was immediate and indignant. "It is of no matter to me. For eight-and-twenty years I have done my duty to my family. My uncle can have nothing to criticise. I have followed his dictates and those of my father to the letter regarding Pemberley and its interests. But this is different. My felicity, as well as that of my future children, is at stake. They cannot expect me to blindly acquiesce to their wishes, hoping all the while that I shall not be made miserable by their edicts. It is short-sighted and selfish, and I cannot adhere to it."

"Your uncle's myopic directives aside, there is no refuting that I am not what he must have envisioned for you, and likely still does."

"Nor are you precisely what *I* had envisioned," Darcy admitted with a rueful smile, "but that does not mean you are lacking. You are a woman to be admired. You are compassionate to a fault and are as handsome, unassuming, and intelligent as you are guileless. Whatever they think of my choice, it is too late. When I have made up my mind, I have made it. What I feel for you will not wane."

"Circumstances change, sir. Opinions alter, especially with the passage of time."

Darcy crossed the room to stand before her. "Elizabeth," he said, and grasped her hands. "I have always known I would never marry Anne. I have told my uncle as much, and my aunt as well, too many times over the years for them to be surprised by my marrying elsewhere. Anne and I have had our entire lives to come to care for each other, yet we barely speak. You know my opinions and preferences regarding what constitutes an advantageous marriage do not align with those of the fashionable world. Their ideals, including those of my relations, are not in accord with my own. Perhaps it has not always been so, but it is so now. Knowing you has changed me and changed me for the better."

He drew closer to her and lowered his voice. "No woman of my acquaintance has ever inspired a fraction of the admiration that I feel for you. I have never liked any of them well enough to dance with more than once, never mind contemplate making an offer of marriage. You are the only woman to ever touch my heart. For the rest of my life, I shall rejoice in our friendship—in our extraordinary communion of souls— and in our love, and I shall thank God each day for his goodness in leading me to you."

And then, without so much as a by-your-leave, he kissed her.

At first, it was nothing more than a gentle press of lips— tender, almost teasing. But soon it became more—deeper and more sensual than any kiss they had shared before. Elizabeth gasped as Darcy's hand grazed her waist and the swell of her hip, while the fingers of his other caressed the sensitive curve where her neck met her shoulder. His touch was tentative and insistent at once.

"I love you," he said on a breath. His voice was endearingly uneven.

"I love you, too," she whispered in reply, touching his face with her hands, wanting nothing more in that moment than to be close to him—as close as humanly possible.

The hand on her hip urged her closer, and Darcy kissed her again.

And that was the state in which her father had found them.

To his credit, Mr Bennet had not yelled, nor had he

lectured or threatened to do Darcy harm. He had told him, quietly but firmly, to go to London to acquire a licence and draw up a settlement, and not to return until he was in possession of both. Then, after a long, appraising look at Elizabeth, he had turned on his heel and left.

Not wishing to further try her father's patience, Darcy and Georgiana had departed for Netherfield soon after.

The Darcys had been fortunate, more fortunate than herself. Not only had her father been in a pensive mood for the rest of the night, but Elizabeth had been obliged to listen to Mr Collins's lengthy recitations of scripture until it was time to retire.

Elizabeth sighed.

Beyond the bedcurtains, with their familiar pattern of white work and rosebuds, the fire had burned low. She moved closer to Jane and tugged the counterpane to her chin. Come morning, Darcy would travel to London, where he would likely remain until his business was complete. In the meantime, Mr Collins would be on hand to entertain them.

Heaven, help us all, she thought as she closed her eyes.

She did not want Darcy to go.

At nine o'clock sharp the following morning, Mr Collins joined the rest of the family in the dining room. No doubt, the scent of buttered toast, ham, and cakes had drawn him to the table like a mouse to cheese. With a wide smile, he wished each of his cousins a hearty good morning, piled his plate with more food than was good for him, claimed the chair beside that of Longbourn's mistress, and began to eat.

Mrs Bennet began speaking to him at once.

"Lord," Lydia muttered to Kitty at the other end of the

table. "Will he burst do you think? Surely, his breeches cannot hold all of that food he intends to eat."

Kitty wrinkled her nose. "I should hope not. That would be a horrid thing, to see such a pudding wearing a preaching collar and torn breeches."

Mary, who was seated beside Kitty, turned as red as a beet. "There is no hope for either of you," she murmured primly, reaching for her water goblet. "You are both wicked and going straight to the devil."

"Oh, please," Lydia snorted. "You cannot tell me you are not put off by the great lump as well."

"Lydia," Jane admonished. "That is unkind."

"It is," Mary agreed. "He is a clergyman and ought to be treated with utmost reverence and respect."

Elizabeth glanced archly at Jane. "Especially considering he is so fortunate as to enjoy the patronage and condescension of Lady Catherine de Bourgh."

Jane cast her a look that was equal parts amusement and exasperation.

Mr Collins raised his head from his plate with eager interest. "Did you mention Lady Catherine, Cousin Elizabeth?"

"Yes, Mr Collins," Jane replied sweetly. "We were just saying how very fortunate you are, sir, to have such a noble and attentive benefactress."

"Now you have done it," Lydia mumbled. "He will talk for half an hour at least."

Mr Collins was still talking when Darcy arrived an hour later.

With Darcy came Miss Darcy, who was excited to spend the day at Longbourn with her new sisters. She was warmly welcomed by all, but by Lydia and Kitty especially. Eager to escape Mr Collins and his sermonising, they took Miss Darcy by the hand and out of the room, chatting about scraps of silk and lace and ribbon. Together, they would pick apart all their old bonnets and make them into something better.

After greeting the rest of her family and assuring her mother he would not forget to come back again once he left for town, Darcy proposed walking out for half an hour.

Elizabeth readily assented.

When they were a fair distance from the house, she said, "I cannot help but notice your sister is no longer quite so shy as she was when I first had the pleasure of her acquaintance."

Darcy shook his head with an infinitesimal smile. "No. Georgiana is happy. She has always wanted a sister. Now she is to gain five."

"Does it bother you?" she asked, biting her lip as she slipped her hand into the crook of his arm.

"Does what bother me?"

"The fact that your sister is so taken with my sisters. Their manners are not what they ought to be, and if they are to spend time together...I know you had hoped Miss Darcy would make friends whom she might eventually take into her confidence, but Kitty and Lydia cannot be what you envisioned to fulfil such a role. I love them both dearly, but I am by no means blind to their faults."

"Yet, despite their faults, I believe neither is beyond hope. They are young, and they lack guidance and consistency."

"Not to mention sense," Elizabeth added with a rueful little smile.

"Even so. They have seen nothing of the world. Removing them from Longbourn and sending them to school would teach them worthy skills. It would broaden their thinking, foster understanding, and greatly improve their minds. In the meantime, I believe your sisters can learn much from Georgiana, just as Georgiana can learn much from them."

She stared at him in consternation, doubtful Darcy's sister, who played the pianoforte with as much mastery as the performers she had seen in London's concert halls, could learn anything exemplary from her own sisters. "And what," she enquired, "would she learn? How to spend all her pin money well before the last quarter day has arrived? How to flirt with officers twice her age and make herself and her family ridiculous?"

Darcy stiffened and Elizabeth immediately regretted her words. "Forgive me. That was uncalled for. My sisters are indeed young and lack maturity and guidance." She endeavoured to smile, but her smile lacked its usual lustre. "Thankfully, your sister is eminently capable of recognising the difference between respectable behaviour and what is not. Hopefully, she will instil some measure of her goodness and self-preservation in Kitty and Lydia. I harbour no doubts they would benefit from emulating her steadiness and restraint."

He stopped walking at once, his countenance impenetrably grave, and ran his hand across his mouth.

Elizabeth could not account for his doing so. "Have I displeased you, sir?"

Darcy glanced at her, then quickly away to stare at some indeterminable point in the distance, in the direction of Oakham Mount. He cleared his throat. "I am not displeased," he replied with unforeseen gravity. "But there is something I must tell you. Now, before we proceed any further."

They found a stone bench nestled in the hermitage, and for the next hour he told her of his history with George Wickham. He told her about Georgiana and what he had found and seen and felt when he surprised her in Ramsgate that awful, fateful day. He told her about the pile of letters he had received from the scoundrel since coming to Hertfordshire, and how they effectively served to increase his torment and compound his fear to near intolerable proportions—fear for Georgiana's reputation and his own. When he was finished, he asked her, "Do you still wish to honour your commitment to me? If you have changed your mind, I shall find some way out of it for you."

Stunned he would even consider releasing her from their engagement, Elizabeth stared at him for what must have been a full minute. "Of course I still wish to marry you. You cannot possibly think I would wish otherwise."

Darcy shook his head. "I cannot imagine you are pleased by what I have related. Shocked. Disgusted. Appalled. Those would be more appropriate responses."

Elizabeth continued to stare at him. He loved her. Of that she was certain. She could see it in his every expression, in the way he spoke to her, listened to her, and touched her. At length, she said, "Is that what you wish, sir? To be rid of me?"

"No," he replied at once. "It is the last thing I would ever wish."

"Are you certain?" she enquired. "Yesterday, I raised similar concerns about you eventually coming to regret your choice."

"And I believe I told you, honestly and openly, that will never come to pass. I know all I need to know of you. For as long as I live, I shall not change my mind."

"Then allow me to ask you this. If the situation was different, would you choose differently? If it were one of my sisters who eloped with a libertine, would you abandon me so readily?"

His answer was fervent and immediate. "There is nothing you could say or do that would deter me from wanting you. Nothing that would drive me away."

"Then consider the matter closed, for neither do I wish to desert you. Georgiana has no mother, no sister, and an aunt who sounds more like an army captain than a maternal figure. I doubt her cousin, Miss de Bourgh, provides any guidance never mind consolation. What kind of sister would I be if I were to abandon her now?"

THE LUXURY OF SILENCE

He opened his mouth as though to answer her, but Elizabeth touched her fingertips to his lips to silence him. "It was a rhetorical question, Fitzwilliam. I require no reply. I require only your safe return as soon as may be. I find I am quite impatient to become Mrs Darcy. Your sister, you see, is not the only Darcy in need of affection, and I am determined that you will have your share."

Shutting his eyes, Darcy kissed her fingertips, grasped her hand, and cradled it against his cheek. "You exceed my every expectation." With unexampled tenderness, he kissed her palm, her wrist, and finally her lips. Then he produced what looked to be a letter from his greatcoat pocket and pressed it into her hand. "Once I have gone, will you do me the honour of reading this letter?"

⁂

"I congratulate you, Eliza. It is not every day a lady has the good fortune to receive a proposal from so handsome and eligible a gentleman as Mr Darcy of Pemberley."

Elizabeth smiled as she checked the strength of the tea. "You mean that you have come to say, 'I told you so', and to gloat. Admit it, Charlotte. You were determined that I should not let Mr Darcy get away, and you are gratified to see that your plans have come to fruition in the end."

"You know me well," said Charlotte with an amused smile. "But I cannot think that you are not also well pleased. Tell me truthfully. Do you like him?"

"I do," she replied. "I do like him. I love him."

Charlotte reached for her hand and gave it an affectionate squeeze. "Then I am truly glad for you."

"If there was only such a man for you," Elizabeth told her impishly. "I daresay Mr Shirley is looking better and better."

"No," her friend insisted. "Not Mr Shirley. As much as I

like him, I have not the fortitude to become the wife of a man who cannot afford to provide me with my own home, nor do I wish to be reliant on the charity of his relations. Esteem and fondness are not enough for me, nor is that likely to change. Given an abundance of material comforts, perhaps it is possible for love to grow from nothing. But regarding Mr Shirley and his situation as a third son, it is not to be. Without an adequate income, any affection I may harbour for him will eventually sink into indifference, resentment, and regret. I would not desire it, for either of us."

Across the room, Mr Collins regaled Sir William and Lady Lucas, Charlotte's sister Maria, and Mrs Bennet with cheerful descriptions of Rosings Park which, by all accounts, sounded very grand. Elizabeth repressed a smile. According to Darcy, his aunt's home was ornate, ostentatious, and uselessly fine, much like the two ladies who lived there.

Charlotte glanced from a plate of biscuits to Mr Collins, her mien thoughtful. "Your cousin seems to be a very amiable gentleman. He also seems quite taken with his patroness and the living she has bestowed upon him."

"Yes," Elizabeth replied, adding cream to two painted china cups before filling them with tea. "Mr Collins is a cordial, attentive sort of person, and most fortunate in his situation. His patroness, Lady Catherine de Bourgh, happens to be Mr Darcy's aunt."

"You are joking, surely."

"I am not," said Elizabeth with an arch look as she handed a steaming cup of tea to her friend. "Mr Collins is in raptures over her ladyship's nobility, her condescension, and her endless stream of advice. It seems that nothing is beneath her notice, for she has opinions regarding all his domestic concerns, and his sermon writing as well."

Charlotte's brows rose to her hairline. "That is...unusual. But, then again, I suppose the rich may do as they like."

Elizabeth smiled as she raised her own teacup to her lips. "Yes. And apparently Lady Catherine likes very much to be of use."

"It does not sound as though Mr Collins minds her interference in his affairs."

"No. I believe Lady Catherine could not have bestowed her generosity upon a more grateful person. Let us hope that the future Mrs Collins, whomever she may be, will look upon her ladyship's condescension with the same appreciative eye."

"Yes," Charlotte agreed. "Let us hope."

❧

It was not until much later, once the Lucases had departed, the supper table was cleared, and her family had all gone to bed, that Elizabeth was finally able to read Darcy's letter. All day long she had felt its presence in her pocket—the weight of it, the significance of it, and the flutter of anticipation that accompanied it, knowing that he had felt the desire to put pen to paper and compose these words to her.

At last, her curiosity would be satisfied.

Ensconced in her bedchamber, Elizabeth took a moment to admire her name as it was written in Darcy's firm, exacting hand. The thick, wax seal on the back bore a design she assumed was his family's crest. Slipping her finger beneath it, she opened her letter and read:

What joy lies within your eyes.

What bliss within the circle of your arms; what succour upon your lips.

One glance from you, one touch of your hand, one word from your mouth, and I am soothed. Yet the pureness of your heart and the sweetness of your beauty stir within my breast a lover's admiration and desire.

Would that you were already my wife, and that your heart and your body yearned for mine as fervently as mine yearn for yours. Would that these words were enough to tempt your lips to bestow upon mine a passionate kiss, and your limbs a most ardent embrace...

My dearest, loveliest, Elizabeth,

I pray that such ardent professions, which I have so boldly put to paper, will not starve away our fine, stout love and cause you to think less of me. I want no secrets between us and look forward to the day when I shall be privileged enough to know all of yours, just as you will soon know all of mine.

Think of me while I am away, for I think of you endlessly, and shall miss you more than you know.

Yours,

Fitzwilliam Darcy

Blushing profusely and moved beyond measure by the sentiments he professed, Elizabeth read Darcy's letter again and again. When she could recite each word from memory, she carefully folded her letter and tucked it in a book of poems in her bedside table, all the while wondering how he could ever think she would wish to be free of him, even for a day.

For a sensible man, in this at least, Darcy had shown himself to be utterly nonsensical.

Regardless, she found it comforting, not to mention gratifying, that he appeared to be as deeply affected by her as she was by him.

SEVENTEEN

❦

A watch is always too fast or too slow.

THE SOUNDS AND SMELLS OF TOWN WERE A STARK
contrast to those of the countryside. In the country, there
were birds and wild creatures and fresh, clean air. Ancient
manor houses dotted the landscape, their holdings extending
over thousands of acres of land, cultivated and kept for
centuries by a privileged legacy of fathers and sons.
Surrounding these great ancestral homes were woods full of
game, rivers and lakes stocked with trout, pike, and tench, and
fields where tenant farmers tended crops in fertile soil. There
were orchards and pastures and manicured parks replete with
pleasure gardens where the scent of flowers pervaded the air
with a sweetness not replicated in a hothouse.

Entering London felt like entering a different world.
Although green spaces existed in the form of residential parks
and open fields in the better neighbourhoods, countless others
were heaving with humanity—the endless bustle of a popula-
tion more than a million strong going about their daily
concerns. The number of wagons and carriages rumbling
through some eight thousand London streets far exceeded
those travelling along the sparse, rural roads of the country.

There were factories, workhouses, rows of shops, and clubs. There were costermongers peddling their wares, street sweepers, and lamp lighters. There were horses and livestock in the streets, sewage in the river Thames, and people. Day or night, fair weather or foul, there were people and there was noise, and the overwhelming stench of city life.

As a boy, London had been an exciting place to visit, full of new experiences, new sights, and new smells. However, by the time Darcy was required to step into his father's shoes as Pemberley's master, the attractions that town offered a man of means appealed to him less and less. True, he still enjoyed frequenting the theatre, attending concerts, and visiting museums, but Darcy's interest in other entertainments had waned. Evening parties were crowded with eager mothers and their unwed daughters. Dinners and balls were much the same. His club, where he had often enjoyed discussing philosophy and politics, was teaming with men whose present ambitions tended more towards arranging introductions to their daughters than to dissecting the latest treatises in the House of Lords, or investment opportunities in Manchester. His friends, even the married ones, spent more time with their mistresses than they did their families and wives.

Darcy lived a quieter life. He preferred country hours and indulging country habits rather than keeping up appearances with the most fashionable people in the most fashionable venues at the most fashionable hours. He had no patience for, nor an interest in, any person who cared too much for his pocketbook and too little for the steadiness of his character. One of those people, Thomas Stotesbury, was currently eyeing him from across the dining room at his club. Darcy promptly returned his attention to his dinner, avoiding eye contact with the man.

I wonder whether he has managed to bankrupt himself yet

or whether he means to renew our acquaintance. Either way, I shall not be marrying his insufferable sister.

"Why do you look like that?" his cousin, Viscount Emerson, enquired as he pushed a boiled potato around his plate with his fork.

"Why do I look like what?" Darcy replied, reaching for his wine glass and raising it to his lips. The incessant hum of conversation in the room was giving him a headache.

"As though you have smelled something unpleasant."

Emerson's father, Lord Carlisle, snorted. "Darcy always looks as though he is displeased with something, Arthur. Once he settles down and marries Anne, that will change."

Shaking his head, Colonel Fitzwilliam gestured for a footman to bring more wine. "I would not count on it," he said pleasantly.

"Anne has thirty-thousand pounds," said Lord Carlisle with the confidence of a man used to having his way. "That is a fine sum."

"For Anne?" Emerson wrinkled his nose, set his fork on his plate, and pushed it aside. "Codswallop. Thirty-thousand pounds for taking Anne is a penance. She is no diamond of the first water, you know. Besides, Darcy is not like the rest of us. He is clever and therefore likes to speak of clever things. Anne is duller than a soup spoon. I doubt she even knows what day of the week it is never mind that we are at war with the French."

"Anne is not altogether ignorant," his lordship insisted, linking his hands over his stomach as he reclined in his chair.

"She is ignorant enough," said Emerson. "I would not take her for thirty thousand, that is for certain. I would not even take her for fifty." He smirked as he glanced at his brother. "Perhaps Richard might want her. Rosings Park is a pretty little piece, even if Anne is not."

Giving Emerson a look that clearly communicated he did not, in fact, want Anne, Fitzwilliam said, "While I would certainly not balk at thirty-thousand pounds, I do prefer my wife to have some meat on her bones, as well as the ability and desire to hold a conversation—any kind of conversation. Anne is not for me."

"Of course she is not," said Lord Carlisle, slapping Darcy's back. "Anne is for Darcy. Always has been."

When Darcy made no effort to refute such a claim but chose to take another gulp of wine from his glass instead, Fitzwilliam kicked him sharply under the table. "You know Lady Catherine has been spouting that nonsense for years, but in the end, nothing will come of it. Darcy has never cared for Anne—none of us have. Nor would Lady Anne Darcy ever have consigned her dear boy to a lifetime of misery with such a dour creature. If Darcy ever did consent to take her on, I doubt Anne would speak two words to him never mind let him in her bed."

Lord Carlisle made a dismissive gesture with his hand. "That hardly signifies. A wife has a duty to provide her husband with an heir. Anne will comply. If she does not, Darcy will simply have to assert his right as her husband. Once he gets her with child, he may look elsewhere for his fun. He need not bother with his wife once he has secured an heir for Pemberley. I doubt Anne will care. She will likely welcome the reprieve. As for Catherine, she will have nothing to repine so long as Darcy is her son."

Fitzwilliam kicked him again, harder this time.

Repressing an oath, Darcy drained the last mouthful of wine from his glass and glared at his overzealous cousin. The last thing he had wanted to do was inform his uncle of his engagement in the middle of White's, but Lord Carlisle's voice had only become firmer and more insistent as the evening progressed, as had Fitzwilliam's aim. Steeling himself for a potentially unpleasant scene, he set his empty glass on the table and said, "Despite what you think Anne and Lady Catherine will or will not tolerate in such a situation, you have overlooked one significant detail in this plan you have concocted."

His uncle frowned. "And what is that detail, Nephew? To what do you refer?"

"I refer to my compliance, your lordship. You never will have it. Anne will never be my wife, and I shall not tolerate everyone in White's thinking otherwise."

Lord Carlisle was poised to speak, but Darcy forged onward and made his announcement. "Saturday last, I made an offer of marriage to Miss Elizabeth Bennet and am delighted to say she has accepted me. Her father's estate is in Hertfordshire, and he has given us both his blessing and his consent. This afternoon I obtained a licence, and my solicitor is drawing up the settlement as we speak. It is as good as done."

All at the table save for Colonel Fitzwilliam, with whom Darcy had shared his happy news the moment he arrived in London that day, stared at him in consternation.

"You cannot be serious," his uncle stammered.

"I am perfectly serious. Miss Elizabeth Bennet will be Mrs Darcy within a month."

"And this woman, whom no one has ever heard of—this Eliza Bennet—is your choice?" Emerson asked, looking as though he could hardly believe his ears.

"She is," said Darcy in a voice that left no room for argument.

Emerson snorted. "I take it she has nothing in common with Anne de Bourgh, then."

One corner of Darcy's mouth lifted as he thought of Elizabeth's intelligence, her impertinence, her beauty, and her smile. "No. They have nothing in common whatsoever."

"What of her fortune?" the earl demanded gruffly. "Is it adequate?"

Darcy brushed a piece of lint from his coat sleeve. "There is no dowry to speak of, but that does not mean Elizabeth comes to me with nothing."

"What the deuce does that mean?" his uncle exclaimed, drawing the attention of several gentlemen dining at a nearby table.

"It means," Darcy told him, pitching his voice low, "that she possesses qualities which I find infinitely more valuable than pound notes. Pray lower your voice else the entire room hears you. We are not in the privacy of Grosvenor Street."

His uncle stared at him as though he was a stranger.

Emerson, however, laughed. "You have stayed in the country too long, Darcy. Your mind has become addled. What you need is a good tup. You need not marry some country girl to get it either. The West End is full of obliging ladies who will have you."

"They will likely have the French disease as well," said Fitzwilliam drily. "Especially if Arthur and his friends have been there first."

Emerson gave his brother a look of utmost annoyance. "Forget about tupping, then," he said with a haughty sniff, "and let us talk of money. You have seen my wife, Darcy. Josephine is not unattractive per se, but she is only marginally better looking than Anne. Aside from a generous bosom, a resentful temper, and titled relations, she came with eighty-thousand pounds. I would have been a fool to ignore such a sum in favour of a pretty face with nothing to her name."

"How fortunate for Lady Josephine that you conde-scended to take her on," Darcy remarked, not even attempting to conceal his sarcasm.

Emerson merely shrugged.

"This is ludicrous," his uncle blustered, thankfully at a volume that did not carry to those beyond their own party. "You cannot ignore your duty to your family by marrying this nobody!"

At this point, Darcy had heard all he was willing to abide from his uncle regarding the subject of marriage and duty. He said, "You, more than anyone, know better than to lecture me about duty. My entire life I have done as I was bid, and while it has given me satisfaction and a sense of pride and fulfilment to please those for whom I care, it has not always brought me happiness. Elizabeth brings me happiness. I shall not give her up to appease Lady Catherine, nor so that you and your friends may collect on a wager you should never have made in the first place."

To emphasise his point, he fixed his uncle with a steely, level look that could not possibly be misinterpreted. "I lost my mother when I was sixteen, and my father when I was not three-and-twenty. I had no choice in the matter, but I persevered. I did my duty. To my family, to Georgiana, and to Pemberley. My personal business does not belong in a betting book, Uncle. In the future, I urge you to remember that before you lay down money and tell your friends what I shall and shall not do." He tossed his napkin on the table, rose from his chair, and quit the room without another word.

Outside White's, the sky was clear, but the night felt as cold as it was dark. Tamping down his annoyance with his uncle, Darcy buttoned his greatcoat to his chin as he waited for his carriage to be brought around to the front entrance. He had passed a long, tedious afternoon travelling from Hertfordshire to town, which was made even longer and more tedious by his spending another hour in Doctors' Commons petitioning the archbishop for a marriage licence. The settlement had been an easier task, but his solicitor required time to draw up the marriage articles, and so Darcy would have to return for them on the morrow.

His carriage appeared at the same moment Colonel Fitzwilliam stepped outside, fastening the buttons on his greatcoat. Although Darcy valued his judgment tremendously, he regretted accompanying him to White's. The earl was not known for being reasonable, especially pertaining to matters of the heart, and Emerson, having a higher opinion of his wife's fortune than his wife, was little better. His announcement had not gone as planned.

"Are you for Darcy House?" his cousin enquired.

"Yes. Do you intend to join me?"

"If you can bear my company. I know you must want to beat me for dragging you to dinner with my father this evening. Nor do I blame you."

"You are always welcome," Darcy told him as his footman opened the door. "Even when your good intentions go amiss." He climbed inside and settled himself on the forward-facing seat with a weary exhalation.

His cousin followed suit and claimed the seat opposite, facing the rear. "You know you could not have kept it from him, Darcy. My father would have heard it all from Lady Catherine soon enough. From what you intimated about her parson, it is likely the man has already written to her of your engagement. It is only a matter of time before she writes to my father. This was the best way to go about it. He will go home now, drink too much port, mutter and complain, and come morning my mother will set him straight."

Darcy turned his attention to the window as the carriage lurched forward and began making its way through the streets of St James towards Mayfair. He could not refute what his cousin had said of Lady Catherine writing to his uncle. Should Mr Collins happen to inform her of his engagement to Elizabeth, she would be furious to say the least. "I know," he muttered in resignation. "It is better this way, although it pains me that your father is more concerned for his pocket-book and his connexions than for my happiness and my peace of mind."

"He will come around eventually. If your Miss Elizabeth is everything you claim, she will do a fine job of charming him into submission. Regardless of his impression of her, he will not dare denounce her publicly, or give any indication he does not approve of your choice. The family," said Fitzwilliam, imitating his father's deep, stuffy baritone, "must always present a united front. We must always consider appearances, et cetera, et cetera...blah, blah, blah."

Darcy rolled his eyes, but what Fitzwilliam said of his father was true. Behind closed doors, Lord Carlisle would pitch a fit and rail until he was blue in the face, but in public he would wear a chipper smile and pretend all was well, even if it was not. For that, Darcy supposed he should be thankful.

"When do you plan to return to Hertfordshire?"

Resting his head against the back of his seat, Darcy rubbed his eyes. "I have another meeting with my solicitor tomorrow morning. If the settlement is in order and nothing else needs to be done, I shall set out after my business with him is complete. I would prefer not to leave Georgiana in the care of Bingley's sisters longer than necessary, although I am certain she will beg Bingley to take her to Longbourn rather than remain at Netherfield with Miss Bingley and Mrs Hurst."

"Would you mind if I accompanied you? To Hertford-shire, I mean. I should like to meet your Miss Elizabeth."

Darcy eyed him speculatively. "If you intend to talk me out of marrying her once you have, you will be wasting your time. Her family is not what I had envisioned when I imag-ined forming an alliance with a woman, but for the most part I have made my peace with their eccentricities and imperfections." He shook his head. "Despite their titles and noble lineage, our own family, you must own, is far from perfect. While most of Elizabeth's relations will likely improve with time and exposure to more superior society, Elizabeth and her eldest sister are both exceptional young women. After knowing her, I cannot imagine my life without her."

"I know. I can see your heart is set on having her. That, in and of itself, must recommend her to me, and her family as well. In any case, I know you, perhaps better than you know yourself. You would never have formed such an attachment to a woman who was unworthy of you, Darcy."

"I fought my attraction to her for weeks," Darcy admitted.

"Because of her imperfect family?"

"Her imperfect family. And her inferior connexions. And her lack of fortune. I was intent upon marrying to please your father and to fulfil the expectations of my friends, not to please myself. At least at first."

Fitzwilliam blinked at him. "You cannot mean to say that you actually entertained the idea of marrying Anne..."

"No," said Darcy with a rueful shake of his head. "I was never going to marry Anne. But I had thought, given time, I would perhaps meet with a respectable woman whose status would further elevate my own, and whose conversation and understanding of the world would be tolerable. Then I met Elizabeth, and all I had previously thought and felt regarding matrimony, not to mention my felicity, changed. It did not change overnight, I grant you, but soon enough the prospect of taking another woman as my wife—even one who possesses those qualities and accomplishments society has deemed so desirable—made me sick to my stomach. I could not so much as think it. I knew better than to believe I could ever bring myself to do it, and so I proposed to the one woman I knew could make me happy—who *has* made me happy. I have no regrets."

"She must be very special to make you feel so much. Miss Elizabeth is most fortunate to have earned your regard."

"Of the two of us, I am the fortunate one. She is...I love her, Fitzwilliam. More than I can ever express."

His cousin smiled. "Then I am certain I shall love her as well. I look forward to making her acquaintance."

"Thank you," he said sincerely. "Your support means the world to me."

"You will always have it, just as I shall always be happy to give it to you. But you did not mention how Georgiana is getting on. I suppose she approves of Miss Elizabeth if she is eager to pass her days at Longbourn?"

Darcy smiled. "Georgiana adores Elizabeth and all her sisters. She is a different person from whom she was a month ago. She is less shy, more confident, and almost completely at ease with the Bennets. Even Mrs Bennet, who is of a nervous disposition and focused upon seeing her daughters well settled, does not put her off. Elizabeth's younger sisters, Miss Catherine and Miss Lydia, are teaching her to be more assured, and she is teaching them restraint. Miss Mary, she is teaching to play duets on the pianoforte. She will be pleased to see you."

"And I her. But what is this about teaching restraint?" the colonel enquired with a frown. "What sort of girls are Miss Elizabeth's sisters?"

Darcy sighed. It was best to reveal all, especially as Fitzwilliam would soon meet them for himself. "Elizabeth has four sisters. The eldest is Bingley's favourite, the middle one is prim and bookish, and the youngest two are near Georgiana's age. Regrettably, they are somewhat silly and in need of guidance, but I have confidence that with time and a firm hand they will become fine young women. I plan to send them to school."

"Why has their father not sent them to school?"

"While Mr Bennet is a scholar and an avid reader, he is more interested in sequestering himself in his book room than overseeing the education of his youngest daughters."

Colonel Fitzwilliam raised his brows. "That is a recipe for disaster if ever I have seen one."

"We are in accord, then." He eyed him for a long moment in silence. "You should know Miss Catherine and Miss Lydia are great admirers of the militia currently quartered in Meryton. Their encampment is but a few miles from Netherfield. Perhaps, if you wear your red coat, their attention may be redirected."

"Not a chance," said his cousin with a laugh. "You are on your own. Send them to school, but do not count on me to improve their manners. If anything, I shall only encourage them towards mischief."

"Enough said," Darcy told him with a wry smile. "In any case, I am certain Miss Bingley will show you every civility in her power. It is not every day the son of the Earl of Carlisle sees fit to grace her home with his presence."

Fitzwilliam snorted. "Arthur is the consequential son. I am only the spare."

"You are more agreeable by far. Emerson is a dandy and a libertine. I do not know how Lady Josephine lives with him."

"As of September, she no longer does. Since she has given Arthur a son at last, he has made good on his promise to establish himself elsewhere. I know he intends to purchase a house in town eventually, but for now he is content to live in the one he purchased for his mistress."

"You mean to say he keeps only one?" Darcy remarked, unable to keep the disgust from his voice.

Fitzwilliam shook his head. "Of late, he has secured the favours of a Miss Dankworth. She is a bit actress, but by no means a good one. To my knowledge, there are no others, at least not presently. But I am not particularly interested in

Arthur's comings and goings. I am far more interested in acquainting myself with your Miss Elizabeth." He grinned. "I believe you mentioned she is impertinent."

The corners of Darcy's lips lifted as he looked out of the window. "Quite."

Darcy glanced at his watch, then returned his gaze to the view outside his carriage. In the distance, he could see Oakham Mount growing ever closer, and he smiled. Along the London Road, shadows lengthened as the sun continued its descent towards the horizon, signalling the end of another day. Since he had left town hours earlier, delicate, frosty etchings had formed on the edges of the windowpanes, and each exhalation of Darcy's breath caused a foggy film to form on the glass. Such an obstruction was remedied easily enough with a swipe of his gloves, but the bricks at his feet, which had come directly from the fire when they had stopped for an hour to rest the horses at The King's Head, had long since lost their warmth.

"How much longer?" Colonel Fitzwilliam enquired, stifling a yawn as he stretched his tall frame along the rear facing seat. "I have grown weary of travelling."

"It is not long now," Darcy told him as his coachman turned onto King Street and entered Meryton.

"I could use a hot bath, a warm fire, and a good meal. I can no longer feel my feet."

"You sound like Emerson instead of a foot soldier. I thought you were made of sterner stuff."

"Because I happen to be a soldier does not mean I am happy to sit in a cold carriage for four hours. Have pity on me. If I happen to freeze to death, who will you look to for sage advice and companionship? And before you tell me you will soon find those comforts, among others, in your future wife, I shall remind you Miss Elizabeth Bennet has not mucked about with you since you were in leading strings, nor is she privy to your most embarrassing secrets." One corner of Fitzwilliam's mouth curled upwards. "If you would like to keep her in ignorance, I urge you to be nice to me, else I accidentally tell her any number of mortifying tales."

Darcy rolled his eyes. Rather than acknowledge his cousin's ribbing, he directed his attention to the window and pointed out the encampment of tents erected on the village green. Colonel Forster's regiment was well known to him, and the man himself possessed an aptitude for strategising that was impressive. Countless red coated officers milled about the encampment, but several were presently gathered on the far side of the street. Darcy recognised Captain Carter and Mr Denny, who were engaged in conversation with several other men. He pointed them out to Fitzwilliam as well.

"If you like, we can pay a call upon Colonel Forster tomorrow. I have found him to be an amicable fellow of considerable intelligence, despite his taking a wife who is barely out of the schoolroom. He would enjoy making your acquaintance. I believe he was in Portugal, although I understand he does not care to speak of it."

Fitzwilliam's countenance revealed his surprise. "I can hardly blame him. Had I been sent to Portugal, I doubt I would wish to speak of it either, especially to my general acquaintance. As for meeting this Colonel Forster, I shall look forward to an introduction if for no reason other than we share a common profession. After all, one never knows when one may need a favour someday, or a friend with other resourceful and well-connected friends."

"True," Darcy muttered absently. In truth, he had been thinking more about seeing Elizabeth than Colonel Forster and whomever he might know beyond Meryton. He was about to avert his eyes from Mr Denny's group, but one of the men turned and Darcy was better able to see his face.

His intake of breath was immediate and sharp.

There, in the middle of Meryton, stood George Wickham.

Sick with dread and sick to his stomach, Darcy tore his eyes from the window as he felt the blood drain from his face.

Fitzwilliam regarded him with concern. "Whatever is the matter?"

Darcy could not speak. He could barely credit what he had seen.

"Darcy," said his cousin with some urgency, leaning forward in his seat. "What has happened? Truly, you look ill."

Darcy passed his hand over his mouth, cursing his wretched luck.

Had Wickham come to Hertfordshire to make more threats? Had he come for Georgiana? How the devil had he found her? Darcy shut his eyes and endeavoured to bring his roiling emotions under regulation.

"For the love of God," Fitzwilliam cried. "Tell me what has happened before I stop this coach and call for a doctor!"

Finally, after swallowing the bile that had risen in his throat, Darcy found his voice. "Wickham," he said tersely, "is in Meryton. I saw him just now. On the green, by the smithy." Although his initial horror remained, another emotion had begun to simmer beneath the surface: outrage.

"Here?" Fitzwilliam cried incredulously, twisting around in his seat. "In Hertfordshire?"

"Yes," Darcy said in annoyance as his temper flared. "Speaking to the officers."

His cousin's countenance turned murderous. "Has he been here the entire time?"

"Of course not! He must have come yesterday or today."

"Why?"

Beyond furious, Darcy uttered an oath. Clearly, the time for complete, scrupulous honesty was upon him, regardless of his disinclination to speak of those damnable letters! Once he made his confession, Fitzwilliam would likely want to thrash him for keeping Wickham's threats and attempted extortion to himself. But there was nothing else to be done. Darcy was in no state to deal with Wickham on his own. He needed his cousin, and he needed a plan.

"I must tell you something," he said darkly. "Something I ought to have told you weeks ago but did not."

Fitzwilliam pursed his lips. If his cousin's stormy countenance was any indication, what Darcy had to relate would not be well received.

Cursing himself and Wickham both, he told Fitzwilliam about the letters. He told him of the appalling things Wickham had to say about Georgiana and what she had consented to in Ramsgate. Then he told him of Wickham's demands for money—the outrageous sum he expected to receive as payment for his silence. When he had finished, he averted his gaze to the window, quietly seething as he imagined choking Wickham within an inch of his life.

Fitzwilliam was silent for what felt like an eternity, his countenance as grim as Darcy had ever seen it. Finally, as the carriage turned onto Netherfield's long, gravel drive, he asked, "Can you afford to pay it?"

"No." It pained Darcy to admit it. He was a prudent man, but the sum Wickham had demanded was in excess of ten thousand pounds. While he *could* pay it, he could not afford to part with such a large amount at once. Not when he had already set aside Georgiana's thirty-thousand pounds. He would be left with a hole in his coffers that would take years of economising, and perhaps even retrenching, to recoup.

There was also a part of him—a stubborn, fed up,

incensed part of him—that flatly refused to part with so much as another shilling to the reprobate, despite the imminent threat to his sister's reputation and his own.

His cousin shook his head. "We shall resolve this," was all he said in reply.

EIGHTEEN

❦

Wickedness is always wickedness,
but folly is not always folly.

"He did not love me," Georgiana whispered miserably, wiping tears from her cheeks. "He wanted my fortune. He wanted to hurt my brother. And he wanted... other things. Things no lady should ever grant any man who is not her husband."

Elizabeth stood alone in the upstairs hall, before the partially closed door of the bedchamber Kitty and Lydia shared. All her sisters, save for Jane, were perched on the roomy four-poster bed with Georgiana in their midst, listening with rapt attention, incredulousness, and horror as she spoke haltingly of Ramsgate and her near elopement with Mr Wickham. Although Darcy had confided the entire incident to Elizabeth yesterday morning, until now she had no tangible knowledge of Georgiana's feelings, only what Darcy had related in addition to her own speculations. Hearing the girl speak of her experience was sobering to say the least; as sobering as seeing the reprobate himself in Meryton that very morning.

"You did not surrender your virtue to him, surely," Mary whispered urgently, leaning forwards and pitching her voice low so as not to be overheard.

"Hush, Mary," said Lydia crossly, wrapping her arm around Georgiana's shoulders. "Can you not see dear Georgiana is upset enough as it is? She is far too proper to behave so inappropriately with any man, especially a man who is as awful as that Mr Wickham. She may have been taken in by him, but she would never have done *that,* I daresay."

Lydia had no sooner finished delivering her speech than Mary's countenance grew heated and her expression contrite. "Of course not. Do forgive me for uttering such nonsense, Georgiana. Your manners are the most elegant of any young lady I know, and your behaviour is always beyond reproach. We would all do well to emulate your comportment."

Nodding her head, Kitty agreed. "Of course Georgiana would never permit any man such liberties. And if Mr Wickham was a gentleman, I am certain he would never have proposed such scandalous activities in the first place." She wrinkled her nose distastefully. "Can you imagine Mr Bingley or Mr Darcy proposing such things to Jane and Lizzy?"

"Certainly not," Mary replied. "Nor would our sisters ever consent to engage in such sinful behaviour. We none of us should ever think of perpetrating such lascivious acts never mind engaging in them."

"Mr Wickham is a hateful man," Lydia proclaimed with vehemence. "He is nothing at all like Mr Darcy and Mr Bingley. They are gentlemen and will always behave as such."

Georgiana, who had been sniffling before, began weeping in earnest as Mary, Kitty, and Lydia persisted in expounding upon her goodness and that of her brother.

Deciding enough had been said of Mr Wickham and his depravity for one afternoon, Elizabeth opened the door and joined them, making sure to close it behind her so their voices would not carry to the rest of the house. "Sisters," she said gently but firmly. "While I am certain Georgiana appreciates your ardent defence of her character, there has been enough talk of the wicked Mr Wickham for today. Pray allow her some time to compose herself and rest before we are called downstairs for tea."

"There is no harm in talking," Lydia informed her. "Aunt Gardiner says it is good to speak of things that pain us. Georgiana has no one in whom to confide, and we are all of us eager to listen. She will likely feel better before long."

"Aunt Gardiner is indeed very wise, but she has also warned against speaking too freely of our most private matters, especially where others are liable to overhear." Elizabeth fixed all her sisters with a steady, serious look and said, "I need not remind you—any of you—that Mr Darcy would not want his sister's distress or his family's concerns to be generally known. I trust that each of you will exercise restraint and repeat nothing of what Georgiana has confided here to anyone, including Mama and Aunt Philips. I love them dearly, but they cannot be trusted to keep a secret to save their souls. Should so much as one word of this business with Mr Wickham leave this house, now or ever, I cannot vouch for Mr Darcy's temper. Georgiana will be our sister, and her reputation, as well as each of our own, is reliant upon the strictest secrecy."

Although seemingly reluctant to abandon their friend, Mary, Kitty, and Lydia rose from the bed with solemn faces.

"We shall not say one word of what you told us to anyone, Georgiana, not even to Mama," Lydia promised, tucking a loose strand of hair behind her ear. "And we certainly shall not give that horrid Mr Wickham the time of day should we ever actually meet him. He is undeserving of our notice and your tears!"

"That is right," Kitty agreed, pressing Georgiana's hand. "We are to be sisters. You will have all of us to confide in from now on, and we shall tell you all of our secrets, too."

"And we shall be as silent as the grave," Lydia assured her with uncharacteristic seriousness, "just as we know you will be. I swear it."

"Of course, we shall," Mary replied. "We must stem the tide of malice and pour into the wounded bosoms of each other the balm of sisterly consolation."

"Thank you, Mary," said Elizabeth while Georgiana continued to weep. "I believe that is more than enough assurance for now."

"Lord, Mary," Lydia muttered, glancing worriedly at Georgiana as she pulled Kitty towards the door. "Such nonsense about wounded bosoms is hardly helpful."

"Standing together in the face of adversity and wickedness," Mary insisted, lifting her chin as she followed them from the room, "is always helpful. I am sure Mr Collins would agree completely."

"Oh, hang Mr Collins," said Kitty as Mary closed the door behind them. "What has he to do with anything? Mr Darcy does not like him any more than the rest of us. If *he* found out about Georgiana's troubles, there would be no peace for a fortnight at least. And that horrid benefactress of his..."

Gradually, their voices became less and less discernible until the only sound to be heard in the room was Georgiana's weeping.

Elizabeth's heart ached for her. *To know so much heartbreak and sorrow at such a young age!*

Not for the first time, she wondered what sort of heartless scoundrel would prey upon an innocent, motherless girl. Although she had seen Mr Wickham with her own eyes, it had been from a distance, and she had observed nothing in his manners or his appearance to indicate he was a villain. If anything, he seemed perfectly amiable as he smiled and talked to the officers in Colonel Forster's regiment. That, in and of itself, posed yet another set of questions:

How did Mr Wickham know them?

How *well* did he know them?

And how well did *they* know him?

Elizabeth had no idea, but the reality of his being in Meryton, so near to her home and her family and friends—and Georgiana—sickened her.

Georgiana had no mother to console her, and Darcy was not expected back until tomorrow at the earliest. Elizabeth climbed onto the bed and embraced her. "Hush, my dear. Pray calm yourself, for you are safe. I am so sorry. Had I known Mr Wickham was in Meryton, I would never have sanctioned walking to Mr Worthington's shop. He has used you most cruelly, and I regret that seeing him again has reopened wounds that are still so fresh." She smoothed her hand over Georgiana's hair, hoping the gesture would soothe her. "Regardless of his perfidy and wickedness, I want you to know the disappointment and heartbreak you feel is a natural and justifiable emotion. You have every right to mourn the loss of the man you believed him to be. No one who loves you will judge you for it."

Georgiana shook her head. "I am not now mourning the loss of Mr Wickham," she said brokenly. "I am not now upset because he did not love me. I am upset because I am as sinful and wicked as he is and—"

"You are neither sinful nor wicked! Far from it. Mr Wickham is a debauched libertine and a fortune hunter, and therefore no gentleman. He was very wrong to take advantage of you."

"I know," said Georgiana, attempting to compose herself and failing utterly. "I know Mr Wickham is all those things, but I am no better." And then, in the most heartbroken voice, she confessed, "I allowed him *liberties*, Lizzy! I have done what no proper lady would ever do with a man not her husband, and I have done it more than once!" She wrenched herself from Elizabeth's grasp, horror apparent in her every feature. "What if he tells everyone here what I have done? What if he tells Fitzwilliam! I could not bear it! And my poor brother—he would be so furious with me and disappointed in me all over again! What if this time he is so angry he decides to send me away?"

Attempting to conceal her own distress, Elizabeth cradled Georgiana's face in her hands, mentally cursing Mr Wickham for his reprehensible treatment of a girl so sweet and innocent and *young*. "I doubt very much that Mr Darcy will ever send you away," she said with certainty. "I do not know Mr Wickham and therefore I cannot say one way or the other what *he* might do, but your brother is not the sort of man who would ever allow such slander to be perpetrated against you, nor against anyone he holds dear. If Mr Wickham threatens you or speaks ill of you, your brother will never put up with it, nor shall I."

Georgiana exhaled a tremulous breath. "I hope Mr Wickham will say nothing to anyone," she whispered feelingly. "I hope he will *do* nothing. I hope he will simply go away again, like he did in Ramsgate, and that I shall never have to see him again for the rest of my life. But I suppose that is terribly naïve of me."

"No," Elizabeth told her. "It is terribly human of you, and perfectly understandable and appropriate given the situation." She withdrew her handkerchief from her pocket and pressed it into Georgiana's hand. Darcy's sister had been entirely innocent until Mr Wickham instigated his seduction and filled her head with lies. Not only had she been manipulated and used, but the unconscionable libertine had convinced her she was in love.

Elizabeth worried her bottom lip. It was impossible not to

wonder *which* liberties he had claimed whenever her chaperon had intentionally left them to themselves. When Darcy had discovered them, his sister had been in a state of dishabille that had both disturbed and infuriated him. But that was only one instance, and Georgiana had mentioned there had been several.

Should Georgiana be with child, more than her own life would be affected by her pregnancy; the birth of her child would have far-reaching consequences for Elizabeth and Darcy as well. After a moment of hesitation, Elizabeth extended her hand to the girl. "Would you mind if I ask you a question?"

Georgiana slipped her hand into Elizabeth's and slowly shook her head.

"I fear it is a very personal question," Elizabeth admitted. "You need not feel as though you must answer if you do not wish to do so. We shall soon be sisters, and I want you to know you can confide in me whenever and whatever you like. I shall not judge you, now or ever, but I promise I shall always listen to you, and endeavour to help you however I am able, regardless of the situation and all it entails."

An infinitesimal, tearful smile appeared on Georgiana's lips. "I am glad that you and I shall be sisters, Lizzy, and that your sisters will also become my own." Then she bowed her head and softly, so softly Elizabeth found herself straining to hear her speak, said, "My brother must love you very much. I know I have said so before, but Fitzwilliam is truly the best brother in all the world. I am confident he will be a devoted husband to you, and a wonderful, caring father to my future nieces and nephews. Duty and honour are of utmost importance to him, but so are loyalty and trust. My brother would never have told you about what happened with Mr Wickham if he did not trust you implicitly, so I shall try to answer your question if I can."

"Tell me then," said Elizabeth, giving Georgiana's hand an encouraging squeeze. "Have you had your courses since the summer?"

Georgiana blushed, but she appeared more confused by Elizabeth's question than anything else. "Yes. I have had my courses each month without fail since I was thirteen years old. I have them still. Is...is there a reason I would not continue to have them?"

The relief Elizabeth felt upon hearing Georgiana's answer was the equivalent of having a weight lifted from her shoulders. There would be time enough to explain the reason behind her question later, when Georgiana was not so distressed. For now, she offered the girl a gentle smile. "No," she replied. "All is as it should be. All is well."

❧

After securing the last button on her pelisse, Elizabeth gathered her gloves from the table in the centre of the ante-room, anticipating the feel of brisk winter air on her face as she indulged her desire for a turn in the garden before the sun sank below the horizon. She was wondering where she had left her bonnet when the front door was suddenly thrown open and Darcy strode unannounced into the house.

Relieved and pleased he had returned so soon, she smiled, but her smile faltered when she noticed the hard, determined set of his jaw. His boots and greatcoat were spattered with mud, as though he had ridden hard through the wet muck of the fields. "Mr Darcy," she said as she curtseyed. "You are very welcome back to Longbourn."

He executed the stiffest, most abrupt bow she had ever seen, but the expression in his eyes, which had conveyed a sense of utmost urgency a moment earlier, softened. "Elizabeth," he said to her, stepping forward until only a few inches remained between them. "I am very glad to see you. You know not how much, but I must beg your forgiveness and enquire after my sister. Mrs Hurst informed me I would find her here. I have not an instant to lose."

"Whatever is the matter?" she cried with more feeling than politeness. Then, recollecting herself, she said, "Forgive me. Of course you may see her, but Georgiana is presently upstairs. She is sleeping."

"Sleeping?" he blurted. "It is nearly suppertime. Is she unwell?"

"Georgiana is well, but you should know that she received a shock this morning."

At once, the confusion Darcy wore transformed into an expression of alarm. "What sort of a shock?" he demanded. "Tell me what has happened."

Elizabeth reached for his hand, which he surrendered almost absently, and gripped it. "I do not know how or why," she said, taking care to speak quietly so as not to alert the rest of the house, "but that horrid man—Mr Wickham—is in Meryton." She glanced towards the drawing room, where she knew her mother and sisters were at that moment taking tea with Mr Bingley and Mr Collins. On the other side of the anteroom was her father's book room. She had no idea whether he was within or without. It hardly signified, as they could not possibly continue such a conversation where they stood. "Pray come with me. We cannot speak of this here."

His countenance was grimmer than she had ever seen it, but Darcy allowed her to tug him towards the front door and out of the house. "What has happened?" he demanded a second time as soon as the door shut soundly behind them.

Elizabeth shook her head as she led him past the front garden and around the western side of the house towards the hermitage, where he had revealed his own dealings with Mr Wickham to her the day before. "Pray be patient, sir."

"I am out of patience," he told her irritably, coming to a stop in the middle of the lawn. "Tell me at once what he has done before I lose my mind as well."

"He has done nothing," Elizabeth replied calmly, although she felt anything but calm at present. Whatever his mood, Darcy was usually in control of his emotions. Rarely had she seen him otherwise. Witnessing his self-possession unravelling was unsettling, especially knowing the cause. She glanced at the house. They were still shy of the hermitage, and she hoped they would not be seen by anyone within, especially her parents, who would likely demand answers Elizabeth felt were not within her power to give. "We had not reached King Street when your sister recognised Mr Wickham standing in front of the butcher's shop speaking to Mr Denny."

Darcy stared at her. "Why in the world was Georgiana in Meryton?"

"She was by no means alone. Your sister and mine were much engaged trimming bonnets for most of the morning, but they wanted to make roses and lamented the selection of ribbons in their work baskets. A trip to Mr Worthington's shop was proposed. I did not think you would approve of Georgiana walking to Meryton with only my sisters for company, and so I enlisted Mr Bingley, who had accompanied her to Longbourn shortly after breakfast, to escort us.

"It was...awful, seeing Mr Wickham so unexpectedly. None of us understood what was happening at first. We only noticed Georgiana had suddenly turned very pale. Truly, she looked ill, else I doubt Lydia and Kitty would have so readily agreed to abandon their scheme of ribbon shopping after we had walked all the way to the town. We returned to Longbourn without delay and have remained here the entire day. No one has called, and Mr Bingley has been so good as to remain with us, although he has been more attentive to Jane than to anything else."

Darcy passed his hand over his mouth in agitation. "His admiration of your sister aside, has Bingley ascertained the truth? Did he recognise Wickham?"

"No. I do not believe so, for he did not mention Mr Wickham's name at all, to any of us. But Georgiana was very upset, and my sisters, as attuned to her as they have been of late, soon realised there was more to her discomposure than a supposed illness. Once we arrived home, I intended to speak to her privately, but she would not have my sisters taken in by Mr Wickham's gentlemanlike appearance and revealed all. I wish she had not done it, but I cannot fault her desire to spare them the pain and heartache she has suffered herself."

Shaking his head, Darcy uttered a harsh, unintelligible oath beneath his breath. "It was foolish of her to say anything at all. The entire town will surely know of her ruination before morning, and I shall be helpless to prevent it!"

"While I understand your concern," Elizabeth told him, endeavouring to keep her own emotions in check, "my sisters are fond of Georgiana and have come to look upon her as their own sister, even more so now that she has confided in them. All have promised to say nothing to anyone, including my mother, but I shall speak to them again in any case and reiterate the necessity for secrecy. Mr Wickham, however, is another matter. I do not like that he is here. No one in Hertfordshire knows who he is or of what he is capable."

"I shall deal with Wickham," Darcy told her with grim assurance. "Would that I had acted when I saw him in Meryton myself an hour ago!" As his agitation increased, he began to pace. At length, he said, "Tomorrow, I shall seek him out and confront him. By then, I hope to be better prepared to deal with him. The damage he can wreak upon a single town is significant. I cannot allow him to do in Hertfordshire as he has done in Derbyshire."

Elizabeth frowned. Although she did not like the idea of Mr Wickham inflicting any sort of damage upon the people of Meryton, she liked the idea of Darcy confronting him even less. He was a man who apparently did not abide by a gentleman's code of honour and embraced idleness and dissipation; he was neither to be trusted nor underestimated. "Will you have Mr Bingley accompany you? I do not like the idea of you confronting him alone."

"No. I do not wish to involve Bingley in my personal affairs. Colonel Fitzwilliam will accompany me. Wickham may not fear me as he ought, but that is not true of my cousin. Had Fitzwilliam been the one to discover Wickham in Ramsgate, he would not now be in Meryton. He would likely be in a shallow grave in Kent, or at the bottom of the sea."

Elizabeth did not want to think of anyone lying dead at the bottom of the sea, even the debauched Mr Wickham, and suppressed a shudder. "Will Colonel Fitzwilliam come all the way to Hertfordshire on such short notice? Is he able to travel, or does his duty keep him elsewhere?"

"Fitzwilliam accompanied me to Netherfield. I saw him while I was in London, and I informed him of our betrothal. Being as close as we are he wished to meet you. He is the very best of men, Elizabeth. I know you will like him prodigiously."

"I am glad he is come and look forward to making his acquaintance. You have spoken of him before. The filial affection you share reminds me of my own closeness to Jane. There is nothing in the world I would not do for her. I imagine it is the same between you and your cousin." Elizabeth shook her head. "It is very good he is here now. You should not be alone at such a time, with such a man as Mr

Wickham, who would do you harm without batting an eyelid, and who cares nothing for anyone but himself."

The grave expression Darcy wore softened, but he looked tired, as though the weight of the world had once more been laid upon his shoulders.

Elizabeth offered him her hand, which he immediately grasped and brought to his lips, bestowing a tender kiss. Then he reached for her other hand and repeated the gesture.

"I am glad you have come back," she told him softly, feeling more than her complexion flush with warmth. "I know you were gone for no more than a day, but I have missed you dearly. Your letter—the professions you made— only made the ache I felt in your absence more pronounced."

"I have missed you as well. I hope my letter did not shock you unduly."

The corners of Elizabeth's lips lifted. "I confess I was surprised at first, but every sentiment was so beautifully expressed. I must have read it fifty times at least, and each new reading made me feel...so very much. Thank you for having the courage to put such words to paper. I had no idea I was to marry a poet. I daresay you are in a fair way of outdoing Mr Hurst's ebullient efforts."

Darcy's laugh was as unexpected as it was welcome. "Hurst's aptitude for verse is singular, to say the least. Hopefully, he will not manage to steal you away by composing a sonnet to honour the black pudding Bingley's cook set before him Sunday last."

"Yes," she said, laughing in turn. "Let us hope."

Their laughter waned, and Elizabeth was disheartened to see Darcy revert to his former gravity.

"Since I first beheld you on Oakham Mount, not a single day has passed that I have not thought of you. I want you to know I consider myself the most fortunate of men, not only to have earned your friendship and your love but your loyalty and your trust. As your friend and your future husband and, also, as a man who is violently in love with you and therefore unwilling and unable to give you up, I would make a request."

His words had the effect of both flattering and discomfiting her. "Of course. You may ask me anything and I shall comply if I am able."

Clearing his throat, Darcy said, "I shall introduce Colonel Fitzwilliam to you tomorrow. I harbour no doubt that he will adore you every bit as much as you deserve, and probably a vast deal more than he should. Pray do me the kindness of endeavouring not to like him as much in return."

Elizabeth frowned. "I do not understand precisely what it is you are asking of me. Are you attempting to dissuade me from becoming good friends with your cousin?"

"No," Darcy said at once. "Of course not. Forgive me. I am expressing myself poorly. My mind is not where it ought to be today. Of course, I would like you and Fitzwilliam to become good friends. He is the closest thing I have to a brother, and I love him beyond measure. There is no better man in all the world."

"I still do not understand what you are saying."

Darcy averted his eyes to their joined hands. "I suppose my objective is the preservation of my own equanimity. Fitzwilliam is possessed of a charm I can never hope to attain. The same is true of his ability to converse with ease on all manner of subjects, with all manner of persons. Had he met you in my stead, he would have smiled at you, and made you laugh, and asked you to dance without hesitation or insult. You would have danced with him, and teased him, and he would have responded to your every provocation with his own. I fear you will find me sorely lacking in comparison."

Elizabeth blinked at him in incomprehension. That Darcy should think anything of the sort was simply absurd. She had given her heart to him. She had accepted him, and they were to be husband and wife. "I believe that I did find you lacking at first. But my initial dislike of you did not last more than a quarter hour at most. If you recall, we made up quite nicely in the end. We even shook hands and parted as friends."

"We did," he allowed. "And now...I hope with all my heart we shall always be as we are now."

"If you do not allow this sudden insecurity of yours to override your filial affection for your cousin or your faith in me, I have no doubt we shall. I shall be your wife, which means that you will never be rid of me. Despite your claim that you are not so very charming and easy as your cousin, I heartily disagree. I love you, and to think I shall change my mind is nonsensical. The wife of Mr Darcy must have such extraordinary sources of happiness necessarily attached to her situation that she could, upon the whole, have no cause to repine."

Without warning, Darcy pulled her into his arms, embracing her tightly—so tightly that not even an inch of space existed between them. Elizabeth pressed her nose to his shoulder and inhaled his familiar, masculine scent—that of sandalwood, soap, and musk mixed with the scent of leather from his greatcoat. She felt each beat of his heart, each breath he expelled from his lungs, each caress of his hand as it followed the curve of her spine to the small of her back, over and over again.

"I love you," he murmured against her hair. "Now that I have found you—now, that you are mine—I cannot return to a life without you. Promise me you will be careful. Promise me you will not walk out alone until I have dealt with Wickham. If he learns of you...if he discovers who you are to me—that you are to become my wife—there is nothing he would not do to make me suffer for what he perceives are my affronts against him, however unfounded they are in reality."

She could do nothing but agree with the hope that he would be appeased. Darcy had enough to worry him. He did not need to worry about her as well. "If you insist upon it, I shall walk out with you, or with my sisters, or with Jane and Mr Bingley. If no one is available or if they are disinclined to accompany me, then I shall not venture beyond Longbourn's gardens, not even to Oakham Mount. I doubt that Mr Wickham will take an interest in me, though. My beauty," she said, endeavouring to introduce some levity to offset the gravity of their exchange, "you early withstood, and we both know I have no fortune with which to tempt him."

"You have plenty with which to tempt him," Darcy insisted. "You are undeniably handsome and charming and are therefore precisely the sort of woman who would tempt him most."

"While I am flattered you think so, I cannot believe you and Mr Wickham share the same opinions about anything. I was also under the impression he intends to make his fortune by marrying an heiress. I am hardly that."

With bitter solemnity, Darcy informed her, "In my lifetime he has ruined maids, tenants' daughters, the daughters of tradesmen, and the daughters of gentlemen. He cared not whether they were well dowered or impoverished, experienced or innocent. He gave no thought to their reputations, their families, or to the consequences that inevitably followed such acts of profligacy. None of the women and girls he ruined meant anything to him, not even my sister. Wickham wanted Georgiana's fortune and to revenge himself upon me. He would use you in a similar fashion and show no remorse once it was done. Believe me when I say he will not hesitate to single you out, for it is the most effective way to hurt me."

Elizabeth swallowed thickly as she thought of Georgiana. Wickham had told her that he loved her and wanted to marry her, but what had he told those other girls? Clearly, Pemberley's maids or the daughters of Darcy's tenant farmers could never tempt him into matrimony; Wickham had seduced them any way and abandoned them as easily. As Darcy said, their ruination had likely meant nothing to him. "He is utterly loathsome," she whispered, feeling a great heaviness in her heart.

"He is," Darcy agreed. "Wickham has lacked ambition all his life, but he certainly has not lacked resources. My father presented him with opportunities and funds that would have enabled him to distinguish himself in a respectable occupation and provide well for himself and a family. Although he denounced taking orders, at one point he professed an interest in studying the law. But that, like everything else that requires diligence and conscious exertion, came to nothing."

Propping her chin upon Darcy's chest, Elizabeth tilted her face to his and looked into his eyes. She touched his cheek. "It is a very good thing you denied him the living your father bequeathed him once it became vacant. Mr Wickham would have made a terrible clergyman. I shudder to think of him in such a role."

Darcy uttered a sound of disgust. "Let us speak no more of Wickham."

That happened to suit Elizabeth perfectly. "What would you prefer to speak of, then, my dearest? Tell me and I shall oblige you."

A lone curl had escaped from its pins and presently rested against the apple of her cheek. With unexampled gentleness, Darcy brushed it aside with his hand and tucked it behind her ear. "I believe that I would rather not speak at all."

Elizabeth looked at him askance, but Darcy cupped her face with his hands, dipped his head, and kissed her. She was happy to comply, and soon there was no further need for words.

NINETEEN

ণ৯৹

What is right to be done, cannot be done too soon.

"AND YOU ARE CERTAIN HE DID NOT RECOGNISE YOU?" Darcy asked for what felt like the hundredth time, trying and failing to keep his voice from sounding stern. "I am not angry, Georgiana. I only wish to know precisely what happened this morning so there is no misunderstanding the situation. I want no repeat of Ramsgate, or anything of the sort."

To her credit, Georgiana did not cower or withdraw, nor did she burst into tears as she had done when she was first questioned at Longbourn. Instead, she looked solemnly from Darcy, who was seated beside her on the tufted leather couch in Netherfield's library, to Colonel Fitzwilliam, who had taken a position by the hearth and was absently stirring the fire. Owing to her earlier bout of weeping, her eyes were red rimmed and puffy.

She shook her head. "I was not close enough to be noticed, nor would I have deigned to acknowledge him if he had seen me. I saw him only from a distance. It was such a shock that I froze and then Elizabeth noticed I had stopped and asked whether I was well. I told her I was not, and...and why. And then I felt even worse, for she looked so alarmed by my communication that she motioned to her sisters and whispered something to Mr Bingley, and we all turned back to Longbourn. Everyone was concerned for me. They were very solicitous and kind."

Rubbing his forehead with his hand, Darcy sighed. It was exactly what she had told him countless times throughout the evening, as had Elizabeth, Miss Bennet, and Bingley. He wondered what he had hoped to gain by repeatedly submitting his sister to such an inquisition. At the end of the day, did he mistrust her as much as he did Wickham? Did he suspect her of believing herself in love with him still? Darcy hardly knew. Georgiana was not the first girl to abandon sense and the protection of her family to throw herself into the power of an dishonourable reprobate.

That she might well be the first girl to attempt to do so twice terrified him beyond all that was holy. He turned towards his cousin, feeling nearly as unsettled as he had that afternoon when he had seen Wickham in Meryton. "What are your thoughts?"

Frowning, Fitzwilliam returned the brass poker to its stand. "Because Wickham did not seem to notice our girl does not mean he is ignorant of her presence here, or yours. I think we should pay him a visit tomorrow and see what he is up to. Or perhaps we ought to visit your friend Colonel Forster first and question him. Wickham was speaking to his officers, was he not? That tells us he either knows them or is interested in knowing them, and I want to know why. Either way, his being here at the same time as Georgiana does not sit well with me."

"But he cannot so much as suspect I am here," Georgiana insisted with no little emotion. "I have written to no one since we arrived, only to you and Aunt Carlisle, and she would never say anything of my being here to anyone who knows Mr Wickham. After what he has done, I cannot imagine he would ever think to come near me again, never mind seek me out on purpose."

"Unfortunately," Darcy remarked tersely, "unscrupulous men do unscrupulous things."

"I would never consent to anything he proposed now, not even a turn in the garden," she proclaimed in distress. "He could ruin me utterly and expose me to the censure of the world, and still, I would never consent to have him. I would rather be sent away and never marry any man than agree to be his wife! George Wickham is *despicable!*"

Fitzwilliam glanced worriedly at Darcy. "Calm yourself, my dear. We do not doubt you. Not for a moment. You must know you need not concern yourself about Wickham in any capacity. He will not come within a hundred feet of you, especially now that I am here to chase him away."

Georgiana expelled a tremulous breath. "I know. I have been so afraid that you would not believe me. I promised you in July never to do anything so foolish and reckless again and I intend to keep my promise."

She glanced at Darcy, then away. "I know there is no excuse for the dreadful mistakes I have made, but I cannot help but wonder if I had not been so lonely, or if Mrs Younge had not encouraged me to receive Mr Wickham whenever he called, perhaps...perhaps I would have better understood what he was about and would not have so readily believed his lies. The things he proposed—the things he said and did—had nothing to do with being in love. I know that now. I have seen what love looks like. I see it whenever you look at Elizabeth, Brother, or when you speak to her of some interest you both share—a favourite book, or a piece of music, or some silly little anecdote about something Solomon has done." She shook her head repentantly. "I shall not be taken in by him, or any man ever again. I swear it."

Fitzwilliam cast another brief, concerned look at Darcy.

Darcy turned aside his head. He desperately wanted to give his sister the benefit of the doubt, but she was a fifteen-year-old girl. She was still lonely, she was still naïve, and she was, to some extent, still heartbroken. Was she still foolish as well? She claimed to have learned her lesson, but the world was full of handsome men with nefarious intentions, weaving their Banbury tales for pretty, gullible girls. Only time would reveal the truth.

Fitzwilliam, likely exasperated by Darcy's silence, said, "Of course you would not be taken in again, my dear. You have learnt your lesson and will not fall victim to such a scoundrel a second time. Your brother and I both have every confidence in your discernment. We know that you would do what is right to be done. Do we not, Darcy?"

Anxious to put an end to the conversation, Darcy made a noncommittal sound and stood. "It has been a long day. Perhaps you would like to retire now, Georgiana?"

The expression on his sister's face was one of relief as much as it was disappointment. She hesitated a moment, then asked in a small voice, "You do believe me, Brother, do you not? You do believe me when I say that Mr Wickham no longer holds any power over me?"

In that moment, Darcy wanted to kick himself. Despite his reservations, the last thing he ought to do was make Georgiana believe he had no confidence in her. "Of course he does not. Forgive me. It was not my intention to make you feel as though that is not the case."

Georgiana twisted her fingers together. "I do not mind answering any other questions you wish to pose. I understand I have given you and Richard little incentive to trust me in the past, but I hope given time that will change."

Darcy cleared his throat. "You have come a long way

since the summer, Georgiana. I have no further questions at present." He inclined his head to her and extended his hand with the intent of encouraging her departure. He was tired and in danger of losing his sanity if this conversation did not soon come to an end.

Accepting his hand and his assistance, she brushed several tears from her cheeks and stood. "Thank you, Brother. I wish you a good night." She turned towards her cousin and another tear escaped, and another. "Good night, Richard. I am very glad you have come to Hertfordshire."

"Come," Darcy told her gently, concerned and disheartened by the return of her tears. "There is no need for more weeping. All is well. Fitzwilliam will still be here in the morning, you know."

"I know," she replied with a tearful smile. "I shall retire, and go right to sleep, and tomorrow I shall be myself again. I do not want either of you to worry over me or feel sorry for me any more. Nor do I intend to feel sorry for myself." And then, to Darcy's astonishment, she laughed. "Because of you, I have *sisters* to confide in now."

Before Darcy could form a response, she kissed his cheek and hastened from the room.

He watched her go with a mixture of concern and awe. There was no denying the girl who had just left them was stronger than the girl he had watched hide herself away from the world in London for months on end.

"She is different," Fitzwilliam observed, his expression reflective. "Hertfordshire has been good for her I think." Shaking his head, he walked to the sideboard and poured himself a generous glass of port. "Would you care for a glass as well?"

"I thank you, no," Darcy muttered absently. Instead, he walked to the window and pushed aside the curtains. As it was nearly nine o'clock at night, there was nothing to see but darkness. He remained in any case as his mind wandered through a host of subjects that he would rather not think on at all:

Georgiana.

Ramsgate.

Wickham.

Eventually, or rather inevitably, his thoughts wandered to Elizabeth.

Before leaving Longbourn, his sister had embraced her every bit as tightly as Darcy had embraced her earlier, when they were alone in the garden before sunset. There was no denying the adoration he glimpsed in Georgiana's eyes, just as there was no denying the deep and abiding love Darcy felt for Elizabeth within his heart. Never in his life had he known any person who possessed such a capacity to love and inspire love in others. As much as he had loved his mother—as much as he missed his mother—even she had not possessed Elizabeth's selflessness and heart.

Closing his eyes, Darcy found himself wishing he could ride back to Longbourn to see her. He would steal into the house and slip into her bed and wrap himself around her until he could no longer tell where he ended and where she began. Elizabeth would soothe him as she always did—with her laughter and her words. And then, while she was tempting him with her dark eyes and her inky lashes and her lovely chestnut curls, he would capture her lips as she had captured his heart, and he would kiss her until she whispered his name like a prayer.

"Darcy," Fitzwilliam called from across the room. "Are you well?"

Opening his eyes with an exhalation, Darcy raked his fingers through his hair and returned to the hearth. "I am well enough," he muttered, propping his arm on the mantelpiece. The fire in the grate licked at the logs within, curling and crackling and radiating warmth; but it was not the soft, companionable, perfect warmth Darcy craved within his soul. With a loud pop, one precariously balanced log slipped from the conflagration and rolled towards the Axminster carpet. Darcy nudged it back into place with his boot.

At length, Fitzwilliam asked the inevitable question. "What are your thoughts about this business with Wickham?"

For a long moment, Darcy did not reply. He was heartily sick of Wickham. Sick of his dissipation and debauchery. Sick of his lies. Sick of paying his creditors. Sick of his threats. Darcy did not care to ever look upon him again. What he wanted was to marry Elizabeth in church—any church—and whisk her and Georgiana off to Pemberley, where Wickham would never be admitted and where they would all be happy and safe.

It was naïve of him, not to mention selfish and irresponsible, he knew.

Darcy had never ignored any responsibility set before him. His staunch sense of duty and his honour, as a gentleman and as Pemberley's master, forbade it. Although he did not like it, protecting the world from Wickham and his wickedness had become his duty. His most unpleasant duty, but his duty, nonetheless. Unless Darcy dealt with him once and for all, swiftly and mercilessly, he would never be rid of him. But that did not automatically negate that part of him that would prefer to ignore the blackguard and hope he would simply go away.

"If I wanted nothing further to do with Wickham, what would you say?"

For a moment, Fitzwilliam said nothing. "I suppose I

would tell you that I shall be glad to handle the reprobate myself, but we both know my methods are not in accord with your own. Also, curiosity demands that I enquire as to your change of heart. It is unlike you to leave anything so personal and delicate, not to mention unpleasant, to another, especially where Wickham is concerned. You are too fastidious and too honourable to do anything less."

"I am sick to my stomach with this business," Darcy told him grimly. "And as much as it pains me to admit it, I suppose I am also afraid."

If Fitzwilliam was surprised by his confession, he did not show it. His expression was inscrutable as he slowly swirled the port in his glass. "What is it that you are afraid of? You are no coward."

Darcy shook his head with a self-deprecating twist of his mouth. "I am afraid that, no matter what I do, his tormenting me and those I love will never end. I am afraid that I shall never be allowed to be truly happy because Wickham, to whom my father showed a decided preference and spoilt with gifts of money and attention, will always be there, lurking in the shadows, making my life and everyone in it miserable."

"Your fear is not unfounded," Fitzwilliam allowed. "But what do you propose to eliminate it? Wickham has had his fun. He has made his demands. He may be a lazy bastard, but I doubt he is bluffing. He would ruin you without batting an eyelid, although I cannot help wondering why he would take such a risk. If he crosses you in this, he must know there will be nothing else for him. Your purse will be closed tight. He will not see so much as a shilling from you for the rest of his life. He will have played his last card so to speak."

"Unfortunately, I have no answer to give that would satisfy us both," Darcy replied. "He has always planned to make his fortune through marriage. Upwards of ten-thousand pounds will serve his purpose admirably until he does."

Fitzwilliam raised his glass to his lips and took a measured sip. "Perhaps. Or perhaps he will burn through it as carelessly as he has every other pound note you have given him over the years. Perhaps he will never be satisfied, and his demands will become increasingly more unreasonable the longer he remains unchecked. Think of the misery he has caused already. If it were me, I would want to be rid of him once and for all. But I am not the one who must live with him on the peripheral edges of my life, forever despising me for being born to a life he was not. Coveting that which he does not have. Making threats time and again until he has reduced me to a shadow of my former self and driven me to act in a manner that is entirely unreminiscent of who I am as a gentleman."

"You would like to call him out, I know."

Shrugging, Fitzwilliam said, "It would certainly serve our purpose, although I doubt the coward would show his face in Battersea Fields were I to issue such a challenge."

"Nor would it be worth hanging for, whether you killed him or not."

"Perhaps I would not hang at all but be lauded for my contribution towards the betterment of society for doing away with the blackguard once and for all."

"Even so, I would not have you risk your life or your commission. Were you my own brother, you could not be more dear to me. I hardly know how I would manage without you."

With a dismissive wave of his hand, Fitzwilliam said, "You have your impertinent Miss Elizabeth to tease you into a better humour. She is likely far more agreeable than I, and far more handsome as well."

The corners of Darcy's mouth lifted infinitesimally. "That goes without saying, but that does not negate the fact that I prefer you alive and breathing. Your parents would agree."

"But not Arthur." Fitzwilliam raised his glass in the air and drained the contents. Then he walked to the sideboard to fill it with more port. "I shall take pity on you and say nothing further about my demise at present, but we do need to form a resolution. As it happens, I may have a solution that will not only ensure my neck and your sanity remain intact but which will also meet with your approval. Come, have a drink, and I shall tell you what I am thinking."

Desperate for any solution that would neither result in the compromising of his principles nor in the termination of his cousin's life or profession, Darcy conceded, and they spent the next hour forming their plan.

❧

"Wickham...Wickham..." Colonel Forster muttered thoughtfully from behind his desk, drumming his fingers on his leather blotter. "Oh, yes. I believe Wickham is Mr Denny's friend. He brought him back from London yesterday, a lieutenancy in his possession. He seems like a learned, amicable gentleman. We are happy to have him." He eyed all three men—Darcy, Colonel Fitzwilliam, and Mr Bennet—sceptically. "What is it you want with him?"

Mr Bennet cleared his throat. "Although I do not know Lieutenant Wickham personally, Mr Darcy has related to me some of his history with the man, which includes an unfortunate habit of running up significant debts of honour and then failing to make payment. I understand Lieutenant Wickham's receipts to his creditors in Derbyshire alone amount to more than five hundred pounds."

"Five hundred pounds," Colonel Forster repeated, straightening in his chair. "Good Lord."

"Regrettably," Darcy told him with grim assurance, "accumulating debts of honour is not Lieutenant Wickham's only offence."

Colonel Forster grew pale. "What do you mean?"

"There were several local girls, mostly maids of all work and tradesmen's daughters, who were compromised in the villages of Lambton and Kympton. Both border Pemberley. Last year, more than half a dozen girls between the ages of fifteen and nineteen became with child after he was known to be in the area. He has behaved similarly in other villages in other parts of the country, and in London and at Cambridge as well."

"Have you proof, sir?"

"I have the assurances of the children's mothers, many of whom are from families well known to me, as my own family has conducted business with theirs all my life. I hold Lieutenant Wickham's debts, as many as I could acquire. The total sum is more than two thousand pounds and goes back several years. Recently, while in Kent, he left behind another hundred pounds in debts and there was...there was another incident," Darcy added darkly. "One I find exceedingly painful to relate."

Although he tried to form the words to communicate what had happened to his sister, they would not come. How could he expose Georgiana to such censure and scorn? She would be ruined and there would be nothing he could do to change the course of her fate. Mr Bennet knew all; Darcy had confided in him that morning and was more grateful than he could say for the compassion Longbourn's master had shown him. It was the last thing he had expected to receive, especially after he had brazenly offered to send Elizabeth's sisters off to school only four days earlier to improve upon *their* comportment.

Agitated, he rose from his chair and strode to the window,

fighting to maintain his equanimity. It would not do to lose his composure when he had yet to face Wickham, who would not hesitate to abuse Darcy to his face once he learned of the fate that awaited him. Hopefully, the blackguard would not mention Georgiana. If he did, Darcy could not vouch for his temper.

Fitzwilliam, as he had done on countless occasions throughout their lives, filled the void. "Forgive my cousin, Colonel. The matter he was about to relate is of a delicate nature and should not be repeated. As Darcy has a young charge of his own, he cannot but feel deeply about such an occurrence. But I digress. It has come to our attention that Lieutenant Wickham orchestrated an elopement between himself and the young daughter of a very wealthy gentleman of some consequence. She was fifteen years old. Fortunately, her family intervened in time, and she was unharmed."

Colonel Forster looked as though he could barely credit what he had heard. "Upon my word," he cried, both outraged and indignant at once. "This sort of behaviour—elopements and the ruination of innocent girls—ought not and will not be tolerated."

Fitzwilliam agreed. "Although I have only just arrived in the area, I can see that Meryton is a fine town with fine people who stand to lose much with such an unscrupulous man living in their midst."

"What do you propose, Colonel Fitzwilliam?"

Fitzwilliam leaned forward in his chair, propped his forearms on his knees, and linked his fingers together. "As Darcy mentioned, he currently holds Lieutenant Wickham's receipts. We intend to speak to him. If he has the funds to settle his debts to my cousin's satisfaction, then we shall be satisfied on that account, but the matter of the young lady will not be so simple, nor so straightforward. We would, of course, prefer to keep her name and that of her family confidential."

"I shall do all in my power to ensure it is so," Colonel Forster replied.

"It is doubtful," Fitzwilliam continued, "that Lieutenant Wickham is in possession of the funds necessary to satisfy his debt to my cousin at this time. We plan to notify the local magistrate here at once and mention *all* his offences. Any cooperation you can extend to us would be appreciated."

"Of course. I am glad to help however I can."

Mr Bennet, who had been silent while the other men spoke of Wickham's perfidy, cleared his throat. "Perhaps, Colonel Forster, you might permit Mr Darcy and Colonel Fitzwilliam the use of your office to speak to Lieutenant Wickham privately. It may also be helpful if you were to summon him here. From what I understand, his past dealings with both gentlemen have been relatively unpleasant. I doubt he will come willingly into the lion's den."

In the end, not only did Colonel Forster summon Wickham, but he abandoned him to Darcy's keeping the moment he walked through the door. Mr Bennet followed his example, but Colonel Fitzwilliam had no intention of leaving Darcy to face Wickham alone. Not wishing to show his hand prematurely, he found a dim corner and claimed a comfortable chair, where he waited in silence for his cousin to do as he wished.

As for Darcy, he had since regained his self-possession and seated himself behind Colonel Forster's desk as though it was his own. He was the one Wickham saw when he entered the room and was pleased to see the blackguard pale as the confident, easy smile slipped from his face.

As was often the case, Wickham managed to recover his composure in little time. "Darcy," he said as his bravado rose. "Well, well. I heard you were in the area, but I did not think I would see you so soon. To what do I owe the pleasure of your company this fine morning? I trust you remembered to bring your pocketbook."

Hearing the tone of his voice, so smooth and unaffected, grated on Darcy's nerves; seeing Wickham's face made Darcy want to hit him. "It is no pleasure," he said, restraining himself.

A low, rueful laugh filled the room as Wickham claimed a chair before the desk, crossed his ankles, and linked his hands behind his head. "On this we agree. Tell me, how does Georgiana? I hear she accompanied you." The smile he wore was insufferable.

Darcy clenched his jaw so hard he felt it pop.

"I hear you have taken to keeping her locked up at your friend's estate—a precious little princess in a fortified tower. Alas, it is too little, too late." His smile widened. "I also hear you are engaged to be married. I would ask for an introduction, but Denny and Chamberlain have already agreed to perform the honour. From what I hear, Miss Elizabeth is a favourite among the officers, although not nearly so spirited as her youngest sister. Perhaps that will change once she marries." His smile became a smirk. "Lord knows that you will never satisfy her. But perhaps for the right price she would—"

Darcy was across the desk in an instant, his hands curled around Wickham's throat. His grip was just tight enough to make drawing breath difficult but not enough to suffocate. "Finish that sentence and it will be your last."

Wickham tugged and clawed at Darcy's hands, but his efforts proved insufficient.

Darcy was not of a mind to let him go. This was not Ramsgate, where he was friendless and therefore forced to remain calm when he felt murderous. There was no need to glean answers to painful, mortifying questions pertaining to his beloved sister while suffering Wickham's arrogance and insolence. There was no need to hold his rage in check while he silently seethed, swallowing the screams that wanted to force their way from his throat.

No. This was altogether different, as was the potent, violent anger that boiled to the surface and erupted in a firestorm the moment Wickham had mentioned Elizabeth by name. Darcy nearly smiled when he saw Wickham had felt the shift in their dynamic; the cathartic, fatalistic moment when Darcy had forsaken his vaunted self-control and seized the mantle of a possessive, irate lover. For the first time in his life, Wickham looked at him with something akin to fear.

Whistling the refrain of *Will Ye Come Back Again*, Colonel Fitzwilliam abandoned his chair in the corner of the room, making his presence known. "Did I not always tell you, Darcy, that Wickham required a firm hand?"

Upon hearing Fitzwilliam's voice, the fear in Wickham's eyes increased tenfold. He ceased his struggling at once.

Darcy knew better than to loosen his grip. As much as he wanted to see the back of him, it was preferable to see Wickham bound and shackled in a magistrate's cart, being hauled through the town to the gaol like a specimen at the London Tower—a fitting punishment for the harm he had done to others over the course of his dissipated life.

As though privy to his thoughts, Fitzwilliam laughed. "You seem to have your hands full for the moment, Cousin. As intimate as we are, I can discern your thoughts easily enough. And yours as well, Wickham." His amicable countenance turned cold. "I wonder whether you can guess mine? In case you cannot, I shall tell you." He took a seat upon the corner of the desk and motioned for Darcy to stand down.

Darcy did so reluctantly, without taking his eyes from Wickham, who was presently gasping for breath. He straightened his coat and reclaimed the chair behind Colonel Forster's desk.

For the most part, Wickham appeared shaken and pale, but a bit of colour was beginning to return to his countenance. He drew a deep, ragged breath, coughed, and made to stand, but Colonel Fitzwilliam's booted foot connected with his sternum and forced him backwards, chair and all, onto the floor. His head hit the polished oak boards with a sickening thud.

"Now," said Fitzwilliam darkly, looming over him like a menacing shadow, his foot planted firmly on Wickham's chest. "Darcy will tell you what we have planned for you, Wickham, and I shall relieve you of your sabre to ensure that you understand."

Darcy had never seen George Wickham so willing to oblige.

Not half an hour later, he stood beside Mr Bennet, watching the magistrate haul his former friend away in irons while townspeople and shopkeepers milled about the street, staring and exclaiming at the spectacle.

Darcy felt myriad emotions, but the most prevalent of those, even more prevalent than relief, was disappointment. Despite his dissolution and depravity, Wickham had been his boyhood friend. Darcy had never understood why he had rejected the path of honour and prosperity his father and Darcy's had set before him. They had lived in the same house. They had been offered the same education. Other boys in similar situations had applied themselves and thrived. Yet Wickham had not. For that, Darcy felt a deep regret and would probably continue to do so for the remainder of his life.

Whether Wickham would ever come to regret his chosen path remained to be seen.

Darcy was jolted from his introspection by Mr Bennet, who slapped him companionably on the back. "It may not mean much coming from me, Mr Darcy, as I am not your father, but I am proud of you. I daresay your own father would be proud of you as well. It was not an easy thing you did, but you have saved this town a considerable amount of trouble and heartache, I think. Whether they realise it or not, the people of Meryton are in your debt."

"Hardly," said Darcy, feeling anything but proud of himself for what he had done. "I should have exposed Wickham long ago."

"What matters, young man, is that you did so now."

Darcy looked towards Longbourn, where Elizabeth was waiting with Georgiana, and frowned. "While I appreciate the sentiment, sir, I cannot say for certain whether my father would have been proud of my actions, today or many years prior. I have failed to protect my sister, who he left in my care. I failed to inspire Wickham, who was once my father's favourite, to follow a repentant course and to be a better man."

Mr Bennet's expression turned thoughtful, almost pensive. "That is quite a burden you have carried. But you need not carry it alone."

Darcy looked at him askance.

"You are engaged to my Lizzy, who is *my* favourite. Whether you like it or not, by marrying into this family you are gaining four opinionated, often silly sisters, an overly affectionate mother, and a father who, although not your own, will be proud to call you his son nonetheless." He squeezed Darcy's shoulder. "Come, Mr Darcy. My wife and daughter await our return, and you have yet to set a date for your wedding. If you do not make haste, Mrs Bennet may grow complacent and insist on a full year to buy wedding clothes."

Darcy blinked at him, horrified by the prospect of waiting a year for his bride.

"Do not look so put out, sir! You have ten thousand a year and a licence. I daresay you will think of something."

Shaking off his astonishment, Darcy managed to find his voice. "I also have a stable of fast horses and an estate in Scotland."

"That is the spirit," said Mr Bennet. "So long as this estate has a decent library and a well-stocked cellar, I shall be your staunchest ally."

TWENTY

⟡

If I have not spoken, it is because I am afraid I will awaken
myself from this dream.

"WITH MY BODY I THEE *WORSHIP*, AND WITH ALL MY
worldly goods I thee endow!" proclaimed the frail Mr Reager
in a strong, zealous voice that rang throughout Longbourn's
little stone church.

Elizabeth pursed her lips, repressing her amusement as
Mr Bingley started, flinched, and dropped Jane's ring on the
floor. He had been in Hertfordshire for three months and had
never quite accustomed himself to the minister's enthusiasm
for preaching the word of the Lord.

From the corner of her eye, she glanced at Darcy, who
stood ramrod straight beside her, endeavouring to appear as
proper and composed as ever while his friend retrieved his
wayward ring. As though he knew precisely what she was
about, he shifted so the sleeve of his coat brushed against her
arm—a silent reproach in a holy place.

And then she felt his fingertips gently caress her hand.

It was the briefest touch, barely anything at all, yet the
gesture itself and the tenderness behind it felt incredibly
significant to Elizabeth. That he had done it—before their
families while in church—made her recent amusement cease
to exist. Her heart filled with affection and gratitude, and she

took a moment to thank God for putting him in her path that wonderful, fateful morning on Oakham Mount.

Their own vows had been exchanged minutes earlier. Darcy had recited his clearly and reverently. When he had finished, he slipped his ring on her finger and, although it was not the done thing, he bowed over her hand and kissed her ring. There were murmurs of surprise, and the tips of his ears had turned red.

Moved beyond measure, Elizabeth had longed to wrap her arms around him. To kiss him. To tell him with more than the expression of her eyes how dearly she appreciated and loved him.

The ceremony was not long. Once Mr Bingley and Jane exchanged their vows and Mr Reager pronounced them man and wife, the newly wedded couples strode up the aisle, signed their names in the register, and burst from the church into the churchyard. Cheers and well wishes from their friends and neighbours greeted them. Feeling uncharacteristically emotional, Elizabeth embraced each one in turn while Darcy stood beside her and shook their hands.

They had not been out of doors for more than a few minutes when it began to snow. While Jane and Mr Bingley hastened to his waiting carriage, Elizabeth tilted her face to the sky. "Shall we walk to Longbourn, my husband?" she enquired with a joyful smile she found impossible to contain.

"If it pleases you, my wife," he replied, gazing at her with such an expression of love it nearly stole her breath. "You will not catch cold, I hope."

Elizabeth slowly shook her head. "Not if you promise to keep me warm."

His response was to draw her close, tuck her hand securely into the crook of his arm, and lead her towards the little path that wound through the woods and on to Longbourn. They assumed a leisurely pace, in no hurry to be reunited with the rest of the throng, or to be confined to the house and likely separated according to the conventions of their sex. Instead, they paused frequently beneath low hanging boughs of fragrant balsams and pine, seeking refuge from the weather, kissing and touching and murmuring endearments as they anticipated what was to come.

By the time they reached Longbourn, their outer clothing sported a dusting of snowflakes, and they were half an hour late to their own breakfast, but neither could find anything to repine, even when Mrs Bennet exclaimed and tutted over Elizabeth's damp hem and ruined slippers.

"And such a lovely gown it is, too," she lamented with a long-suffering sigh. Her eyes lingered on the intricate embroidery at the hem, the velvet trim at the waist and cuffs, and the lovely Brussels lace at the neck. Then she met Elizabeth's gaze and her expression, which betrayed her vexation, softened. "Oh, well. What is done is done. I do not suppose it even matters. Not today. Mr Darcy is so besotted I daresay he will not notice a thing beyond how beautiful you look."

"But not nearly so beautiful as Jane," Elizabeth replied flippantly. "Until I have her goodness, I can never hope to have her beauty."

She was startled when her mother stepped forward and took her hand.

"I should never have compared you, or any of your sisters, to Jane. You are all very different, and those differences should be lauded, not criticised, especially by me. Jane is beautiful to be sure, but you are every bit as beautiful, inside and out." Then, in a rare show of affection, her mother pressed a kiss to her cheek. "Come, Mrs Darcy. Let us re-join the others. Mrs Long has been asking about the lace on your gown all morning." She patted Elizabeth's hand and turned, emitting a delighted little laugh. "Mrs Darcy," she repeated. "Bless me. How well that sounds...!"

Dear Mama...! Elizabeth mused with a diverted twist of her lips. *I suppose there must be some consistency, or the world may stop spinning on its axis.* Compulsively, she hugged her well-meaning, often frustrating mother, and set off to speak to Mrs Long.

That evening Mr Bingley finally held his promised ball. The invitations had come two months late, but, as it was in honour of his new wife and he was such an amicable, agreeable gentleman, his neighbours easily forgave him.

The décor was lavish and elegant. Flowers from Netherfield's conservatory adorned the tables and swaths of rich silk draped the walls. The ballroom was aglow with hundreds of candles and the musicians had been brought up from London. It was rumoured there would be a waltz.

Elizabeth had opened the ball with Darcy, but their set had no sooner come to an end when she was approached by Mr Bingley, who solicited her hand for the next. Colonel Fitzwilliam requested the third, and Mr Shirley claimed the fourth. Then Mr Collins asked her, and Robert Goulding, and Dick and John Lucas, and countless other gentlemen she had known all her life. To her chagrin, and Darcy's annoyance, Colonel Fitzwilliam, who was every bit the charming flirt Darcy claimed, insisted on dancing with her twice.

Finally, sometime after eating supper and dancing once more with her husband, Elizabeth begged a seat beside Charlotte, who welcomed her warmly. As no one appeared to be paying them any mind, she removed her slippers, tucked her stockinged feet beneath her ball gown, and smiled affectionately at her friend. "I am so glad you have come. I would have missed you today. Indeed, I *have* missed you."

"As I have missed you. You look lovely, Eliza. Marriage to Mr Darcy will agree with you, mark my words."

"Your marriage appears to agree with you as well," Elizabeth replied with an arch smile. "Mr Collins is a most attentive husband. Save for standing up with me and my sisters, he has barely left your side for ten minutes together."

"Mr Collins is most attentive," Charlotte agreed, "but I have nothing to repine. He is a respectable man, and our home is very comfortable. I could not have asked for a better situation."

They spoke of Mr Collins's parishioners and her chickens and the former Anne de Bourgh, who was lately married to a distant cousin on her father's side more than twice her age. The gentleman, a Mr Blatchford, was also worth twice Darcy's consequence, and so Lady Catherine was satisfied enough with her new son-in-law that she had forgiven her nephew for failing to fulfil what had once been her dearest wish.

For all intents and purposes, Charlotte appeared content with her lot, but Elizabeth could not help but notice her eyes would often find Mr Shirley—wherever he happened to be— and linger. Such conduct did not bode well for her friend's domestic felicity. Whether Charlotte was truly happy or regretful was of little consequence at this point. She had set her cap at Mr Collins the day they were introduced, secured his regard by the end of the week, and married him a month later. There was no chance of undoing what had already been done.

Eventually, Mr Collins returned to his wife's side to solicit her hand for the *Allemande* and Elizabeth was left to herself. The reality of Charlotte's situation—being forever bound to one man while preferring another—made her appreciate the mutual love and respect she had found with Darcy even more. She sought him with her eyes and discovered him standing across the ballroom beside Georgiana, Lydia, and Mary, who were deep in conversation. Miss Bingley and Mrs

Hurst were on Darcy's right, talking at him without pause. The expression on his face was reminiscent of one he had worn at the Meryton assembly three months prior: haughty and aloof. Occasionally, he would offer an inclination of his head or, at most, a monosyllable. More often than not, his lips formed the shape of the word 'no'.

As though he felt her eyes upon him, Darcy's disinterested gaze met Elizabeth's and softened. A small, infinitesimal smile lifted the corners of his mouth. He turned towards Miss Bingley and made several attempts to disengage himself from what was clearly a one-sided conversation, but she talked on, Mrs Hurst tittered, and they were joined by Mr Bingley and Jane.

As Darcy could not be so rude as to ignore his new sister on her wedding day, he greeted Jane and was promptly drawn into conversation with Mr Bingley, who was intent upon talking as much as his sisters. Before long, Darcy's polite demeanour showed signs of strain. When Elizabeth saw him roll his eyes, she decided the time had come to rescue him before he did something truly abhorrent. She had just worked her toes into her discarded slippers when Colonel Fitzwilliam claimed the chair beside her own.

"He is miserable," he said without preamble, grinning at his cousin's discomfiture. "You should rescue him before he loses his wits as well as his composure. From what I know of you, Mrs Darcy, you would not suffer a stupid husband with equanimity."

"No," she agreed blithely. "I certainly would not. But surely you are more qualified than I to lead such a campaign, Colonel Fitzwilliam. Why must such an office fall to a lady? Or is your plan based solely upon the fact I am now your cousin's wife?"

"Not at all," he conceded with ease. "It is because I have often heard my sister-in-law proclaim that if there is anything disagreeable going on, men are sure to get out of it. As she is disagreeable herself, I cannot imagine you would wish me to incur her ire by proving her wrong."

His explanation was so unexpected and ridiculous, Elizabeth laughed. "You are awful, and not nearly as gallant as you believe yourself to be for having made such a speech in the first place."

"Listening to Miss Bingley rattle away about the puffed-up importance of the *ton* for half an hour is awful," he told her with a teasing smile. He rose from his chair and extended his hand to her. "Come. Let us both go. I shall distract the troops while you and Darcy make your escape. It is nearly three o'clock in the morning. He has endured enough."

Colonel Fitzwilliam performed his office admirably, and Darcy and Elizabeth were able to slip away with little fanfare. They made their way through the maze of adjoining rooms with alacrity, but once they reached the main anteroom, they slowed. Just ahead, the grand staircase loomed. Rather than ascend it, Darcy tugged her towards the row of paintings displayed on the wall beside it.

More specifically, to the painting of Ramsgate's coast.

Elizabeth expelled a wistful sigh. "It is still every bit as lovely as it was on the morning when we first stood in this spot and admired it together."

Darcy gave her hand an affectionate squeeze. "You admired it. I was very nearly discomposed by it. But you, my darling, discomposed me most of all."

"Did I?" she said in surprise, turning from the painting to look at him. She searched his eyes and saw his sincerity, and something else; something she remembered seeing that morning as she talked to him and listened to him and longed to touch his face. She had loved him then, although they had not yet moved beyond the friendship they shared. Touching him at all would have been inappropriate. Now, everything had changed. While they remained the dearest of friends, they were also husband and wife. The reality of being Darcy's wife filled her with such joy as she had never known. Simply because she could, Elizabeth raised her hand and caressed his cheek with her fingertips, exactly as she had wanted to do that day.

Without hesitation, he leaned into her touch and kissed her palm. "If you will recall," he said quietly, "my sister had played Mozart the night before. It was my mother's favourite piece in all the world, and one reason why I was so distracted during her performance. Your distress, your solicitude, and your tempting proximity added greatly to my agitation.

"The next morning you were here, standing beside this painting. I had spent the entire night thinking of you, imagining what it might be like to surrender my heart to your keeping. The idea of it appealed to me like nothing else, but it also terrified me."

Darcy shook his head with a rueful twist of his mouth. "After much deliberation, I decided I would not do it. I would not give in to your lure. And so, I determined to guard my heart at all costs. It was not until I recited that passage from *The Seafarer* to you, however, and heard you speak the next line of it to me, that I knew resisting you was a hopeless task. You understood precisely what I had meant—what I had felt. Much as I was unprepared to face the evolution of my feelings for you then, my heart was no longer my own. It was yours, and no matter how much I told myself otherwise, I knew I would never get it back."

"I am glad of it," she said, and pressed his hand. "I have never been so happy. Today has been wonderful, but it has also been long, and I have seen far too little of you, my husband."

"And I of you, my wife." Darcy drew her close, touched his forehead to hers, and sighed. "I am worn out with civility.

I am tired of speaking to everyone of everything and nothing at once and not nearly enough to you. With you, there is no need for pretence or polite formality. With you, there is only ease and familiarity and a sense of *rightness*. You make no demands of me I cannot meet and do not judge me harshly when I am disinclined towards conversation. With you, I may have peace."

"You may have anything you wish," she assured him. "You need only ask, and whatever you desire shall be yours."

"And if what I desire is you?"

"Then you may have me. Whenever and however you wish."

He kissed her then, a slow, heartfelt kiss that tugged at her senses and warmed her blood. Before he could deepen it, Elizabeth encouraged him towards the stairs. "Come, Fitzwilliam," she murmured. "I have no intention of spending my wedding night in this chilly anteroom."

Feeling they had been separated enough for one night, she bypassed her own apartment and boldly entered Darcy's. It was a rich, masculine space, with dark colours and dark wood. It was nothing like the room she had been given—a light, airy confection draped in pinks and creams and white.

The door closed with a quiet, but decided, click. Darcy turned the key in the lock, ensuring they would receive no interruptions. No candles were lit. The only light in the room came from the fire.

"Will you take down your hair?" he enquired softly.

It was such an innocent request compared to others he might have made that Elizabeth could not help but smile. "As you like," she replied as softly.

Discarding her gloves on a chair, she stood before an elaborate full-length mirror framed with dark wood that matched the rest of the room, plucking decorative pins from her hair. Long, thick curls tumbled down her back, caressing her shoulders, which were bare but for the tiny, capped sleeves of her ball gown. Darcy stood behind her, so close she could almost feel him. His proximity and the look in his eyes as he watched her, as though he had never seen anything more captivating in his life, made Elizabeth feel desirable and bold and innocent all at once.

When she had cast off the last pin, Darcy embraced her from behind, pressed his nose to her hair, and inhaled deeply. The heat of his body warmed her like a flame. She felt each exhalation of his breath, the solidness of him against her back, and the strong, reassuring cadence of his heart. His hands, large and warm and sure, slid from her waist to her hips in a manner that both enticed and tormented her in equal measure.

With unexampled gentleness, he swept her hair aside and kissed her neck. His fingers found the buttons at the back of her gown, and he began to work them free with a deftness and efficiency Elizabeth had not known he possessed. Each time his fingertips grazed her skin her breath hitched, and her body flushed with warmth, making her feel almost heady.

When he had done away with the last button, he eased the layers of silk, embellished with thousands of tiny seed pearls, from her shoulders and started on her stays. Her gown pooled around her hips, leaving her exposed in a way she had never been before any man.

With one fingertip, Darcy traced a slow, tantalising path from the nape of her neck to the base of her spine. "I love you," he whispered against her pulse. His voice sounded endearingly uneven.

Elizabeth shivered, both emotional and aroused. "I love you," she said on a breath, turning so she could see his beloved face. She had never felt so exposed nor so protected, so uncertain yet so self-assured as she did in that moment. She ought to have known it would be like this; she ought to have known there would be only sweetness and reassurance, adoration and love. Her mother had explained the mechanics of the act to her, but she had said nothing of the closeness, or the feeling of rightness, or the lovely, exquisite little ache in her belly that intensified with her desire. "I love you," she whispered again, pressing a kiss to the sliver of skin just visible above his cravat, beneath his jaw. Her voice was as unsteady as his own.

With a ragged breath, Darcy relieved her of her stays and kissed her shoulder, the sensitive curve where her shoulder met her neck, and finally her lips—tender, extravagant kisses meant to soothe as much as to seduce.

Overwhelmed by his ministrations and the powerful desire she felt for him, Elizabeth pressed herself closer until not even a hairsbreadth remained.

An unintelligible sound rose in Darcy's throat, and he pushed her gown to the floor, lifted her in his arms, carried her to the bed, and laid her upon it. Her eyelids fluttered closed as he joined her, kissing her deeply, and Elizabeth, knowing she was wholly, completely in his thrall, surrendered to him.

Every breath, every touch, every sensation was amplified by the darkness.

An ardent kiss.

A tender caress.

The warm, wet velvet of Darcy's tongue.

Never had she imagined such pleasure.

Slowly, devotedly, Darcy relieved her of her inhibitions with the same tenderness with which he had eased her clothes from her body.

The curve of her shoulder; the soft, round slope of her breast; the sensitive skin of her inner thigh. There was nothing he would not do for her. Elizabeth melted into ecstasy again and again.

When at last he settled himself within her embrace, smoothed a rebellious curl from her forehead with a slightly shaking hand, and gazed into her eyes with a look of such heartfelt adoration it made her breath catch, Elizabeth's soul had been laid bare to him every bit as much as her flesh.

Now, he would know all her secrets.

It was well, for she would know all his secrets, too.

In the early hours of the morning, as the first slim rays of the sun crept above the horizon, she wound her fingers through Darcy's hair and her legs around his hips as her pleasure wound its way through her body, washed over her like a cresting wave, and left her gasping.

EPILOGUE

⚜

A little sea bathing would set me up forever.

Weymouth, August 1818

THE CRIES OF THE GULLS COULD BE HEARD FROM THE house, even though the weather was overcast and disagreeable, and the windows were closed tight to keep the chill and the incessant rain from dampening the home's comfortable interior.

They had been married six years, and in that time the Darcys had come to the shore nearly every summer without fail. Elizabeth had been so taken with the painting of Ramsgate's chalk cliffs hanging on the wall at Netherfield that Darcy had proposed travelling there to experience their majesty first-hand. To his consternation, she professed a desire to visit Devon or Lyme instead. As he adored his wife far more than he had adored his time in Ramsgate, he arranged to take a house in Lyme Regis that first July they were married.

The Dorset coast was a long drive from London—one hundred-fifty miles—and the house, though charming and well kept, was smaller than Darcy had expected, with a single bedchamber, a drawing room, a dining parlour, and a kitchen, where a capable maid of all work prepared their meals. Despite its humble size, they spent four glorious weeks there sightseeing, exploring the village, and walking along the Cobb. While the surrounding cliffs were not chalk but sandstone, the shore situated in their shadow was a veritable treasure-trove for fossil hunters, and the bay provided a sheltered strip of golden sand and calm water perfect for bathing. Every aspect of Lyme Regis delighted Elizabeth, including their cosy little house, and her affection for the seaside became fixed.

The following year they went to Devon, and the year after that to Cornwall.

Now they were in Weymouth, where the house Darcy had taken was fashionable and large, and the weather was uncooperative and wet. They had arrived the previous day and had seen no sights, nor had they been able to walk to the shore or bathe in the sea. As he lay abed listening to the rain lash against the windows, Darcy lamented the fact they had come amidst such poor weather.

But then his wife combed her fingers through his hair, slid her leg along his hip, and kissed his neck in a manner that never failed to warm his blood. Immediately, all thoughts of the weather ceased.

Outside, the rain continued unabated, pounding against the house with unrelenting force.

Inside, Darcy urged Elizabeth closer, kissing her deeply until they both knew nothing beyond each other.

❧

"Are you certain you are feeling well enough to walk out this morning?"

"I am very well this morning, Fitzwilliam," Elizabeth replied, her tone one of patient forbearance as she secured the rich, emerald ribbons of her bonnet beneath her chin. "Shall we go before all the prettiest shells are reclaimed by the sea?"

"Elizabeth," he began, but ceased speaking at once when she expelled a sudden, startled gasp.

Grasping his hand, she placed it just below the thickening curve of her belly, holding it there as she smiled up at him with such a look of heartfelt delight that his breath caught in his throat. Her eyes, which Darcy had admired since the very first moments of their acquaintance, had become even lovelier and more expressive since she had become with child. "It seems your son is eager as well, sir. Surely, you would not wish to suspend any pleasure of his!"

His son.

Beneath his hand, Darcy felt a slight, almost infinitesimal movement, and was powerless to repress his smile. The idea of having a son filled him with such elation, though he knew in his heart he would be equally elated and grateful to have a daughter. It had been only the two of them for so long he had nearly given up hope. Jane was with child within a few months of being married to Bingley. For Catherine and Mary and their husbands it had been much the same.

The Bennets were a hale, fecund family—the opposite of his own relations.

Lord and Lady Carlisle were married for six years before Emerson was born, and five more passed before Fitzwilliam followed. Lady Catherine and Sir Lewis had waited seven years for Anne. It had taken Darcy's own parents nearly five years to conceive him, and Georgiana came along twelve years later with no other pregnancies in between.

Elizabeth would be brought to bed in January.

"Come, husband," she said, throwing open the front door

of the house with an incandescent smile. "The day is wasting, and I am impatient to be reunited with the sea."

In that moment she looked so beautiful, so vibrant and full of life, that he could not help kissing her tempting lips. It was broad daylight, and they were in the middle of the main vestibule, where any number of servants or passers-by could happen upon them, but Darcy cared not. He merely grinned at his wife and her happy, blushing countenance, placed her hand on his arm, and escorted her down the steps and into the street.

They made their way at a leisurely pace towards the esplanade, admiring the sights and sounds of Weymouth in the early morning hours. Linking both hands around Darcy's arm, Elizabeth drew close to him and said, "I received a letter from Lydia the other day."

"You have been remiss," he replied, drawing her closer still. "You mentioned nothing of receiving any letters. Tell me, how does your sister? Is she enjoying herself in Brighton?"

"She is, and Georgiana as well. Colonel Fitzwilliam, on the other hand, sounds as though he has reached his wits' end."

After marrying Elizabeth, Darcy had made good on his promise to send all their sisters to school, where far more than their comportment and their manners saw improvement. At school, under the tutelage of masters and school mistresses, all four girls not only blossomed, but thrived. While Mary and Kitty were presently married to excellent men and enjoying the delights of motherhood, Lydia and Georgiana, at one-and-twenty, appeared in no hurry to follow their elder sisters to the altar.

Darcy shook his head. "I cannot imagine either of them giving Fitzwilliam any trouble."

"Oh, it is not our sisters who try his patience," his wife

replied equitably, "but the gentlemen whose notice they have attracted. There are balls and parties nearly every night and, as Lydia and Georgiana have a fondness for society and dancing, poor Richard must attend every engagement put before him."

Darcy snorted. "'Poor Richard' indeed. He does not have to attend every engagement, you know. Lady Carlisle is in residence there as well and has agreed to perform the office of chaperone for the duration of their stay."

"True, but it seems as though the colonel does not wish to leave anything to chance. If there are gentlemen about, he is determined to keep them at bay. According to my sister, he has done an admirable job of driving away several would be suitors, although Lydia did admit that none of the gentlemen had made a very favourable impression."

"They are good girls."

Elizabeth raised one brow in an arch manner. "On the subject of their goodness I am inclined to agree, but Georgiana and Lydia are no longer girls, Fitzwilliam. They are proper young women."

Darcy frowned at this pronouncement. So long as Georgiana remained under his care, she would be his *sister*. Once she left his protection for that of her future husband's, which Darcy was in no hurry to see happen, then, and only then, would he acknowledge she was no longer a girl but a grown woman. The same rationale applied to Lydia.

As she often did in such circumstances, Elizabeth ignored his long face and attempted to coax him into a more acquiescent mood. "Regardless of your sentiments, you and your cousin must know your efforts to deter potential suitors will ultimately end in failure. Even as we speak, there are two determined gentlemen who have succeeded in attracting the notice of both our sisters, and it sounds as though their admiration is not only welcomed but reciprocated wholeheartedly."

"Who are they?" Darcy demanded, wondering how two such men had gotten past his cousin's eagle-eyed vigilance. "Fitzwilliam has mentioned no determined young men by name. In fact, he has made no mention of any young men at all."

"Likely, because he does not wish to disturb your peace of mind," she said amicably. "Or your seaside holiday with your wife! In this case, there is little cause for concern, as I happen to know the gentlemen in question are none other than Lord Ridgefield's eldest sons. Your acquaintance with their family is of some duration, is it not?"

"Robert and James Morland? Are they in Brighton?"

His wife inclined her head in answer.

Darcy rubbed his brow. Georgiana and Lydia, he knew, could do far worse than Lord Ridgefield's heir and his brother. Both were fine young men from a well-known, well-respected family. In truth, he knew nothing but good of them, and he had known them all their lives.

Even so, Darcy thought to himself with a stubbornness that would not be denied, *they are men all the same.*

Elizabeth's laughter rang throughout the empty street. "I know that look, sir, but there is little you can do at this point except wait and see what happens. In the meantime, they are frequent callers in Marlborough Row, though I believe most of their visits have occurred when your cousin was known to be elsewhere."

Darcy shook his head. "I shall have to remedy that at once."

"You will do no such thing. Colonel Fitzwilliam has business to attend to—important business for his commanding officer—and our sisters are well chaperoned by your aunt. Lady Carlisle is more fastidious than you are regarding their respectability and proper comportment. There is no need to bring Richard into the mix. He shall only be in the way. Oh, Fitzwilliam, look!" she cried. "How wonderful!"

If Darcy had not placed his hand atop hers, restraining her, he suspected his wife would have sprinted across the street and onto the sandy expanse of beach beyond the esplanade. Not fifty feet away, the bay shimmered in the morning sun. A short distance from where they stood, a handsome pier extended into the water; but Elizabeth's object was the soft, golden sand of the shore.

For over an hour, they walked along the beach, skirting the incoming tide as they collected limpet shells and periwinkles and colourful turban tops. Elizabeth's pleasure knew no bounds. Darcy observed her with an affectionate smile, his heart full as he listened to her delighted exclamations intermingled with the cries of the gulls and terns. She had just bent down to claim a particularly fine specimen near the waterline when he noticed a large wave rolling headlong towards the shore.

Elizabeth's attention was solely on her prize as she endeavoured to pry it from the sand.

In an instant, Darcy lifted her in his arms and carried her to higher ground. Elizabeth shrieked in surprise and rang a peal over him for his forwardness, but by the time he had set her gently upon her feet where the waves would not reach her, she was laughing.

Darcy's boots had gotten wet, but they were so thick and sturdy, and so highly polished, that the water rolled right off. Elizabeth's pretty shell was unfortunately lost, but the look in her eyes as she gazed at him made Darcy wish they were not in public, but in the privacy of their comfortable rented home.

"You rescued me," she told him with a smile so bright it rivalled the sun.

"Of course, I did," he allowed as his lips turned upward.

Gripping his hand, Elizabeth tugged him closer until they were separated by naught but a few inches. "As I am exceedingly fond of this gown, Mr Darcy, I must thank you. I would have been wet through had you not come when you did."

Though he wanted nothing more than to pull her into his arms and kiss her thoroughly, he settled for gently brushing a wayward curl from her cheek instead. "I shall always come, Mrs Darcy, whenever you have need of me."

Her smile softened, as did her voice, and she touched his face tenderly in return. "I shall always have need of you."

⁂

Elizabeth's day of reckoning came early, a week before Christmas. They were dining in Grosvenor Street with Lord and Lady Carlisle, Viscount Emerson, and Colonel Fitzwilliam. Earlier that evening, the weather had been cold and dry, but it had quickly turned cold and wet. When Elizabeth voiced her intent to finish her supper, then return to their home in Brook Street, Darcy stared at her in incredulous disbelief. Outside, the rain had turned to sleet, making the cobbled streets slick and treacherous. Elizabeth was petite, but her belly had grown large with their child; far more so, he thought, than any other woman he had ever seen. He had no desire to risk her safety, or, God forbid, have his child enter the world in the middle of Davies Street on the forward-facing seat of his carriage.

Lady Carlisle patted his hand with an indulgent smile, assuring him it would be many hours yet before the babe was born and, therefore, they had plenty of time to see Elizabeth returned safely to Brook Street; but Darcy was determined. He would take no chances with Elizabeth and their babe in such weather. At Grosvenor Street they would remain.

Later, after receiving no word of his wife for nearly seven hours, he regretted his intractability. Thoughts of barging into Elizabeth's bedchamber and spiriting her from the house consumed him almost as much as the horrifying possibility that something had gone terribly wrong. Lady Carlisle, who adored Elizabeth the moment they were introduced, had bustled off to be of use to her and to assist the midwife. Except for Colonel Fitzwilliam, Darcy's remaining relations had been neither supportive, nor helpful.

His uncle, who was snoring on the tufted leather couch before the fire, had not understood why his nephew was so anxious and on edge, and Emerson, who had no fondness for his own wife, had been incapable of keeping his boorish opinions to himself.

"What you need is a stiff drink," he said to Darcy as he ·pressed a glass of port on him. "I cannot imagine why you insist upon remaining sober. When Josephine was brought to bed I was at my club, well and truly foxed, and better for it. You will soon wear a hole in the Axminster at this rate."

Darcy accepted the port, stared at it for an indeterminable amount of time, and eventually set the glass on the table untouched. Though he was tempted to partake simply to settle his nerves, he was not so selfish or unfeeling as to drink himself into oblivion while his wife laboured to bring his child into the world.

"Suit yourself," Emerson told him, draining the last mouthful of port from his own glass. "In such a circumstance as this, being in one's cups is preferable to sobriety. If you are concerned about your wife finding out, I daresay she is in the thick of it now and will likely never know."

Colonel Fitzwilliam snorted. "As impossible as it must be for you to comprehend, Arthur, Darcy happens to like his wife, whereas you are barely civil to yours. For God's sake, you do not even live in the same house, but with your mistress."

Rather than take offense, Emerson merely shrugged his shoulders and strolled to the sideboard to refill his glass. "I cannot see how any of what you just uttered is pertinent, Richard. I will be the first to admit Elizabeth is delightful. Josephine, however, you must own is a miserable, harping shrew. That I have ended up shackled to such a woman and must therefore find my pleasure elsewhere is no fault of mine."

"Of course, not, Emerson," Darcy muttered, his voice heavy with sarcasm. "After all, what truly affable wife would disapprove of her husband cavorting with bit actresses and prostitutes? Presently, I can think of none."

Rolling his eyes, Emerson drank half the port in his glass in one gulp. "You have no sense of adventure, Darcy, and far too much money for your own good."

Shaking his head at his brother, Fitzwilliam set his glass on a nearby table with a resounding thud. "If you are amenable, Darcy, I could use a change of scenery. I have lost my taste for port."

Glad to escape Emerson's inebriated prattle, Darcy consented, and they quit the room and went in search of another. The house was eerily quiet as they made their way through the darkened corridors. Their footsteps echoed off the pristine marble floors and the decorative wainscoting on the walls. There was a hollowness present, a loneliness, that only succeeded in putting Darcy that much more on edge. *All is well,* he told himself, exhaling a slow, measured breath. *Elizabeth is well. The babe is well. Everything is well.*

They ended up in the library, where the only source of light came from a low burning fire crackling in the grate. Fitzwilliam shut the door behind them, walked to the hearth, and stared at the flames. At length, he said, "I received an express a week ago."

"From whom?" Darcy enquired distractedly. He had responded only to be polite. Presently, his thoughts were focused overwhelmingly on what was happening in the bedchamber above his head.

"From a friend of mine," Fitzwilliam replied with undue seriousness, "who happened to have news of a former friend of yours."

A familiar feeling of dread he had not experienced in years spread through Darcy's chest. News of George Wickham and his perfidy was the last thing he needed at such a moment. Swallowing a vicious oath, he walked to the window and then to the fire, where he grabbed the poker from its stand and stabbed at the logs in the grate. "What new unspeakable offense has the contemptible blackguard committed now?"

Beside him, Fitzwilliam cleared his throat. "None."

Darcy gave him a sardonic, albeit dubious, look.

"He is dead, Darcy."

The words hung in the air between them, taking up space as though they were tangible.

It took Darcy nearly five minutes to find his voice. "Did he die in the gaol?"

"No. On a transport ship bound for Australia." Fitzwilliam laid his hand on Darcy's shoulder. "I know you hated the scoundrel, but I can easily recall a time when you did not. He never changed. At least not for the better. I am sorry."

Before Darcy could contemplate what that meant, or even how he felt about it, the library door opened, and Lady Carlisle entered the room. Her countenance was impenetrably grave.

"Nephew."

In the library's dim interior, her voice sounded too abrupt, too sharp, and too loud. "Elizabeth is...that is to say..." With a long-suffering sigh, she looked to the ceiling and pursed her lips. "Pray go upstairs at once."

All thoughts of Wickham were immediately forgot.

Darcy quit the room. As he strode through the darkened corridor and took the stairs two at a time, his heart felt as though it had lodged in his throat. The bedchamber his wife had been given loomed ahead. Without pause, he grasped the door handle and threw open the door.

The midwife was before him in an instant, preventing him from entering. "That is far enough!" she told him in a voice as stern as her countenance. "We will send for you when it is over, Mr Darcy. Be off with you now and re-join the men."

From the large, four poster bed in the centre of the room, he heard Elizabeth call to him. Her voice, usually so rich and clear, sounded hoarse and strained. "Do not dare leave this room, sir. I have no intention of bearing this burden alone."

The midwife, however, would not hear of such an impropriety being perpetrated on her watch. "Mrs Darcy," she said, marching swiftly to her side. "A birthing room is no place for a man."

"It is as fine a place as any," Elizabeth informed her, wincing at what Darcy assumed was likely the onset of a labour pain. Curling her fingers into the counterpane, she gasped, "Since Mr Darcy was instrumental in the conceiving of this child, it is only fitting that he is present for its ejection!"

Shocked to hear such a pronouncement from his wife, Darcy stared at her.

Even from the corridor, he could tell the room was unbearably hot. The bed, where Elizabeth was propped up with bolsters and pillows, was piled with rugs and counterpanes. A sheen of perspiration glistened on her skin, soaking her shift. Her hair was long and loose—a riot of damp curls on her pillow—and she was flushed and gasping and obviously in a great deal of pain. Though her eyes were as lovely and dark as ever, in their depths, Darcy saw something he had never seen before: a stark frisson of fear.

As quickly as her pain had begun, it passed. The midwife mopped her brow with a clean, damp cloth and offered her a cup of caudle.

Elizabeth pushed it away with a shaking hand. "Please," she pleaded, and reached for Darcy instead.

By then, Darcy had seen enough. Ignoring the exasperated glare of the midwife, he stepped into the room, shut the door firmly behind him, and strode to his wife's side.

✥

Many hours later, bright fingers of sunlight slipped through the gaps in the curtains. Once the room was freshened, and Elizabeth had been made comfortable, Darcy settled himself beside her on the bed.

"We have a son," she whispered with a tremulous smile.

"And a daughter," Darcy murmured, awestruck and enchanted by the tiny, beloved image of perfection swaddled in his arms. Feeling uncharacteristically emotional, he pressed a reverent kiss to Elizabeth's brow, then her cheek, and finally her lips. "I would have been grateful for one child, my darling, never mind two. Once again, you have exceeded my expectations."

Wiping a tear from her cheek, Elizabeth laughed. Her eyes were focused entirely on the sleeping babe she cradled in her arms—her son. "Our children have exceeded mine. I had despaired of ever giving you any child, never mind an heir. It took us *six years,* Fitzwilliam."

"The fault is my own. Your family is hale and hearty, while mine is considerably less so. Because of you, Elizabeth, I have become a father twice in one morning."

"My heartiness," she remarked wryly, "must be owed to my country upbringing."

"In case you have failed to notice, Pemberley is very much a country house."

"And it is also ten times grander than Longbourn, in both appearance and consequence."

Darcy could not disagree. "It has always been a grand house, but it is you who have made it a warm and loving home."

She looked at him then, and Darcy was startled by the sadness he saw in her eyes. "It pains me to hear you speak so. As though you had nothing before me."

With care, Darcy shifted his daughter in his arms so he could gently touch his wife's cheek. "I was not alone, Elizabeth. I had my aunt and uncle. I had Bingley. I had Georgiana and Fitzwilliam. When I needed him, Fitzwilliam always came, no matter where he was or what he was doing."

"I know, and I am glad. But for Richard to come to you, first you must send for him, which I happen to know you rarely did."

How well she knew him.

Darcy had once told her he wanted no secrets between them, and so, nearly seven years later, none remained. Regardless of Elizabeth's present distress, he could not regret their sincerity and frankness with each other. He could not regret their forthrightness and honesty. They were important aspects of their marriage—of their beautiful communion of souls—and they had been there from the beginning.

"No," he allowed. "But on those few occasions when I felt I had real cause to send for him, Fitzwilliam came to me, fair weather or foul, day or night, wherever I happened to be."

"Thank you," Elizabeth said softly, but with considerable feeling, "for coming to me today when I wanted you. I know it was highly improper, and not at all the done thing, but I needed you with me." She shook her head and shifted her gaze to their son. "I cannot explain it."

"Nor do I require an explanation," Darcy said as softly. "Not from you. I was happy to come to you today, even though, as you said, it is not done."

"Poor Mrs Chapman! She was fit to be tied, and your aunt as well. I have never seen Lady Carlisle so mortified and vexed."

Darcy shook his head. "It does not matter. What matters is that you are well, and our children are well. It has been a long night. A long day, and you have barely slept."

The expression in Elizabeth's eyes was as warm as her voice was tender. "Are *you* well, my husband?"

Darcy's gaze drifted to his daughter, then to his son, and finally, to his beautiful wife. His heart had never felt so full— full of joy, full of hope, and full of love for this remarkable, compassionate, intelligent woman who teased him, and trusted him, and loved him in turn.

He pressed a lingering kiss to her lips, and another and another, and smiled. "Yes, my darling friend, my dearest love —*my wife*. I have never been better."

The End

ACKNOWLEDGMENTS

My sincere gratitude to my wonderful editors, Kristi Rawley , Jo Abbott, and Jan Ashton. After months of obsessing over sentence structure and cadence and dialog and plot holes and words until I was losing my sanity, you ladies swooped in with friendly faces and red pens and suggestions to make this story better.

Heartfelt thanks as well to all of you who have generously chosen to spend your time reading my book instead of tidying your homes or cooking supper or going to sleep at a reasonable hour. A huge portion of the enjoyment I receive from writing is owed to you.

ABOUT THE AUTHOR

When she was five, Susan Adriani wanted to be an opera singer, but changed her mind when she realized she would have to perform in front of an audience instead of her bedroom mirror. She attended art school instead and became a graphic designer who spends more time writing stories and researching the social niceties of Regency England than she does cleaning her house. She has a teenage daughter who dearly loves to laugh, and a handsome husband who is not the least bit intimidated by Mr Darcy. She makes her home in New England, and cannot imagine a world without books, Google Maps, copious amounts of tea, or Jane Austen.

 facebook.com/susan.adriani.7

bookbub.com/authors/susan-adriani

ALSO BY SUSAN ADRIANI

Misunderstandings & Ardent Love

"I have never been able to forget you...I am yours, in body and soul, for as long as I am able to draw breath."

After months of brooding despair while Bingley prepares to wed Jane Bennet, Fitzwilliam Darcy realises he has no choice but to put his heart at risk and try to win the only woman he will ever love.

Elizabeth Bennet would more than welcome his return to Longbourn. Yet despite such mutually ardent feelings, her most beloved sister and Darcy's own uncle hold quite the opposite points of view.

Torn between personal loyalties and responsibilities, the couple must balance finding a discreet solution for a family scandal in London and dealing with new outrageous actions by Mr and Mrs Wickham, all while facing a Jane Bennet who cannot forgive Darcy his interference in her love story.

Can the two overcome misunderstandings and meddling and find their way to one another at last?

Call It Hope

There is no one's society I find more acceptable than your own; no one whose friendship I have longed for as I have longed for yours.

As Christmas approaches, it appears to Elizabeth Bennet that only Shakespeare himself could have devised a more wretched comedy of errors.

Jane is now Mrs Bingley, and in her desire to be away from Longbourn and its long-settled guests, the Wickhams, Elizabeth has travelled to Kent to spend the Yuletide holiday with her friend Charlotte Collins. Yet not only have odd circumstances--and a snowstorm--fated her to spend the Yuletide holiday at Rosings Park, she must do so with the elusive Mr Darcy and all his Fitzwilliam relations. Neither of their hearts has healed from their mutual disappointment, and now they each must navigate his family's ridiculous antics and their own apprehensions to reach a new beginning. While each is eager, neither is certain of the power they may hold over the other's affections.

Once Darcy and Elizabeth get past mishaps and misunderstandings--and at least one mortifying moment--they each may receive the only Christmas gift they truly wish for: the other's love.

The Truth About Mr Darcy

The truth always has consequences...

Mr Darcy has a dilemma. Should he tell the truth about his old nemesis George Wickham in order to protect the good citizens of Meryton from Wickham's lies and deceits? Doing so will force Darcy to reveal family secrets that he'd prefer never come to light. The alternative is keeping the man's criminal nature to himself and hoping he leaves the area before doing significant harm.

But as Wickham's attentions to Elizabeth increase, Darcy knows if he's to win the one woman he's set his heart on, he's going to have to make one of the most difficult decisions of his life. And what he ultimately does sets in motion a shocking chain of events neither he nor Elizabeth could possibly have predicted.

FROM THE PUBLISHER

The publisher and the author thank you for choosing *The Luxury of Silence*. The favor of your rating or review would be greatly appreciated.

You are cordially invited to become a subscriber to the Quills & Quartos newsletter. Subscribers to the newsletter receive advance notice of sales, bonus content, and give-aways. You can join at www.QuillsandQuartos.com where you will also find excerpts from recent releases.

Made in United States
Troutdale, OR
11/07/2023